Dear Reader,

Are you like me?

Do you love houses rich with history and rooms that echo with phantom sounds at midnight? If so, you'll feel right at home at Draycott Abbey, with its shadowed walls overhung with fragrant Centifolia roses.

One day the swans on the moat floated into my mind—followed in short order by the imperious guardian ghost and his faithful cat Gideon.

Since then, Draycott Abbey has never been far from my thoughts. A place of magic.

A house of many secrets.

And there are more secrets yet to be revealed.

You've asked me so many times when these crucial, first stories of the Draycott series would be brought back into print. Now, after ten years, you are holding the first new volume in your hands! There are more stories coming, rich with suspense, dark with history and magic. Adrian and Gideon would have it no other way.

Meanwhile, feel the moonlight. Smell the perfume of banked old roses. Enjoy the abbey's promise of beauty and eternal love.

With my very best wishes,

Christina

CHRISTINA SKYE

ENCHANTMENT &
BRIDGE OF DREAMS

HQN™

ISBN-13: 978-0-373-77262-9
ISBN-10:   0-373-77262-9

ENCHANTMENT & BRIDGE OF DREAMS

Copyright © 2007 by Harlequin Books S.A.

The publisher acknowledges the copyright holder of the
individual works as follows:

ENCHANTMENT
Copyright © 1991 by Roberta Helmer
First Published by Avon Books in 1991

BRIDGE OF DREAMS
Copyright © 1995 by Roberta Helmer
First Published by Avon Books in 1995

CONTENTS

ENCHANTMENT 9

BRIDGE OF DREAMS 141

ENCHANTMENT

PROLOGUE

HE SAT IN SULLEN SHADOWS, staring pensively at his own portrait. Dark-eyed, velvet-clad, he stroked a great gray cat, which drowsed on his knee.

Around him the granite house seemed to sleep, intensely quiet, caught in wistful, yearning dreams.

So different, the man thought sadly. How could the same house be so very different?

He frowned, realizing that no one would notice him here. Here he was just another shadow in the darkness, just a still figure slumped in a faded damask armchair, studying his own proud features with self-loathing.

Once it had been different, of course. Once the house had rung to his shouted orders, and an army of servants had scuttled to anticipate his slightest bidding. Once *she* had walked here, and to look upon her had been his greatest joy.

But times change; he should have known that better than anyone.

No, the figure in the chair thought, he liked this graceless age not at all. But then liking was not what had brought him here. Love perhaps, but not liking.

His long pale fingers tensed and halted their rhythmic stroking of the cat. "Ah, Gideon, it is hard, much harder than I'd thought, this business of coming back."

In his lap, the cat arched slightly, nuzzling the man's cold hand.

He smiled bitterly. "Nothing is as I expected. Everything feels wrong. Too slow. Too heavy. Too clumsy. Too—"

He thought for a moment. *Solid.* Yes, that was precisely the word. And that sense of solidity was what bothered him most.

At the cat's sharp meow, the black-clad figure looked down, and his hands resumed their lulling movements; a deep purring sound spilled from the animal's throat.

"Yes, old friend, it will be hard—dangerous even. Should I fail, my torment will be magnified a thousandfold. But we knew that already, did we not?"

The cat's hair seemed to bristle for a moment. His tail arched and flicked sharply from side to side.

"Very true. But what choice have we?"

Gideon's eyes narrowed, gleaming golden from the darkness.

The ghost of Draycott Abbey merely frowned and shook his head. "That would not be permitted, I'm afraid."

For a moment anger boiled up in him—savage and lethal. Around him the room seemed to grow chill, the darkness to heave and tremble.

Then with a ragged sigh, the man closed his eyes, struggling vainly to forget how far his jealousy had driven her and how much he had hurt her.

His beloved stone walls were intact, at least. Down to the last capstone and merlon, they stood inviolate.

And they were still his. That much had not changed.

Now would it ever, the ghost vowed grimly. In the shadows, his proud, gaunt features seemed to gleam and shimmer, suddenly merciless.

CHAPTER ONE

Spring 1991
Sussex, England.

LATER ON, AFTER THE FEAR had fled and the hurting stopped, she would realize it was the house that she had fallen in love with first. But for now Kacey Mallory could only stare, speechless and dreamy, at the towering walls of weathered stone before her.

Lichen-covered, with climbing roses spilling color over its ancient gray towers, Draycott Abbey was a vision of heart-stopping beauty.

Even more jarring, it was somehow familiar.

In some strange way, she felt as if she were coming home. But that was impossible, of course. Home was three thousand miles away, where a small clapboard saltbox nestled amid the rolling hills of western Connecticut.

And this vision before her was a universe apart from that—a granite Jacobean moat house whose crenellated roofs and twisting chimneys floated like a summer dream over the Wealden Hills of southern Kent.

Kacey felt her breath catch. The sun was going down behind her, pouring golden light over the valley, painting the mullioned windows a fiery crimson.

To be here at last. To feel so strangely at home, as if she were returning from years of wandering.

Frowning, Kacey tossed back a wind-blown lock of honey-colored hair. What in the name of heaven was wrong with her? This massive granite structure was no more hers than was Balmoral Castle!

And yet the dark feeling of familiarity persisted. Along with something else—a hunger so tangible that it hurt.

Abruptly she dropped her canvas bag and rubbed a slim hand across her weary eyes. The blurring was only to be expected after twenty-two straight hours of traveling. Yes, of course—that must be the source of this strange disorientation.

She closed her smoky-green eyes, then warily reopened them.

Nothing had changed. Just as before, the abbey gleamed back at her.

Like a jewel, Kacey thought. Set within an emerald ocean of manicured lawns. And flowers everywhere, a scattering of pinks, sweet alyssum and madonna lilies.

Something had told her there would be lilies.

A shiver ran down her spine.

"Next thing, you'll be following a white rabbit right down its little hole, Katharine Chelsea." Still muttering, she tossed her bag up over her shoulder and crossed the last feet of lawn onto a narrow graveled path that wound up to the house.

So this was Draycott Abbey—or what was left of the medieval structure. Built in 1255. Nearly burned to the ground in 1645 during the "troubles" with Cromwell. Partially restored a year later, and entirely refurbished in 1793, after the eighth Viscount Draycott made a number of clever investments in the Orient.

Kacey could have gone on forever about this house, quoting chapter and verse of its long, rich history—right down to the ghost of an ancient ancestor who was said to pace the battlements on moonless nights, sad-eyed and travel-weary, a rose crushed between his long fingers.

Yes, she knew the gray granite structure by heart, from its

Jacobean long gallery on the fourth floor to the fine stained-glass windows on the north front facing the quiet moat.

It was an imposing house. A magical house.

A house of many secrets, she suspected.

Once again, a shiver worked its way down her spine.

But it was not the house she had come to see, though that alone would have been the dream of a lifetime. No, it was a different task that brought her to this small corner of England— equally the dream of a lifetime to an art conservator like herself.

Somewhere inside the abbey was a newly discovered canvas carrying the signature of James Whistler. An uncatalogued canvas that appeared in none of the artist's correspondence. A painting unseen since the day it was completed. Ever the temperamental artist, Whistler had ordered it destroyed along with all the other pieces he felt were inadequate to bear the scrutiny of posterity.

If the canvas actually *was* by Whistler, Kacey reminded herself sharply. It was far too soon to hope, especially since the odds of its being real were very small.

Yet a part of her dared to hope. The canvas had been discovered two months ago by the present owner of Draycott Abbey. Wrapped in linen, it had remained unseen and forgotten for over a century. Kacey's job was to verify the painting's authenticity and to undertake any restoration that might be required.

Her pulse quickened at the thought of such a discovery, and at her rare good fortune in being involved in the recovery of such a masterpiece.

Not that luck had much to do with it, of course, for Kacey was one of a mere handful of experts who specialized in Whistler. After completing her doctoral work, she had gone on to further study in pigment and canvas restoration at the Louvre.

Her own articles on Whistler had soon become widely circulated, provoking a good deal of controversy. Perhaps it was

because K. C. Mallory's passion for Whistler shone through
every word she wrote. Or perhaps it was just that she seemed to
have a skill for seeing beyond the layers of color right into the
heart of the canvas, sensing the unspoken motivations of the
painter's soul.

For whatever reason, Whistler had been her life and love.

And now here she stood, wind-blown and weary, at the foot
of an awesome stone edifice, surrounded by a scene of timeless
pastoral beauty.

In the shadow of Draycott Abbey.

Almost within reach of her long-dreamed-of Whistler.

Nocturne in Lavender and Silver: Southampton Pier. An
unseen, unrecorded masterpiece by probably the greatest
American painter of the nineteenth century. Along with the
canvas, the present viscount had discovered a scribbled note, apparently from Whistler himself, directing his assistant to destroy
the canvas.

The slim beauty frowned, worrying her full lower lip with
her teeth. *Authentic?* Or simply another one of the Whistler
hoaxes so common in the last decade, since Japanese collectors had driven the prices sky-high? The painter's spare brush-
strokes and flat washes of color made him damnably easy to
forge, after all.

Kacey tried to calm her racing pulse, knowing that in a few
hours she would have her answer. Gripping her bag, she started
toward the gatehouse perched just outside the silver moat.

As she walked, she flung back a handful of honey-gold hair,
entirely unaware of the way the sun gilded her high, fragile
cheekbones to a warm, glowing porcelain. Entirely unaware of
the way her hair flashed like liquid gold upon her slim shoulders.

Had she known what was waiting for her just beyond the
crenellated stone gatehouse, Kacey Mallory might never have
taken another step.

TOO LATE...TOO LATE...

He could feel it even as he jumped from his horse and lunged up the cold marble steps to an unlit house. He knew it even before he threw open the heavy door and plunged into the leaden shadows.

She had gone, taking the child with her. Sweeping away all his hope, all his chances to atone for his unforgivable stupidity.

With a harsh curse, he turned and stumbled back into the lashing wind, his eyes narrowed on the dim line where the chalk escarpment fell away six hundred feet to meet the frigid swells of the English Channel.

She would have taken the old path along the cliffs. That way she would be least likely to encounter anyone who would try to stop her.

Like him....

Dear God, out there on the cliffs—in such a storm!

Tossing his greatcoat about his shoulders, he plunged forward, shouting her name wildly.

But no sound drifted back to him. Only the wind wept a shrill answer, its fierce blasts whipping black strands across his face. As he struggled south the last frayed edges of sky bled from indigo to black far out over the channel.

Too late, the wind keened.

All gone.

And then he heard another sound, more like the wild shriek of a bird than any human cry. The sharp stiffening of muscles along his neck and the twisting stab of fear in his stomach told him that could be only one person's voice.

"Katharine!" he screamed, pounding forward blindly. "Wait for me! Let me—"

A second later, the earth tore free. With a muffled explosion, a thousand tons of chalk and granite smashed down toward the narrow shingle, drowning out her last, shrill cry.

And then only the long darkness.

"Nooo!" His heart pounding, Nicholas Draycott jerked upright in the chill silence, sweat-soaked and heartsick, listening to the telephone ring. After two days of insomnia, he'd finally fallen into a ragged sleep, only to be shaken awake by the old nightmare.

Just a dream, he tried to tell himself. Just an illusion, like all the others. It was the quiet that did it, or maybe it was the drinking and the endless stream of late nights.

At his sides, his strong fingers clenched into fists. He stared into the room's shadows, fighting a choking wave of loss and regret. Let it go, he told himself harshly, listening to a branch whip against the window. Put it behind you—it's only a damn dream, after all.

Once again, the phone rang; Draycott made no move to answer it.

That, too, was over, he told himself harshly.

But there were some things a person never got over. And a ten-month hell of jungle captivity in southeast Asia was probably one of them.

A muscle flashing at his jaw, the hard-faced Englishman reached across the bed for the pack of cigarettes on the side table.

At that moment, the phone again began its insistent ringing, the sound echoing loudly in the deathly silence of the house. On and on it rang, shrill peal after shrill peal.

Draycott didn't move. His silver-gray eyes narrowed, studying the receiver.

The ringing stopped for a few moments only to begin anew. Slowly the Englishman bent down and lifted the receiver, not saying a word.

"Ah, Lord Draycott. You respond at last. Have you given any more thought to our proposal?"

Nicholas did not answer.

"Still stubborn, are you? Such a pity, that." The voice was flat and faintly accented.

Just like all the other callers.

Murderous visions burned through Draycott's brain, but he knew that expressing them would only give these men what they wanted. So he held his silence instead, making the most of the lessons a year in hell had taught him.

"So. You have made your choice, Lord Draycott. That makes my own choice so much easier." The man on the other end of the phone chuckled. It was a cold sound, harsh with finality. "There will be no more warnings. You have four days, Lord Draycott. The next time we will not miss, I assure you."

A second later, the connection broke off into scattered static.

Draycott's left hand slowly tightened, crushing the cigarette package into a shapeless mass. A muscle flashed at his temple. In the gathering dusk, his face looked very hard.

Goddamn the man with the voice like sandpaper. Goddamn the people who came spying, day after day.

Goddamn them all!

But the twelfth Viscount Draycott knew that the man had spoken the truth. Unless he came up with a miracle by Friday, he was a dead man.

Awkwardly, he came to his feet and tossed the crumpled cigarette pack down onto his dresser. The muscles at his chest rippled as he rubbed his neck tiredly, then bent down and tugged on a pair of charcoal trousers.

In the darkened room, the scars at his left thigh were barely visible. No more than a phantom network, they radiated from his pelvic bone to the outside of his knee.

He barely noticed them now, beyond a stiffness when he overexerted himself. His silver eyes narrowed. Someday maybe the rest of the scars from Bhanlai would fade, too.

Frowning, he strode to the telephone and punched out a number.

"Six-two-one-five" came a clipped voice at the other end.

"Inspector Jamieson. Nicholas Draycott calling." His face dark, Draycott stared down at the crumbled cigarette pack.

"Lord Draycott? Has something—"

"Nothing new, inspector. I merely wanted to see if you'd got anything on the men who took my Turners."

"I'm afraid not, Lord Draycott. These were no amateurs, unfortunately. We're tracking our regular sources just in case the stolen paintings surface, but it could take weeks…"

And time is the one thing I don't have, Nicholas thought grimly. "What about Trang? Anything new there?"

From the other end of the line came the rustle of papers. "There has been some revived activity in his part of Burma. A few munitions purchases, the usual opium deals. Nothing significant, however. The villagers swear they saw this man Trang cut down in the barrage after your release and that he is buried in the hills outside Bhanlai. Which leaves me wondering why you'd doubt their opinion. Is there perhaps something you're not telling us, Lord Draycott?"

For a moment, rage darkened Nicholas's vision. There was a bloody lot he wasn't telling the inspector—but only because it was none of his damn business. And as for Bhanlai's grimy little dictator—Nicholas, too, had seen him fall in the gunfire when he was rescued. And yet who else but Trang could be behind the harassing phone calls he'd been getting? Who else but Trang knew the details of those last desperate days at Bhanlai and a woman who had betrayed him?

One of the warlord's men, perhaps? Or one of that motley horde of a hundred different nationalities who drifted around Trang, men of no allegiance to anything except themselves? And what did they want from him anyway?

Nicholas's hands tightened as he felt the old gnawing sense of powerlessness begin to choke him.

"Lord Draycott? Are you there?"

"I'm here, inspector."

"Are you going to answer my question?"

Draycott's eyes were unreadable. "Just call it an instinct. Trang and I got to know each other pretty well up there in the jungle. I guess it's often that way between captor and captive. And lately I've had the feeling…" *That I'm being watched. That I'm walking right on the edge of a precipice.*

But Nicholas didn't tell Jamieson that. It would only bring another horde of police flocking down to Draycott Abbey, and all he wanted now was to be left alone.

"Just a feeling, Lord Draycott?" The inspector's voice was sharp with disbelief. "You won't be more specific than that?"

"No."

"Did you know that Trang was supposed to have buried a fortune in jewels somewhere in those hills? Not one piece has ever been recovered, as a matter of fact."

"Are you calling me a liar, inspector?"

There was a silence at the other end. "Not a liar. Not quite. But I think there's a damn sight more that you're not telling us, my lord."

"I can't remember, damn it!" Draycott's hand clenched and unclenched at his side. Even this much he hated to reveal.

The inspector's next words were slow and careful. "There are ways of remembering, you know. Relaxation techniques. Hypnosis." A momentary silence. "Drugs."

Draycott cursed low and graphically. "And have my brain ripped open all over again, so that some stranger can pick through whatever bits he finds interesting? Thanks but no bloody thanks, inspector. I'm done with Bhanlai. All I want now is to get on with my life!" Nicholas's fingers whitened on the receiver. *If I ever can.*

"I'm sorry to hear that, Lord Draycott. Because I'm afraid there is very little we can do for you in that case. Not until you give us something more concrete to go on."

Nicholas's jaw hardened to a rigid line. He'd expected nothing more than this, of course. Were he in Jamieson's shoes, Nicholas supposed he'd have said the same. But time was running out, and he was nowhere nearer to an answer than before.

"Of course, inspector," he said flatly. "Good night."

After cradling the receiver, he stalked to the window and pulled aside the curtain. To the east, the valley was tinged with purple shadows, while the distant Wealden Hills beyond shone vermillion in the setting sun.

And that's when he saw her—a long, cool column of womanhood poured into a pair of expensive denims so favored by the bloody Americans. A mane of blond hair spilled about her shoulders. On her feet were a pair of lavishly hand-tooled leather boots.

A muscle flashed at Draycott's jaw as he watched the woman move around to the side of the house. In the slanting sunlight, her hair shone honey-gold, the color of the finest Burmese silk.

He cursed, long and savagely. So she was another gossip hunter. Another maggot come to feed off the wounds of Bhanlai. When would they learn that his privacy was not for sale? That he refused to see his story become cheap copy to fuel tabloid sales? Photojournalists! A fancy word for voyeurs, he thought angrily.

But this one would be no more successful than any of the others who'd come in search of a story, he swore, even though she was stunning.

Trust Edward Armistead, one of Fleet Street's most ruthless gossip peddlers, to find someone like her. Armistead was an expert when it came to acquiring gossip, and he never stinted on money or personnel when tracking down a story.

Furious, Draycott turned from the window, a wild plan already forming in his head. Yes, the woman deserved exactly what she got, he decided.

For right now, Nicholas Draycott was no longer a gentleman. No longer the hero of Bhanlai.

Tonight he was only a man—a man who had reached the end of his rope.

CHAPTER TWO

THE AIR WAS STILL AND heavy, rich with the scent of thyme and hyacinth as Kacey moved forward into the cool shadows of the stable. She called out several times, but no one answered.

Frowning, she tried to gather the few scraps of information she'd been given before leaving New York.

"Lord Draycott is an unusual man," Kacey's employer, Cassandra Edwards, had announced. "He's intensely protective of his privacy. Obnoxiously so, in fact. You'd do best just to keep out of his way. I imagine his staff will provide you with anything you need. The man probably won't even be in residence at the abbey—he has homes all over England, did you know?"

As it happened, Kacey hadn't known, but that suited her just fine. The last thing she wanted was a nervous owner hovering about while she examined the would-be Whistler canvas.

And with several million dollars riding on her decision, she couldn't blame an owner for being a little nervous about her findings.

Still, she hadn't thought the earl would be quite so eccentric as to leave the house closed up and silent, with no one at all to meet her. After all, he had stipulated this weekend as the best time for her to arrive.

Kacey pulled her case higher on her shoulder, frowning. Perhaps money and pedigree did that to a person—made him cold and careless of others. She made a mental note to avoid the viscount at all costs.

Inside the stables, the air was still and cool, little motes of dust dancing across the last golden beams of sun slanting down through the high windows.

Kacey's breath caught. Even here, the sense of timelessness, of being caught in a dream, lingered, for the stalls were all empty, pooled with shadows.

So where was everyone? she wondered crossly. She had been punctual to the dot. The bus had dropped her at the foot of the home wood, as the driver referred to the dark expanse of beeches and elms. He had provided her with careful directions to the abbey, but his look, Kacey recalled now, had been frankly curious.

And faintly hostile.

Her brow creased in thought, she dropped her canvas bag and sat down on an upturned wooden crate. She tugged off her right boot, massaging her cramped and blistered toes.

Her gaze wandered up to the ceiling, crisscrossed by massive overhanging beams. That was when she first noticed the meticulous carving atop the first stall—three horses in full gallop, tails flying, hooves aloft.

On an impulse, she unzipped her bag and extracted her camera. Unless she missed her guess, that detail was an eighteenth-century masterpiece, perhaps the work of Grinling Gibbons himself! Quickly she switched on her flash and began to shoot. She would ask the viscount for permission when she saw him, of course, but meanwhile, this was just too good a chance to pass up, especially since Cassandra had just received a commission to restore a pair of sculptures by Gibbons in Cheshire.

In the excitement of her discovery, Kacey forgot that she should be looking for the man who belonged to that sleek black sports car parked outside or tracking down a place to sleep. Already the sun was melting over the treetops.

Instead, she saw only the fine details of wood and plaster, intent on capturing them on film.

Concentrating on her documentation, she didn't notice the tall shadow which separated from the darkness of the front court.

Nor did she see the glittering eyes which scrutinized her, harder than burnished steel.

"Nice…very nice," a hard voice growled. "And it's about bloody time you got here."

Her breath checked, Kacey spun about.

He stood well over six feet, broad-shouldered and lean, eased into a battered tweed jacket and form-fitting charcoal trousers. His face was a fascinating play of angles and shadows in the darkness of the stables.

His eyes smoldered.

Dangerous, she thought dimly, sensing an aura of power about him that fairly crackled.

And made her own skin tingle in response.

Frowning, Kacey tamped down her rioting pulse. "Who—" To her fury, she found she had to swallow before continuing. "Who are you? You nearly terrified me."

The man continued to study her in silence, a lock of black hair fallen across his brow.

Her frown grew. "Lord Draycott? But I thought…" For the first time, Kacey noticed the faint silver scar running across the man's cheekbone.

It gave him the cold look of a pirate—a modern-day pirate, the sort who would raid corporations rather than coastal settlements.

One dark brow slanted up, mocking her.

The sight made Kacey lift her chin and stare back coolly, her green eyes glittering.

"Don't let them intimidate you, love," Cassandra had warned her back in New York. "These wretched bluebloods will walk all over you if you give them half a chance. Don't forget, it's still the sixteenth century as far as they're concerned."

Only Kacey wasn't about to be any man's doormat.

Her lips tight, she shot him a challenging look. "I'm K. C. Mallory. Cassandra Edwards sent me."

The man's expression did not change. "Cassandra Edwards?" He seemed to find the name unfamiliar.

His voice was dark silk, and it made Kacey's skin tighten and prickle. The sight of that dark hair shadowing his open collar was doing equally strange things to her pulse.

Get a hold of yourself, Kacey girl.

"I've come about the—" She started to say "the Whistler," then recalled that Lord Draycott had stipulated that the project be kept totally secret. "About the research work," she finished carefully.

His eyes slid from her windblown hair to the tips of her boots, missing no detail. Finally his full lips curved in the ghost of a smile.

"Nice. Yes, very nice, indeed. I shall have to thank—Cassandra, did you say her name was?" He moved a step closer, his face made even leaner by the shadows.

"Cassandra Edwards," Kacey repeated impatiently, trying to ignore the sudden trip beat of her heart. She saw his lips tense in a hard line, as if he were struggling to retain his control.

Dimly, Kacey found herself wondering just what it would take to make him lose that control, to melt the ice in those wintry eyes. She shivered slightly, her pulse jerky. "You *are* Lord Draycott, aren't you?"

"Does it matter?"

Kacey frowned. What was wrong with the man, anyway? "I'd like an answer. *Now.* If you are not Lord Draycott, then I'm wasting my time here."

"Oh, you're not wasting your time, my dear. I assure you of that." Smiling, the man moved a step closer, so close now that Kacey could feel the heat of his hard body. "The Cassandra Edwards in New York, is it, by any chance?"

"Of course it is. She received your cable last—" Kacey had

time for no more. Somehow his fingers were cradling her face, his thumb tracing the curve of her cheek.

She froze. "What do you think you're—"

"First things first, my dear," he murmured, moving closer, so that she felt his heat in earnest, along with the barely unleashed power of his lean body.

Until she wanted to feel much, much more.

What in the name of heaven was happening to her?

As she stumbled away from him, his lips quirked in a mocking challenge. "I shall have to assess your qualifications before we talk business, my dear."

Kacey took another step back. Her pulse was wild, her heart slamming against her ribs. Something was very, very wrong here.

"Cassandra sent my *vita* ages ago," she snapped. "Or are you having second thoughts because I'm a woman?"

"Oh, I wouldn't have it any other way, my dear," he said silkily.

Their eyes locked, slate-gray to jade-green. The force of the contact was enough to make her jump.

Kacey's jaw set in a mutinous line. The man was a bastard, no mistake about it, but this job was too important to risk losing. *Steady, kiddo. Show him that it takes a damn sight more than one insolent Englishman to frighten you away!*

She was just getting ready to tell him so when his hand curved around her shoulder, slipping deep into the warm hair at the back of her neck. Her eyes widened in shocked inquiry. She tried to speak, but her throat was suddenly too dry.

"Very nice indeed," he murmured. "Kacey, did you say your name was? Let me see—personable. Intelligent. Open to new ideas. Everything I requested. You are all those things, aren't you?" His voice, just beside her ear, was low and darkly intimate, as if they were sharing a private joke.

"Yes, I suppose so," Kacey began impatiently. "But—"

And then his mouth came down on hers, darker than the

shadows gathering through the stable. As electric as the bright, jagged bolts playing out over the channel.

As fiercely erotic as any of those forbidden thoughts she had been trying so hard to ignore.

His mouth opened, urgent and persuasive, demanding a response. And somehow Kacey gave it, her lips softening beneath his.

His breath hissed out in a hot growl of triumph.

He wanted her, she thought dimly.

And, dear God, she *wanted* him to want her. Suddenly it seemed as if her whole life had been no more than a prelude to this moment.

She didn't move, dizzy with shock. *What was happening to her?* For wild heartbeats, she stood paralyzed beneath his touch, aware of a thousand different sensations at once.

The cold still air on her face and neck. The lingering smell of hay and old leather. The distracting tickle of his tweed collar against her neck.

And always there was the raw awareness of the man himself. His mouth hot against hers. His fingers, powerful and demanding, where they teased her neck to electric awareness. His restless tongue exploring the locked barrier of her lips.

He moved over her like a man with a mission, and dimly Kacey realized that right now she was the mission.

She caught back a moan. Suddenly she was dizzy and spinning and nothing else in the world mattered but that he stop.

And that he *never* stop.

His ribs crushed her chest, and his taut thighs backed her against the wall. She blinked, stunned by the hardness of his body pressing against her softness.

A raw, choked moan escaped her dry throat. Was she mad? She drew her palms up to his chest, meaning to push him away.

But he caught the sound of her moan between his open lips and answered with a hoarse groan of his own. He seemed to sense exactly where to skim her neck to drive her wild, exactly how to stroke her tongue until she was shivering with need.

And somehow Kacey seemed to know the same. How to smooth the hard, corded muscles at his shoulders. How to feather her fingers through the black hair at his temples. How much he enjoyed it when she tightened her lips around his restless tongue and drew a ragged moan from him in turn.

Not *if,* but *when.* As if she'd done this all a thousand times before.

Her fingers tensed at his chest. *But you have touched him like this before,* a dark voice whispered. *And he's touched you just the same. Until you begged him for more—much more—than this.*

Dark, heated images swept over her.

Images of hard thighs and soft, yielding hips.

Images of his long fingers, sure and urgent, feathering over her naked thighs, parting her softness. His body rising over her.

Kacey's breath caught in a ragged gasp. *Madness!*

"St-stop!" she hissed, even then feeling the pull of those erotic images. She balled her hands into fists and shoved desperately at his chest. "Let—let me go!"

But her protests came too late to be believable, and they both knew it.

The next minute, she was swept up in his arms and tossed facedown over his shoulder. Blood surged in hot waves to her head as she fought her way through the drugging storm of passion he had aroused so unerringly. Furiously, Kacey flayed at his back and shoulders, kicking her booted feet wildly. All the time, she cursed herself for being the worst sort of fool. "What in the name of heaven do you think you're—"

The next minute, she was spinning through space, landing with a sharp jolt in a mound of sun-warmed hay. Far above, a ray of fading sunlight slanted down through a mullioned window, one faint golden gleam amid the shadows.

He had tossed her down in one of the stalls! Was the man completely insane?

Or was *she*?

With trembling fingers, Kacey pushed up onto one elbow and swept a tangled mass of hair from her eyes. She'd had more than enough of this fool and his arrogance—and more than enough of her own strange reaction to him!

"I don't know who you are or what you think you're doing, but I'll see that you're struck from Cassandra's client list. You'll never get another researcher down here ever again, I promise you that! So your precious Lord Draycott can just kiss off any other restoration projects he might have in mind. Believe me, when I'm done, you won't be able to find a restorer in Timbuktu who'd work here!"

The man's only answer was a sardonic smile. In horrified silence, Kacey watched his long fingers drop to his belt.

A deep red blush stained her pale cheeks. "Just what in the name of hell do you think you're doing now?" she demanded.

The slate eyes narrowed. His belt slid free with a soft hiss, darkly intimate in the confined space of the stall. "Doing, my dear? Why, I'm getting ready to screw you, of course."

CHAPTER THREE

THE SILVER EYES NARROWED, smoldering. "That *is* how you say it on your side of the Atlantic, is it not? If you can supply a better word, of course I'd be happy to use it." His hard fingers tossed the belt to the stable floor. "I don't believe I've ever had an American before. I find I'm rather looking forward to the experience."

White-hot fury exploded through Kacey's veins. None of this could actually be happening, could it?

But the tingling of her lips where his mouth had savaged hers told Kacey this was no dream. The urgent tension of her skin, clamoring for more of his heat, told her the same thing.

She pushed unsteadily to her knees, brushing wildly at the errant bits of straw clinging to her hair and face. "Now just wait one damn minute! You can't really believe—" Her voice died away sharply when she saw his fingers fall to his zipper.

"We can discuss your terms later. Of course they will depend on just how well you…perform for me."

Kacey's heart slammed against her chest. "Perform! *T-terms!*" she croaked. Her breath was coming in jerky little gusts now. "Listen—this is some kind of joke, right? You can't possibly believe that—"

Wide-eyed, she stared at the place where his hands worked. The fabric was stretched taut, she saw.

The realization of just why it was so tight sent a wave of crimson shooting through Kacey's cheeks and neck.

Her heart was hammering so loudly she could barely hear. "Well, you—you can just take your fine title, your expensive car, and your fancy belt and—and—stow them where you sit!"

His only answer was a dry chuckle.

And then, with a sharp metallic snap, his zipper slid free.

Kacey's eyes fixed in horrified fascination on that tight square of charcoal wool. "You—you wouldn't *dare!* You couldn't—"

Hard, work-callused fingers began to pull the zipper.

Down.

Lower and lower.

The fabric parted slowly, inch by inch, to reveal more bronzed skin, sprinkled with springy black hair.

Hungry skin. All aroused male.

Kacey's tongue was wedged in her mouth. Her pulse was out of control. That's when it hit her.

There was nothing beneath the cloth—nothing but taut bronzed skin and a mat of dark hair, a denser version of that shadowing his open collar.

And in a few more seconds he would—

Suddenly the man's fingers went still. "You *are* the call girl I phoned for, aren't you?"

Kacey's eyes widened. A firestorm of fury ripped through her at his cold question. Dear God, he thought she was a—

She took a ragged breath, focusing her fury on his mocking eyes. Even now she found it difficult to forget that tantalizing V of bronzes skin beneath his hard fingers.

"Get this through your thick skull because I'll tell you only once," she hissed. "I'm an art restorer, damn it! Cassandra Edwards sent me to see Lord Draycott. About a project *he* requested."

The man's eyes narrowed, running thoughtfully over her heaving breasts, noting the taut nipples clearly outlined against the fine lawn of her shirt.

Exquisite, Nicholas Draycott decided. And even more dangerous than he'd thought.

Almost too damn hot to handle.

Almost, he told himself grimly. "What sort of project?" he drawled, clearly skeptical. "A project of Edward Armistead's perhaps?"

"I'm not at liberty to discuss it," Kacey countered. "Only with Lord Draycott."

The slate-gray eyes narrowed. "Indeed. Only with Lord Draycott, is it? Well, I'm afraid he's busy. As his estate manager, I'm the one you'll have to deal with."

"You *were* his estate manager," Kacey hissed. "When I'm done with you, no one will even open a door to you."

"So, the little cat has claws, does it?" Draycott moved closer. "At least we're getting down to the truth."

"Call Cassandra, if you doubt my word. Or call that bloody procuress in London and—"

"Procuress. How quaint."

"Oh, I'm sure *you* know all the proper terms. Having never had dealings in such things before, I confess to complete and total ignorance on that score. My work is rather different, you see. It's honest work. Work performed out of love rather than greed."

"You—an art restorer? Come, come, my dear." His mocking words hit her like a knife. "When was an artisan ever so lovely? So seductively packaged? No, no, let's just dispense with the charade, shall we? I didn't ask for any particular erotic fantasy. I thought I made that very clear to your employer. Simple sex, that's all I require. Maybe later we can try something more—"

Kacey threw back her head and screamed. The gambit had always been useful in silencing her younger siblings when their bickering reached intolerable proportions.

It had the same effect on the Englishman now.

"Now you listen to me, you—you bacon-brained, boneheaded

pile of horse dung." At least she had his complete attention, Kacey thought.

"A mixed metaphor to say the least," he said dryly. "Obviously, English isn't your strong suit."

"No, *art* is, damn you! Now are you going to move back and let me out of here or not? Lord Draycott," she added a moment later, crossing her arms mutinously at her chest.

"Didn't fool you, eh? What a pity." His keen eyes scoured her face. "And the answer's no. Not on your goddamn life, Miss K. C. Mallory."

Kacey's lips tightened as she fought to salvage her rapidly splintering control. Suddenly she went very still, a plan creeping into her head. An outrageous plan. Something entirely out of character.

And then Kacey found herself smiling, a tiny smile that began at the corners of her generous mouth and worked up to glint from her jade eyes. Yes, it would be the perfect thing. And she would get her look at the Whistler, too.

Slowly, she sat back in the straw, studying him through lowered lashes. *Careful now, Katherine Chelsea,* she told herself. *This man's no fool.*

Her tongue gently swept her upper lip.

Lord Draycott's silver-gray eyes narrowed, fixed on the sight. "What the devil—"

He never had time to finish. His breath caught in a rush as the woman in the straw smiled up at him with wanton promise.

Her upper lip was too full. Her forehead was too wide, her neck too long. She had straw scattered all over her hair, for God's sake, Draycott told himself sternly.

And in spite of that she was blindingly beautiful. So beautiful it made him ache.

The sight of her smile was like a fifty-thousand-volt electric current plugged directly into his heart.

Or into his groin, to be more precise.

Her slim fingers moved to the top of her shirt and slipped the first button free.

Slowly. Teasingly. With total awareness of the infinite torture it was causing him.

Draycott growled a curse.

His jade-eyed temptress merely smiled and moved on to the next button.

Suddenly Draycott was on fire, in a way he hadn't been for months. With a pain that had nothing to do with burns or reconstructive surgery.

It was a fire of wanting, of needing. A fire for total possession.

Just as he had possessed this woman long before.

Nicholas frowned, wondering where that crazy thought had come from. Perhaps he was farther gone than he'd realized, cooped up here in the country. Yes, maybe this idea of paid companionship was something he should have considered sooner.

Then his lips twisted in distaste. It was always for payment anyway. There was invariably a price—it was simply paid in different ways.

And then his mind went blank, for the woman's hand was at mid-chest and a pink expanse of skin mocked him along the faint shadow between her breasts.

Two buttons more, Draycott found himself thinking. His breath was coming strangely heavy now, and the pain at his groin didn't even bear thinking about.

The woman smiled slowly, her head tilting back. Showing him she knew damn well what she was doing. And was enjoying the effect thoroughly.

"How do you like my performance so far?" Kacey murmured huskily, her voice as rich and textured as the erotic current flowing between them.

To Draycott's infinite disgust, he had to clear his throat before

he could answer. "Just—fine. But I think I'll suspend judgment…
until I've seen everything you're offering."

Strange, he thought absently—her hand seemed to quiver for
a moment at his words. But then the next button slipped free,
and he forgot everything but how the full upper swell of her
breasts beckoned, gently shadowed in the growing twilight of
the stable.

Dear God, don't stop now, Draycott found himself praying,
only to tamp down the thought a moment later. It was never
meant to go this far, after all. Just far enough to scare her off.

And to see that she scared off anyone else with similar plans.

Only now, with her before him like this, half-clothed, her
smile warm and inviting, Nicholas was finding it hard to breathe,
much less to think clearly.

"Oh, you'll like it," the woman whispered, rising slowly to her
feet. Deeply V-ed, the white fabric strained against her breasts,
lovingly cupping the lush curves beneath.

Draycott felt beads of sweat break out on his brow. "Perhaps
we should discuss terms now, after all," he muttered, unable to
tear his eyes away from that erotic shadow.

From the dusky, upthrust nipples tormentingly outlined
against the thin lawn.

"Oh, not yet, surely. I've so much more to show you, my lord.
And you *will* show me that pretty painting of yours in return,
won't you? I've heard so much about it." Kacey managed a husky
giggle. "I just can't wait to tell all my friends I've seen it!" Her
fingers slipped lower, tugging the white shirt free of the waist-
band of her jeans.

Draycott had to struggle to hear anything she was saying.
Painting? Good sweet Jesus, she was the painting! A perfect Bot-
ticelli masterpiece. He could look at her forever, he thought dimly.

"You do remember the painting," Kacey prompted, her voice
a sultry caress. "In the long gallery, isn't it?"

"The painting," he repeated mechanically. "On the fourth floor." He had to tell her to stop, Nicholas thought.

He had to tell her *not* to stop.

Her full mouth curved in a blinding smile, and the sight was like a shaft of sunlight plunged right into his heart.

He wanted to see her smile like that always, the Englishman thought. When she awoke, her hair tousled on his pillow. When he slipped off her clothes and plunged deep inside her.

When he felt her convulse in wild, breathless passion beneath him, whispering his name.

Dear God, what was wrong with him? Had he lost the last ragged shreds of his sanity?

"Now you listen to me, young lady," Draycott began, feeling priggish and a complete fool.

She didn't listen.

Instead, her slim hands drifted down to the last, tantalizing button of her shirt. A secret smile on her face, she began to inch toward him. "Oh, I'm listening, my lord. You have my total attention, I assure you."

Draycott couldn't have moved even if the stables were on fire and the roof falling on his head.

Which in a way, they were, at least as far as his screaming senses were concerned.

Her eyes challenging, the beautiful intruder slipped past him. One hand trailing across his tensed shoulders, she teased the bunched muscles at his neck. The faint scent of gardenias rose from her warm skin, inundating his senses. Tightening muscles already taut past enduring.

She was all woman—all soft, yielding desire. She was the fire that lit his restless nights, the dream that tormented his lonely days.

His breath hissed out with the nearness of her. He felt her slip around him, then draw close to his back. He was on fire with wanting her; he was driven by an infinite need to touch her.

In every way that a man had ever touched a woman—and then some.

He was—

Falling?

With his next heartbeat, Draycott was spinning down, his legs kicked straight out from under him. Gasping, he hit the cold cobblestone floor, breaking his fall with knees and wrists. What in the name of bloody everlasting hell?

He cursed harshly, struggling to stand, fighting the raw agony radiating from his kneecaps. He was still cursing when he heard the doors to the stall slam shut behind him. With a sharp thump, a piece of wood was wedged between the handles on the outside of the door.

"Enjoy your evening, Lord Draycott," the woman outside said sweetly. "I'm afraid it will be rather colder than the night you had planned, but maybe you'll learn something in there—not that I count on it overly much. Oh, and don't hold your breath waiting for Cassandra to send down another restorer. You've had your chance, and frankly, you've just blown it."

Fury swept through Nicholas—fury at his own stupidity. Fury at her cunning.

Fury at how much he wanted her still, in spite of everything.

What would the little bitch do now?

Exactly what she'd come here to do, of course. And like a fool he'd told her exactly where to find the Whistler.

Kiss it goodbye, imbecile. If it's the Whistler she's after she knows how to get it. If it's information she wants she can get that, too. And she'll be long gone before you can even work that bloody door free!

The viscount's eyes rose, smoking with rage, assessing the twelve-foot walls around him with disgust.

Bloody blazing hell, Nicholas Draycott thought grimly.

How could he possibly be such a damn fool?

Again.

CHAPTER FOUR

KACEY WAS GASPING BY THE time she reached the front of the stable. Just beyond, sheer granite walls beckoned across a silver sheet of water, shadowed and smooth in the gathering darkness.

Somewhere to the south, heat lightning dug phosphorous fingers into the channel, but she barely noticed.

He must have come out this way. There had to be a wretched door here somewhere! Breathlessly, she ran over the narrow two-arched stone bridge that spanned the moat. And then she saw the door, tucked behind the base of a chimney, painted gray to blend in with the granite walls.

Kacey's heart raced. Did she dare? What if she met someone—a servant or a relative?

A wife?

She resolutely ignored the faint sliver of emotion that pricked her at the thought, seizing the doorknob and twisting violently.

The door slid open smoothly before her, revealing a long corridor of spotless, sparkling marble. She stopped, turning back to listen to the night.

No noise, no angry shouting. Good, he must have given up. Now to find the stairway.

Warily, she slipped inside, feeling a shiver work down her spine as the silence of the abbey's interior fell over her like a cool, enveloping cloak.

Welcome, the house seemed to say. *We've been waiting for you...*

Kacey caught her breath, fighting her dark fancies. Too much traveling, she told herself. Too little to eat.

Of course—it was all so simple. There was nothing wrong with her that a decent meal and a full night's sleep wouldn't cure.

She stopped only long enough to tug off her boots and tuck them under one arm. Then, soundless and graceful, she darted off toward the stairway and her waiting Whistler, determined to have at least one sight of the tantalizing canvas before she turned her back on this place forever.

Never say forever, the house seemed to whisper.

Forever has a way of happening. In places and ways you haven't begun to imagine.

That dim warning, too, Kacey ignored, gripping her lip between her teeth and telling herself to get on with this wild escapade and then get the devil out of here.

It took her only seconds to find the massive oak staircase. She looked neither right nor left, denying herself the pleasure of that rare and ancient house. Somehow she knew she must close her eyes to its beauty, that if she dropped her guard even once she would never find the strength to leave.

And now there was a clock ticking in her head, telling her that a silver-eyed predator was only minutes behind her. Driven by sheer adrenaline, she found her way to the top floor.

And there she forgot her fear. For now the luminous canvas was before her, shimmering in the first faint rays of moonlight spilling through the long gallery's tall windows.

There Kacey made her last, and most deadly, mistake, which was to underestimate the man with the voice like silk and the eyes like beaten silver.

Eyes that she seemed to have known forever.

HE FOUND HER AT THE SOUTH wall of the long gallery, seated before the great canvas. Her long legs were tucked beneath her, and her eyes were radiant.

The Englishman's face filled with awe at the picture she made, her long hair gleaming silver in the moonlight, her whole being suffused with love for the canvas before her.

Suddenly he was ripped by jealousy at the warmth that glowed from her eyes, angry that he wasn't the one who'd put it there.

Suddenly he wanted to be an artist so he could paint her.

A poet so he could capture her in exquisite words.

Most of all, he wanted to be her lover so he could know her warmth always and in a thousand intimate ways.

And then, like a dirty tide, memories of Bhanlai washed over him. Memories of betrayal. Memories of deceit and the blinding pain and rage that came in its aftermath.

Memories of the other woman for whom he had also wanted to be all those things—a woman who'd taught him everything there was to know about betrayal.

Draycott's jaw clenched. In the moonlight, the muscles at his neck stood out clearly. He fought down the urge to stride through the gallery and shake her. He shook beneath a fierce need to touch her—to crush her against the wall and bury himself deep in her heat and softness.

Unaware of the brooding presence behind her, the woman came slowly to her feet. She shook herself slightly, as if fighting the spell of the great canvas. Her eyes were fixed still on the dim, phantom boat that rocked in timeless silence beneath a lavender moon.

Her heart filled with its beauty, Kacey breathed a silent song of thanks for this rare gift she'd been given.

For having glimpsed such a masterpiece, even once. Most of all, for the knowledge, deep in her heart, that it was indeed from Whistler's hand.

A tear slipped down her cheek, For long moments, she didn't move, struggling with nameless regrets and disturbing memories, shadowed fragments that clamored up from some dark place inside her, so deep that she had never before guessed they existed.

Go now, Katherine Chelsea. Go now, or you'll never go!

One hand to her lips, she spun about and stumbled toward the door. In her desperation to be away, she didn't notice the tall shadow unmoving amid the other shadows of the silent room.

Her trembling fingers rose, sweeping her eyes blindly, and then she was gone.

HIDDEN IN THE SHADOWS OF the long gallery, Nicholas Draycott stood frozen, his hard fingers clenched into fists. His head spun as he tried to grasp what he'd just seen. She hadn't taken the painting after all. And that meant—

Abruptly his expression hardened. *It means nothing, you fool. It means that she wants photographs and juicy gossip, not canvases. She probably doesn't even now what the hell she's looking at.*

Draycott reminded himself what she'd said back in the stable. She'd called the canvas a pretty picture, for God's sake!

But try as he might, he couldn't forget her hesitation and the dreamy look on her face. Right now, every sense was clamoring that he was wrong about her.

In spite of that instinct, something made him hold back, waiting silently in the shadows outside the door.

Merely the logical need to learn her real intentions, he told himself coldly. Merely a natural desire to see that she took nothing with her when she left.

By the time she reached the front staircase, he was gone, melting back into the darkness, where an ancient rear staircase ran down to a hidden passage leading out to the gatehouse.

Just in case she stole something else on her way out, Draycott told himself.

But he knew that, too, was a lie.

THE FIRST FAT DROPS OF rain had just begun to fall when Kacey jerked open the side door. Her shoulders slumped as she stood staring out into the night. A long sigh escaped her tense lips.

So this was it—no way out except to walk to town. So be it. She absolutely refused to go back and ask that misbegotten swine in the stable for anything, not even if her life depended on it!

She tossed her bag firmly over her shoulder. At least these wretched boots might actually prove to be of some use, she thought, smiling grimly.

She turned up her collar, then tugged the top of her trench coat up over her head, fighting to see through the slanting sheets of wind-driven rain.

Far to the south, ghostly fingers of fire ripped the sky, and a tremor snaked through her. Fear? Or was it regret?

No, something else, she decided.

But then Kacey had all she could do to keep herself upright as she tottered over the rain-slick grass. Unused to the new boots she was wearing, she tripped painfully and often. Each time she bit her lip against the pain and forced herself forward into the rushing darkness.

It couldn't be more than five miles to town, after all. Her bus ride from the village had taken no more than fifteen minutes, surely.

But in the night and the lashing rain, five miles seemed like the other side of the world.

Which means you'd better get started, she thought. At least she would have the memory of the painting to warm her. Yes, that memory would last her for a very long time.

Fifteen minutes later her hair was plastered to her ashen cheeks and her lips were blue-tinged, even though she hadn't reached the bottom of the hill. The lightning was much closer now, her only beacon in the sullen darkness of the storm.

She would be dangerously exposed out here in the middle of

the sweeping lawns, Kacey realized. Soon she'd have to cut west, toward that dim line of beeches, silver against the darkness.

She stumbled again and bit back a moan of pain, feeling her ankle swell.

Surely no more than four miles to go, she told herself optimistically.

Suddenly she stiffened, listening to the wind howl through the trees. Somewhere a branch ripped free and plummeted past her.

She frowned, tugging her coat tighter over her head. She was just asking herself how she'd gotten into this mess when she heard the other sound.

It came from nowhere and everywhere, and the hands were from the fabric of night itself, jerking her around and holding her rigid.

Kacey screamed.

His face was a cold mask of anger, etched by deep lines at his forehead and cheeks. But then Kacey saw something else—the buried traces of anxiety and concern. For *her,* in spite of what she'd done.

For a wild instant, she felt a primal desire to brush the lines from that brooding face. To set the fires of passion aglow in those silver eyes once again.

His fingers bit into her shivering shoulders. "Just where in the name of God do you think you're going?" he growled, struggling to be heard against the wind.

"Back to Alfriston," she cried. "Back to sanity. Back to civilization. Anyplace that's away from *you!*"

A muscle flashed at the granite line of his jaw. His fingers tightened. "It's eight miles to the village. You'll never make it in the dark."

"Why not? I happen to like walking!"

His smoldering eyes settled on her mud-stained boots. "Especially in *those,* no doubt," he said disgustedly.

"Then I'll just have to take them off, won't I?" Kacey jerked free and bent down to tug at her boots. One came free and went flying, hitting him in the knee. He winced, she noticed happily. A moment later, the other spun off, sailing into the darkness.

Catching back an angry sob, she plunged forward toward a bleak cluster of yew trees, trying to ignore the paralyzing cold seeping into her bare feet.

"You crazy, headstrong—" With a ragged curse, Draycott seized her and swung her up over his shoulder.

"Let me go! Put me down this instant, you bastard!"

But the Englishman's hard, pounding gait did not slacken. Her bag bouncing over the grass, he set off over the rolling lawns to the house.

Gasping, Kacey hammered his sodden back, tugged at his hair, and lashed out with her bare feet, all without the slightest apparent effect.

"Put me down!" she screamed. This time, her voice was ragged with fear.

Draycott went absolutely still. "You promise not to bolt if I do?"

Her heart thundering, Kacey considered her answer. She could lie, of course, but somehow she felt it necessary to meet him head on, with total honesty. "I won't run. Not yet, anyway."

Grim-faced, Draycott pulled her from his shoulder. The next instant Kacey was sliding slowly down his rain-slick body.

He was all hardness, bone and muscle against her softness. And Kacey felt his need revealed clearly in every taut, wet inch.

Her feet touched the grass, and his eyes fell to the small dark crests upthrust against the near transparency of her wet shirt.

Draycott's breath checked. The pain at his groin returned, far worse than before.

"Dear God, who are you?" he said hoarsely. "What are you doing to me?"

Kacey stared back at him, equally dazed. His words drove straight into her heart, echoing the same turmoil she was feeling.

The storm around them paled to insignificance beside the savage, wordless emotions that rocked them both.

Their eyes locked. She felt all his need, his shock, his fury... His vulnerability, no matter how hard he tried to hide it.

Around them, the air shimmered, supercharged, crackling with electricity and the relentless force of their opposing wills.

Time shuddered and then ground slowly to a halt.

Above them, the wind raged on, hurling sheets of rain down onto their frozen bodies. Lightning split the sky, sending an ancient beech smoking to the ground. The world seemed to cry out and twist on its axis, unable to endure this confrontation of relentless opposites.

And then suddenly there was no world and no time, only the two of them. Only the naked need that swept out of some other place to engulf them.

Kacey shuddered, rain sliding chill and forgotten down her face.

Draycott frowned. "You're freezing," he muttered, almost to himself. "You'll catch pneumonia out here." Unconsciously, his grip softened, his fingers cupping her shivering shoulders. "Come back to the abbey with me, Kacey Mallory. Let's begin again." There was a note of desperation in his voice. "I'm afraid I've been a bloody fool. You don't have to be one, too."

Kacey could barely breathe for the intensity of the feelings flowing over her. For the touch of his hard body from her neck to her knees. For the need to feel him far closer still, bodies bared, skin pressed inch to sweat-slick inch.

As they slid into passion's raw center.

When had everything changed? she asked herself dimly. When had she become this strange new person, this wanton creature of hot desire and reckless need?

Dear God, what was happening to her? His touch was too keen, her need too raw.

Settle down, Katharine Chelsea. It's just all those female hormones talking. Maybe you've gone too long without listening to what they had to say.

And they were certainly talking right now—with a vengeance, she thought.

"Kacey?"

One word, but the way he said it, slow and uncertain, nearly pushed her over the edge.

"I—I can't go back." Her words were no more than a whisper. "I won't. I can't ever go back. Not *there*—not with *you!*"

"You must. The Whistler's waiting for you." He paused, studying her tense features. "I saw you in the long gallery, you know. You loved looking at it. You adored it with your eyes. No, don't try to deny it, Kacey. Your eyes couldn't lie—not about a thing like that."

Another shudder ripped through her. It was madness even to consider what he asked. She knew instinctively that she had to get away from this place, from this man. Yes, far away—before she did something crazier still. "Please…"

"Think of it," Draycott whispered, his lips feathering over the chill curve of her ear. "No one else has even seen the canvas for one hundred years. You'll be the first to touch it, to learn its secrets. It's waiting there right now, Kacey. All you have to do is come back with me."

It was the lowest sort of bribe, but Nicholas Draycott didn't care. He couldn't let her go—not this way. Not yet. She was either his sweetest dream or his worst nightmare, and he had to find out which.

Kacey gnawed at her bottom lip. Her body shook, from the cold and the struggle to control some dark, nameless yearning.

But she was losing. Nicholas could feel it in the quiver that ran through her shoulders.

"*Now*, Kacey."

"Oh, all right. Yes, damn you. *Yes!*"

His smile was dark triumph itself. But when he took her hand and tried to pull her back toward the house, Draycott found it was going to be a little more difficult than he'd thought.

Scowling, Kacey dug in her heels. "On three conditions," she shouted against the wind.

"Name them," he yelled back.

"First, we call New York and verify my credentials. I want no more questions on that score."

"Done."

"Second, you move my things—such as they are—into the gatehouse."

Draycott's response was slower this time. "Very well."

"Third, you give me the gatehouse key. No, make that *all* the gatehouse keys."

The Englishman's eyes darkened. "I can't do that," he countered flatly. "There are reasons—"

Kacey spun about and began to stride over the downs toward the village.

"Oh, all right, damn it! One of us has to be sensible about this."

Muttering darkly, Draycott searched for her boots and bent down to shove them on her feet. Scowling, he shrugged out of his coat and pulled it over her head. In the process, his arm encircled her shoulder. Her breast grazed his rib.

They froze, while the rain hammered down on his makeshift tent. For long breathless moments neither moved, caught in the warmth and darkness beneath.

Her hip nudged his thigh; her chin brushed the naked skin at his neck.

Draycott muttered a curse.

You think you're safe, but you're not, Kacey Mallory, his eyes warned from the darkness. *I'll have you. I'll have you every way there is to have a woman. You couldn't stop me if you wanted to. And you don't.*

Somehow she heard his silent challenge, attuned to him as she had never been to any other man. *Not now,* her jade eyes answered. *Not ever, Englishman. You can look forever, but you'll never find me.*

With a little gasp, Kacey broke free and stumbled forward over the grass, knowing no danger could match that of being caught in this man's arms.

Almost immediately she slipped in the wet grass and fell to her knees. Without a word, Draycott swept her up into his arms and strode forward across the glistening sweep of lawn.

Somehow her hands slid around his neck; somehow her fingers combed through his wet hair.

Kacey felt him shudder.

And then the shuddering was hers.

The gatehouse before them, Kacey raised wild, dazed eyes. In the darkness, the towers stood stark and forbidding. The house seemed almost to watch them, a thing of power and tangible will.

Determined to hold sway forever over these ancient acres. In spite of whatever frail, hapless humans might stumble across its shadowed paths.

Kacey frowned, trying to ignore the chill tendrils of fear that swept down her spine. Trying to ignore the angry power of Draycott's tensed shoulders beneath her hands.

How did I ever consider this place comforting? she wondered as the brooding Englishman carried her beneath the stone arch into the silence of the abbey's watchful, waiting walls.

THE STORM PASSED ON TO the north soon after their return. In careful silence, a white-haired butler showed Kacey to a room on the gatehouse's second floor. After reminding her to lock her door, he walked downstairs. A few moments later she heard him lock the ground-level entrance door.

Somehow the sound did little to reassure her.

She walked slowly to the bed and was asleep by the time her head touched the large and ornately embroidered feather pillow.

Twice she came awake during the night, her breath jerky, her muscles tense. But each time, the room was just as she'd left it—velvet bed curtains half pulled, behind a damask wing chair that had seen better days.

Moonlight spilled through the casement windows.

Rat-a-tat-tat-tat. Rat-a-tat. Rat-a-tat.

So that was it! Kacey felt a surge of relief. Just the wind shaking the glass. Just the wooden window frame creaking.

She lay back slowly, holding the bed linens protectively against her neck. It was cold for a June night, and she found herself wishing once again for her bags, which had been lost on the flight from New York. Back at Heathrow, she'd requested that they be shipped on to the abbey, when they were found.

She was reminding herself to phone the airline once again in the morning when her eyelids grew heavy. Her fingers twisted in the pristine sheets, monogrammed with dragon-entwined coronets.

How good it feels to be home again, she thought dimly just before her eyelids closed for good.

IN HIS BEDROOM, NICHOLAS tossed down the agricultural journal he'd been reading and began to pace. The article had been boring enough—he should have fallen asleep hours ago. But sea-green eyes drifted before him, and a vision of tawny-colored hair.

Lips soft and proud by turns, and a body sweet beyond imagining.

With a low curse, he tried to fight the haunting pull of her, to forget the dreams.

But it was no good.

He knew without the slightest hint of a doubt that *she* was the woman in those dreams.

And he the man.

When finally he could pace no more, Nicholas sank tiredly into a chair by the window. The moon was thin and chill, like cobwebs on his face.

He slept—and was tossed instantly into dreams.

Thunder. The slash of rain and wind.

His hands fought the empty air. "Katharine! Come back—you must not go!" His eyes were stark, desperate with fear.

The wind swept back her cloak, and he saw her face. Green-eyed, chiseled beauty at cheek and chin. Her porcelain skin glazed with tears.

Guilt wedged in his throat. He had driven her away. He and Adrian, with their constant quarreling and their everlasting jealousy.

And then her wild, shrill scream, twisting his heart into a thousand pieces.

"*Nooooooo!*" His pulse thundering, Nicholas jerked upright in the chair. At the window a tree branch scraped the glass.

Only the dream, he told himself, trying to steady his breathing. Only an illusion.

But tonight the pain was far worse, because tonight Nicholas had sensed that it all might have turned out differently if he hadn't been so bloody stupid.

He stared out into the silver night, choked by a wave of regret, realizing that this dream was more real than anything he'd ever known.

SILENT AND SILVER, THE moon rose over moat and meadow, dappling yew forest and hedgerow in ice and shadow. Beneath its molten light, the walls of the abbey seemed to shimmer and change, rendered faint and then finally insubstantial.

Like a paper castle in a paper landscape.

An owl cried once from the dark stand of yews at the brow of the hill. A night creature rustled and scurried through the dense shrubbery lining the moat.

Wrapped in a timeless dream, like a sleeper waiting to be kissed back to life, the ancient stones slept on.

The eyes were keen and clear in the moonlight.

Dark and bottomless, they studied the home wood, then swept down to the darkened windows of the turreted gatehouse.

There, the motionless figure thought. So close.

And yet she might just as well have been an eternity away.

The eyes clouded, harsh with regret. But regret was a useless thing. "Regret is life's bitterest poison." Hadn't he read that somewhere, eons ago?

Noiseless, the figure glided across the clipped lawns. The night seemed to hold its breath, the wind to still. As if of its own accord, the oak door swung open.

No light was lit to guide him, nor did the dark figure require any. He found the bedroom by feel and memory alone. He had memories enough for a hundred lifetimes, after all.

And then the moon met him in greeting, poured in a luminous pool on the bare wooden floor. Almost as bright as her hair spilling over the white linen pillow, he thought. Almost as beautiful as her smile, faint and soft and infinitely sweet now in sleep.

The darkness trembled. Will became being. Emotion turned to brooding substance.

A shadow fell over the sleeping woman's face.

Outside the wind rose, shaking the casement, tossing gravel and broken twigs against the gatehouse.

Dreaming still, she twisted restlessly, dimly sensing nature's distant warning.

The glass panes shuddered, and the shuddering turned to rapping. Then the rapping, too, changed—became low, urgent drumming. Beside the window, the thick damask curtains rippled and flared out, with the slow grace of an underwater scene.

The brooding eyes swept over the sleeper's face, issuing a silent command:

Wake up, they whispered. *We have waited long for you, and now the time for sleep is past.*

The phantom eyes waited, raw with hunger.

But for now, seeing her was enough. There would be time for all the rest in the long dreaming midnights of summer yet to come.

Since, of course, she could never be allowed to leave this place again.

CHAPTER FIVE

THE SUN SHONE FROM A cloudless sky the following morning as Kacey halted at the door to a sunny dining room overlooking the moat and western lawns.

His face expressionless, Nicholas Draycott held out a chair for her. "I trust you slept well, Miss Mallory."

He was clean-shaven and perfectly dressed, and the sight only made Kacey angry, since she had been reduced to wearing the same rumpled shirt and creased jeans from yesterday. "Perfectly, thank you," she lied, sliding into her seat, knowing full well that the dark circles under her eyes must belie her words.

"In that case, let's get right down to business," Draycott said in that abrupt, intense way that Kacey was coming to see was a habit with him. "As I see it, we have two choices."

"Aren't you forgetting something?" Kacey countered.

"I don't believe so."

"You agreed to call New York."

"Ah." Draycott paused, his eyes unreadable. "It seems that Ms. Edwards is unavailable. Her answering service said that she had gone on holiday."

Damn! Kacey looked down. Cassandra hadn't told her she was planning to go away. It complicated everything! Frowning, she looked back at Draycott. "Well?"

"Well, what, Miss Mallory?"

"What are you going to do about it?"

"Since I can't very well summon Miss Edwards back from her vacation, we'll just have to proceed as planned—until she returns, at least. I'm prepared to do that much."

Kacey was prepared to do that much, too, but she wasn't about to like it. But what choice had she, really?

Partly to avoid those piercing silver-gray eyes, Kacey looked out the window, where bright morning sunlight streamed through emerald velvet curtains worked with a dragon crest and an entwined D.

The Draycott coat of arms, no doubt, she thought sourly.

In the aftermath of the storm, the air was crystal clear and the lawns hung with diamonds of dew. From somewhere over the hill, she heard the distant bleating of sheep. Today even the sheer granite walls seemed less forbidding—sunwarmed, dappled by scattered patches of lichen.

Almost protective, somehow.

Yes, in the bright light of day Kacey could almost convince herself that yesterday had been a bad dream.

Until she looked up into Draycott's piercing eyes, that was. Into his chiseled, brooding face, which quickly reminded her that what had happened in the stable was anything but a dream.

There was no way to forget how those eyes had stripped her bare. How his hard body had felt when he'd swept her up and carried her back to the gatehouse.

Her throat turned dry; heat swirled through her.

Just simple, low-grade lust, Kacey told herself flatly. *He's one damn handsome man, and it's been far too long since you've had a good case of lust.*

Dark and unreadable, his eyes grazed her lips. Suddenly Draycott smiled as if he'd read her guilty thoughts.

Heat swept across Kacey's high cheekbones, staining her face and neck. At that moment Draycott's daunting butler entered bearing steaming trays of eggs, crisp bacon, toast points and an array of condiments.

"Ah, Marston. Thank you." Nicholas settled back in his chair, waiting for the servant to finish before resuming the conversation.

In the interim, Kacey studied the room. Everything was exceedingly civilized. Fine old china. Gleaming crystal. A blinding array of silver—all sporting the Draycott dragon crest, of course.

The butler served discreetly while the earl murmured polite suggestions to Kacey. But by the time the servant withdrew, she was feeling very much the interloper, the clumsy colonial upstart. She knew she had faint shadows under her eyes, and her coloring was just short of cadaverous. Her hair must have looked a total disaster. She sat in the blinding sunlight, feeling like a grubby schoolgirl summoned before the lord of the manor, who sat infuriatingly neat and crisp in a white shirt, tailored wool pants, and a much-worn wool jacket in a muted gray tweed.

Kacey began to toy with her eggs.

"You may eat them, you know. They're neither drugged nor poisoned, I assure you."

But at that moment she couldn't have swallowed anything. "I'm—I'm not very hungry," she lied. Unfortunately her stomach chose that precise instant to growl—quite loudly.

Draycott's brows slanted upward. "Indeed."

There it was again. That irritating word which could mean a thousand things—or nothing at all.

"As I was saying, we appear to have two choices, Miss Mallory."

"Indeed," Kacey said silkily, managing to force down a spoonful of eggs.

Something flared deep in Draycott's eyes for a moment, but he ignored her mocking imitation. "One is for you to leave today, as you seem so dead-set on doing. That would hurt both of us. You, because you'll never get to see the Whistler again, and me, because something tells me I'll never find another conservator with even half your skill."

His calm assessment stunned Kacey. "And the second option?" she asked, somewhat breathlessly.

"Is that you stay on here at the abbey. I'll see that you have free access to the painting, along whatever materials and tools you require. Your hours will be entirely your own. That, my dear Miss Mallory, would be to both our benefits."

It was tempting, Kacey had to admit. By daylight, the man looked almost human.

Almost, she reminded herself quickly. *He tossed you over his shoulder like a caveman yesterday, remember? He thought you were a call girl hired for a night's pleasure.*

"So which is it to be, Miss Mallory?" Draycott's gray eyes taunted her. "Or do you perhaps feel unequal to the job?"

Kacey stiffened. "I'm more than up to any job you can give me, Lord Draycott." Her jade eyes glittering, she shot him a furious look. "And don't you have a real-life name? We Yanks have never cared much for ranks and titles, you know."

The dark brow slanted higher. "Nicholas is my given name. You may use it, if you prefer, since my title seems to make you uncomfortable. But if it's not the work you're afraid of, then perhaps it's something else." His slate eyes narrowed. "Me, perhaps?"

"In a pig's eye!"

"Yourself then? After all, your performance last night was quite convincing. One might almost say you put your heart and soul into the act. Perhaps *that's* what's really troubling you, Miss Mallory—the thought that you're just not up to the temptation of staying at Draycott Abbey. With me," he added.

"Don't flatter yourself, Lord—Nicholas! Resisting you will be the easiest thing I've ever done!"

"In that case, I fail to see any reason for your reluctance. It will be a simple business proposition, nothing more."

Kacey frowned. He was right, of course. There was no reason for all this anxiety. Her days would be spent in solitude up in the long gallery, doing the work that she loved best.

Her frown deepened. *But there'd always be the nights,* a voice whispered. *And you're not half so immune to this man as you'd like to believe.*

She looked down at her plate, all fruit and florals coiling against a pink porcelain background. Like everything about this house, the china was old and tasteful and colossally expensive.

In tense silence, she pushed the plate away.

So what's the problem? she asked herself. Just say no and be done with it.

Her lips moved. To her total shock, the words that tumbled out sounded strangely like "All right, I'll do it."

A hint of emotion flickered over Draycott's chiseled features—a look that was too hard for relief and too wary for triumph. "I'm pleased to hear it. I'll have a suite prepared for you on the second floor. Marston will see to whatever you require in the way of materials and supplies, although I expect you will have brought most of that sort of thing with you. And if you need anything else, just—"

"Impossible," Kacey said flatly, already regretting her moment of weakness. "No suite—not here in the main house. It's the gatehouse or nothing at all."

Draycott eased back in his chair. The sun on his white shirt was very nearly blinding, enhancing the dark bronze of his neck and face.

His eyes began to glitter dangerously. He took his time about answering, studying the wave of crimson that swept her cheeks. "That would be entirely out of the question, I'm afraid," he said flatly.

"Now, how did I know you were going to say that?" Kacey snapped. "In that case, our arrangement is off, too." She tossed down her napkin and pushed up from her chair. "Good day, Lord Draycott. I wish I could say it's been a pleasure."

The Englishman's eyes narrowed. "Are you always this irascible, Miss Mallory? Or is it merely I who have the dubious honor of being able to provoke you to fury?"

Dimly, Kacey realized her behavior was totally out of character, but she wasn't about to admit that to this insufferable egotist!

Draycott's dark eyes mocked her. "I see. In that case, I must remember to stay well out of your way in the future."

It was a complete and total lie, of course. Nicholas Draycott only intended to get closer and closer to her. For some reason, that challenge had become at least as important to him as the restoration of the Whistler.

Kacey's fingers gripped the back of her chair. "That will hardly be necessary. For we have no future, you and I. That, I promise you!"

Draycott looked down. "I see I shall have to tell you the truth. You see, in the last weeks there have been several…incidents here at the abbey. Oh, nothing serious—a rake disappearing here, a chair there. Nothing to worry about." He eyes turned hard. "Until last week, that is."

"And then?"

"Someone broke into the gatehouse—ransacked the place royally. One very fine Turner landscape was slashed and two more were stolen. No one was hurt, thank goodness."

"Was the thief caught?"

"Unfortunately, no. The police have had a look, but the culprit was damnably thorough. No prints. No clues of any sort."

That was not quite true either, Draycott thought. There had been clues—if a person knew what to look for.

"Can't you just replace the locks?" Kacey demanded, clinging stubbornly to her original plan.

"They had been changed the day before the robbery. The

man—or men—simply broke through the gatehouse windows. It's far enough from the main house that we could hear nothing." Draycott's face hardened. "So you see it would be quite out of the question for you to stay out there. Not now at any rate."

Kacey's breath caught as she realized there was something he wasn't telling her. "And you expect whoever it is to return, don't you?"

For a fleeting moment, Draycott looked startled. "I do. Especially now."

"You mean once the news of your Whistler starts trickling out."

He nodded grimly.

"Perhaps it already has."

"The thought has crossed my mind, too."

"Is that why you were so suspicious of me last night?"

"That reason—among other reasons," Draycott answered cryptically.

"How do you know that I'm not? One of *them,* I mean?"

"I don't," the Englishman said bluntly. "But I mean to find out very soon. And if you are—one of them, as you put it—I'd rather have you here where I can see you than somewhere else," he added.

"I see." Suddenly Kacey did see. That his performance last night was simply to smoke out a thief. That his passion had been no more than a clever ruse.

She refused to consider why the idea should leave her with a lingering sense of regret. Meanwhile it seemed she had no choice but to do as Draycott required—if she wanted to see the Whistler again.

Her fingers twisted back and forth on the chair rung. "Very well. I'll stay here in the abbey," she said at last. "As long as *you* agree to stay out of my way while I'm working."

His eyes followed her, dark with challenge. "And the rest of the time, Miss Mallory?"

"The same condition applies."

Very carefully, the earl dropped his damask napkin on the

table. He uncoiled his tall frame slowly and came to his feet, his eyes never leaving her face. "Then of course I must not interfere in your work. Beyond that—I promise to do nothing you don't wish me to do, Kacey Mallory."

A faint flush swept her cheeks, but he was gone before she could tell him that the only thing she wanted from him was to be left alone.

Damn the man's arrogance! If he thought she was open to a casual flirtation, he'd find himself snapping at thin air.

Yes, I'll see you in hell first, Nicholas Draycott, Kacey swore silently.

Behind her, the air seemed to shimmer and tremble. A shadow fell across the corridor. *That, too, might be arranged, Katharine,* the darkness seemed to whisper. *For there are many different kinds of hell, and a great many are right here on earth. Hell is wanting what you can never again have. Hell is facing something that was once yours and knowing that you destroyed it wantonly.*

So speak that word carefully, the darkness murmured. *Lest you find it sooner than you think.*

And the ghost of Draycott Abbey had reason to know that particular lesson better than most.

THIRTY MINUTES LATER, Kacey closed her mind to the viscount and every other concern, settling down to her work.

In the daylight, the painting was even more magnificent than it had appeared the night before. Now every subtle stroke of muted gray, lavender and turquoise was clearly visible.

A masterpiece of design, the canvas showed a river scene captured at jewellike twilight, with a single gray figure standing at the end of a shadowy pier. In the distance rocked a phantom ship, lanterns lit, agleam from empty masts.

But was it a genuine Whistler? Kacey asked herself. Her

heart said yes, but her mind warned her to stay cautious as she considered a thousand questions of pigment, brushstroke, and canvas treatment.

From somewhere outside came the crunch of feet on gravel, then the creak of a car door opening. A motor roared to life, smooth and powerful.

The sleek two-door number in black, no doubt. Kacey had to fight an errant compulsion to peek out the window.

With an explosive roar, car and driver were gone, gravel skittering in their wake.

Kacey felt her heart give a little lurch. Silence fell once more, heavier now. She tried to tell herself everything was the same, but somehow without Draycott, the house felt different—hushed, waiting. Without fire or heart.

Just as she waited?

Forget him, will you!

Suppressing an irritated sigh, she carried the bulky painting to a chair near the window. Carefully, she tilted it back to catch the full rays of the midmorning sun. Despite modern technology, there was simply nothing like natural sunlight to reveal faint details in painting.

The canvas was clearly fragile, weakened by the hard treatment Whistler was famous for meting out to his paintings. Never content with a single stroke, he often scoured the cloth, digging with brush and file to soften the background for the muted subtlety he prized.

But a few hours of exposure would not harm this one, Kacey decided. There seemed to be little damage beyond a slight buckling of the wooden struts and some crackling of the paint near the signature. In several spots, the pigment appeared to be losing tone—a constant problem with works by Whistler, who grandly ignored every rule of chemistry and artistic practice in mixing his colors.

Her green eyes lit with excitement, Kacey pulled out her jeweler's loupe. There by the window she knelt and began meticulously inspecting the canvas, inch by inch.

KACEY WAS STILL HUNCHED in that same position two hours later when Marston came to inquire if she would care to take tea downstairs.

At first his soft question did not register.

She blinked, squinting through the small frame of the magnifying lens. The question came again.

Frowning, Kacey looked up, her eyes vague and confused. Only then did she register the butler's presence. Slowly she sat back, rubbing her sore back and shoulders. Unfortunately, she had discovered long ago that aching muscles were an occupational hazard for a restorer.

Yes, it was definitely time for a break, she decided, trying to fight the excitement bubbling up inside her. The pigments were of the correct composition, range, and period; the canvas preparation appeared entirely in keeping with Whistler's practice. With any luck at all, this just might turn out to be the lost Whistler she so hoped it was!

"Might I suggest the front salon?" the butler murmured as she tucked back a long strand of tawny hair and flexed her shoulders wearily. "That room is very pleasant this time of day, with the light reflected from the moat."

A few minutes later, he pushed open a polished wooden door and stood back while Kacey entered a bright room filled with chintz, Chinese blue and white porcelain, and freshly cut flowers. At the center of the far wall, an unbroken expanse of leaded windows opened onto the glittering sweep of the lily-strewn moat and the dark woods beyond.

Kacey caught her breath at the beauty of the scene, moving to the window for a closer look.

Somewhere nearby, a telephone pealed shrilly.

A flicker of annoyance—and something more?—crossed the butler's face as he excused himself to answer.

He returned far sooner than she'd expected. "You have a telephone call, Miss Mallory. You may take it across the hall in the library."

Kacey followed him to a book-lined retreat whose French windows overlooked the rolling lawns to the south and the faint blue haze of the channel. Marston held out a telephone, then retired silently.

"Hello? This is Kacey Mallory."

"Any luck?" It was a low dark murmur, just as if they'd picked up their conversation after a lapse of mere seconds.

"Luck?" Despite her firmest intentions, Kacey's heart lurched uncomfortably. "Oh—you mean about the painting." Of course Draycott meant the painting! "I'm afraid it's far too soon to say anything definite. I thought I explained that to you this morning, Lord Draycott."

"Nicholas."

Kacey plunged ahead, ignoring him. "The choice of subject is quite acceptable, the brushwork extremely good. Masterful even. All of that is very promising, of course, but I must remind you that there are still any number of tests to be done—chemical analysis, canvas inspection, possibly even U-V photography."

"Is it or is it not a forgery, Miss Mallory?" he asked impatiently. "Or aren't you capable of telling me that?"

Kacey's face went white with fury. "No, I can't tell you that. Not yet, at least. No reputable appraiser could, without doing one or two tests. And anyone who tells you otherwise is a damn charlatan! *Lord Draycott,*" she added furiously.

A faint whisper of sound crossed the line. A sigh? And if so, was it of relief, of regret, or of exasperation?

"Very well," the viscount said. "We dine at seven. Try to be prompt, if you please." With that brusque utterance, the phone went dead in her hand.

Kacey put down the receiver, seething at this latest insult. She was still standing that way when the phone rang again.

So now he meant to apologize, did he? Her lips set in a line of sheer stubbornness. This was one apology she wasn't going to miss!

She jerked the phone to her ear. "Draycott Abbey," she purred.

Silence met her—five seconds, then ten.

"Hello?" Kacey repeated irritably. She was nearing the end of her patience with this infuriating man!

"Tell Lord Draycott that my patience is nearly at an end. He now has two days left." It was a male voice, low and clipped.

English with a faint touch of something else, Kacey thought. "Two days? What do you mean?"

"Draycott will know what I mean. I wonder if he will die well. I shall enjoy finding out, I think. And…" There was the faintest calculated pause. "Enjoy your stay at the abbey, Miss Mallory."

Kacey's heart began to pound. The last two words were spoken slowly and very precisely, as if the person at the other end wanted to make it clear that he knew every detail of what went on at the abbey.

Was this Draycott's thief? she wondered wildly. "Who—who is this?" The line went dead.

Her fingers gripped the receiver, white with tension. Suddenly Kacey felt painfully vulnerable and exposed.

Most of all, she found herself wishing that Nicholas Draycott was a great deal closer at hand.

TEATIME CAME AND WENT, then dinner. Lord Draycott was nowhere to be seen.

In the end, Kacey took her dinner on a tray in the long gallery, where she could enjoy the beauty of the golden-tinged Wealden Hills.

The food had been excellent, the setting exquisite. And yet she'd eaten almost nothing.

She returned to work, weary and on edge. Several times she spun about, certain she was being watched. But there was no one behind her—nothing but shadows.

And the taste of her own fear.

Finally, her nerves drawn taut as a bowstring, Kacey angled the mounted canvas back against the wall and stood up. So far, every detail had been absolutely accurate—the physical details, at least. Pigment, backing, canvas, and stroke detail—all appeared correct.

But most of all, the painting *felt* real. Of course, Kacey was wise enough to admit that she *wanted* the canvas to be genuine. And that was very dangerous, because experience had taught her that skepticism was her only true friend when it came to the exacting work she did.

A cool draft brushed her cheek, lifting a long strand of honey-gold hair. Kacey frowned, feeling her muscles throb in the aftermath of her meticulous work.

And yes, God help her, with expectancy and an excitement she could barely contain.

The laugh came at her ear, low and dark with triumph. "You just can't keep away from it, can you, Kacey Mallory?"

CHAPTER SIX

KACEY WENT TOTALLY STILL, her fingers clenched on the wooden slats of the painting. Every muscle leaped to aching attention. Every inch of feminine skin flushed with tense awareness.

Until she could calm her rioting pulse, she refused to turn around.

But that just might be never, with this man around you, a mocking voice whispered.

His warm breath teased her neck, playing over her unbound hair. She felt the force of his silver eyes sweep over her, and the power of it made the tiny hairs at the back of her neck tingle.

"Go away," Kacey said flatly. "I'm working, and you are most definitely bothering me."

Draycott made a muffled noise somewhere between a laugh and a curse. Slowly he pulled the frame from her fingers, then tilted it to rest against an antique armchair with gilt legs.

What a ridiculous chair, Kacey thought, her eyes stubbornly glued to its spindly gold legs.

"Stand up, Kacey."

She didn't move.

"Look at me." It was a husky growl.

She tried to ignore him. With every straining fiber of her body, she tried. But it was useless.

His hand fell to her shoulder, and the touch was like a jolt of raw energy. Kacey flinched, her muscles throbbing.

In places she shouldn't even be aware of. In ways she shouldn't be imagining.

The long fingers curved over her skin and then slowly tightened. As if he felt her stiffness, Nicholas began to smooth the taut muscles aching from a day of painstaking detail work.

His thumb hit a knot of angry, corded muscle. Kacey gasped softly. Instantly his fingers stilled. "Kacey? What is it?"

She wouldn't face him. Somehow that would make this moment, these feelings, all too real.

Draycott's mouth was at her ear. "Look at me, damn it! Tell me what's wrong."

As if in a dream, Kacey angled her head, staring up at him through a curtain of tawny lashes, her long legs tucked useless and immobile beneath her.

The sight of her creamy skin and wide, haunted eyes stunned Draycott, even though by now he should have become used to her beauty. But something told him he would never become used to the sight of her, nor ever take this woman for granted.

And then hunger was a tangible thing, a painful thing, twisting through every inch of his body. Suddenly he was restless and hungry.

For her. Somehow it had always been her, Nicholas Draycott thought dimly. "Did I hurt you?" he demanded.

Oh, you hurt me all right, Kacey thought. *You hurt me the very first second I laid eyes on you.*

Maybe even before.

"It's—it's my neck." Her eyes fell, wide and smoky, riveted to his hard mouth. She blinked, trying to forget what it felt like to be flush against him, his lips hard and seeking. His body hot, hungry with need. "It—it always happens. When I work. No time. I—forget—"

She was babbling, but she couldn't seem to stop. Besides, Kacey realized if she stopped she might do something really crazy.

Like pull him down to kiss her. Like comb her fingers through that dense black hair teasing her from the opening of his white shirt.

"Let me touch you, Kacey." It was an urgent command, raw with infinite hunger.

Her heart slammed against her ribs. She couldn't have spoken if she'd been drowning.

Which she was, suddenly. In the dark, hard textures of him. In the heated memories his closeness provoked.

Draycott smothered a curse. With one swift, fluid movement, he came down to kneel beside her, his slate eyes never leaving her face.

Beautiful cheeks, he thought dimly. Beautiful mouth. Beautiful everything. "Don't worry—I'm simply protecting my investment," he murmured, trying hard to believe it himself. Before she could protest, he pulled her between his thighs and drew her back against his chest. His fingers cupped her shoulders and dug smoothly at the knots of tension, splaying and contracting rhythmically. "You're very expensive, Yank, in case you didn't know it."

Kacey's eyes closed, then jerked open sharply as she fought the power of those masterful fingers. "Oh, I do—know it. But…something tells me—ummm—you're very good at…protecting your investments."

Draycott laughed huskily. Strong and certain, his hands played over her shoulders while pleasure lapped through her in drugging waves. "Tell me how it feels, Kacey." His voice was a dark caress against the lobe of her ear.

"Good," she whispered, barely realizing she'd spoken. "*Too* good." Her eyelids fluttered down, and this time they did not reopen.

Nicholas's mouth curved up. Soon I'll make it feel even better, he promised silently.

His hands followed the slim line of her neck downward, picking out the exact inch of skin where a cluster of muscles screamed in agony. With practiced skill, he circled the tense center, gradually narrowing the circle. Long weeks in the hospital had taught him a great deal about physical suffering, after all. Now he knew all there was to know about pain and the thousand ways of releasing it. In the weeks after Bhanlai, physical therapy had helped him survive and restored his sanity.

"How did you know? Who…" With a sigh, Kacey gave up trying to talk, her question forgotten midsentence.

Draycott's laugh was a dark, intimate thing. "You work too hard, Connecticut. It's unhealthy, too much work, don't you know that?"

Kacey's eye cracked open. "Who—who told you I was from Connecticut?" she muttered.

Draycott's fingers paused for a fraction of a second. "Your address was there in your letters of recommendation. I looked them over this morning."

"Oh." Kacey's frown faded and her eyes closed once more. "And now I suppose you're gong to tell me—ummm—that you're the very person to teach me how to relax?"

Draycott's smile widened. "However did you guess?"

She tried to scoff, to tense, to push him away. But she couldn't, because his fingers were heaven itself. Dear God, her bones were turning to jelly, and Kacey realized she would do anything to ensure that he didn't stop.

For the span of a heartbeat, he hesitated.

Her soft protest tumbled out before she knew it.

Even before that, Draycott had felt the exact moment she stopped fighting him. The instant her mind let down its barriers, and her body surrendered to his pleasure.

He knew, and the knowledge stabbed him with hot, primal, male triumph. *First round to me, Kacey Mallory.*

Her head fell back, cradled against his forearm and chest. Her breath escaped in a sigh—soft and husky and endlessly female.

Mine, Draycott thought. Every silken inch, every sweet sigh mine. And suddenly he felt a reckless need to make her sigh that way again. But this time with a woman's pleasure.

At that moment, a high-pitched hum swept the room, followed

by a faint click. A second later, every bulb in the long gallery flickered and went out.

The bloody power was out again, Draycott realized.

He looked down at the woman in his arms, his eyes already adapted to the darkness. Her eyes were closed, Draycott saw, her head tilted back. Her hair spilled like a warm honey cloud over his chest and shoulders.

Fire pooled heavy in his groin. He felt himself harden and swell with a passion he hadn't known for months. But he didn't move, wanting to savor the sweet, aching need.

She hadn't noticed the sudden darkness, he realized. Right now, she felt nothing but the dark power of his kneading fingers. Right now, she was intensely vulnerable, infinitely female.

And that realization gave Nicholas Draycott stunning pleasure.

When her fingers moved a moment later, cupping his taut thigh, he felt it right down to the tip of his toes, right out to his fingernails, right up to the fevered pleasure centers of his brain.

So this is what it's supposed to feel like, the hard-eyed Englishman thought in wonder.

Wanting—a thousand kinds of wanting.

Needing—in ways that hadn't even been invented yet.

And through it all, feeling that somehow he had done all these things before.

He didn't notice her stiffening until her breathless gasp caught him short. Suddenly her fingers were hard on his thigh—and this time she was pushing him away.

"L-let me go!"

"Kacey, don't—"

"Right now, damn you!" She twisted back and stumbled to her feet, blind in the encompassing darkness. "You arrogant bastard! You misbegotten slime! What have you done with the lights?"

What have you done to *me?* Kacey screamed inwardly.

Draycott's jaw tightened. He had an advantage over her,

knowing exactly where he was in spite of the darkness. Right now, for example, she was only inches from a sixteenth-century marquetry card table.

He smiled faintly, the movement a slash of white against the darkness. "I did nothing. The electricity's merely gone out again. The construction teams nick a cable every few weeks. They're in too much of a rush to bother reading utility maps."

He heard her stumble, then curse beneath her breath. A moment later, the card table crashed to the floor.

"Aren't you going to do something?" Kacey demanded irritably.

"I thought I was. And very nicely, too."

He was laughing at her! Kacey thought. Damn the man! How could she have been so stupid as to trust him? To let him touch here, to allow herself to feel so—so safe in his arms?

It's only lust, Katharine Chelsea. Only a matter of hormones. After all, it's been almost a year since—

She closed her mind to that particular avenue of thought. "Well, if *you* want to sit here like a fool, then go ahead. But I'm going down to find a candle."

"You'll never make it in the dark."

"Wanna bet?"

"It's three flights down to the kitchen."

"Ask real nice, and I might bring back a candle for you. No, on second thought—"

"You'd bloody well try it, wouldn't you? And in the process, you'd stumble and break that stubborn neck of yours. Then, no doubt, you'd try to sue me for aggravated assault. No thanks— you're going to stay right here while I go and get the candle. Then I'll see you safely to your room. And you'll damn well stay there until the power is restored."

She heard him turn, his soft soles padding over the wooden floor.

Kacey's fingers clenched into fists. The man was a complete throwback to the Dark Ages! "Now just wait one minute!" She started after him and promptly stumbled. The next second, she felt hard fingers grip her arm.

"Has anybody ever told you you're too bloody stubborn for your own good, woman?" Draycott growled.

"A few times. How about you?" She expected him to snap back a denial, and so his silence surprised her.

His fingers tightened. "Only once. It was a very long time ago." His voice hardened. "I didn't listen then, either."

A thousand questions sprang to her lips. Questions Kacey knew she had no right to ask.

Questions, she reminded herself grimly, that she hadn't the slightest interest in having answers for!

The Englishman muttered something under his breath and pulled her along after him. "Come on then. At least I can keep you from breaking your bloody neck!"

At that moment, he sounded as if the prospect of getting rid of her held definite appeal.

In the engulfing silence, their footsteps echoed noisily. Every breath was sharp, every rustle intensified. And the infuriating man knew exactly where he was going, Kacey soon realized.

"Stop," she hissed. "I can't keep up! It's pitch-black in here, remember?"

Draycott muttered something beneath his breath and slowed his pace.

Reaching out, Kacey felt the banister beneath her fingers, velvet-smooth with centuries of beeswax and careful polishing. Five hundred years ago, the house must have been much the same as this, she thought. No lights, no whirring machines. Only this total, encompassing silence.

Down the stairwell they went, and to Kacey, it was as if they'd found the path straight into the house's heart. The ancient walls seemed to hum and close around them, as if welcoming them down a long corridor.

Of time. Of dreams.

To a place they both dimly remembered.

"Don't you have a generator or something?" Kacey asked irritably, to cover her growing uneasiness. "After all, this *is* the twentieth century."

They were at the second-floor landing. Draycott led her confidently to the right, his fingers hard on her wrist. "Marston will be on to it already, I'm sure."

She frowned, trying to tug free, only to feel his fingers tighten. "Stop fighting me, Kacey. You'll never win."

"That's where you're wrong, Nicholas Draycott!"

He stopped so abruptly that she stumbled into him. Without a second's hesitation, he twisted back against the wall, taking her with him. His arms slid to her ribs and crushed her against his chest.

The next moment Kacey found herself captured between rigid thighs.

"Do you really believe that?" he asked. "Let's find out, shall we?"

Disoriented, she reached out blindly in the darkness. The hard contours of his shoulders flexed rigid beneath her searching fingers.

Somehow her hands curved, digging into those taut muscles.

Somehow his hands shifted, burying themselves in her silken hair.

"Katharine—sweet, soft Katharine." His breath hissed free in a dark, erotic groan.

The sound went straight to her heart, setting off sensual explosions that jolted bone by tiny bone all the way down Kacey's spine. "St-stop, Nicholas."

His mouth cut off her half-formed protest. He kissed her urgently, unthinkingly. All his calculation was gone now—all that remained was raw male need. He took without asking, commanded without speaking.

He shaped her mouth, then remade it in his desire, and he didn't stop until her lips softened beneath him and her breath fled sharply.

Only then did he part her lips and fill her with his heat.

Perfectly.

Agonizingly.

Until the kiss seemed to go on forever, blinding in its power and sweetness.

When he released her at last, her mouth was throbbing, and the old Kacey was gone, swept away forever. Now a new Kacey burned in the darkness, consumed by yearnings she had never before known.

The Englishman just smiled. Without a word, he turned and tugged her after him into the darkness, moving noiselessly and with total certainty. Dimly, Kacey heard a door open, then felt a chair probe the side of her knee. A moment later he pushed her down into a stiff-backed wing chair.

"Stay put. I'll be back in a few minutes."

"Nicholas, wait! Let me—"

Too late. She heard him move away.

Her heart was pounding. Only anger, she told herself and tried to believe it.

Later she was to wonder why she hadn't been more afraid at that moment. Oddly enough, she wasn't, though she was sitting in utter darkness in the middle of a strange room in an unfamiliar house.

As her eyes gradually grew accustomed to the dark, she began to make out faint details. The rectangle of gray at a window. The dim, gleaming oval of a clock face, its hands at eight o'clock.

Since it was too late to go after Nicholas, Kacey decided to pass the time trying to imagine what the room looked like. Vaulted ceiling? Tall bookcases? Paintings covering every inch of its silk-lined walls?

She frowned. The image came to her suddenly, without warning or prethought.

Oak paneling. Gleaming brass sconces and a great crystal

chandelier. Floor-to-ceiling French windows hung with sapphire velvet curtains.

A gilt desk with claw feet. A vast canvas of Henry VIII, fisted hands on his hips, dominating the room from the opposite wall.

Kacey shook her head, but the image persisted. No, somehow more than an image. *A memory.*

Now the silent shadows mocked her, no longer friendly.

Without warning, she felt a current of air brush past her feet. She stiffened at the sound of faint scratching near the floor. Two eyes gleamed up at her from the darkness. A moment later, warm fur rippled past her ankle.

Just a cat, she thought, smiling unsteadily. A very clever cat, however, to find its way in past bolted doors and locked windows.

"I wonder what *your* name is?" she mused, her fingers curving over the soft fur.

The amber eyes shifted up to study her, unblinking in the darkness. The cat meowed once, deep and fluidly.

Kacey relaxed in her chair, enjoying the low hum that radiated into her fingers. The cat shifted slightly, maneuvering closer against her leg.

Gideon.

The word just popped into her head. Somehow she knew with perfect certainty that if she spoke the word, the cat would slant his head and meow softly at her.

Enough, Kacey! she thought, scrambling to her feet, her thoughts reeling.

And then, with a click and a faint pop, the power returned. The room filled suddenly with warm, golden light.

She saw with relief that there was no gleaming chandelier before her.

No gilt desk with claw feet.

Only pamphlets and ancient leather volumes, rising in a haphazard mound atop a massive desk—rosewood surely? A bronze bust of George III cheek by jowl with a little ormolu clock. A row of cut-glass tumblers and a decanter alongside a collection of sherry and whiskey bottles.

A very lived-in room, full of that cheerful clutter her countrymen liked to call the English country house style.

Then Kacey's breath caught in her throat. Her eyes widened.

For now she saw the oak paneling—just as she'd imagined it. The brass wall sconces gleamed back at her—shoulder-high, just where she'd envisioned them.

And there was the lusty monarch himself, swaggering from a gilt frame just above the darkened fireplace.

She sank down slowly, her fingers digging into the padded damask arms of the wing chair.

At her feet the cat shifted and meowed softly.

Slow down, she thought. *You've got a good, healthy imagination, but this is just too weird. Madame Blavatsky you're not.*

But the proof was right there before her, tangible and irrefutable. Blinking her eyes did not make it go away.

She frowned, looking at the large gray cat with ink-black paws. The amber eyes seemed to narrow, staring back at her intently.

"What am I looking at *you* for?" she asked shakily. "I'm not likely to be getting any answers from you!"

She took a deep breath, trying to calm her racing pulse. Perhaps she'd seen the room before in a guidebook. The abbey must have been photographed often, after all. Yes, that must be the answer!

But something told Kacey that the abbey's hard-faced owner would refuse to allow anything but the public rooms to be photographed for publication.

Which left her right back where she'd started. In the middle of a strange, unsettling house with a sinking feeling in the pit of her stomach.

And the total conviction that she had been in this room before.

Trying to deny the dangerous course her thoughts were taking, Kacey jerked to her feet, sending the cat running. Then her eyes flickered across the cluttered desk. They said you could tell everything about a person by what he read. So what would this desk tell her about Nicholas Draycott?

She riffled a leather-bound volume of *Richard III,* lying atop the latest thriller by Tom Clancy. Nearby were four thin gardening manuals. She lifted one and glanced inside the front cover. Published by the Royal Horticultural Society, no less.

A pile of letters—opened and unopened.

A children's book with wildly colorful pictures.

Kacey's brow wrinkled. So Nicholas Draycott had eclectic tastes, did he? She moved closer, pulling a file folder out from beneath the slim leather volume of Shakespeare.

"Armistead," the file was labeled.

Her eyes narrowed. Hadn't Draycott said something about that name last night in the stable? Her curiosity piqued, Kacey opened the folder, resolutely pushing away a pang of guilt at poking into what might be private papers.

But there were no letters inside, only carefully clipped newspaper articles. From the lowest and sleaziest of the English tabloids, judging by the lurid headlines and sensational photographs.

And then her fingers froze. A caption screamed out at her.

"English Diplomat Freed in Burma." A gaunt face stared back at her from a newspaper clipping, the eyes oddly flat and unfocused.

Nicholas Draycott's face—forty pounds thinner and a hundred years older. A face dominated by the savage will to survive, even when logic dictated that all hope should have fled.

Her eyes had just flashed to the smaller text below when the lights flickered. Kacey smothered a curse as the room was flooded with darkness once more.

Scowling, she carried the file to the window and pulled aside the curtain, hoping for enough light to read by. Outside, the wind had risen to a wild, steady rush, and the moon hung huge and silver above shuddering trees.

Kacey shivered, feeling a chill seep across the room, and with it a nearly tangible sense of sadness.

Moonlight glittered on the carpet, pale and cold as frost. Somewhere in the house, a clock chimed. Far away in the distance, across the Wealden Hills, she heard the echo of other bells, low and faint. Something about the sound was infinitely disturbing, as if they did not belong to this world.

And Kacey could have sworn they chimed thirteen times.

Her fingers tightened on the file.

She squinted down at the dim lines of script, barely visible in the moonlight.

Without the slightest sound, the French doors slid open before her. The curtains began to flap wildly.

Cold air lashed her face, making her take a step back.

The file in her hands fell forgotten to the carpet as the curtains surged up, then parted to reveal broad shoulders encased in black velvet, long legs eased into breeches and knee-high boots.

His cascading ruffles gleamed white beneath a flowing beard, and his raven hair was cinched in a long queue. Kacey tried to speak, but only a raw squeak emerged.

Hard and shadowed, the man's eyes watched her, his broad shoulders almost filling the doorway. "At last! I've managed it well and truly. About bloody time."

The words coursed across Kacey's skin in the chill wind, a rich current of sound. "Wh-who are you?" she stammered, sinking away from the door.

Her heart pounded as he strode past her to the unlit fireplace. Without a word, he stripped off his cloak and bent down, his face taking on a fiery glow.

Bathed in the light of a fire that did not exist.

Phantom steam began rising in thick clouds from his sodden

cloak as he tossed it over the nearby chair. Briskly, he held his hands out to the dark grate.

"Cold, as usual. I see I shall have to—" His voice halted abruptly. He seemed to stiffen. "Sit down, Katharine Mallory," he commanded, not turning. "I'm afraid I haven't a great deal of time."

Kacey pinched her palm to see if she was dreaming.

The laugh from the fireplace was deep and harsh. "No, you're not dreaming. Not unless *all* life is a dream and death its waking. Some philosophers would have it so, I believe. Now do sit down," he added sharply. "You're making me deucedly uncomfortable standing there with your mouth hanging open, looking for all the world like a beached mackerel."

Had she walked into a madhouse? Kacey wondered. Her heart racing, she glared back at the dark figure.

Once more, the curtains fluttered. Through the open window glided a second shadow—sleek and gray, legs capped with black paws.

"Ah, Gideon, there you are. All clear?"

The cat made a low purring sound.

"Excellent. Now perhaps *you* can do something to convince her."

Kacey gaped as she watched the sleek creature steal with noiseless footfalls across the thick carpet. With a sharp meow, the animal jumped into an armchair near the fire and curled up in a ball.

And there, his intelligent head slanted at an angle to study her better the cat began to purr. As if summoning her.

Gideon. So she had gotten the name right after all.

Hard on the heels of that wild realization, Kacey began to tremble. She bit her lip, fighting down her fear. "Now wait j-just one d-damn minute."

The bearded head turned, one brow raised, black eyes snapping. "I'm afraid I've no time for your hysterics, Katharine. So you will oblige me by taking yourself in hand, sitting down, and listening." He pointed to the armchair where Gideon sat studying her. *"Now,"* he barked.

Without thinking why, Kacey found herself moving where he pointed. Immediately the cat shifted, then settled in her lap. The room seemed to shimmer, picking up the light of a dying fire.

A fire that did not exist.

Kacey bit back a moan. Dear God, she was going totally mad, without the slightest hint of a doubt!

The man at the grate came slowly to his feet. His face was lean, filled with shadows. Somehow it reminded her of Nicholas's face. "Not mad, my dear, or even dreaming. Had we more time, I would try to explain this the slow way, the patient way, but—circumstances…prevent that." He frowned. "You're still thinking about that bloody file of my brother's?"

"Brother?" Kacey croaked. So that explained the similarity of proud nose and angular jaw. The familiar curve of the sensual lips. She hadn't realized that the viscount had an older brother, but then she was no expert on the Draycott family tree.

"His twin, to be exact. Fraternal twin. Unfortunately, I had a bit of an accident when I was seven years old. We were exploring along the foot of the cliffs, and I was trapped in a cave when the tide came in."

He studied her for long seconds, his eyes as black as Gideon's paws. "My brother managed to escape, but I, unfortunately, did not."

Kacey's eyes widened "I b-beg your pardon?"

"Drowning isn't really such a bad way to go, all in all. First the cold, then the gradual numbing. And then—" He seemed to catch himself. "But I digress. My brother's labors over that generator will not keep him away much longer, and he had better not find the two of us here when that happens. It would raise all the old jealousies…" The shadowed mouth curved in a faint smile. "Not that he would see me. He never does. But it would make things deucedly unpleasant for you to be seen speaking to thin air, my dear Katharine."

A thousand wild questions flew to Kacey's lips. In her lap, Gideon began to purr softly, and somehow the noise only made her more uncomfortable. "You—you can't really expect me to—to believe—"

"That I'm a ghost?" he finished for her. "No, I suppose I don't expect you to believe that. Not yet. But I do expect you to listen. For a man needs your help this night. Two men, in fact," he muttered, turning to stoke the fire that was not there. Warming his long fingers at flames that did not exist.

Kacey started to protest, to hurl a barrage of cold, hard questions at him, but his head turned just then. His eyes changed, naked and vulnerable now. "Once again it is the three of us, just as it was all those years ago. You can remember none of it?"

Kacey shook her head blindly, fighting down the beginnings of hysteria. "I don't know who you are or what you want, but—"

The figure smiled rather sadly. "I am Adrian, Nicholas's brother, Katharine. Just as I was his brother then. And what I want is to help you."

A raw laugh escaped her locked lips. "A ghost? Just grand! You're telling me I'm talking to a *ghost?*"

"Please, my dear—just listen. Do it for Nicholas. Do it for me. Most of all, do it for yourself." The man's gaze swept her face, chill and light as fingers of mist. "Between us, we tore you apart, Katharine. Neither one of us could let you go, even though we should have seen what it was doing to you."

Unable to speak, Kacey only shook her head. It must be some sort of joke! Of course she couldn't be sitting her conversing with a—

The man at the grate frowned. "I see it will take something more to convince you, stubborn one." On the floor, the forgotten file fluttered open. Suddenly the pages began to turn.

Soundlessly. By hands unseen.

All at once, images began pouring through Kacey's mind,

images of lush rice fields, of ancient stone cities hidden beneath an emerald jungle. She saw Nicholas Draycott—young, ambitious and driven.

Then the walls closed in, and the darkness began to crush her. The silent screaming began.

Bhanlai. The word hissed down, burning like acid into her head. She understood it all so clearly now.

For she saw—no, she *became* his past, tried it on like a coat, felt it ripple and surge over her like a river of light and sound.

Now she knew why Draycott was hounded by the tabloids for his story. Now she understood the ghosts that returned, night after night, haunting him, shaking him tense and screaming from sleep.

An ambitious Englishman trying just a little too hard to do his job. A Golden Triangle drug lord flexing his muscle. A dirty little war in a dirty little village in a very dirty little corner of Asia.

And Nicholas Draycott had landed in the middle of the crossfire as three countries scrambled for the pickings. Tossed in a dark, muddy hole, he had become the symbol of everything Trang wanted to destroy.

Stunned, Kacey stared at the man beside the fire, tears sliding down her pale cheeks.

"He's a lucky fool, my brother. I only hope he realizes that in time. If things were different—if I had the chance—I'd take you away from him," Adrian Draycott said fiercely. "Just as I did *then.*" His face turned shuttered, and he seemed to give himself a shake. "But things aren't different, are they? And it's his chance now, not mine," he muttered bitterly.

Kacey could only stare at him, aghast, unable to believe what he was saying.

For a moment his face burned with the dark flares of remembrance. "There was never anyone else like you, Katharine. No one who even came close, though you refused to believe that. That was always your greatest mistake, in fact—underestimating yourself."

Kacey shivered. Why did he say her name just so, as if there were a lifetime of feeling behind the word? And why did it affect her so strongly?

She raised a trembling hand, trying to fight the chill that gripped the room. She felt a sudden, gnawing premonition that he was about to reveal some frightening truth.

His gaze burned over her.

Suddenly he stiffened, his eyebrows raised in imperious slants. "Good God, woman, what are those unspeakable things on your feet?"

Trancelike, Kacey looked down. What was wrong with her boots?

She gave herself a mental shake. Who was he really? A relative of Draycott's who'd come to play a little trick on the visiting Yank? Or merely a neighbor who'd had too much to drink?

"No neighbor. No relative. Draycott has none left, poor fellow. Not alive, that is."

Kacey stiffened. She hadn't *said* anything, only thought it. "How—"

"A simple enough thing, actually. For one of *us*. And one of the bloody few vices we're still permitted."

Suddenly Kacey pushed to her feet, grim-lipped, paying no attention as she dumped an irate Gideon hissing to the floor. "I— I won't listen, do you hear? It's all a trick!" she cried wildly. "An illusion. I'm leaving now, before you can toy with me any more!"

Slowly, Adrian Draycott rose and braced his long body against the mantel. His eyes narrowed. "How would you like to know Whistler's favorite pigment? Shall I tell you the exact proportions to match that *Nocturne* upstairs?"

Sheet-white, Kacey took a step back. "Stop it! I refuse to listen to another word!"

The strange eyes darkened. Across the room, they seemed to seek her out, to glow and widen, fire-flecked. "You *must* listen,

Katharine—before it is too late. You are in gravest danger here, as is my stubborn, arrogant brother. No, don't interrupt—I can only manage this materialization for a few more minutes, I fear."

Gasping, Kacey spun about, refusing to listen. Immediately she felt a faint stirring of wind across her shoulders. Her neck began to prickle, almost as if shot through with static electricity.

"Maybe it's because I loved you once," the dark voice continued. "Or maybe it's because of the harm I did you both then." The sound moved closer, low and rough and bitter. "Damn it, perhaps the whys aren't important. What *is* important is that I've been given the chance to come back. To warn you both, so that things do not end as they did before—out there on the cliffs in the slashing wind. So heed this warning well, my dearest heart. There is greed and great hatred at work here, along with something even darker."

Dimly, Kacey felt herself fall beneath the dark rhythm of his words, pulled deep into his spell. Even as she fought him, his voice rippled over her, became part of her. "It was never suicide, though they found your bodies together at the base of the collapsed cliff. No, if anything it was murder—and *I* was the murderer." His voice caught for a moment. "But I never thought you'd take it so hard, Katharine. And I couldn't marry you, don't you see? I had the estate and the Draycott name to think of. You were just a village girl—and an artist's model to boot."

Kacey heard him curse, and then, feather-light, a current of air rose and skimmed her cheek. "You *can* remember what happened then. It is with you even now. All you lack is the desire to know."

Even as he spoke, Kacey had a queer vision of silver cliffs above a leaden sea, of horse's hooves pounding through the rain-swept night.

And then raw terror as the ground fell away beneath her and she plummeted down...

Down...

Into darkness.

She froze, rigid with fear.

Suddenly the scent of roses surrounded her. "But now I must say goodbye, my beautiful Katharine," the wind whispered, combing through her long hair. "I can come only once more. And it must be through *you*, since Nicholas refuses to see me or allow me in. The rest is up to the two of you. Until then…tell my brother not to grieve about what happened in the cave all those years ago. Tell him it was—necessary, for many, many reasons. Had I lived…well, I am just coming to understand all of that myself."

The rich voice wavered for a moment. "Just tell him Adrian found the pirate treasure after all, though it cost him dear. I pray to God he will not make the same mistakes that I did. As for you, my beautiful Katharine—trust in Nicholas. Help him trust in himself. He loved you very much then—far more than I did. He deserved better than what he got. *My* fault, again."

The words seemed to fade. And then out of the darkness behind her came the whisper of fluttering curtains.

Her heart slamming against her ribs, Kacey summoned her courage and slowly turned.

The dark figure was gone.

Only a quiet room remained, and a file that lay closed on the rug, exactly where she had dropped it long minutes before.

Only a locked door and tightly drawn curtains.

Only a dark fireplace and a chill room, with no one in it but her.

CHAPTER SEVEN

A RAGGED CRY RIPPED FROM Kacey's throat. White-faced, she moved to pick up the file, which lay forgotten on the carpet.

At that moment, the door burst open behind her. Nicholas's face was outlined against the bright rectangle of light from the doorway. "The bloody power's still out, and I'm afraid the generator won't—" Suddenly he stopped, his silver-gray eyes narrowed on the file Kacey clutched to her chest.

A vein beat at his temple, and the scar at his cheekbone gleamed silver in the light of the desk lamp.

Suddenly Kacey saw the image of a different man in that doorway—a man taller and slightly leaner, clad in sapphire velvet. In his hand, he carried a single candle that flickered in a ceaseless play of light and shadow over his deeply lined face.

A beloved face. The face of a man who loved too much…

And then her breath snagged as she had a keen image of those strong, callused fingers loosening her long gown.

Gown? she thought, frowning.

Next, her lace-edged chemise and a boned undergarment of some sort opened, and then his naked skin met hers.

She caught back a moan, feeling the touch of his hand at her breast, the steely length of his thigh. Pleasure shot through her— *remembered* pleasure. Kacey realized that she knew just how to make this man groan with ecstasy, just when to stop to make him wild with desire.

Could it possibly be true? Had she and Nicholas really been lovers in some other time? Had they somehow managed to find each other again, haunted by a tragedy that had separated them two hundred years before?

No, it couldn't be! She was a nice, normal person; things like this didn't happen to *normal* people!

Kacey shivered in the chill grip of hysteria. She started to offer the file to him, only to feel the string closure snag on her blouse. With trembling fingers, she ripped it free, sending a button flying onto the carpet.

But she barely noticed. Suddenly she had to know for certain whether Adrian had spoken the truth. Her hands clenched, and she studied Nicholas's face. "You really should stop feeling guilty for what happened…back in that cave. It was meant to be."

The only sign that Draycott heard came in the tensing of his fingers on the door frame. "Cave? I haven't the faintest idea what you're—"

"There were just the two of you." Kacey watched his face for a response—and saw none. "The tide came in. You didn't notice until the cave was half covered."

Suddenly, just as before, images began to flood into her mind, like slides clicking in a swift, ceaseless flow across a bright screen. First came the image of two boys, dark-haired and slate-eyed, scrambling over a beach of white sand. She could hear their high, reckless laughter above the crash of the surf.

"It was a dare. His dare." She frowned, concentrating—and then tried not to concentrate as she discovered it was best just to let the images flow over her. "It was your—your seventh birthday. You were sick from too much cake. Plum cake—it was always your favorite, though Adrian—"

Draycott's breath exploded in a curse. "You bloody little liar!"

Kacey flinched beneath the force of his anger, but she had come too far to stop now. Most of all, she had to have an end to this terrible uncertainty. "You called and called, but he wouldn't come away from the tunnel he was searching. And then the tide surged."

"Don't do this, Kacey," Nicholas rasped. "I can't take much more tonight, I warn you."

And then she saw it all, as clear as the pages in a book. "Dear God, you just managed to get out and—and Adrian didn't."

Draycott's curse cut her off. "Who told you those things? *Who,* damn you?"

"*He* told me."

"He? Armistead, you mean?" Nicholas pounded across the room, seizing her shoulders in a hard grip. "How much did he pay you to—"

"Can't you stop looking for villains? I didn't say anything about Armistead. It wasn't Armistead who told me. It was—" Kacey took a quick, unsteady breath. "It was…Adrian."

A muscle flashed at his jaw. "Stop this bloody charade, Kacey. My brother has been dead for almost thirty years."

"I didn't believe it either. Not at first. But I saw him, can't you understand? He was standing right there by the French doors, his cloak steaming, his shirt fluttering in the wind. He said…he said we were both in danger."

Nicholas's mouth twisted. "In danger, are we? So that's where all this is leading. How much? How bloody much do you expect me to pay you?"

"Stop it, Nicholas. Just listen to me!"

But he didn't stop. Grim-faced, he pressed her back, step by step, until a ridge of books bit into her spine.

Struggling vainly, Kacey closed her eyes, trying to ignore the fire of him, the searing steel of him, desperate to make him listen.

"Do you think that you're the first to try this scam?" the Englishman growled. "Over the last ten years, dozens of helpful mediums have written to offer their services so that I might escape a terrible fate that's supposedly hanging over me."

Kacey's shot open. "And you paid no attention?"

"Half of England must know the story of the Draycott ghost. Any one of those people could tell you that the ghost appears only when a member of the family is in danger. Why should I listen to every crackpot who—"

"But you must! There's a reason the ghost is appearing, don't you see? If we don't listen, he said it will happen all over again. Dear God, the storm—the cliffs—" She swayed as the dark images flashed over her again: lashing wind, ragged lightning, the explosive fury of collapsing earth.

And then the thunder was beside her, in the growl that ripped from Nicholas's throat. In the savage force of his body wedged against hers.

"How did you know, Kacey? No one but Adrian and I knew those things! And did you guess the rest of it—that I was jealous of Adrian? Dear God, maybe I even…wanted him to die."

Suddenly Nicholas stiffened. His glittering eyes seemed to look right through her. "So you think you know the whole of it, do you, my sweet?" He laughed mildly, mirthlessly. "You never could let it alone, could you? You just couldn't accept the fact that Adrian and I were enemies, and you the cause of that enmity. No, you always had to be about your infernal meddling, determined to smooth over what could never be set right." His fingers tightened on her wrists. "He doesn't love you, Katharine, haven't you realized that by now? Adrian is incapable of love—except for himself. And perhaps for that great gray cat of his!"

Kacey's breath caught. She had the riveting sensation that she was looking into the blank eyes of a stranger.

The man he had been two hundred years ago?

Nicholas's eyes smoldered silver, scouring her face. "But you're mine, do you hear? You were always meant for me. I won't let Adrian hurt you anymore, and I'll see to it that you have the things he would never give you. I'll give you the security of my name—a home. A family." His voice turned raw and hoarse. "Oh, God, Katharine, how I want to see you heavy with our child."

His eyes narrowed on her face, and Kacey had the feeling that he was more than a little mad at that moment. Desperately, she lashed out with her foot and struck him soundly in the ankle.

Draycott flinched. With a start, his eyes refocused. For long moments, he simply stared down at her, frowning. "What did I—" He shook his head sharply. "Do you still think you're the only one with questions, Kacey? There are other kinds of ghosts, you know. Do you want to hear about those?"

"Let me go, Nicholas," she gasped, trying to ignore the heat seeping through her shirt. Trying to ignore the hot hard length of his body, which was doing crazy things to her pulse.

"Not until you answer a few questions for me, I think."

"*Now*, Nicholas. I'm tired of these games. I've an immense amount of work to complete tomorrow before—" A tiny, breathless sound escaped her drawn lips as his thumb rose to trace her cheek.

Once again, Kacey caught the fleeting scent of roses. The air around her seemed to hang heavy with regret and the acrid bite of sadness.

He is your life now, the darkness seemed to whisper. *Let the rest go. Forget how it ended all those years ago. Teach him to trust you, Katharine. Then take this happiness and never look back.*

Kacey shivered as Nicholas's finger slid along the arch of her lower lip. "Why do you fight it? Is there a boyfriend waiting somewhere back in the States?"

Kacey stiffened instantly.

"Ah. A no. Are you married?"

"Never!"

"Now that, my sweet Kacey, would be a terrible waste." His eyes fixed on her lips.

"What in the—are you—" She swallowed and tried again. "Just what do you think you're doing?"

"Doing? I'm asking some questions of my own, Kacey. Like how you can feel so bloody soft. How that sexy mouth of yours can rip me apart. And I'm going to find out just what excites you in turn." Even as he spoke, Nicholas's thumb teased the locked line of her lips.

Kacey shuddered. First had come Adrian's revelations. And now she was caught in dark sensations stronger than anything she'd ever known. Were they *both* going mad?

"Get—get away from me," she whispered, her mind reeling. "You promised not to—"

"I promised to do nothing you didn't want me to do, Kacey. And you've been wanting me to touch you like this since the first moment you got here. Which is just as long as I've wanted to do the touching," Draycott added hoarsely.

"That's a lie!"

"Is it?" he growled. His fingers brushed the line of crimson staining Kacey's cheeks. "This heat says no." His hands moved to the pulse point just behind her ear. "This skittish pulse says the same." His eyes searched her face. "There's no need for lies between us, Kacey. We're both adults. I'll make it good between us—incredibly good. I've thought about this since the first moment I set eyes on you. Maybe even before that," he muttered, half to himself. "Maybe I've been waiting my whole bloody life for this moment."

Kacey tried to steady her plunging pulse. What was he up to now? Or was this Adrian's doing?

With a groan, Nicholas splayed his fingers open over her ribs, measuring her resistance ridge by ridge before coming to a halt just beneath the yearning swell of her breasts. His mouth was at her ear, low and hard and hungry. "I want to see you wrapped in moonlight, Kacey. In warm moonlight and cold shadows and not a stitch of anything else." Each word was a fierce, erotic rasp, punctuated by the sleek velvet stroke of his tongue against her neck. "I want to hear you when I fit myself all the way inside your heat. I want it to be *my* name you whisper, *my* shoulders you dig your fingers into when you go spinning away into space. And, by God, it'll be *my* body you want deep inside you when the pleasure shatters you into a thousand pieces."

One by one, the dark images triggered shock waves down Kacey's spine. Too late, she realized he had freed her shirt from her jeans. Moving across her naked skin, his hard fingers subverted her last vestige of stubborn resistance.

Dear God, why do I want those things, too? Gasping, Kacey tried to break free, realizing clearly that with this man things could never be halfway or halfhearted. Yes, this man would sweep inside and claim her very soul.

And she would welcome his fierce claiming, which could bring her only searing pain and loneliness.

For whatever was happening between them was too strange, too powerful to be real or lasting. "*No,* Nicholas. This is all wrong!" Kacey caught back a moan. Her hand broke free and flattened against his chest. When she felt hot naked skin and crisp wiry hair beneath her fingers, a shudder stabbed through her.

Nicholas smothered a curse. "You're trying to tell me you don't want this, Kacey?"

"No, I—I don't!"

A dark light flashed in his eyes and then disappeared. Kacey watched a hard line settle over his jaw.

"Then you'll have to prove it to me, because I'm afraid I just don't believe you."

In taut silence, Nicholas's silver gaze stripped her bare. He had to find out how far he could push her, and not just for the painting. He had already accepted the fact that there was more than the Whistler at stake here.

"I don't have to prove anything, damn it!"

"Try to tell me you haven't felt it too, Kacey. Tell me you haven't had the crazy feeling that this has all happened before between us. You know *exactly* how it feels when I kiss you, when you wrap your sweet legs around me and take me all the way home inside you."

Kacey heard the desperation driving his words, since it mirrored her own. Her breath caught sharply. So he *had* felt the same thing she had. Something naked and visceral. Something terrifying familiar.

She shivered as his warm breath teased her neck. She felt his body tense.

She looked down to see his gaze smoldering across the closing of her shirt, where white cloth had parted to reveal one perfect, upthrust pink nipple.

"Good sweet Jesus," Nicholas muttered hoarsely. "You're so beautiful that it hurts, Kacey Mallory." Rough and heated, his gaze swept over her silken skin. Abruptly his voice dropped. "You have a birthmark on your right breast, just where the lace edge of your gown ends. It's small and smoky and crescent-shaped. You've got another one—"

Kacey's breath caught. "How—"

He went on hoarsely, as if she hadn't spoken. "—at the base of your neck. You tuck your right hand beneath your chin when you sleep. You never use a pillow. And you always sleep without a stitch, just the way you were born, my sweet Kacey." As he spoke, Nicholas made no move to touch her, only gaze down, his face dark with an endless, tormenting hunger.

Kacey's face turned white. How did this stranger know such things about her? "It's—it's another trick! You're just—"

A muscle flashed at Nicholas's jaw, the only movement in his rigid body. "Is it, Kacey? Then tell me you haven't the birthmarks where I said." His voice dropped lower, husky with arousal. "Better yet, show me."

Kacey swallowed, fighting a wild urge to do just as he asked.

"Tell me that I don't remember every details of how it feels to love you. That the dreams haven't haunted me for weeks, starting at Bhanlai. God, I almost wish I didn't know how your eyes darken with passion. How your breath comes and goes in soft little gasps. The way you moan when I fill you."

Kacey bit back a gasp. He was frightening her now. "St-stop, Nicholas. If this is some sort of joke—"

"It's no joke, Kacey. From the first second I saw you, I knew you were the one, even though in the dreams I never could quite make out your face. Maybe that was why I fought the knowledge so hard, why from the beginning I found the sight of you so damn frightening."

"You're lying!"

"Am I, Kacey? You've felt it too, haven't you? The pooling heat. The sweet, aching restlessness."

She shook her head wildly. "You're stark, raving mad, do you hear? Whacko. Crazy as a loon. Definitely unhinged!"

A vein began to hammer just above the jagged scar over Draycott's cheekbone. "Now *you're* lying, Kacey. I can see it. I can *feel* it."

"And you're one prime, grade-A bastard, Nicholas Draycott. A miserable, rotten egotist. Can't you get it straight? Whatever you're feeling is all in your own head, and has nothing to do with me!" Her desperation made the lie convincing.

Or it would have, to anyone except this man, who knew her as well as he knew himself.

"Then why is your voice shaking, Kacey? Why is your breath so jerky?"

"Because I'm scared, damn it! *You* scare me—with all this ridiculous talk!"

Draycott went completely still, his eyes fixed on her face. "So you still refuse to admit it?"

Kacey nodded her head mutely.

"No matter, I remember enough for both of us. I remember enough for a whole lifetime—and maybe even *more* than a lifetime. And what I remember most is wanting you, the way I want you right now. With your honey hair tangled across my chest. With your emerald eyes glazed with passion when I bury myself inside you—as far as a man can go. Until you're wild, my sweet Kacey—as wild as a woman can be."

There was something more—something Nicholas should have remembered, but couldn't. Something that seemed important.

Then Kacey shivered against him, and the elusive thread of thought was shattered. Hunger tightened; need threatened to overwhelm him.

Silence fell around them, tense and brittle.

Very slowly, as if in a dream, his head slanted down, raven hair lying thick and straight against her ivory skin as he worshipped the pink bud that furled beneath his lips.

Pleasure coursed through her, hot and achingly familiar. Just as his mouth was hot and familiar against her. After all the long, lonely nights and empty years.

Why only with *him* all these intense feelings? Kacey asked herself over and over. Why only with this man, who was a complete stranger?

She had her answer a moment later. It came in the fierce rush of heated images. He and she, bodies intertwined.

Frenzied and reckless. Not as strangers but as lovers, skilled and intimate with the secrets of each other's pleasure. Knowing every curve and lithe movement until each body was simply an extension of the other.

Kacey began to tremble. "St-stop, Nicholas." It was a plea and a silent admission.

An end and a beginning.

"Never, Katharine," he whispered, his lips hungry against her flushed skin. "Not until you tell me that you feel it too. Dear God, whatever I have is yours—whatever I *am* is yours. Just tell me what's happening to us."

Kacey's eyelids fluttered as his lips closed around her, fierce with a velvet fury that strained to break free of his rigid control.

His strong fingers swept her neck, easing the shirt down until it balanced precariously at the very edge of her shoulders.

But no lower. Not yet. Nicholas Draycott wanted to make this moment last forever. He wanted to make her feel every inch as hungry as he was.

So that she'd never think about leaving him again.

"I don't understand—it isn't—" Kacey swallowed audibly. "Nicholas, we can't—"

Nicholas raised his head. His eyes raked over her, dark with need. Suddenly Kacey saw a pair of entwined bodies reflected there.

Their bodies. In that moment, she accepted the fact that she'd loved this man a thousand times. But she knew she could never tell him that, because then he'd never let her go.

Warm and wet, his lips traced the swell of her breast. "Don't be sensible, Kacey. Not tonight. Tonight just forget sense and logic. Forget anything else but us." His fingers curved over her hips, drawing her flush into the heated line of his arousal. "Dear God, forget anything but this."

Kacey felt his need burn through her clear up to her forehead. Right down to her toes.

Most of all in her heart, which was naked and vulnerable.

For him alone, deny it as she might.

Nicholas gasped, reading the dark shimmer of passion in her eyes. The sight of it made his breath snag and his body catch fire.

Then it was Kacey who gasped as his teeth limned her breast. Her head fell back, the slim column of her throat revealed as pleasure flowed over her like a river.

Like a tide of dreams, a current of beauty.

And with the pleasure came a dark, swift flood of memories.

Memories of him. Of her. Of all the other times they'd touched and moved and loved, just like this.

Each one different and yet somehow the same.

Driven always by a love that didn't die, only surged and frothed and tumbled forward in a forever twisting course, spilling over its banks from one life to the next, its molten ripples gleaming down through time.

Nicholas felt her answer before he heard it. It was there in her soft, jerky gasp. In the restless shifting of her hips, which sought his heat. In the hot tide of crimson that stained her chest and neck.

Dear God, she was more beautiful than the silken petals of any rose. And though it was hell, Nicholas made himself wait, desperately afraid that this dream would suddenly end, just as all the others had done.

He held himself still, hoping—no, *aching* for her to say the words he'd waited two hundred years to hear.

"Don't—don't ask this of me, Nicholas."

"I must, Kacey. Just once," he said hoarsely. "Dear God, it's driving me crazy, don't you see? Dreaming of this—of *you*—was the only thing that kept me going through those long months in captivity. Now I've got to find out if it was nothing more than a dream. I've got to know if I left my sanity back there in Bhanlai, along with everything else."

His body shifted, his hips teasing and then mastering in turn as they flexed in the ancient, drugging rhythms of passion and seduction.

He eased open her shirt with his mouth, then slowly traced the soft swell of her breast. Her breath caught when he coaxed the tight bud at its center even tighter.

Inch by smooth inch, the fabric slipped down her shoulders, one more exquisite texture among so many.

Suddenly Kacey was drowning in sensation—the rough velvet of his mouth, the sleek thrust of his tongue, the hot granite of his rippling thighs.

When he loosed his belt and let it fall to the floor with a raw, sensual snap, she caught back a restless moan. When his teeth nipped her naked shoulder, she arched wantonly.

She felt Nicholas shudder. And then his hard fingers eased the cloth lower until it wedged over her arms, holding her captive.

"N-Nicholas!"

"Hush, my love."

He found the birthmark at the base of her neck and traced it lovingly. With a growl of triumph, he found the other on her right breast, which he suckled reverently.

Too reverently for the way Kacey wanted his claiming now.

Her hips shifted, seeking his heat, pleading for it.

He tugged her zipper free and eased her jeans lower. A moment later, his callused fingers glided over her ribs and her belly, settling on the wild tangle of hair at the joining of her thighs.

Slowly he coaxed an entrance, then slid in search of her heat. Deep, so deep.

Unforgettable…

"Tell me, Kacey. Tell me that you want this—that you want *me*."

Kacey shuddered beneath his exquisite caress, overwhelmed by need and raw sensation. How could it all be so familiar?

"Do you feel it, Kacey?" Nicholas demanded hoarsely. "Can you remember every sweet detail as clearly as I do? Oh, God, tell me I haven't lost my mind!"

Kacey heard the catch in his voice and realized he was as overwhelmed as she. Words, that was what he wanted. But how could she speak, how could she begin to explain the storm of memories breaking over her all at once?

Words?

She tried to find them, digging deep, down below the fires of desire fanned by his expert touch, down below the hard-built layers of defense, deep down into the dark silence of remembrance, where words did not exist or ever would.

No use. Nothing could reflect the intensity of what she was feeling right then.

So, forsaking words, she found emotion and shaped it into movement. With movement she answered him, and every movement was a discovering, every sigh a claiming.

Her senses bold, she ventured out with her answer and prayed it would be enough. As she sensed that the last time, two hundred years ago on the eve of tragedy, it had not been.

Her fingers found his hair and slid deep. Her mouth found his shoulder and nipped urgently. Her eyes found his, and her gaze was open, wanting, infinitely vulnerable.

For you, Nicholas, her eyes promised. *Only and ever.*

Desire slammed through him. Heat exploded to his groin. In that instant, Nicholas Draycott learned a thousand new meanings of word "torment."

But he wanted that sweet torment from her, too. And he wasn't about to be rushed in anything he did this night. "Look at me, Kacey," he rasped.

She only tossed her head, arching restlessly.

"How long has it been?" His voice was raw with passion.

She mumbled a mindless protest, half lost already, seeking the heat of his hand.

"Since you've had a man, sweetheart."

Her head rose at that, her beautiful eyes flashing open, dark and unfocused, hazy with passion.

So beautiful, she made Nicholas grimace with new pain.

"A man?"

"A lover, Kacey. How long?" he repeated urgently, nearly unhinged by her honest, open need.

For him, only him.

Slowly comprehension tightened her features. "I—six months. A year, maybe…"

Her answer nearly unmanned Nicholas, even though it was no more than his first touch had intimated. All of which explained why she was so sleek and tight against his fingers. Sweet Jesus, just thinking of it nearly drove him over the edge.

Her, narrow and sleek.

Him, big and painfully hard.

Nicholas's jaw clenched savagely. Dear God, he'd tear her apart, he thought dimly.

And then he smiled, a dark, primal twist of lips. He turned and swept the desk clear in one wild, powerful stroke and then lifted her up into his arms. A moment later, he arched her back onto the cool, smooth wood.

Gently, gently, his mouth traced a hot path down her chest to her navel.

"Wh-what—"

"Trust me, love," he murmured thickly. "Just trust me. It will be good, I promise."

"Nicholas, what are you—"

With a rich, sensuous whisper, the last barriers of cloth slipped free of her arms and hissed to the floor. Kacey's skin burned beneath him, glowing with an inner fire.

The fire of love, Nicholas thought, awed beyond words.

Knowing his own skin burned the same way.

In that moment he knew that all his life, he'd somehow been a taker. But now all he wanted to do was give. To atone, with body and soul, for a mistake he couldn't even remember.

And somehow Nicholas realized that this would be the very last chance he would be given.

Then he thought not at all. All heat and hard planes, his body glided down her nakedness. His head slanted forward.

"Nicholas—" Kacey gasped, restless, totally urgent. She tensed, realizing his intent.

"No, don't stop me, love," he said roughly, aflame at her sultry beauty. At the sight of her burnished golden fur. Wanting to taste every sweet inch of her. "It's been a long time since I've been a knight—in shining armor or any other sort."

She started to disagree, to say that wasn't the way she'd heard the story of Bhanlai from Adrian.

But then she froze. Fear ripped through her. "I—I can't, Nicholas! I promised myself—never again. Not unless it was on *my* terms. By my own choosing. Safe—and it can never be safe with you."

"It's never safe, my love, don't you see that? It's only good when you give it all, when you've got everything to lose. It might be easier the other way, but it would be a damn sight less interesting," he muttered.

And then his mouth traced the softness of her thigh.

Kacey tensed.

"Smooth and easy," he rasped. "Let it happen, love—just feel it. Me wanting you. You needing me."

His lips teased aching skin. His tongue found her flowering need.

Gently, then not so gently.

"I love you, Kacey." His voice was a raw blur of sound. "Feel me loving you."

And then conscious thought shattered as Kacey's body spun away, raw and desperate, awakened to infinite pleasure.

Her heart trembled and convulsed. Her spirit leaped free.

She cried out wildly.

And because it was Nicholas, and the night silence was lush with promise—because his touch was nothing but magic, pure, primal magic, she let the last wall topple and fled the bonds to find paradise breaking over her.

AT THE WINDOW THE CURTAINS rippled faintly. Wind growled and tapped at the pane.

Outside, Gideon floated comfortably in space one minute, then tensed abruptly and hit the ground with a muffled thud.

A low curse split the night air. "So sorry, old friend. I fear I've—miscalculated—once again." The voice was gruff. "This whole thing is damnably awkward. It's been thirty years, after all. And two hundred before that. One forgets…"

There was a faint shimmering just beyond the glass windows, where a pair of shadows arched, then slid together into one. The air hung chill and sullen for a moment.

"One forgets a great deal. And now, seeing her again, like this—" The pale fingers clenched convulsively for a moment. "Yes, far better for me to go. But keep watch, old friend. On her. On them both. If it comes, it will be soon. That much I can feel. These men of Trang's are desperate."

The gray cat meowed once, his long tail high and arched. Then Gideon turned and trotted obediently to the ancient wall, where he jumped noiselessly to a high perch. And there, his sleek body simply another shadow on the dappled stone, he lay down to wait.

Beyond the window, out in the darkness, the air spun wildly, rising in a vortex of twigs and fallen leaves. Then, slowly, the currents subsided and the shimmering began to fade, bleeding away into a silence that was night, and no more than night.

Until finally only the faint, lingering scent of roses remained in the chill air.

HE HELD HER WHILE HER breath stilled, stroked her while the tremors ebbed.

Lifetimes later she shifted, breathless, dazed.

Nicholas's eyes smoldered silver above her.

"Are you protected, my love?" His voice was raw silk.

Kacey's eyes cracked open dreamily. "I...I had all the shots before I left New York. The usual—smallpox, gamma globulin."

She felt a sudden spasm work across his broad chest. "Nicholas?"

The rumble reached his throat and burst free in dark laughter. "Sweet, soft Kacey. Where have you been all my life?" Draycott turned and reached for the pocket of his pants.

Kacey's cheeks flamed as she saw the small packet in his hands. His eyes smoldered over her face, one dark brow raised. "This is hardly the eighteenth century, after all. But I can and will protect you, my love. Every way I know how. Remember that."

Kacey's heart lurched and sank into the dark current of his eyes. Even now he thought of her, he wanted to be sure—

Like a great effervescent bubble, joy burst through her.

And then she gasped as Nicholas molded her against him, skin to naked skin. Hands dark and hungry.

Discovering passion, in all its infinite variations.

For a ragged infinity, he let her feel him—wanting her.

He made her feel herself—wanting him back.

He eased her down onto the soft carpet. "I warn you, Kacey, the knight's gone now, and all that's left is the man. Tonight he's hungry. He's dangerous, I promise you. Because he's remembering all the things he's had before and all the things he's never gotten to have. Things he never even dreamed existed until now. If your mind's in a different place, then you'd better get away as fast and as far as you can, because in a few seconds, the man's going to be beyond stopping. He's going to do something crazy. And completely irreversible."

"Take me, Nicholas." Kacey's voice was breathless, husky with her own need. "Now. Beneath you. With you. I don't want to wait another second to know how you feel inside me."

And when she looked up at him then, love-dazed and passion-slick, skin turned inside out, heart shining on her shoulder, he found his way home inside her, all the way home.

Heaven, Kacey thought, and told him so.

"Sweet love—ahhh. So bloody good…so tight." He tensed suddenly. "I'm not—oh, God, Kacey—hurting you, am I?"

She moaned breathlessly beneath him, adrift in dark, mindless currents of pleasure, past and present like a split image suddenly focused into one.

"Kacey?" he muttered hoarsely.

"More—now. Oh, please…"

His smile was a fierce, feral thing, full of the heat of conquest, dark with triumph. A moment later, he did just as she wanted. As they both needed.

With a raw groan, he caught her to him and slid deep, rocking her to the very center of her soul, shaking himself to the roots of his being.

Crying out her name when he felt her silken contractions begin again.

Gripping him infinitely. Dragging him off to paradise.

Just the way it always was when he loved her.

Above them, half-shadowed in the gentle glow of the room's single light, the portrait of Henry VIII seemed to wink and smile down benignly.

CHAPTER EIGHT

THEY FELL ASLEEP THERE ON the carpet, Kacey's long hair spilling golden over Nicholas's bronzed chest, his hard hand molded protectively around her thigh.

Once and then twice more they awakened in the long night, lips urgent, breath fled, fingers sure and swift, drawing each other to wordless, shattering passion.

Until Kacey sank down with something between a laugh and a breathless moan, and Nicholas began to have serious doubts about whether he would ever walk again.

But he merely smiled.

After all, giving up walking was a small price to pay for the exquisite pleasure he'd just experienced in her arms.

THE CALL CAME IN THE LAST chill hour before dawn. The sharp peals shook Draycott awake as he drowsed somewhere between sleep and dreams, body and soul satiated in a way he had never before imagined possible.

The Englishman frowned, making no move to answer. Her cheek to his chest, Kacey stirred restlessly, mumbling a protest at the intrusive noise. When the shrill ringing continued, her fingers tensed on Nicholas's thigh.

At last the insistent peals stopped.

Draycott watched Kacey's eyelids flutter, relieved that she did not wake.

And then the ringing began again.

With a smothered curse, Nicholas slipped from beneath Kacey's warm body, twisted across the desk, and jerked the receiver to his ear. "Who is it?"

Silence.

And then from the other end of the line came the faint hiss of indrawn breath. "Dreaming again, Lord Draycott? Such a pity. But perhaps the American will ease your painful memories. Is she good in bed, by the way? Does she make you hard with desire? So different from Su Win, of course, for *she* knew how to pleasure you in the thousand ways of hand and tongue."

Not Trang, Nicholas thought, but who? And what was Trang's part in all this?

"Leave me alone," he snarled.

"So sorry, Lord Draycott, but that is quite impossible. You have something of mine, you see, and I'm afraid I need it back." Silence fell for a moment, punctuated by another sharp hiss of breath as the caller's lungs again filled with smoke.

"I don't have anything of yours. I took nothing with me from Bhanlai, you bastard. You should know that better than anyone!"

A soft chuckle. "Really, Lord Draycott, do you think me such a fool?" And then the soft voice dropped, ruthless beneath its silken timbre. Ruthless as only one who has lived long amid the poverty of Asia can be. "You have one more day to give me what I want. If not, you die. And your death will be the old way— the hard way. The way you saw all the others die at Bhanlai. And your American lover, she will die too. Just as Su Win died—after she betrayed you." The chuckle that followed was low and coarse.

A vein began a wild staccato throb at Nicholas's temple. Anger roared through him, along with the ragged edge of fear. Who, damn it? Who was it this time?

It could be any number of people, of course. The warlord,

Trang, had had dealings with many nations. He must have double-crossed them all at one time or another—Russian, American and Chinese. Even the British had had their reasons for approaching the ruthless warlord on occasion.

And Trang would deal with anyone for hard cash. His trade was infinitely accommodating—any commodity of worth to the buyer. Information. Poppy. Planes.

But it was the human trade Trang liked most. And he was very good at it.

Bloody, sodding dung-eater!

Lips clenched, Nicholas waited for the cold, precise voice to finish, fighting his rage and saying nothing because he knew that this would goad his caller most.

Long minutes later, his face a mask of unrelenting fury, he lowered the telephone back to its cradle.

Slowly. Very carefully.

Trying to ignore the wild, ragged laughter that erupted in a shrill din just before the line clicked dead beneath his fingers.

One more day to give them what they wanted.

One more day—and then they would kill him and everyone in the abbey.

SOMETHING WARM ON HER cheeks. Something soft at her breast.

Sweet fatigue and dark, silken memories.

"Mmm." Smiling dreamily, Kacey curved her body into that heavenly softness. Her fingers moved, seeking the warm, muscled length that had pillowed her, teased her, and coaxed her to wild abandon throughout the long night.

But her hands met only cold cloth.

"Nicholas?" she cried, jerking upright, her eyes fixed on an unfamiliar room. Heavy velvet draperies on a huge mahogany four-poster. Spare, bold prints on pale silk walls.

Nicholas's room. Nicholas's bed...

She remembered all of it now and couldn't help smiling even as her cheeks reddened at the memories of the night before.

But where was *he?*

She frowned, sensing a strange emptiness. The air did not hum or the room shimmer as it always did when he was near.

Slowly she lay back, wincing at the protest of hidden muscles. Where had he gone? Was he already regretting last night? Had something happened to him?

Unbidden, a new image sprang to her mind.

Lightning over a jagged silver shore. A riderless horse, hooves pounding out of the darkness. "Wait!"

And then a scream, ragged with terror.

Her scream.

Kacey tensed, feeling the fear slam through her even now. What was wrong with her? Was this the dream that shook Nicholas from sleep night after night? Was this the past that Adrian had warned her would be repeated?

Was there a curse on this house, after all? Or was it perhaps *she* who was cursed?

She slipped from the bed, her eyes widening as she took in the dress and lacy lingerie laid out on a nearby chair. She picked up the accompanying note, its lettering angular, elongated and bold. Nicholas's writing—there could be no doubt about that.

My sweet Kacey,

Had to go out. Ought to be back in good time for lunch. Meanwhile, try this on. It was my grandmother's, and I rather think it will fit you. There's a brooch of hers on the dresser. Wear it, won't you?

Nicholas

P.S. Did I tell you that you snore? Low and soft—very erotic, actually.

P.P.S. Did I tell you that I love you? I do, you know.

Her eyes glistening, Kacey lifted the silken dress, mesmerized by the way the soft mauve folds fell about her, as smoothly sensual as Nicholas's hands had been the night before. A collar of handworked lace framed the old-fashioned square neck— richly feminine with just a hint of sensuality.

Oh, yes, trust Nicholas Draycott to choose well, she thought.

Her carry-on bag lay on the dresser, and she realized Nicholas must have put it there before he left. Deftly, she fished out the pink ballet slippers she had packed for comfort on the long flight.

Then, fully dressed, she smoothed down her long skirt, feeling every inch a princess or a heroine in an old novel.

Feeling, best of all, like the woman Nicholas loved. Which was all she wanted to be, anyway.

There was a soft tap at the door. "I beg your pardon, Miss Mallory." It was Marston's voice, low and acutely uncomfortable.

Kacey opened the door. "Yes?"

The butler's eyes were carefully averted, and a hint of color streaked his cheeks. *So you're not accustomed to seeing strange women in Nicholas's bed, are you?* Kacey's heart, already humming, took a serious, high-voltage leap at that realization.

"Lord Draycott was called out some two hours ago, Miss Mallory. Before going, he left instructions that you were not to be disturbed." The splash of red across the butler's cheeks darkened.

God bless you, Marston, Kacey thought. But she was careful to keep her thoughts from showing. "And?" she prompted, sensing that there was more.

"As it happens, there is a police officer below requesting to speak with you, miss. I asked the nature of his business, but he declined to say. Shall I...?" The servant's voice trailed away suggestively.

"No, of course I'll speak with him."

The broad-shouldered officer was waiting before the mullioned windows in the salon. He turned as Kacey came in, his eyes blue and very keen, his smile expectant. He was much younger than she'd expected.

Marston left them, closing the door softly.

"Ah, there you are. Miss Mallory, isn't it? That Marston chap's always so tight-lipped. One can't ever get a bloody thing out of him." He took her hand in a quick, brisk grip. "I expect you'll be wondering why I've come. Business, I'm afraid." His eyes flickered over her face, assessing her reaction. "But I haven't even told you my name. How silly—" He extended a hand a second time. "Detective Chief Inspector Gerald Parks, Hastings Police. But perhaps…yes, I think you'd better sit down before I continue."

Kacey paled. "Go on," she whispered, sinking into the nearest armchair.

"Yes, well, there's been an accident, I'm afraid. Or at least we believe it was an accident. We found Lord Draycott on the coast road slumped over his steering wheel about ten miles from here. Engine still running—but the Alfa was pretty badly banged up. Before he passed out, the viscount muttered something about another car trying to run him off the road."

Kacey felt the room begin to spin. "Is he—dear God, will he—"

"I expect he'll pull through, Miss Mallory. They've taken him to hospital in Hastings. We've an excellent staff there—no need to fret. But before he went under, Lord Draycott asked…for you." The policeman's blue eyes were kind.

And very curious.

But Kacey barely noticed, already lurching to her feet. "What are we waiting for, inspector?" She ran to the door. "I'll just tell Marston where I'm going and—"

The inspector's eyes narrowed. "I'd prefer that you didn't do that." It was soft, but an order just the same.

Kacey looked back, frowning. "Why not?"

"The fewer people who know about this, the better, Miss

Mallory. Lord Draycott was being harassed and…well, it's strictly on a need-to-know basis, I'm afraid. The only reason we're telling *you* is because he specifically asked. You do understand, don't you?"

Kacey didn't understand, not entirely, but she nodded anyway, desperate to get to Nicholas.

The young inspector nodded approvingly, then patted her shoulder—a quick, professional touch. "You're very brave, you know."

Kacey bit her lip. She didn't feel brave. Right now, all she felt was wobbly and sick and horribly afraid. Somehow she managed a bleak smile before following the inspector outside to a dusty blue Mini with a badly rusted fender. An older man, dark-haired with a creased, lived-in face, nodded to her from the front seat.

"My partner," the inspector explained. "Right now he's got a nasty case of laryngitis. Too many late nights, eh, William? When are you going to learn it's no good burning the candle at both ends?"

The older man shrugged, smiling grimly.

The next moment the engine coughed to life and they were bowling down the long, twisting drive. Kacey's eyes blurred, and she had to resist an urge to turn and stare back at the abbey's ancient walls, warm and mellow in the morning sun. Suddenly it seemed as if the last two days had been a dream. Nicholas, the Whistler, Marston even—all a dream.

Why did she have the odd feeling that when she returned, it would all be gone?

She gave herself a shake, fighting down a sick stab of fear. "Have you—have you had any luck with your search?" she asked, trying vainly to think of anything but Nicholas lying white-faced and silent in a hospital bed somewhere.

"Luck?" The blue eyes flickered to her face in the rearview mirror.

"With the search for the thieves. Nicholas—Lord Draycott—mentioned what happened to the gatehouse."

"Not much, I'm afraid. No trace of the paintings. In fact, no clues of any sort." The inspector frowned. "Damn good, these fellows."

Kacey barely heard him. *Hold on, love. You can't get away from me now—not when I've just found you. I'm coming, Nicholas...*

"How about you?"

"Me?" Kacey blinked.

"With the painting Lord Draycott discovered. It's become quite the focus of local gossip, you know. Down here, everyone knows everyone else's business."

Remembering Nicholas's insistence on secrecy, Kacey bit off what she'd been about to say. "Not yet. It's still too soon to say."

The driver nodded. "I suppose your work is rather a lot like ours, in the end. Chasing down clues, sorting through all the possibilities. And something tells me you're very good at what you do, Miss Mallory." The keen eyes studied her in the mirror. "The very best, in fact."

Kacey managed a vague answer, staring blindly at the landscape hurtling past. There was a time when she would have said that being the very best at her job was the most important thing in her life.

But now she would have traded all her skill, all her experience, to have Nicholas here beside her, safe and sound.

"You're very fond of him, aren't you?"

Kacey dropped her head, brushing furtively at her eyes. *Fond?* The word didn't even begin to describe her feelings for Nicholas Draycott.

The driver nodded. "Not that I'm surprised. Quite a few people hereabout feel that way about Viscount Draycott. With his wealth, he can do a great deal of good for the area." Abruptly the inspector's voice hardened. "Unfortunately, not everyone feels the same way that you do."

Kacey's eyes fixed blindly on the window as the road dipped and twisted past thatched, timber-framed cottages and grand estates hidden behind stone fences.

The young inspector drove quickly and efficiently, just the way he did everything, she imagined. In fact, he drove rather too fast for comfort, but then he must know these narrow roads well. Out of the corner of her eye, Kacey saw the inspector's partner click open a lighter.

Dear God, he wasn't going to smoke! She would be sick, she knew it! Quickly she leaned forward and rolled down her window.

A little better.

Breathing deeply, she watched the earth flatten and empty, trees gone now, houses too. The ground stretched away to right and left, myriad rich shades of green. Here and there was a nearly black tangle of gorse, orange-blossomed now in summer.

But all Kacey *really* saw was the image of Nicholas's pale face, his body shattered and unmoving.

Somewhere in the distance came the glint of water. The channel, she thought. To the west rose the treeless slopes of the Seven Sisters, their white cliffs bared to the ceaseless hammering of the sea far below.

The road was empty now, and they began to pick up speed. On and on the man in front smoked until the car was thick with fumes and Kacey felt her stomach lurch.

They slowed at a small intersection, and Kacey noticed a point jutting out into the channel. But that had to be Beachy Head! And that meant they were going west, while Hastings lay to the east.

"Excuse me, inspector but—haven't you made a mistake? This *is* the road to Eastbourne, isn't it? Hastings would be the other way, surely."

The inspector's clear blue eyes met hers in the rearview mirror. He nodded briskly. "Quite right. This road loops about though, and with less traffic we'll make better time."

Kacey managed a faint smile, feeling rather foolish.

"You know the area then, Miss Mallory?"

"Not really. I took the bus from Hastings on the way to the abbey, though, and I remember the route." Her voice trailed away and she found herself blinking back tears. How long ago that all seemed—how different she had been then.

A tear slipped down Kacey's cheek, and then another. *Oh, Nicholas, hold on!*

It was a moment or two before the sound penetrated her consciousness—very soft, like a sigh.

A sound she'd heard before...

Her eyes narrowed. She sat up straighter.

Then the realization slammed into her like a fist. Her heart began to pound. Dear God, she hadn't even asked for any identification. They hadn't let her tell Marston that she was leaving...

"Did you..." Kacey swallowed, trying to steady her voice. "Was Nicholas's wound better when you saw him?"

"Wound?" The blond brow framed in the rearview mirror slanted up.

"On his cheek. He fell when the power was off last night. It was quite a bad cut."

"Ah." The driver nodded thoughtfully. "No, there didn't seem to be any bleeding." His tone was faintly apologetic. "I can't say for certain, though, since the bandage was still in place."

Through the wild hammering of her blood, Kacey managed to smile naturally and nod. Dear God, it was true then. Nicholas had no wound on his cheek, of course, or any bandage. If these men had seen him, as they claimed, they would surely have known that.

Again came that faint hiss of air...

Now Kacey knew without any doubt that the man in the front seat was her unknown caller of yesterday!

Her fingers locked in her lap. At least they didn't know she'd found them out—not yet. *Think, Katharine Chelsea—think!* If they didn't have Nicholas, then where was he? And what would he want her to do?

Escape.

The word simply dropped into her mind, then hung there, resonating faintly.

Kacey blinked. *And how exactly am I supposed to do that?*

She didn't realize she'd asked the silent question until an answer flashed back to her.

There's a door right beside you, my dear, the voice said dryly. *I suggest you use it.*

Only he didn't speak in words, of course. He communicated in quick bursts of meaning, in bold, concrete pictures.

And the speaker was most certainly a *he.* She could feel the dark force of him most clearly.

Adrian? she queried.

None other. But you must make haste.

That's easy for you to say, Adrian Draycott! You're a ghost—you can walk through walls! came Kacey's angry, silent answer.

Static ripped through her thoughts for a moment, and then the voice in her mind returned, needle-sharp this time. *Now, Katharine! Before they realize you've seen through their desperate little masquerade. Get out of there!*

Still wearing a crooked smile, Kacey moved her fingers down in search of the door handle. They were going about forty miles an hour, she estimated—enough to do quite a bit of damage to whatever part of her anatomy hit first. At least she was on the left side of the car, which meant she would land on grass rather than pavement.

For a long, breathless moment, she fought down wild laughter.

And then, with a gasp, she yanked open the door and dove from the Mini.

The ground exploded toward her, a swirl of green, and she heard the driver shout. "She's bolted, damn it! Stop her!"

Dimly, Kacey heard the shrill scream of braking tires. An instant later her vision filled with shards of light and then went blank as the darkness claimed her.

She heard a shrill whine. Her head felt huge and heavy. Savage hammering split her left temple.

What…

And then Kacey heard the dim scream of grinding gears.

Run, Katharine! Cross the fields to your left, toward the cliffs.

Kacey brushed a shaky hand across her temple and frowned to see it covered with blood. She must have hit her head on a rock when she'd jumped from the car.

Now, woman! the voice broke in, harshly this time.

Wincing with pain, Kacey stumbled to her feet and began to weave toward the distant slash of silver, where the cliffs turned to chalk below the green turf of the downs.

Nicholas? she queried wildly.

Unharmed. But he'll need time.

Kacey no longer even wondered at this strange, wordless form of communication. In fact, all she heard was the first word. It burned through her with a rich glow, giving her the strength to plunge ahead.

Good girl! That's it, steady on—now to the left.

Abruptly the voice receded, as if Adrian had moved away.

Kacey fought down a feeling of fear at the sudden severing of their unspoken contact. Not human contact, she could accept that now, but contact with someone who had once been very dear to her.

Gasping, she ran over the flat green earth, her eyes fixed on the distant azure glint of the channel.

And then she heard a low growl, felt the ground begin to vibrate. Still running, she turned her head and saw the blue Mini swerve sharply and head off the road onto the grass.

Coming directly toward her.

Adrian! What do I d-do now?

No answer.

Kacey swept her hair from her eyes, fighting the razor-sharp pain in her head. Something slipped into her eye, blinding her, and she brushed it away roughly.

Sticky. More blood...

Just like *that* night, when she'd run away toward the village, unable to bear the pain of being caught in the middle any longer.

Kacey shuddered as the growling behind her grew louder. She heard the muffled thump of tires and the metallic creak of the car frame protesting as the Mini took bump after bump far too fast.

It came to her then, with total, blinding clarity. She'd never make it. She could never hope to outrun the car, not on this flat downland, without trees or any place of concealment.

Adrian's warning had come in vain after all.

A wave of despair slammed into her, black and suffocating. It was not for herself that she grieved, but for the love severed fragile and newborn, like a green shoot trampled just as it pushed free of the earth.

"No!" Her wild, angry cry split the air. She had to think—there must be something she could do! Time, that's what Adrian had whispered to her.

And then she saw it—a narrow, gorse-fringed basin dotted with boulders at its lowest point.

Enough gorse to slow a car. Enough stones to savage the car's underbody and perhaps even destroy the engine floor. And if she circled around gradually, the basin would be totally invisible from above, until one was almost upon it...

Kacey's breath was coming ragged in her ears when she shifted course. Behind her, the motor droned louder.

"Stop, you fool. You can't hope to outrun us!"

Sheet-white, she closed her mind to the angry shouts. It must be the other man, the smoker. The man who had phoned the abbey yesterday expecting to reach Draycott with his warning.

Oh, Nicholas—hurry!

Her throat was raw and her knees shaking as she stumbled down the slope toward the basin, calculating the remaining distance. Twenty-five feet, with luck. Maybe a little more.

Behind her, she heard the man curse. A second later a bullet whined past her head, and she ducked reflexively.

Dear God, not a gun too!

Fifteen. Twelve.

Her heart felt like it would explode from her chest.

Ten. Nine. Eight.

And then the roar was beside her. From the corner of her eye, Kacey saw a door swing open. They meant to ram her!

Somehow, at the last second, she managed to dodge and stumble to her knees, then right herself drunkenly. A moment later she felt the sharp arms of the gorse spear her ankles. Just in time she jumped across and dropped out of sight, flat against the ground.

A stream of curses ripped the air. An instant later the Mini came sailing over her head, tires spinning uselessly, engine whining, only to land with an explosive crash atop the rugged line of boulders at the center of the green crater.

Without a backward look, Kacey pushed to her feet and lurched back up the incline, away from the muffled shouts, a silent prayer fixed in her head.

She had just cleared the gorse when she heard a shrill crack. White-hot metal bored through her shoulder. Gripping her forearm, she tried to fight back tears.

Adrian…where in the name of heaven are you? Now would be…nice…very nice…

She swayed, closing her eyes to the tears and pain, feeling hysteria weave its seductive web around her. She caught back wild laughter. Asking help from a ghost, no less!

When her tear-streaked eyes opened, she saw a gray shape dart over the slope, moving downhill.

Kacey squinted in disbelief. "G-Gideon?"

But the cat was gone, no more than a slash of gray as he surged down the hill out of sight. From the hollow came angry curses, grunts, and the whine of spinning wheels.

Go, Katharine. Head east! The voice took her by surprise.

She stumbled to the left. Adrian?

No, east, to the right. That's it—steady now, love.

Her hair tossing wildly about her face, Kacey did as the voice bade her, too tired to wonder at his return, too tired now to think of anything but escape.

Panting, she wobbled up the incline, trying to focus on the cloud-dappled earth stretching flat to Eastbourne and beyond that rising sharply to the ruined battlements of Hastings.

Her eyes glazed with tears, Kacey didn't see the dark shape at first. Only gradually did the shadow resolve into an oval, then into a horse with flying feet—and a rider.

"N-Nicholas!" she cried raggedly, lurching over the grass, one hand to her shoulder, the other scrubbing away tears of pain, now turned to tears of joy.

Such fierce joy that she didn't hear the low, feral purr until the Mini was nearly upon her.

Turn! The raw order rang out in the depths of her mind.

She moved by pure instinct, just as Nicholas's hoarse warning filled her ears a split second later. Horrified, she watched a blue door go whipping past, only inches away from her knee. If she hadn't moved it would have broken her kneecap—and possibly much more.

This time, however, the car kept going, picking up speed. Dear God, they were heading straight for Nicholas!

In mute horror, Kacey watched the two adversaries surge together on a collision course, car and rider implacable. She caught a glimpse of Nicholas's face, dark with fury, before he pulled his mount aside at the final instant, barely managing to avoid impact with the Mini.

He pounded past her a moment later, shouting a question. "—all right?" she heard.

"Yes! Be careful! They've got a gun!"

But he was already gone, streaking toward the coast. In that instant Kacey felt her stomach wrench as she realized his intent.

To save her, he meant to draw them off, toward the cliffs.

Be careful. Oh, be very careful, my dearest love. At first, she didn't realize that she'd spoken with her thoughts rather than with speech. Raw static filled her mind for an instant, and with it came a burning sensation like acid. Like bitter sadness and aching regret...

She turned, her legs wobbling, her lungs aching. Horrified, she saw the Mini wrench about in pursuit of Nicholas. As if caught in a nightmare, she watched the car streak after horse and rider. In the bright sunlight, the jaws of the cliffs gleamed silver above the sea, and Kacey realized that this deadly game of cat and mouse would soon be pushed to a bloody conclusion.

Help him, Adrian! Please, if you love me—if you ever loved me, help him now! Tears spilling from her eyes, Kacey put all the force of her yearning heart into her plea.

Suddenly the swirling static receded; now only chill silence remained. Kacey tasted the sick-sweet tang of fear on her tongue as the two shapes began to converge.

They were gaining on him! It was only a matter of yards to the edge now! Nicholas kneed the horse in a sharp turn, but the car followed, its angry wheels jolting over the earth.

"Dear God, no!" Kacey's shrill scream echoed across the downs.

And then out of nowhere came the gray blur, flashing from behind the gorse and streaking over the flat earth. Only feet from the Mini, he lengthened stride and leaped into the air, legs flexed, a study in grace and power.

A second later, the cat lay flat against the windshield, his black paws braced against the wiper blades as he clung to the glass.

Kacey never knew exactly what happened next. It would always remain a blur of noise and movement interwoven with the sound of her own screams.

An angry shout. The wild neighing of a horse. The scream of grinding gears…

And then the dark rectangle of the car, rising as if in slow motion and arcing in sudden, dreamlike silence over the ragged edge of the cliffs to plunge out of sight into the snarling waters six hundred feet below.

"N-Nicholas…" Kacey never finished her hoarse cry. Already swaying, she felt her legs give way. That was the last thing she felt before crumpling slowly to the ground.

CHAPTER NINE

IT IS DONE. I MUST GO NOW, Katharine.

Kacey frowned, hearing—no, *feeling*—the words slip down to the dark place where she floated, mind asleep, thoughts closed off to the outside world.

A-Adrian?

Yes, my heart. I'm here.

Thank you—for saving him.

Silence, bleak and total, for long moments. In those empty seconds, Kacey realized exactly how much he loved her.

And just how much he regretted having to give her up.

Suddenly the scent of roses filled her mind, along with the gentle kiss of spring wind. *Nonsense,* the voice whispered. *It is no more than I came to do. Now you, my stubborn woman, must rest. There will be time enough for all the other things. For now, just rest...*

Kacey tensed, caught up in the terror of those last, chilling moments. But—Gideon? He was—

Gideon will be with me, which is where he belongs. And then, as if he'd seen her frown, *No, don't fret, Katharine. Not for what you cannot begin to understand...just accept this thing I tell you.*

Then...thank him, at least.

A smile. She could feel it crinkle through her, warm and slightly chiding. *No need, sweeting. Gideon has already heard. You might try the aquamarine, you know. Whistler vows it was always his most difficult pigment in the Nocturnes. And be bold—add ocher to your aquamarine and lavender to your grays, then dilute the lot with a liberal dash of turpentine. This is his way of thanking you for caring. But then you were always a rare one for caring, weren't you, my love? Even while Nicholas and I tore you in two...*

The scent of roses lay heavy upon her, almost like a lover's caress. And then Kacey's thoughts began to scatter, exhaustion overtaking her, the fragile thread of contact beginning to unravel, Adrian? she asked drowsily.

Sleep. It was a brisk command, almost paternal now.

She felt the last thread break, then slipped deep into a cloud of dreams.

Into forgetting. Just as Adrian had intended.

Goodbye, my heart, the voice in her mind whispered softly, knowing she could not hear. Regret hung heavy on him as he began the last difficult step of easing the contact which had become the sweetest thing in his long and very tattered existence.

His bitter sigh mingled with the wild channel winds. *My three visits have been given and used. There can be no more, my love.*

Someday, perhaps, you will remember—when the pain has faded and this day is no more than a faint shadow in your memory. And on that day, perhaps you will remember just how much I loved you, Katharine, though my damnable pride always got in the way.

Until then, forget me and everything about me. Just forget...

The voice fell away, ebbing into a raw swirl of noise for a moment.

He collected himself, but only with great difficulty. *Until then, mind my roses, if you will, sweeting. Them I have loved full well. But not as much as I have loved you, Katharine. And always will love you...*

Then the voice melted away, buffeted by the chill currents from the sea, swallowed up by the cry of gull and curlew.

Soon even the scent of roses was swept away on the churning channel winds.

SOMETHING PRODDING—SQUEEZING her fiercely.

Go away!

"Kacey!"

No more—leave me alone. World surging in, and all she wanted was forgetting—no, *remembering,* in a way more intense than any waking thought.

"Sweet God, Kacey, wake up!"

Once again the probing fingers. This time they shook her, then slapped her cheeks.

She started to reach out with her mind, then stopped short, frowning.

Reaching out for what? For whom?

No answer came back from the chill shadows around her. Only sheer blackness, like a slate washed pure and clean.

"Kacey, can you hear me?"

Something about the raw plea in that voice pierced the dark veil of her thoughts. She opened one eye warily, wincing at the light that flooded in. Her head immediately began to throb, and pain broke over every inch of her body.

It was a hard face Kacey saw above her then—eyes smoldering silver, lips full, tense now with fear. So very tense…

Slowly she reached up and traced the taut line of that mouth. A beloved mouth? A beloved face, she realized.

In one sharp stroke, recognition burst over her, and the lingering traces of her dreams were swept away.

"N-Nicholas? Is it really you?"

The hands tensed and crushed her to his chest. "Thank God," Draycott muttered thickly, his fingers buried in her hair, his breath warm on her cheek. A faint line of moisture worked down his face.

"You came," Kacey whispered. "I hoped…I tried to believe…"

"Of course I came. I'll always come, my brave, sweet love."

Then no more words, just two bodies crushed together, heart

to wild heart, breaths raw with thanksgiving. And then, as the fear slowly ebbed, they were caught up in feelings far different…

Driven by a need too long unassuaged.

Driven by a need that felt two hundred years old.

He would have taken her then, fiercely, out of a raw desperation to prove that they were both alive, with a future yet to share. But at that moment Marston tapped at the door and entered, followed by a tall, gray-haired visitor.

The Englishman with the silver eyes smothered a curse. Not yet, it appeared, were they to have their moment of peace.

It was a strange scene, even in this room that must have witnessed many strange scenes in its time. The golden-haired woman, pale still, propped against the flowered chintz cushions, an ice bag on her temple and a bandage wound around her forearm.

The dark-haired man on the sofa beside her, his eyes tense on her face, full of the consciousness of how close they had both come to dying.

The butler, stealing discreet, sidelong looks at the other two, holding back a smile, content with all he saw.

Last of all was the irritated police inspector, who plunged a hand through his disheveled gray hair, understanding nothing at all. "But I still don't see how you knew where they'd gone, Lord Draycott," the inspector began, moving directly to the question that had been bothering him the last two hours. "The coast road could have taken them any number of places."

Nicholas's eyes fixed on Kacey's face, drinking in the beauty of her smile. He muttered a curse, desperately wishing the officer would go away.

Draycott said nothing about the voice he'd heard, of course. Nothing about the swift, sharp images or the absolute certainty he'd had of her location. No, that would be for another time, he decided. Preferably after he'd come to understand it more himself.

Inspector Jamieson muttered something beneath his breath as Draycott bent and feathered a soft but very thorough kiss across Kacey's parted lips. The officer scratched his gray head, distinctly ill at ease, but determined to have some answers all the same. There were forms to be completed, after all. Forms in bloody triplicate! And this was one case he wanted closed—once and for all! "I'm terribly sorry to intrude, Lord Draycott, but I really must ask—"

Nicholas sat up slightly, his lips curved in a dark smile. "I'm afraid I haven't the slightest idea, inspector. Just a lucky guess, perhaps."

The officer gave an exasperated sigh. If only the man would concentrate for a moment...

Then, as he saw the radiance that filled Kacey's eyes, saw the blinding force of her answering smile, Inspector Jamieson began to understand exactly why Nicholas Draycott was having trouble breathing, or of thinking about anything else right now.

But business was business, the officer told himself firmly, squaring his shoulders. "I don't believe in guesses, Lord Draycott. It's hard work that solves crimes." Jamieson frowned for a moment, considering his next words. "Shall I be frank?"

"Of course." Just as long as you make it quick and then leave us bloody alone, Nicholas thought, his irritation growing more pronounced by the second.

"Special Investigations knew that Trang had secured a movable fortune somewhere close at hand for a fast escape. It was there all along, hidden in the mud of your cell—an ancient Buddhist reliquary urn set with a fortune in cabochon gems. And inside was a microfilm list of all Trang's contacts—in Asia as well as Europe. That's what your two friends were after." The inspector's eyes narrowed. "They'd been involved with Trang long enough to learn about his little stash, and when the choppers came in for you, Lord Draycott, they were already scrambling for the urn. They never found it, though, because by then soldiers were swarming everywhere and they didn't have a clear chance to look. By the time things settled down after Trang's death, the urn had disappeared. That's where SI came in. They found out about the contents of the jar last week and grew distinctly uneasy when…" The inspector cleared his throat, clearly uncomfortable. "That is, just in case…"

With a sharp curse, Nicholas jerked to his feet. "Just in case what, inspector?"

"In case Miss Mallory might be, er…" The officer's eyes flashed to Kacey's face, and he cleared his throat again.

"Go on, spit it out, man!"

"Well, be working with one of those fellows from Bhanlai. Someone up in London was worried that—"

Draycott plunged across the room toward the telephone, muttering a long and very graphic stream of curses with every step. "The bloody, interfering imbeciles! What have they got, oatmeal for brains? Someone's head is going to roll for this, by God. Just see if it doesn't!" His hand was on the receiver when Kacey's breathless protest brought him to a halt.

The inspector never did see what passed between them, as Nicholas's back was turned. Ever after, he was to puzzle about that.

But whatever it was, the effect was swift and totally persuasive, for a moment later Draycott ran a hand through his unruly hair and slowly came back to his seat. Silently, Kacey reached out, drawing his hand to her cheek. That much Inspector Jamieson did see, and the jolt of naked longing he'd seen on her face was enough to stun him speechless.

His discomfort increasing by the second, the inspector plunged ahead. "By the way, the two of you were bloody lucky out there on the downs today. That's a damn unstable stretch of cliffs. It could have given way any moment, especially with the weight of the car." Jamieson's brow creased. "Good God, didn't one of your ancestors fall from the cliffs somewhere near there, Draycott?"

A closer ancestor than you'll ever know, Nicholas thought grimly. And luck had absolutely nothing to do with the events that took place out on the cliffs today, he added silently.

No, love and not luck had saved them today. Love along with trust. And perhaps a little help from Draycott Abbey's proud and stubborn ghost...

Nicholas's fingers tightened as he felt Kacey shudder.

Jamieson saw, too, and that more than anything else decided him it was time to leave. His only regret was that he wouldn't get a chance to interrogate those two ruffians in the Mini, particularly that fellow with the acrid cigarettes and the arrest record stretching from here to Brighton.

But neither of those men would be talking to anyone—ever again. And that left the urn in limbo.

Too bad, that. Still, someday Draycott might remember exactly what had happened to it. Until then, SI would just have to wait.

Jamieson smiled grimly at the thought of those tight-lipped bureaucrats up in Whitehall waiting patiently for anything.

Yes, nothing else needed tending to here, the gray-haired officer decided. "I expect I'll be going then. Tomorrow one of my men will pop round with the Turners we recovered, Lord Draycott." He darted a last, sidelong glance at the pair of oblivious lovers. "On second thought, perhaps next week might be a better idea," he revised softly.

When he took his hat and left the room, Marston, efficient as usual, was waiting to show him out.

"Bloody strange business," the inspector muttered, half to himself.

"But it ended well for all that, I believe."

Jamieson merely frowned, cramming his hat down on his

head with unnecessary force. "A lucky guess indeed! What kind of fool does the man take me for?"

Still muttering, he walked into the courtyard. "It's going to look damn odd on the paperwork, I can tell you that!"

The inspector was still frowning when he got into his car and slammed the door.

"YOU WERE SHAMEFUL WITH that poor man, Nicholas." Kacey shot the viscount a chiding smile. "No, we were *both* shameful," she added ruefully.

"Nonsense. The bloody fellow should have left hours ago. Anyone could see we had other things on our minds than police business."

"The inspector was only doing his job. And we certainly didn't give him much help." Kacey's eyes darkened, probing his face. "How *did* you know—where they'd taken me, I mean?"

Nicholas ran the pad of his thumb tenderly over her brow where a white bandage covered the lacerated skin at her temple. He gave a soft sigh. "Something told me you were going to ask that... Hmmm—let's just say that a bird told me."

"Indeed." Kacey's brow rose in a devastating imitation of the viscount's own arrogant gesture.

"It's the only answer you're going to get from me. After all, who are you to complain? You claim to have conversed with a ghost," Draycott growled, bending down for another kiss, this one long and devouring, not nearly as gentle as the last.

Long minutes later, when they finally began to resurface, Kacey slanted her head back, frowning. "Ghost? I don't believe in ghosts."

It was Draycott's turn to look skeptical. "No? Very well then, let's just drop the whole business, shall we? But one day I'll work it all out of you, I promise. And I can be most persuasive when I wish to be, Kacey Mallory."

Kacey's tawny brow arched. "Prove it," she whispered silkily.

With a low growl, the Englishman did just that, leaving no weapon in his vast arsenal unused.

When Kacey's breath was ragged and her pulse beat a wild staccato, Nicholas slid forward and drew her head onto his lap. He twined her slim fingers through his. "I love you, Kacey," he said huskily. "You know that, don't you?"

Her eyes radiant, Kacey nodded up at him, too full of emotion to speak just yet, still floating on the rich currents of the love that surrounded them.

The brisk tapping at the door barely registered at first. When neither answered, the door opened.

"Excuse me, your lordship, but it *is* nearly noon. Shall I serve luncheon now?" Brisk and correct, Marston stood just outside the door.

Draycott smothered a very graphic curse.

Marston's face remained entirely impassive. "I take that for a no. In that case, will you be requiring me for anything further?"

"Take the night off, Marston." Nicholas's smile widened, decidedly wolfish now. He did not take his eyes from Kacey's flushed face. "On second thought, take the whole bloody month."

The butler's lips twitched, but to his credit, he did not give way to the smile sneaking over his mouth. "Thank you, my lord. You are very generous. And may I be the first to wish you both happy?"

Nicholas turned at that, shooting Marston a grin that was swift and lopsided, making the viscount look boyish and slightly uncertain.

It was a smile that made Kacey's heart ache. A smile that made her vow to see that he looked like that often.

"Always on the mark, aren't you?" Then, turning to Kacey, "Yes, I rather think you *may* wish me happy, Marston."

"By the way, your automobile has been repaired, my lord. I've taken the liberty of returning it to the garage."

"Ah. Thank you for the loan of your Alfa."

There was a decided glint in the butler's eyes as he caught Kacey's look of surprise. "His lordship is rather conservative when it comes to automobiles, Miss Mallory. You might as well learn that now. The Alfa Romeo is mine, in fact. The Land Rover is his—and a greater pile of junk never existed. If I may say so, my lord," he added smoothly.

Nicholas's grin widened, but he still did not turn, enjoying Kacey's confusion. "No, you may *not* say so, Marston."

The butler merely nodded. This argument was clearly one of long standing between them. "Very well, my lord. Consider the remark unsaid." His eyes still glittering, Marston turned and left them then, closing the door softly behind him.

"That gorgeous sports car—it's Marston's?" Kacey couldn't keep the incredulity from her voice.

"Quite a first-rate amateur in the racing circuit is our Marston. Rather the ladies' man, too."

Kacey could only shake her head, amazed.

And then Nicholas shifted, bending down and sweeping her into his arms.

"What…whatever are you doing?"

"I'm carrying you upstairs, my heart. I find I've had entirely enough talking for one day."

"P-put me down this instant, Nicholas! I'm perfectly able to walk."

"Ah, but I like carrying you, Kacey Mallory from Connecticut. I plan on carrying you quite often, as a matter of fact. Up my steps. Over my threshold." His voice grew taut. "Into my bed. And right now I have a very important question to put to you, but I mean to render you entirely mindless with lust before I risk it."

Kacey smiled. Her fingers eased deep into his dark, unruly hair. "Indeed." It was a perfect imitation of his own imperious tone.

Nicholas's laugh was silk over steel. "You dare to provoke

me? For that you'll pay most dearly, I warn you. Do you know that my aunt has been calling all morning? I really should throw you to the wolves, you know. She's just itching to get her hands on you—she's got an attic chock full of art up at that ruin of hers in Yorkshire. But I told her you'd be tied up until after the honeymoon. We've decided on Lake Como, by the way."

"Have we indeed? And what else have *we* decided upon?" Kacey demanded silkily, her voice low and very provocative.

Nicholas's eyes narrowed to silver slits. The pain at his groin was growing worse by the minute. "That it must be soon." His eyes closed as her fingers eased open the top button of his shirt. "Oh, God, very soon," he muttered thickly.

Kacey merely smiled, her lips following a moment later, teasing a hot, wet trail down his neck.

Nicholas's fingers tightened on her hips. "I'll never get enough of you, Kacey, I warn you here and now. In fact, I probably won't let you out of my bed for a week."

The smile she gave him was instant and breathtaking. "Promises, promises."

"And just in case you change your mind at the last minute, I have a little bribe for you, my dear Miss Mallory. It's upstairs in the long gallery. Would you care to see it?"

Kacey nodded dreamily, thinking the only bribe she needed was him—the things he did to her, the cherished way he made her feel.

He carried her upstairs, then lowered her gently to the ground before the door to the long gallery, frowning. "That's odd. I could have sworn I left that door closed this morning…"

He glanced quickly through the room. The curtains were drawn now, as Kacey had instructed, to protect the fine old tapestries and Oriental carpets from the damaging effects of the sun. The quick inspection told Nicholas everything was as he'd left it.

With a faint shrug, he took Kacey's hand and led her to the canvas propped on a chair by the far wall. "It's yours, my love.

That's the least I can do. Without it, I might never have found you. Although sometimes I wonder..."

A startled protest broke from her lips. "Nicholas! You can't! I *couldn't*—it's far too valuable for—" Kacey's breath caught. "It's genuine, you see. I should have told you yesterday, but—"

He stopped her with one finger soft upon her lips. "All the better, my heart. The perfect bribe, isn't it? My only condition is that it not hang in *our* bedroom." His eyes darkened. "I want neither distractions nor onlookers when I have my way with you, woman. Or shall I take you back to the stables, perhaps?"

Kacey decided not to argue with him about the canvas now. Instead, she slanted her head and studied him through half-lowered eyelids. "Indeed, your lordship? The way I remember it, *you* were the one sizzling like a lit stick of dynamite back there in the stables." Her hands climbed slowly to the buttons at her collar. "Maybe I should..." The first came free, and then the second. Her fingers slipped lower, freeing a third. "And what about when *I* have my way with *you*, my lord?" she purred.

Nicholas's eyes darkened, shot through with molten specks. "Promises, promises," he whispered thickly.

Clear laughter spilled around them, dispelling the gallery's lingering shadows, along with any ghosts that might have haunted that ancient room. Nicholas pulled her to him, easing her between his taut thighs until she felt the hard evidence of the passion she had so skillfully provoked.

Kacey's hips shifted against his thighs, restless and sweetly urgent. Her eyes darkened, fixed on his hard mouth.

It was a silent plea, and one which the Englishman resolutely ignored. This time he would make her wait, Nicholas vowed, firing her need until it was just as great as his.

His hand dropped, gliding over her ribs until his fingers skirted the full swell of her breast. He didn't even try to resist the urge to move higher and palm her rich, seductive curves. Fire shot through him when he heard her breathy sigh, saw her eyes close, felt the nipple bud sweetly beneath his touch.

"God, Kacey…"

"Please, Nicholas…"

Fingers laced, hearts meshed, they moved unsteadily to the door. They were almost at the threshold when Kacey stiffened, staring at the massive portrait that hung beside the entrance. "Do you see it?"

"See what, love?"

"There—the portrait!"

Draycott studied the gaunt figure of his ancestor impatiently. Clad in velvet and lace, the eighth viscount wore a faint, sad smile on his proud lips. "Am I supposed to see something?"

"Adrian…" Kacey seemed to hear a faint humming in the air around her. With it came the drifting scent of roses. She frowned, trying to place something—something about that smell. Something that seemed very important.

Her eyes narrowed. "I could swear there's something different about it. The face…the stance, maybe." After a moment more, she gave up, shrugging. "Oh, I don't know. Maybe I'm just imagining it. This house has always done strange things to me."

"I was hoping you'd say it was the house's *owner* who did strange things to you," Draycott muttered, oddly jealous of the portrait that had captured all her attention.

Suddenly with a little cry, Kacey pointed lower. "There—that's it! The rose. He didn't have a rose before, I'm sure of it. I worked here for a whole day and I never before saw that rose!"

Nicholas studied the portrait more carefully this time. The figure carried a single rose in full bloom, not a modern hybrid but one of the old, wide-petaled varieties. Just the same sort as those growing over the stone face at the front of the house. "*Cuisse de nymphe*—maiden's blush. One of the old reprobate's favorites." He frowned. "To tell the truth, I never paid much attention to the portrait before. Of course, all of these have been reproduced in some collection or another. We'll have a look in the library and check on it."

Kacey was still staring at the portrait, a crease working across her brow, when Nicholas pulled her around to face him. "*Tomorrow,* that is. Right now, I've got other things on my mind than paint and canvas, no matter how old or cleverly executed."

With a tremulous smile, Kacey turned into his embrace, combing her fingers through his thick hair and then rising to brush a kiss across his lips. Hard-faced, fierce with a need that was hunger and far, far more, Nicholas swept her up and strode down the hall to his bedroom.

A vein throbbed at his forehead as he laid Kacey back against the sapphire coverlet. "How right you look there."

A muscle flashed at his jaw when he slipped the buttons of her dress free and tossed it away, feasting on her pure ivory nakedness.

In a wild flurry of rustling, he tugged his shirt from his pants and fumbled at his zipper with fingers suddenly unsteady.

Seconds later—seconds that seemed like an aching eternity— his clothes went flying atop hers. Slowly Nicholas laced his fingers through hers and stretched her arms above her, every movement deliberate as he covered her with his hard body. "Marry me, Kacey Mallory," he ordered huskily. "Spend the rest of your life making me hungry, happy, and very crazy. Ferret through my mail. Sneak files out of my desk. Knock over my plants. Lock me in my own stables." His eyes darkened, searching her face for her answer. "Make me the happiest man on earth, in short."

"Yes—a thousand times yes, my love." As Kacey spoke, a tear worked from the corner of her eye. Her love poured over him in a golden flow, nearly tangible.

At last some of Nicholas's fear began to ebb. His head dropped, and he tongued one furled pink nipple to exquisite arousal. "Are you sure, Kacey? Are all the ghosts gone now?

There's room for only two in this bed, you know." His fingers shifted, seeking her sweetness.

Jade eyes dazed with passion, Kacey stared up at him. "I—I told you I don't believe in ghosts, Nicholas."

"What *do* you believe in, green eyes?" he muttered, sliding his fingers deep, shifting his hips against her until she was mindless and gasping with the pleasure he brought her.

"*You,* Nicholas Draycott. Oh—"

"Prove it," he muttered, arching his back and filling her with the steel of his own need.

Instantly Kacey's fingers dug into his back. Her legs wrapped around him. "Please, Nicholas…" she moaned.

The Englishman's face darkened with the strain of control. "God, Kacey, I wanted to make it last…but—ahhh—I don't think I can. No, don't touch me or I'll—"

Her hands moved. Her soft, breathy gasps rocked through Nicholas like an explosion. He felt her tighten, convulsing around him, her eyes dazed as she pleaded for him to follow.

With a raw groan he did, sliding deep, oh, so deep, until time shimmered and wove its glowing strands around them, long spirals crossing and then meeting again, past, present and future caught together in the beauty the lovers wove with hearts and minds and bodies one.

Somewhere far out over the downs, a church bell rang twelve times—and then once more, one could have sworn, the last peal low and faint but clearly audible. A freak of nature, the experts called it. The product of high humidity and low temperature—or perhaps the opposite. Experts could never agree about such things, of course.

But the locals only shook their heads, knowing it was something very different. They knew the work of a ghost when they heard it—the work of the Draycott ghost, to be exact, signaling his presence with that phantom thirteenth stroke.

Upstairs in the long gallery, a dark portrait began to shimmer in an errant beam of sunlight from a not quite closed curtain. Golden light played over the man's lips, carved in a proud, bittersweet smile.

In his hands, the blush-pink rose seemed to gleam, its petals slowly unfolding while rich perfume filled the air.

One petal moved, detached from the corona, and fell dreamlike to the floor.

And then, as the sun moved behind a cloud, the beam shifted and the portrait was cast back into shadow, resolving into a flat plane of oil and canvas once more.

From the end of the hall came the creak of wood, followed by soft, breathless laughter.

"Again?" Kacey's voice was startled. "Nicholas, you wouldn't— *I couldn't possibly—*"

"Wanna bet?" It was a low, primal growl, dark with triumph, rich with promise. "Sweet Jesus, you make me feel like a randy sixteen-year-old, Kacey Mallory. Like a man's who's got two hundred years to make up."

Which, in a way, he did. Perhaps they both did.

So it was no surprise that neither noticed the sleek gray form ghosting past the door and down the corridor. On velvet paws, the cat found the long gallery and came to rest before the portrait of Adrian Draycott.

His long tail arched, the great creature sniffed at the fallen rose petals, then turned to stare up at the painting.

For a moment, the air seemed to hum.

The cat fell back, legs tensed, tail high. He jumped...

Up, and then higher...

Right into the portrait, which shimmered and seemed to open as the gray body sailed inside, then disappeared from view completely, to the sound of low, welcoming laughter.

BRIDGE OF DREAMS

PART I

A Door of Shadows

PROLOGUE

Kent, England
Draycott Abbey
May 6, 1794

GABRIEL MONTSERRAT, THE fifth earl of Ashton, stood in the candlelight, letting the silence wash around him.

He was going to die. There was no escaping it now.

But it didn't matter. Everything he had loved and valued was already gone, so what greater pain could death hold?

He touched the damp stone walls of Draycott's wine cellar, feeling everywhere its vast age. A grand old house, it had witnessed so much of his life's joy—and all its bitter sorrow.

Draycott Abbey alone he might miss. And also its arrogant master. But the rest?

No, not the London glitter. Not the jeweled, laughing women who ever sought his bed. Not the gaming, nor the vice. Certainly not the heady danger he had taken to courting ever more recklessly of late. He was the Rook, after all. Such excesses were expected of the man famous for saving French aristocrats from the guillotine. Yes, Gabriel was a man who would dare all, even if his exploits in revolutionary France left nothing but ashes in his mouth.

Now that *she* was gone.

Gabriel's head was pounding and the wound in his side had

settled into a vast, icy chill. Something was sticking to the lace of his shirt. Glancing down, he saw that it was his own drying blood. He raised a glass of wine to the darkness. "To you, Devere. You have won, damn you. I shall die in here behind this wall with my wine."

He should have been terrified or furious, but he wasn't. He'd lost too much to care. And, as he studied the case of wine, a strange smile twisted Ashton's lips. Yes, it was over. Devere had seen to that when he'd shot the one woman Gabriel had ever loved.

But maybe there was a different way. Maybe in some other time, everything could be different. Maybe somewhere in the soul everyone carried memories of lovers lost and vows shared in palaces that had long since turned to dust.

For a moment the tall man with the sun-bronzed face and the unfashionably unpowdered hair studied the bottles nestled in a case of wood shavings and cotton batting—bottles which he had escorted all the way from the misty valleys of the Garonne in France, where the fires of revolution yet raged.

He had slipped through death, eluding his pursuers again and again, and in the process he had saved the family of the woman he loved. But he had returned to find death leering from his own doorstep.

Still, maybe there was a way.

A wild blaze filled his eyes. As hope lit his face, a fragment of the earl of Ashton's notorious bravado returned.

The recklessness that Geneva had loved so well.

Before she'd breathed her last. Before she'd died in his arms. *Yes, I will manage it somehow, my love,* he vowed.

Because some things had power beyond belief or explaining. Perhaps beyond time itself.

Gritting his teeth against the pain tearing through his chest, Ashton pulled quill and ink from the small writing desk that Adrian Draycott kept by the far wall of his wine cellar. Slowly he began to write...

I, Gabriel Ashton, being whole of body and sound in mind and spirit, do hereby warrant this document as the final addition to my legal disposition of worldly goods and lands. Only one change is to be made, and that will be entered below…

His face gaunt with strain, the dying earl wrote on by the light of a guttering candle. Each sharp stroke that slashed at the vellum sent fresh blood oozing onto his white lace.

The contents of the case of superior Sauternes wine from the Garonne Valley of France, lately acquired by myself and now settled at my feet, are to be handled exactly as detailed below. Let it be recorded that ANY DEVIATIONS FROM MY WISHES WILL NEGATE THE TERMS OF THIS WILL. In that event, this wine is to be destroyed, with no benefit accruing to anyone. I hereby charge the heirs of my friend, Adrian Draycott, to see to the terms, and warn that WHOSOEVER SHALL TAMPER WITH THESE WORDS WILL FEEL THE FULL FORCE OF MY FURY.

Ashton coughed painfully. A dark blotch slid onto the sheet that was an addendum to his last will and testament, a document as reckless and outrageous as the fifth earl of Ashton had been in life.

And when he was finally done, when the last word lay like a black gash upon the page, the man who had once been the most dashing scoundrel and the greatest hero in all England gave a despairing cry and fell forward onto the desk, where his lifeblood mingled with the still-wet ink.

He whispered Geneva's name with his last breath.

Kent, England
Draycott Abbey
April 16, 1994

SOMEWHERE OVER THE WEALDEN hills of Kent a church bell was chiming.

The brawny mason from London barely noticed, too busy looking for the end of the rusted water pipe. Cursing, he inched along the wall, reaching fruitlessly through the suffocating darkness of Draycott Abbey's wine cellars. With every cramped movement his oaths grew more colorful.

Suddenly his foot caught on a slab of uneven granite. He toppled forward, his ten-pound wrench slamming against the wall.

Somewhere beyond the granite slab came a low rumble, then the heave of rotting mortar. Moments later a six-foot section of wall gave way, toppling to the stone floor.

A square of darkness gaped from the far side of the cellar, where a narrow room now lay revealed.

"Well, I'll be blowed," the big man whispered.

"Bloody likely," his companion answered. But as he spoke, he surreptitiously made the sign of the cross.

Suddenly, William Jones wasn't feeling so grand himself. "Go and fetch his lordship. Reckon he's going to want to see this for himself."

But the man at his side didn't move, transfixed by the opening in the wall that led away into darkness.

To a room that had lain sealed and secret for two hundred years.

"Whatta you reckon's hidden in there, Will?"

"How in bleedin' hell should *I* know?" There was nervousness in the big man's voice now. Suddenly he wanted to be back in London, back in the crowded streets filled with lights and laughter and people.

Anywhere but *here,* with its odd silence.

With its strange, clinging darkness.

"Will?"

"Just go and *get* him, blast you!"

With the other man gone, the silence in the wine cellar grew choking. And although the brawny stonemason would forever afterward try to deny his memories and convince himself it had been no more than a freak of his imagination, at that moment he found himself implacably drawn toward that cold square of darkness.

Slowly, he raised his flashlight. Just beyond the jagged edge of the wall, light played over an old wooden crate thick with dust and cobwebs. Inside the rough planks he could just make out the outline of eight bottles of wine, dark streaks of mold straddling their corks.

And draped across the case, quill intact, lay a set of white bones, still cradled in fragments of lace and velvet.

Will Jones's broad face went pale. His flashlight glinted off a jewel winking amid the network of bones, all that remained of a man who had died here two centuries ago and had been interred in this dusty grave. Then the stonemason saw the diamond ring and the sheet of vellum that lay scrolled between the white, bony fingers.

Not much frightened William Jones. He had fought in the Falklands and done a tour of hard labor in the emerald mines of Brazil, where greed and death lay thick as the stink of human sweat. But he had never known real terror until now as he stood with his flashlight playing through Draycott's inky darkness.

Because suddenly he had the feeling he was not alone. Something seemed to push him inexorably forward, almost as if a hand had settled on his shoulder, forcing him toward that jagged piece of darkness. His jaw clenched as he fought the urge. Muscles bunched over his brawny shoulders. Against every wish, he felt his hand rise toward the dusty crate of wine. As it did, William Jones felt something move past his fingers, almost like the brush of cold water.

With a cry, he lashed out with his hammer, fighting the insane urge he couldn't even name. "No, damn it. I won't. I *won't!*"

Stumbling like a drunken man, he lurched around and fought his way back toward the cellar door.

Toward the lights. Toward the noise and the life.

Not all the money in the world could keep him in that cold, restless tomb full of secrets.

OUTSIDE DRAYCOTT ABBEY the wind played through the elms and hawthorns. A bird cried once, high and shrill.

But within the shimmering moat, within the circling walls, all was silent. Deep in the wine cellars, light tore away from darkness, form from nothingness.

A shape emerged. A man, yet not quite a man.

His eyes glinted with the clear azure of a tropical sea and his hair shone the unrelenting black of a northern sky.

Alive, he was, light shimmering about his shoulders, catching in the fine lace that fell across his wrists.

Alive, yet not quite alive.

Back and forth the ghost of Draycott Abbey paced the cold floor, brows knit, hands locked behind his back. His eyes were fixed on a past half-forgotten and a future that refused to be revealed.

For a moment anger filled the darkness. Anger and a wanting that stretched down through the long, sad centuries.

I tried, Gabriel, but God help me I came too late. By then you were both gone. But where? What happened here in my absence?

The words drifted on the soft wind. They sighed through the roses wrapped about the abbey walls.

Of course, there was no answer. Adrian Draycott had long ago given up expecting one.

Only now the past stood open, unsealed with the stroke of a wrench, and Adrian was determined to see the old mystery solved. It was his sworn duty, in fact, as the guardian ghost of

Draycott Abbey. On and on he paced, fire in his eyes and cold in his heart, walking this house he loved so well.

He wished he could change the past, but it was not possible. One could only go forward, trying desperately to remember all the old lessons while mastering the new ones. Sometimes the process left him very tired.

He made his way to the gray parapets. There he touched the lace that drifted at his cuff, lost in memories of a bolder time, when the abbey had rung to his shouted commands and fourscore servants had rushed to do his slightest bidding.

But no more. Now he was just another shadow at the edge of the roof, just another memory among all the others that filled this great, grand house. And he found himself wondering if his long-dead friend Gabriel had been right. Maybe there was a way that the past could finally be set to rights.

It all depended on the wine, of course. And the hearts of two stubborn people. But Adrian swore that if it was even remotely possible to see Gabriel's mystery solved, he would somehow see it done.

Deep in the night the church bells chimed, twelve times and then once more, a low, ghostly hum. The scent of lilacs seemed to drift upon the still air, while the dreaming house slept on. And Adrian's tall form shimmered, moving restlessly among the abbey's shadows.

CHAPTER ONE

"ONE MILLIONS POUNDS?" Dominic Alexander Montserrat, the tenth earl of Ashton, sank down in a chintz wing chair at the sunny corner of Nicholas Draycott's study. Below the window, Draycott Abbey's moat shimmered and danced, but Dominic barely noticed. "I don't believe it."

Nicholas Draycott smiled broadly. "Then you'd better start. As a matter of fact, the solicitor tells me the figure might be closer to *two* million."

Dominic's strong fingers, callused from months of stripping oak casks and pruning grapevines, dived through his long black hair. "But *how*, Nicholas? Why? And when—"

His old friend, now the twelfth Viscount Draycott and devoted inheritor of the beautiful Jacobean moat house called Draycott Abbey, interrupted with a laugh. "Hold on, Dominic. I realize this must be a huge shock—it bloody well was to me, too. At least *you* didn't have to go down and confront a skeleton that had been immured for two hundred years in your wine cellar."

"I still can't believe it!"

"According to the date on the will, that's when he died. And this man Gabriel, your ancestor, was most precise in how he wanted that wine of his to be treated. With a million pounds at stake, I suggest that it's worth taking the trouble to comply with his conditions. Not to mention the fact that he threatened anyone who tried to obstruct his plans. 'Whosoever shall tamper with these words will feel the full force of my fury,' was how he phrased it."

"Sounds damned Gothic." Dominic's lean, suntanned face still carried signs of disbelief. "Look, Nicholas, I'm finding all this very hard to accept. Maybe I've been too long at my vineyards and I'm accustomed to hearing nothing but French morning, noon, and night." There was indeed a hint of an accent in his voice. "Let's try it again, shall we? You're telling me that an ancestor of mine left a case of Château d'Yquem 1792 down in your cellars. A case of vintage Sauternes in perfect condition that could bring, even conservatively, over a million pounds at auction?"

"That's what I said. The man was Gabriel Ashton. The fifth earl of Ashton, to be exact."

"Bloody hell." Dominic ran his hands through his hair, burned by the French sun to a rich mahogany. "Since I was a boy I've heard stories about mad Uncle Gabriel. Many a night my sister and I went to sleep shivering from some horrendous tale our father had told us. The man was either a black-hearted scoundrel or the most reckless hero England ever knew, snatching French aristocrats from the very shadow of the guillotine. But no one in the family ever knew what happened to him. He simply vanished one day without a trace."

"Well, now you know *where* he died, at least," Nicholas said grimly. "The why remains a mystery, however." He sat back, noticing how fit his old friend looked sporting a new set of muscles and skin baked copper by the French sun. The last time they'd met, Dominic had been guarding the Prince of Wales on a state visit to Thailand, and the strain of Dominic's work as a royal bodyguard had been all too apparent.

That vineyard he'd bought in France three years ago had to be good for him, Nicholas decided. La Trouvaille, wasn't it called? "That's it in a nutshell. And it's all yours, Dominic." A speculative light entered Nicholas's green eyes. "Well, half of it at least."

"Mad Uncle Gabriel. A million bloody pounds." Dominic stared blankly at his glass of sherry. "My God, I could finally start setting in those new Sémillon vines that I've been wanting to get my hands on. Then maybe I'll commission some new oak casks for—" Abruptly his head rose. "*Half?* What happens to the rest of the money?"

"I'm afraid that's where things turn a bit tricky. As I said, your ancestor was most precise about how the funds were to be disposed of." Nicholas cleared his throat, turning a jewel-studded Fabergé egg in his fingers.

"Out with it, Nicky. What do I have to do, spend a night down in that haunted wine cellar with Mad Uncle Gabriel's ghost?" Dominic laughed softly. "For a million pounds, I'd spend a *week* down there, ghosts and all."

"You'd be surprised what you might find in this house, Dominic. But it's not so simple. Someone else is involved in the bequest. And I feel that the two of you are honor bound to solve the mystery of that skeleton I happened across."

Dominic barked out a laugh. "I have to split with you, is that what you're saying? If so, out with it, my friend. After all, I owe you Draycotts something for keeping that wine safe all these years."

"No, not me." Nicholas looked at his friend, noting the calluses from hard field work and the little lines at the edges of his eyes. From days squinting in the sun, days of backbreaking physical labor setting in vines, stringing protective nets, and harvesting grapes, Nicholas knew.

If he didn't love Draycott Abbey so well, Nicholas would envy his friend, who had beautiful rolling acres of vines in one of the loveliest valleys in France. He worked hard, lived well, ate wonderfully, and the little lines at his eyes attested to the fact that Dominic Montserrat laughed often and hard. Life didn't get much better than that, Nicholas thought. Surely that was the right kind of work, healthy labor that made things grow where before there had been nothing. Not like the other kind, the work that had carried Dominic to tense meetings with suspicious men in far-flung cities with unpronounceable names.

But Nicholas knew he couldn't put off the rest of his news any longer.

"So who's the lucky man? He's going to get one hell of a surprise when he finds he's just inherited a case of priceless sweet white Bordeaux." Dominic's eyes crinkled at the thought. "*I* certainly did."

"Not he, *she*."

"That's better yet. Maybe she'll be so overcome with delight at the news that she—"

"It's someone we both know." Nicholas's fingers tightened. "Donnell O'Neill's daughter."

Dominic went very still, his eyes on the sunlight spilling through the study windows. "Cathlin O'Neill?"

"One and the same."

The silence unraveled until the whole room was filled with it.

Dominic strode to the window and stared out at the moat. "Cathlin O'Neill, the girl whose mother died here? I remember your father was off in Brazil at the time, buying a copper mine. We were up at school when you found out. Bloody awful."

Nicholas nodded grimly. "We never found out exactly what happened to the mother. When my father came back, the police told him it was probably a simple accident. Or…"

"Or what?"

Nicholas shrugged. "Or it might have been something else. Elizabeth Russell O'Neill was here to examine some textile samples that needed restoring. My father was very keen that it should be done right and had insisted on hiring the best authority, which Elizabeth O'Neill was. She'd brought her young daughter along with her for the weekend and even though Cathlin was only ten, she loved this place as much as her mother did."

Nicholas turned the priceless jeweled egg, frowning as it caught the light. "You know the rest. That first night they were here, her mother went out and never came back. There were only a few servants on duty in my father's absence, but none of them saw or heard anything odd and there was no sign of foul play. But the next morning little Cathlin found her mother's body beside the moat, where she'd plunged from the roof."

"Good God." Dominic looked at his friend. "Possibly suicide?"

Nicholas shook his head. "She had no history of instability and she was happy in her marriage, by all accounts."

"And there's nothing more? You never discovered how it happened?"

"Never. The girl remembered nothing—the result of trauma, we were told. At the time there was some talk of a political connection, since her father had been involved in government work. But nothing concrete ever turned up. I can't believe this is all coming up again." Nicholas glared out the window. "I'm almost tempted to pitch that wine into the moat, since the last thing I want is all this muck dredged up again. Believe me, the press will have a field day when they find out." He sighed and set down the jeweled egg. "I don't want Kacey and little Genevieve upset by this either." Nicholas studied a framed photo of his laughing wife and five-year-old daughter. "I think it best we leave as soon as the conditions of your ancestor's will have been put into motion. Perhaps some digging in London will turn up new answers about the mystery of Gabriel Ashton."

"But what do Cathlin O'Neill and I have to do with this wine? I don't understand."

"Your ancestor insisted that the two eldest living descendants of himself and one Geneva Russell spend seven days and nights here at Draycott Abbey. Then—and only then—the wine would be theirs. Cathlin is the oldest living relative of that Geneva Russell, through her mother."

Dominic stared at his friend. "You're kidding, aren't you?"

"I'm afraid not. And this will was quite specific, Dominic. In fact, the legal terms are enforceable even today. You can see why I feel I have to carry out those terms exactly as Gabriel Ashton asked."

Dominic cursed softly. Already he could see his hopes of expansion at La Trouvaille vanishing like early morning mist in the French sun. "But what's all this business about seven days and nights?"

"Assuming that these descendants are of an age of independence and of sound mind and body, they must spend seven nights together here at Draycott Abbey. It was Gabriel's express wish."

"Isn't this all rather farfetched, Nicky? The man's been dead for two hundred years and from all I've heard he was far from a saint himself. Why not just forget all this folderol? *He* certainly isn't going to know."

A frown worked down Nicholas's handsome face. "He won't, but I will. Dominic, the man wrote his will as he lay dying. He signed his name in his own blood. How can I ignore such a request?"

"It's probably some kind of trick one of your demented ancestors thought up. You Draycotts seem to have a damned morbid sense of humor, especially that ghost you always talked about as a boy."

"This is no trick, Dominic. I had an architect in to look at that wall, and the bricks were authentic for their period, and the mortar was brittle with age—two hundred years of age."

"I don't *believe* this."

"You'd better start. La Trouvaille's future is going to depend on how seriously you take what I'm telling you. A great old vintage like that Château d'Yquem is worth a fortune now."

Dominic's jaw hardened. "You don't have to tell *me* what a rare Sauternes is worth!"

"Stop it, Dominic. I know this is hard for you, but it's the very thing to get you back on your feet at La Trouvaille. That vineyard has drained your pockets since day one, and you know it. Your father left you damned comfortable, but a million pounds will buy a hell of a lot of new vines and every kind of technology you could ever want."

"But why do we have to go through with this farce about the will? I've got grapes to tend and wine to get into cask. Can't we just take the wine and sell it now?"

"Out of the question. The heirs of Adrian Draycott were assigned to oversee the terms of the will, and I mean to comply with the man's wishes." A challenging gleam lit Nicholas's eyes. "Which means I'll just have to toss the wine off the abbey roof and leave it in the moat to feed the fish."

Dominic went still. "The will specified *that?*"

"Afraid so."

The earl of Ashton rubbed his jaw, calculating exactly how many oak casks, stainless steel distilling vats, and computer-scanned irrigation pumps he could buy with half a million pounds. "Damned expensive fish food."

"Isn't it though."

Dominic muttered something low and graphic and shoved his hands into his pockets, trying not to think about how much good that money would do at La Trouvaille.

"There's something else you should know, Dominic."

"Sweet God, what *now?*"

Nicholas looked grim. "This kind of news is going to interest a whole lot of people. I'll try to keep the wine secret as long as I can. I've already paid the plumbers to keep their mouths shut, in fact, but eventually one of them is bound to let something slip. And since the will is a legal document, I will eventually have to see that it is publicly recorded. When I do…"

"Go on, Nicholas."

"Let's just say that I suggest you find Cathlin O'Neill and get her up here where you can keep your eye on her."

"You think she's in danger?"

"It's only logical, considering the value of this wine. Wouldn't you be interested in possessing such a treasure?"

"If I had the money to spare, of course."

"There are other people with fewer scruples. They'll try to get it any way they can."

"Kidnappers?"

"Would you give up the wine if Cathlin were taken?"

"Of course. But it won't come to that." Dominic thought about the dangers he had confronted while guarding presidents and kings in every corner of the globe. He found it hard to imagine that he'd meet his end back in sedate, stuffy England, trying to protect a case of wine.

Then again, he hadn't made it to the relatively ripe old age of thirty-five by underestimating any kind of danger. "Have you spoken to Cathlin O'Neill about any of this?"

"I've tried, but she hasn't returned my calls. Draycott Abbey can hardly hold fond memories for her, of course."

Dominic's jaw clenched. "If I should decide to look up Cathlin O'Neill—and I do mean *if*—where would I find her?"

"She has a wine shop on Regent Street. No, wait a minute." Nicholas delved through a pile of papers on the edge of his desk and pulled out a sheet of thick vellum stock. "If I remember correctly—yes, here it is. Cathlin's on the program of a charity auction to be held at the British Museum next week." Nicholas held out the engraved invitation. "And do it right, if you please. I don't want any more restless ghosts pacing the parapets and wrecking my sleep."

"Any more? You mean those stories you told me in school were true?"

Nicholas frowned. "Never mind. Just find Cathlin and convince her somehow. Use that famous Ashton charm I keep hearing about."

Dominic shook his head. "I'm making no promises,

Nicholas." He swung his jacket over his shoulder. "How can you expect her to come back here after what happened? Who would want to face all that again? I certainly wouldn't."

"Maybe it's time she did. No matter what she decides, she's involved, and she's going to need someone to keep her safe when this news gets out. And you were always the very best, Dominic."

"Not anymore. I'm out of that world, Nicholas. You'll have to find another bulletcatcher."

"Why? You never told me what happened," Nicholas said softly.

Dominic watched his shadow slant across the lush peach carpet. Outside, the air filled with birdsong. "Because it almost killed me, Nicholas. After a while I saw shadows everywhere and I couldn't tell my friends from my enemies. I can't go back, not to the shadows, not to the adrenaline highs and the cold sweats. Not even for a million pounds."

And when Dominic left the abbey, he didn't look back. Danger had once been a way of life for him. He had been a cold professional, a man who had learned the hard way to trust no one.

But France had softened him, taught him balance. The long sunny days and lazy velvet nights of his fields along the Garonne had wiped away some of the anger and most of the bad memories.

And Dominic liked it that way.

So he would go see Ms. Cathlin O'Neill in all her glory at a society wine auction. He was curious to see how good she really was. But that was the beginning and end to it.

Nothing was going to pull him back into the shadows, not even the last, desperate words of a dying ancestor.

Or so he told himself.

CHAPTER TWO

THE STATELY VESTIBULE OF the British Museum was filled with the glitterati of four continents. Amid the Indonesian orchids and dwarf oranges, royal dukes rubbed elbows with English rock stars, California winemakers and unsmiling Japanese investors. Champagne flowed, diamonds glittered; the suits were strictly Armani and the gowns were all haute couture.

Cathlin O'Neill looked on and stifled a sigh. It was the world she'd made her own, the world she'd become intimately familiar with since she'd come to England to expand her business as an appraiser and dealer in rare old wines. She knew that tonight the bidding would be fierce, all proceeds from the charity auction going to benefit a popular wildlife trust. It didn't hurt that more than a few in attendance expected the Prince of Wales to put in an appearance before the evening was out.

Cathlin entered the antique-strewn ladies' room and turned before the mirror, straightening her elegantly severe black velvet suit. She looked like what she was: young and clever and very American. If the stuffed shirts around her didn't like it, then too bad for them. She'd had to deal with too many condescending aristocrats since coming to London and she had done it smoothly and well—but she hadn't liked it. She was tired of the formality and tired of the condescension. All she wanted was to finish her work here and go back to her little apartment off Piccadilly Circus, kick off her heels, and finish an article commissioned by a major wine journal on the pitfalls of sulfites in the winemaking process.

Hardly light reading, Cathlin thought.

But most of her thoughts had been far from light these last months. She had begun to have serious doubts about staying on in England. She disliked the climate and disliked the tone of the city and wanted nothing more than to return to her plant-filled rooms in the sunny Philadelphia shop she kept off Rittenhouse Square.

In addition to her subjective biases against London, the last months had stirred up memories of her English mother, memories that Cathlin preferred to leave buried. But she found she had little choice. The images seemed to come and go at will, and they'd been coming more often since she'd returned to England. Cathlin knew she'd have to make up her mind soon just how much longer to stay. When her friend, formerly the head of Harrods Wine Department, had first called, a partnership had seemed a good idea. Now Cathlin wasn't so sure.

She shoved back her glossy black hair and frowned into the mirror. Outside, the premier auction event of the season was about to begin, and her partner, an old friend from college days in Ithaca, had talked Cathlin into gaveling the Sauternes segment. As an expert in the early sweet white wines of Bordeaux, Cathlin knew how to fill her patter with a running commentary on good wines, bad wines, and how to know the difference between them. She named names and quoted prices, when no one else dared. As a result, she'd been the hit of two similar London auctions, especially when she'd poured out a sample taste of one of the offerings, then tossed the bottle over her shoulder, saying no one needed to be afflicted with an unfortunate mistake like that year was.

The charity council had nearly succumbed to cardiac arrest and the owning wine company had been apoplectic. But Cathlin had been dead on target and the rest of the audience had laughed wholeheartedly.

The next day the phone at her shop on Regent Street had rung right off the wall.

So tonight Cathlin forced a smile and straightened her hair, reminding herself that this exposure helped her business and gave her access to the stuffed shirts she needed, even if she *did* find them incredibly irritating.

"Ready to go?" A jeweled finger pressed her shoulder.

"Serita, you pest, why do I ever agree to do these things? If I die of Joy inhalation, it will be your fault and yours alone."

"But what a way to go." Serita McCall, Cathlin's partner, stood six feet tall and drop-dead gorgeous in gold lamé. She knew everyone worth knowing and all their various wine preferences. For five years she'd badgered Cathlin to come to London, and now that Cathlin was here, her friend was determined to see her paired off and happy.

Cathlin had very different ideas. Serita's string of introductions had left her utterly bored, and she was having no more of them.

But suspicion was a hard habit to break, and Serita had that old gleam in her eye again. "What is it, Serita? Don't tell me there's another sweet, dear man you want me to meet. I warn you, I've had it with making small talk with strangers."

Her friend gave her a sympathetic look. "I was terrible, wasn't I? Well, you can breathe easily, because I'm done with all that. I'm only thinking about that man who's been asking about you. See, over there." She opened the door and pointed. "Beside the Japanese contingent."

Cathlin studied the tall man striding past a marble column. She had time for only a dim impression of broad shoulders and dark hair before he disappeared into the jeweled throng. "Am I supposed to know him?"

"No, but I am. His name is Dominic Alexander Montserrat. He's the tenth earl of Ashton, actually."

Cathlin's lips pursed.

"Don't go all New World snob on *me*, Cathlin O'Neill. Dominic is a perfectly nice man who asked me to point you out. For purely business reasons, I might add. He owns a vineyard himself."

"Great. Another dissipated absentee landlord. Forget it, Serita."

"You're wrong, Cathlin. He's very quiet about his involvement, but he does take a great interest in his wine and he's very knowledgeable, believe me. I'd tell you more, but he'd shoot me, since he's very sensitive about his privacy."

"So am *I*."

Serita smiled. "As a matter of fact, he said you were far too young to be an expert on anything so subtle as nineteenth century Sauternes."

"Just what I need, another pompous ass. I dearly love you, Serita, but really, you English seem to grow pompous asses the way we grow Florida oranges. And these auctions just seem to pull them out in droves."

"But he is a most attractive man, Cathlin. There's something different about Dominic. It's his eyes, I think. He looks at you and really *sees* you. There's something seductive, but dangerous about that kind of total focus in a man." She shrugged. "Then again, I've already had two glasses of Taittinger, so my judgment is probably a tad hazy. Now I must be off. There's a man waiting for me outside who has a blank check from a very fine department store in Texas and I mean to see he spends every cent of it here tonight." She winked at Cathlin. "And a few more after that."

Knowing Serita, she'd do just that, Cathlin thought, as her partner moved back into the crowd. For a moment Cathlin was envious of her ebullient friend, who always seemed to know just how to put people at their ease and bring out their best points.

Unlike Cathlin, who seemed too serious, too competent, too—

Capable. Yes, that was the word. She'd had to be capable, losing her mother so young. Worrying about her footloose father. Then losing him, too.

Sighing, Cathlin picked up her repoussé gold evening bag and headed for the columned auction room. Capable or not, she had made a promise to Serita and that meant she had some very old and very valuable Bordeaux to sell.

Halfway between the potted palms and the carved ice swans a man blocked her way. A very tall man with hair the color of the oak casks used to age the finest Dom Pèrignon.

"Ms. O'Neill?" His black brow arched.

Cathlin looked into his cool green eyes and thought they were too knowing, far too confident. Not that he didn't have reason to be. His formal black jacket was just about perfection and his bronzed face spoke of just the right amount of time shuttling between Cap d'Antibes and the latest haunt in Mustique.

Which meant that in Cathlin's eyes he was a grade-A washout.

"Maybe." Her eyes skimmed his body, noting the exquisitely cut white shirt that came from one of the finest tailors on Savile Row. His wrist held a worn but extremely valuable Swiss designer watch that would have bought a year's lease on her shop back in Rittenhouse Square. "But probably not."

There was a flare of emotion in his eyes, something that Cathlin decided was a mix of anger and humor. She found the combination startling.

"Why not?"

"Because I don't like how you talk."

A muscle flashed at his bronzed jaw. "You haven't heard me talk yet."

Cathlin pursed her lips. "Then because I don't like how you look."

"I can take off the suit if it will help."

"Not interested. You're too high on the food chain and I don't like your attitude." Cathlin smiled sweetly. "Is that reason enough?"

Again the flare of mingled emotions, only this time the anger was winning out over the humor. "My credit is good and my references are excellent. As for my attitude—" His lips curved slightly. "I'd be glad to discuss that further over dinner."

Cathlin had heard it all too many times before. As a woman in a man's world, she was considered fair game for every Bond Street Lothario and would-be Don Juan with a storefront and a two-line wine list. It was true back in Philadelphia and it was equally true here in London. "Sorry, I never mix business with pleasure." She turned to leave.

He moved in front of her with a silent grace that left Cathlin frowning. "Then let's leave the pleasure for later and focus on business. I have a proposition for you."

"I'll just bet you do."

"A business proposition."

"Let me guess. You need to decide between an imperial of Château Lafite-Rothschild '71 and a 1912 Château d'Yquem Sauternes and you simply *must* ask my advice."

His eyes weren't just green, Cathlin saw then. They were smoky, the color of the finest China jade. Too hard to be carved, the stone could only be shaped by the slow and laborious abrasion of some harder substance like crushed garnets or rubies.

The result was objects of phenomenal price but extraordinary beauty.

Looking into those eyes, Cathlin thought of the imperial archer's ring her father had brought back to her after one of his frequent Far Eastern trips.

Cathlin had found the piece lovely—at first. Soon she had come to hate it, because it represented the government work that kept him away from home for months at a time, constantly on the move—and perpetually in danger.

And the work had finally killed him, before Cathlin had ever really gotten a chance to know him.

The green eyes narrowed, hardened. "Sorry, no Lafite."

"No? How disappointing. Good-bye." Cathlin saw his eyes

change again. She sensed a raw edge of violence, not quite hidden by that sleek, cool veneer.

If so, that was *his* problem.

She was turning away when his hand snagged her wrist. She felt the hard palm and the ridge of calluses lining his fingers. Not exactly the hand of a playboy, she thought. But he'd probably gotten the calluses from counting tax write-offs and opening bottles of tanning oil for Victoria's Secret models. "Let go of my hand."

"The Lafite '71 has definite potential, but hasn't opened up and come into its own yet. The d'Yquem '12 was a flat-out disappointment." A slow, cocky grin. The kind of grin that said he was smart and good to look at and he knew it.

"Now."

"Maybe I don't want to let go of your hand."

"There are two kinds of women in this world. Those who say no and mean it. And those who say no and mean it."

"Very clever, Ms. O'Neill. But there are two kinds of men in the world—those who think there are two kinds of women, and those who know they'll never know the first thing about the incredible subtlety of the female mind. I happen to fall in the second group. Now what about my proposition?"

Cathlin shook her head in disbelief. "There are probably four hundred women in this room right now. Most of them would seriously consider armed robbery to hear a proposition from you. Go pick on one of them."

The jade eyes glinted. "I don't want one of them. I want you."

"So call my shop. It's on Regent Street. Right under *H* for hard to get."

"This is important, damn it. I need to talk to you."

Somewhere out in the auction area, a man's voice announced that the final lot of champagnes had just been sold, tallying up to a grand total of fifty thousand pounds.

Which meant Cathlin was on next.

She stared at their overlaid hands, trying to ignore his carefully controlled power. Her jaw hardened. "For your information, the Lafite '71 is more than passable even now and its potential is tremendous. The d'Yquem '12 was intense but quite uneven. Both are better than anything that could be said for *you*." She jerked her hand from beneath his. "And if you ever try that again, I'll break your wrist."

Dark glints lit the jade eyes. "What if I let you be on top next time?"

"Certainly. *If* I were wearing cement boots—with a whole lot of spikes."

"Have you ever eaten Bordeaux oysters fresh from the salt marshes on the Seudre River, Ms. O'Neill? With just a hint of lemon juice and nothing more. You'd like them. Then we'd add some hot sausages and a little pastry from Gascony. Maybe a foie gras or two and a big white Burgundy. Or perhaps a bottle of Sauternes, since that's your specialty." His eyes narrowed, considering. "A Château Climens '71, I'd say. Big and gorgeous and magnificently well bred." His eyes followed the curves suggested but not quite revealed by the black velvet of Cathlin's jacket. "Chilled just fractionally to give an edge, of course."

The man was smooth, all right. And he bloody well knew his wines. He also didn't give up. "I don't eat oysters and I don't mix business with pleasure, Mr.—"

"Montserrat," he finished smoothly. "Dominic, since we're going to be on a first name basis."

"Not in this lifetime we aren't. Lord Ashton," Cathlin added a moment later, remembering what Serita had told her of the man's background.

In the next room a very Oxonian voice announced that the Sauternes category was next and that this year's auctioneer would be Ms. Cathlin O'Neill of Nonesuch Wines, Philadelphia and London.

There was a ripple of applause.

"Very impressive, Ms. O'Neill."

"Not as impressive as I'm going to be if you hold me up any longer."

"Tell me which Sauternes I should bid on."

She looked him over thoroughly. "A '61 Climens, I think. Pleasant but hardly exciting. Impeccable opening aroma, but a thoroughly disappointing finish."

With that, she pushed off through the crowds already thronging the auction floor.

Dominic Montserrat's lips curved up in a hard smile. "Tough, aren't you? But let's see how a case of Château d'Yquem vintage 1792 worth two million dollars grabs you, Ms. O'Neill."

"NEXT ON OUR PROGRAM WE have a very fine Château Climens '71. This, as you all know, is a superb sweet white Bordeaux with excellent balance, exquisite overtones and a fine finish. It would make a perfect companion to some of the chocolate trifle I had here earlier. Now who will give me fifty? No one? Come, come, Mr. Smythe-Hampton." Cathlin made the words a sultry caress as she smiled at a tall man in an $8,000 Patek Phillipe watch.

He smiled. His pale fingers wobbled.

The man beside him muttered something and stabbed at the air.

Two minutes later the sale was closed at two thousand pounds.

Cathlin breathed an inward sigh of relief. Her feet were killing her and her shoulder itched. But there was one lot left to go.

"Our last lot tonight is a very special bottle of Château d'Yquem 1870. It is, quite simply, a legend that deserves being a legend, with marvelous texture, perfect balance, and wonderful finesse. It is also distinguished by a resolute finish. I suggest you offer it with a wedge of Grand Marnier soufflé and a bit of Vivaldi. In a Georgian drawn-stem wineglass, of course." Her lips curved. "Except for you, Reginald." She gestured at Mr. Smythe-Hampton, who was sweating openly now. "You can drink it out of that gold bullion you keep in your vault. My partner Serita will no doubt be happy to help you carve it into a suitable-size container."

Amid the laughter, the rare bottle was carefully lifted for display, to a host of muffled sighs.

"Let's be dangerous, shall we? No need for preliminaries." Cathlin swept a curve of satin hair back off her cheek. "Do I hear, say, three hundred pounds?"

"Five hundred."

Heads crooked. Women whispered at the unorthodox size of the bid.

And Cathlin felt a sinking sensation in her stomach.

The voice was cool and correct and utterly brash. It could belong to only one man.

Dominic Montserrat.

Cathlin made a point of not looking. "Do I hear six? Six hundred pounds?"

Mr. Smythe-Hampton nodded.

"Six hundred. Do I hear—"

"A thousand."

Cathlin looked up and met piercing jade eyes. "Perhaps our mystery bidder has a few chunks of gold bullion of his own lying around among the Bentleys. I have a thousand," she repeated. "Do I hear a thousand one?"

Smythe-Hampton wiggled uncomfortably and inched up one finger.

"One thousand one."

Two rows away a well-groomed man in a Turnbull and Asser shirt raised a manicured finger.

"I have one thousand two. You'd like this one, Richard." Cathlin smiled at the well-groomed international financier she had worked with on several occasions. "Much better than that last batch of erratic '83 Burgundies you bought."

Richard Severance smiled tightly and raised his hand.

Cathlin's comments were dead on target, of course, so he shrugged gracefully.

"I have one thousand two. Do I hear one thousand three for this brilliant Château d'Yquem? Come now, ladies and gentlemen. One of our most famous statesmen and presidents admired this wine greatly. You do remember Thomas Jefferson, don't you? He was on the other side of that little war we fought a few years back. But really, no hard feelings. You got to keep the peerage and we got to keep the tea, even if it was at the bottom of Boston Harbor. So now, for Mr. Jefferson, do I hear—"

"Five thousand pounds."

Cathlin swallowed. The man was mad, utterly mad.

She saw heads bend and mouths gape open. She saw bejeweled women turn clear around in their seats.

And she saw the president of the wildlife fund smiling broadly in the front row, already counting his money.

Cathlin took a breath. "Five thousand pounds. Do I hear six? Six thousand for this memorable vintage?" She waited, glancing at Mr. Smythe-Hampton, who looked flushed and sulky. He shook his head.

Cathlin's eyes swept the room. "Do I hear six?"

Richard Severance frowned and looked away.

Cathlin brought down her silver gavel. "Sold for five thousand pounds. End of lot. End of category. Thank you for all your warm participation. I'm sure our lucky buyers will enjoy these exceptional Sauternes and that the proceeds will go to help a very good cause."

She moved out, fast and silent, but she wasn't fast enough.

He closed in on her before she even got to the bottom of the stairs. "Go away," she hissed. A countess in too many opals and too little silk blinked at her and sniffed.

"Now that one's a Chablis." Dominic moved right in behind her. "An '82, I'd say. Overweight and overpriced." He slid into step, his breath tickling the soft skin at her neck.

Cathlin tried to ignore him.

"That one's an '80." He pointed to a man in polished loafers and a head of hair that was obviously not his own. "He's had his good moments, but now he's fading fast."

Cathlin felt her lips curve into a reluctant smile.

"And then there's that one." Dominic pointed to a woman in a black dress whose brevity barely qualified as decent. She looked very glossy and expensive to maintain. "Definitely a '75."

"A keep-away vintage?"

"At all costs."

So he really did know his wines. Cathlin studied him closer, noting the tiny lines around his mouth and eyes. From too much beach time or something else? "And what exactly are you, Mr. Montserrat?" Not that it mattered, of course.

"Oh, I'm definitely Château d'Yquem 1870, the exact lot you sold to me. I'm all marvelous texture and wonderful finesse." His eyes burned over her face and settled on her full lips. "Especially the resolute finish. Care to try it out with me?"

"The wine?"

"Of course. Did you think I meant something else?"

Definitely. His eyes were hinting at something much more earthy. Cathlin shrugged. She'd heard all the innuendos before. At least this man did it with panache. "You're asking me to share the bottle you just bought for five thousands pounds?"

"I could always get something more expensive, if it's not enough."

"Are you serious? Does money mean nothing to you?"

"You might be surprised."

"I doubt it."

He moved ahead of her, blocking her way. "I've just spent a great deal of money to secure your good opinion, Ms. O'Neill, but it looks like I'm failing. Help me a little here." The mockery was gone from his voice. He seemed almost sincere.

As sincere as a car dealer at a convention of little old ladies, Cathlin thought sourly. "Listen closely, Lord Ashton. I can't. I won't. I'm not interested. End of lot. End of category." The bluntness had always worked before. Somehow Cathlin found herself regretting that it would work again now.

"It's important, damn it. I need to talk to you. Now."

This time his voice was taut. Could he possibly be serious? She looked pointedly at her watch. "You have thirty seconds."

He glanced at the throngs around them. "I can't. Not like this."

"Five seconds."

"Not here, damn it."

"Ten."

"It's—confidential. I have a letter to show you, but it will have to be done somewhere more private."

Cathlin shook her head, angry at herself for believing him, even for a moment. He was just like all the others, men with smooth smiles and sleazy agendas. "I see, someplace private. Back at your apartment, no doubt. Probably with our clothes off on the middle of the bed." She stepped forward and ran her hand along his lapel. "Sorry, Lord Ashton, but I'm not impressed. You're several centuries too late with that Don Juan routine." She smiled sweetly. "But maybe the Chablis '75 would think differently. She hasn't looked away from you once. Good night—and happy hunting."

Cathlin felt his eyes burn into her all the way to the door.

HE CURSED.

Softly. Then not so softly.

Two men frowned at him and a woman in a backless Yves St. Laurent sheath giggled.

Dominic saw a familiar face and caught her wrist. "Serita? Come here and talk to me."

"You found her, I see."

"I found her all right. I have the wounds to prove it."

"Sorry, Dominic. I'm afraid Cathlin's a little prickly these days."

"Prickly wasn't exactly the word I had in mind," Dominic said grimly.

"It hasn't been easy for her, you know. She's young and lovely and very honest, Dominic. That's a difficult combination for this set. It's still very much a man's world over here, you know. Half the men in this room act as if Lord Nelson still rules the seas and America is just one of our colonies."

Dominic cocked a brow dramatically. "You mean it isn't?"

"Repulsive insect." But her eyes were admiring. "That tan becomes you. How are you doing? Really doing?"

"A decent yield." Dominic thought of his neat rows of vines marching over the hills of his holding in the Garonne. He was turning out his fourth vintage this year and already his vineyard, La Trouvaille, was making a solid profit from its rich, complex wines. It had been hard work, but the very best work of his life. "The sugar levels could be better, but we're working on that. So far no problem with quality, but—"

"No, I mean *you*. You inside."

He shrugged. "I'm surviving."

"That tells me next to nothing."

"Maybe I like it that way." Dominic gave her a lopsided smile that took the sting from his answer. "Tell me about her, Serita." He said the words tightly.

"Look, Dominic, she's not one of your usual runway beauties or extrovert actresses. She's nice and she's vulnerable. Leave her alone." Serita's voice was surprisingly hard.

"I don't plan on bodily physical harm, my dear. I have a business offer for her, that's all. But the lady seems determined not to hear it. Tell me why."

Serita sighed. "She lost her mother young, Dominic. Then she lost her father when she was just getting to know him. He was in security, I gather. Among other things," Serita said. "Oh, she doesn't talk about it much. She says she's put it all behind her. But she's lying. And that's one of the reasons she doesn't care for pomp and circumstance English-style."

Dominic laughed shortly. "So I've noticed."

"Unfortunately, *you're* very long on both, my dear man."

"Who me? I'm just your average working stiff."

Serita studied his lean, chiseled face. "Not in a million years. You're too bloody handsome for comfort. You're also too arrogant."

Dominic frowned as he saw Richard Severance stride up to Cathlin and slide his arm casually around her shoulder. When he laughed—and he seemed to laugh a great deal—Dominic saw that he had very regular white teeth. "What about *him?*"

Serita turned. "Richard? Oh, there might have been something between them once. I didn't ask and Cathlin never told me. But if so, it was nothing serious. Now it's just business."

Dominic watched Cathlin's slender back disappear through the doorway. She was beautiful and clever and he'd be a bloody fool to get within two counties of her. "I heard a saying over in Thailand once, Serita. It went something like this. Woe to any man who trusts a clever woman, because she'll drive him to all fours and leave him howling like a scrawny dog in the market square." Particularly, Dominic added silently, if the woman in question had black hair as soft as China satin and burning amber eyes.

Serita brushed his cheek. "Maybe, with the right person, howling can be fun."

"About as much fun as taking a heavy caliber .357 Magnum slug in the leg," Dominic muttered. He knew, because he'd done it. More than once.

But that life was behind him. Wine was what he cared about now, and if getting the funds to improve his acreage in France meant being nice to bloody Miss High-and-Mighty O'Neill, maybe he'd have to consider it. Besides, he had a personal score to settle now. "Where's she spending the weekend?" he asked tightly.

"Forget it. You'll never find her."

Dominic turned, his eyes urgent. "Please, Serita. I won't charm her and I won't push her. I just need a chance to talk to her in private, away from all this. It's important. To *both* of us."

Something about the urgency in his voice cut through Serita's obvious reluctance. "I don't suppose you'd care to be more specific."

"Sorry, Serita, I can't."

She sighed. "You promise you won't be an utter pest?"

"Who, me?" He gave her an innocent look.

"You."

"I promise. On my honor as a good Etonian."

"Etonians don't *have* any honor, only a universe of charm. Dangerous charm." Serita had been involved with enough of them to know.

Dominic frowned. "If I have any charm, Cathlin O'Neill didn't see it."

"Didn't fall for you? Come to think of it, this might be a very salutary experience for you, Dominic." Serita nodded decisively. "She's got a big, rambling house on the southeast coast, overlooking Romney Marsh."

"Near Rye? How in the world did she manage that?"

"Seacliffe came to her through her mother's family. Cathlin hasn't been there often since her father's death last year. Oh, the place is beautiful, but very expensive. The house itself is early seventeenth century and there's a ruined thirteenth century priory on the grounds."

Since Dominic had just finished renovating a fourteenth century chateau in France at La Trouvaille, he'd seen enough crumbling plaster and rotting wood to last a lifetime. He also knew firsthand just how expensive—and how infuriating—such a project could be.

Which meant that things were definitely looking up. "So she'll need lots of money?"

"Don't we all?" Serita asked cynically.

"I can help her then. Tell me how to find her, Serita. Just to talk to her. It's urgent."

After a moment Serita sighed and reached into her purse. "She'll kill me if she finds out I gave this to you, but—" She pulled out a pen and scribbled on a sheet of paper. "Good luck. You're definitely going to need it."

"Thanks, my dearest Serita." Dominic bent and kissed his companion's cheek. Smiling slightly, he pocketed the precious address.

And now I have you, Ms. O'Neill, he vowed darkly.

CHAPTER THREE

Southeastern England
Romney Marsh

WATER.

Reeds.

A thin black ribbon of road and beyond it the coast of Kent in May, all shadows and cold silver.

Out in the English Channel, lightning forked through the darkening afternoon sky. A storm over Dieppe, Dominic thought. Or maybe above Dunkirk to the north.

Some days in summer, France must look close enough to touch, he mused. But not today, with rain racing over the channel and the thermometer dropping by the hour.

He squinted into the windshield, past the fingers of mist that drifted over the glimmering silver pools. How far was it to Seacliffe? He'd stopped in Rye for directions and had been told to take the coast road. Now, as the sun slanted low and golden over the hillside, over the barren marshes where two hundred years before smugglers must have plied their desperate trade, Dominic felt as if he'd stepped straight back into the past, a past without highways, electric wires, or telephone poles. And there was something very beautiful about that past.

He swung his battered Triumph around a sharp curve and crossed a narrow granite bridge. To his right a pair of Sussex sheep stood grazing beside a granite boulder that marked the gravel road up to Seacliffe. Slowing, Dominic studied the landscape. The wind was picking up now, and through the tossing reeds he finally made out a winding drive that led up the hill.

He was a fool to have come here, Dominic thought as he eased the Triumph over the deep ruts. His old car, which he kept at his family estate near Tunbridge, was well loved. He had hand-nursed it for too many years to see it wrecked on a gravel road now.

Suddenly there was a crack of lightning and a wave of sand struck the windshield, driven by the first gusts of the coming storm. Dominic downshifted, trying to see in front of him, and cursed when he heard a thump, followed by the hiss of leaves. The next moment the Triumph struck what felt like a wall of cement and his head smashed down against the windshield.

SLOWLY, DOMINIC FOUGHT his way back to consciousness. His head was throbbing and through the sand scattered on the cracked glass he made out a tree blocking the road five feet ahead of him.

So that's what had left him with the fifty-piece orchestra hammering inside his head, he thought irritably.

Scowling, he shoved open the door, but his initial hope of moving the tree aside quickly faded. The lightning had broken, but not severed, the huge trunk and the roots were still half-embedded in the sandy soil. It would take at least three men to wrench them free and cart the tree off the road.

He would just have to walk the rest of the way.

Muttering uncharitable words against a woman who kept a house in such isolated countryside, Dominic grabbed his single bag, turned toward the hill, and began to walk.

But as he strode through the wild, beautiful terrain of the marsh and the lapping sea, his thoughts grew calmer. Even with the rising wind, the place had a brooding beauty that went right to Dominic's soul. With every cool cry of a passing kestrel,

Dominic again felt that strange sense that he had been carried back in time.

He laughed softly and hiked his bag over his shoulder. Places of beauty and isolation had always intrigued him. It was half the reason he'd fallen in love with La Trouvaille, gleaming in the early morning sun.

Off to his right came the distant clang of sheep bells. The sound rose and fell, carried on the gusting wind, first loud then wavering sharply. Strange, Dominic thought, he'd never been here before. In spite of that, the sound was almost familiar.

Shrugging, he walked on, letting the low hiss of his feet on the sand settle into a rhythm.

Again the bells rose. *Clang-clang,* they called out, tugging at his mind. He frowned, studying the hills that rose lush and green above the sandy slope. Where had he heard that sound before?

Again it came, making him think of the wood slamming against stone. The sound was restless and sad in the last hour of daylight.

Clang-clang.

Suddenly, as sweat trickled over his forehead, Dominic knew that something about the sound was infinitely important to him.

He closed his eyes, letting the noise roll over him, opening deeply to its meaning.

He had a sudden image of a house. A house with no lights.

Clang-clang.

A big gray house with weathered green shutters. A house by water, full of noisy people. A house where something very important had once happened to him.

He cut off his reverie with a low laugh. He'd never seen any house like that, although he'd been in enough grimy waterfronts in his life.

Yet with every distant clang Dominic felt his hair rise at his neck.

Clang-clang. Clang-clang.

What did it mean? And why did the sound seem to mock him,

rising in gray waves that filled his head until he could think of nothing else.

Tendrils of mist curled about his feet and the wind pulled at his clothes. He thought of water and night and an infinite loneliness.

Most of all Dominic thought of honor—and a vow betrayed. On he walked, fog at his feet, wind in his hair. And as he walked, his mind drifted, coiling like the mist.

Imagining.

Or was he really remembering?

London
The Crown and Dragon
April 1794

OUTSIDE *the inn a loose shutter was banging in the wind.*

Frowning, Gabriel Ashton tossed off the last of his brandy, cursing the noise, cursing the ache in his side, most of all cursing his memories. For once he'd actually succeeded in forgetting, putting the death and blood of the Paris streets out of his head.

Then she had swept into the noisy inn that squatted on the mist-covered bank of the Thames.

Clang-clang.

The same wind that banged the shutters sent her perfume wafting through the smoky room filled with gamesters and footpads and thieves. Roses, perhaps? Or was it something more subtle?

The fifth earl of Ashton scowled down at his empty glass. Damned if he cared. He was only here to forget. To drink himself into the darkness of utter oblivion, where he could finally escape the cries of the hungry children in the Paris streets.

As he poured himself another drink, her perfume mocked him yet again. Lilacs, he decided, with just a hint of cinnamon. It was as unusual as the woman herself, her fine-boned face framed by the hood of her velvet cloak, with blue satin shimmering at one hem.

Hardly the usual attire of the women who conducted their profitable trade at the Crown and Dragon, Gabriel thought grimly.

And those eyes of hers. Dear God, they reminded him of Baltic amber shot through with flecks of gold. How young those eyes were. And how achingly innocent. But beneath the cloak came the shimmer of satin that hinted at a body tantalizingly ripe.

He must be drunk, Ashton thought cynically. Not that it had helped him forget.

A slender shadow fell against the grimy table where he sat.

"May I sit down?"

Gabriel looked the woman up and down, striving to be as rude as possible. Her face was even finer than he'd thought, which meant she had no business being in a place like the Crown and Dragon. "No," he snapped.

Color flared across those impossibly creamy cheeks, but for some reason Dominic wasn't pleased at the sight.

She gnawed at her full lower lip, then sat down anyway. "I am looking for someone, you see." Her voice was cultured, yet with a rural softness.

"Aren't we all?" Gabriel was surprised to hear that his words were faintly slurred. Ah, well, a bottle of brandy would make even King George himself slur his words. Except that these days the unfortunate, mad king always slurred his words.

"My name is Geneva Ru—"

He cut her off abruptly. "Not a place f'r real names. Not by the likes of you anyway." Gabriel scowled at her wishing she would go away. Wishing she would stop blushing.

Most of all wishing he could see the color of her hair beneath that soft, flowing hood she wore.

"*You are drunk, sir!*"

"*That was my plan,*" the earl agreed easily. "*Care to join me, m'lady?*"

Her eyes widened. Ashton saw her lips tremble in their haste to form a denial. And then she went quite still. "*I see. This is the test he told me about.*"

"*Test? I should like to offer you many things, my dear,*" the earl said huskily, "*starting with a roll between my sheets. But not a test.*"

"*You are vastly rude.*"

"*That was also my intention.*" *And so it was, Ashton thought. Perhaps the bloodstained streets of France had left him unable to look upon such innocence without feeling resentful.*

Abruptly the candle fluttered. A cold wind rushed through the room, and the door was thrown open by a crowd of noisy sailors.

Drunk, no doubt, Gabriel thought. And so would he have been if she had not interrupted him like some avenging angel. "*Go away.*"

"*But I need your help.*"

Ashton's eyes narrowed on her fine kid gloves. "*If you're looking for help, you've come to the wrong place. Certainly to the wrong man.*"

But she was as stubborn as she was unsuited to her sordid setting. "*I think not. I have heard about the many brave things you've done.*" *She glanced about and lowered her voice.* "*You once helped a friend of mine.*" *She drew something from her pocket and laid it on the grimy table.* "*He said to show you this.*"

It was a rook's feather, the sign of the man who was wanted throughout France for snatching aristocrats from the very shadow of the guillotine.

Gabriel's eyes hardened. "How come you by that, young woman?"

"From my friend, Lord Draycott."

"From Adrian, you say?" Gabriel finished his brandy. Determined to be discourteous, he immediately poured another. "Are you lovers?" Adrian Draycott, plump of pocket and striking in his dark good looks, was notorious for his unquenchable appetites.

"That is none of your affair, I believe."

"Ah, but it is. If you ask a man's help, then everything becomes his business." He steepled his hands. "Well, are you?"

"No," she said flatly. "Though for his part—" She looked down, coloring.

"So he wants you for his bed, does he?" Maybe it was the brandy that made Gabriel speak so crudely. Or maybe it was the fineness of her eyes, eyes that urged him to be the hero she took him for.

Which, of course, was entirely absurd. Gabriel Ashton was no hero.

"Go back to Adrian. His wealth will buy all the assistance you need. I can do nothing for you."

"But it is an affair most grave!"

"Aren't they all?" The earl studied her over the rim of his glass. "Have you lost a bundle of love letters and fear that your husband will find them and toss you out on your lovely backside? Or have you been indiscreet with a mercenary cad who means you to buy his silence after a night of passion?"

Her chin rose and she clasped her hands before her with infinite dignity. "Lord Draycott told me it would be exactly so with you. First you would bait me, then you would be vastly cynical and refuse me. But I told him he must be wrong. The man called the Rook would never turn down such a desperate request. And you are that man," she said firmly. "You are the hero I seek."

"*My dear woman,*" *Ashton said, his voice as cynical as she'd predicted,* "*the notorious Lord Draycott was correct for once. I do refuse you. And I know nothing of this person you call the Rook. Now if you will kindly hie yourself off, I have a glass of brandy here that requires my immediate attention.*"

And a host of nightmares to forget, *Gabriel thought bitterly.*

"*But you can't! Truly, you are my last hope.*"

The earl turned away, hardening his heart. He'd heard too many sad tales over the last two years. Why should he take time for hers?

Frowning, he tossed back the last of his brandy, then refilled his glass. As he emptied it, he felt a pleasant numbness steal over him.

Much better, he decided.

Looking up, he saw blue satin blur into white lace. "*What? You still here? Go away. 've got no time f'r angels.*"

Somewhere there were three more angels tonight, he thought dimly. Three children with frightened faces who'd fallen to the blades of the Tribunal, their only crime to be born with blood too blue. Gabriel knew he'd never forget them.

Her gloved fingers settled resolutely on the table. "*I see I must make myself very clear. I am prepared to give you whatever fee you ask for your services, my lord. Anything at all.*"

"*Anything?*" *the earl asked brutally.* "*Best be careful with that particular word, m' dear.*"

"*I am. I would only make the offer to a man of honor like yourself.*"

"*Then your faith is sadly misplaced.*"

"*Not at all. The Rook is a man of great honor!*"

Ashton laughed bitterly. "*He might be, but I'm not.*"

"*I think not. You are known to a cousin of mine, you see. You must remember the comte de Broussard. Last month the two of you were engaged to fight a duel. Although he is little more than a boy, his honor was touched, and nothing would do but for him to call you out."* Her eyes took on a gleam. *"You devolved most nobly, after appearing to stumble."*

"Didn't pretend anything," Ashton muttered. "Exceedingly drunk at the time and m' hand slipped."

"On the contrary, my lord. You merely pretended to be drunk."

"And on what d' you base this masterpiece of deduction?"

"One simple fact—when you entered your carriage after the seconds had been satisfied, you were again the soul of sobriety."

An odd look crossed Ashton's face. "And how, young woman, would you know a thing like that?"

"Because I was right behind you."

"You?"

"You do not recall me?"

"I think not!"

"Hardly surprising, I suppose, since I was dressed in the yellow livery of your house at the time."

"Impossible!"

Her amber eyes gleamed. *"Not at all, my lord. You were wearing a vastly elegant sapphire waistcoat with an exquisite fall of white lace about your neck. In the lace was nestled a diamond stickpin carrying the Ashton crest. In addition you wore one of the Ashton emeralds on your left forefinger."*

The earl shrugged. "Anyone could have told you that."

"But you cursed as the stairs were lowered. And then you vowed that you would never again drink port at White's with young cubs just up from Sussex."

An arrested look crossed Ashton's face. "You were the clumsy cockney lad? The one who earned my abuse for failing to see the coach door fastened properly?"

Miss Geneva Russell nodded gracefully. *"Verbal abuse only, for which I much thank you. Other masters would have used a cane on me. I fear I would have found that most unpleasant."*

"What audacity! You are monstrous impertinent, miss."

Her chin rose defiantly. "And you, my lord, are monstrous foxed."

"Not foxed enough." But Gabriel knew he'd have to be dead drunk to be immune to this woman's charm. "What d'y' say y'r name was?"

"I didn't. You warned me that I should not."

"Did I? Can't think why. Unless y've something to hide."

"I do not," Geneva said with great dignity. "My name is Geneva R—"

Gabriel sat forward so swiftly that his head swam. "No names," he said gravely, in blithe ignorance of his own pronouncement. "Dressed as a footman, you say? By God, I should turn you over my knee to repay such trickery."

"You would have to catch me first."

"Did I catch you, you would soon be sorry. Now off with you!"

"Not until you agree to help me. It is the Rook I need and the Rook I mean to have."

Gabriel's eyes narrowed in anger, but she met his gaze without flinching. "You were very kind to let my poor cousin go free, for he is a dreadful shot and he did malign your honor most shamefully. In truth, I thought you most handsome. And wonderfully noble."

Gabriel Simon Montserrat, Lord Ashton, hardened roué and lifelong cynic, could only stare in disbelief. "Noble?" He thought of the three soldiers he'd left in the mud outside Calais. He thought of the French children whose cries still haunted his dreams.

Bottle in hand, he pushed away from the table. She would betray him, as all other women had done. He could not trust her or anyone else with his dangerous secret. "Enough of this. I've a bottle to finish and a pair of willing arms to find. Unless you'd

care to join me in my bed?" He tossed down a gold sovereign as
a final insult. He saw her cheeks darken and laughed harshly.
"No? I thought not. Women like you always offer the world, then
forget it a moment later."

　　"But—"

　　Gabriel turned away. "Go back where you came from, Geneva
of the golden eyes. Go back to your satins and velvets and forget
you ever saw me." His jaw hardened and he lied to her with the
cool ease of a man whose lies had often saved his life. "For my
part, I've already forgotten that I ever met you."

THE SUN HAD GONE BY THE time Dominic felt himself slip out
of his odd reverie. His head was aching where he'd struck the
dashboard and he couldn't seem to clear the odd fragments of
images from his mind. It must be the strange desolation of the
marsh, hugging the shore of the channel. Perhaps its weight of
ghostly history had played tricks with his mind. Or perhaps it was
the thought of his ancestor's exploits, resurfacing in all this attention to the will.

　　Dominic was near the crest of the hill now, and a cold wind
drove over the reeds, carrying the sharp salt tang of the sea. Yes,
it was simply the storm and the shadows that brought him such
odd thoughts.

　　As he walked through the gathering shadows he tried not to
think about a woman with golden eyes. He tried not to hear the
distant clang of a wooden shutter.

　　But he didn't quite succeed.

CHAPTER FOUR

CATHLIN FROWNED AS SHE trudged over the crest of the hill that ran from a copse of gnarled oaks down to the lawn skirting Seacliffe's weathered walls.

Out to sea dark clouds piled in toward the land. Just what she needed, more rain! Seacliffe's gabled old roof already leaked in half a dozen places and Cathlin doubted it would bear the assault of another full-fledged gale.

She gnawed at her lip, calculating the cost of the repairs that would be required after another storm. More money than she had, certainly, which meant that she'd have to take on new clients.

She sighed. She and Serita had finally built up a successful list of customers with the palate and the pocketbook to appreciate their choices. But with the demands of renovating Seacliffe, all that would have to change. Cathlin knew she'd have to take on additional commissions and broaden her clientele, taking on the high rollers she had always avoided, men with far more money than taste, whose only concern was buying high-ticket and making sure everyone knew it.

Was this wonderful old house she'd inherited worth it? True, it was a thing of beauty and her only concrete connection to the mother she'd lost so young, but would Seacliffe simply awaken the old memories?

Cathlin shivered and hunched her shoulders against the rising wind, then set off through a tangle of berry vines. Seacliffe's broad green lawns were only yards away, but the air was filled with fine bits of sand and gravel, which left her cheeks flushed and stinging.

She stared out at the marsh, looking for a car. She was expecting a structural engineer from Hastings later that afternoon, but it was possible that with the coming storm, he might not make the trip. She only prayed that if he came, he wouldn't ask for a bank draft up front.

And then Cathlin went still as she saw someone striding up the hill. Some instinct made her pull back behind a hawthorn tree so that she could watch unobserved. He ran for the porticoed front entrance just as the first fat drops hit the gravel drive. Frowning, he propped one broad shoulder against the weathered granite and turned to survey the house. Fawn corduroy trousers hugged his lean hips below a shirt of tailored blue denim. A slash of dark hair curved down into his eyes. In the gloom of the storm, Cathlin couldn't make out much more than this—except that he looked cool and quiet and dangerous.

Then he turned toward the sea, and Cathlin felt her breath catch. Dominic Montserrat? How had *he* gotten her address?

She strode over the gravel, not bothering with a smile. "What do *you* want?"

One dark brow crooked. "How about shelter from the storm?"

"I'm waiting, Mr. Montserrat." Cathlin didn't like the peerage in general and she certainly wasn't going to make an exception for *him*.

Dominic sighed. "As I told you in London, I need to talk to you about some wine. You didn't return my calls, remember?"

"I've been busy," Cathlin said curtly.

"This is no game, Ms. O'Neill."

"Talk to Serita. She's got a tremendous knowledge of wine. Besides that, she actually appears to like you."

Her visitor looked Cathlin over slowly, taking in her faded

blue jeans and baggy Montreal Canadiens sweatshirt. His gaze went to the matching Canadiens cap that covered her sleek black hair. "Very nice. I think I like it even more than the black velvet."

"Good-bye, Lord Ashton."

"You can't just throw me out. The road is blocked down there by a fallen tree, and I can't go anywhere."

"So walk back to Rye. You're certainly not staying here. As you can see, I'm busy. I've got to see a man about my roof. Assuming that it's still there, of course."

Dominic's keen eyes narrowed. "What's wrong with your roof?"

"Rain damage from our last gale. And about two hundred or so before that one." Cathlin shoved the Canadiens cap lower on her head. "Something like a century of neglect isn't helping either. Why?"

"Just curious."

"Don't tell me. In addition to dabbling in wines, you just happen to be an authority on roofs."

"As it happens, I am."

The man's gall was beyond belief. "And I'm the Royal Mum," Cathlin snapped. She stiffened as his eyes slid over her. "May I ask why you're staring at me?"

"You're different out here. Younger. Softer. Then again, appearances are usually a trap."

Great, now he was a philosopher. A philosopher with something cold and hard at the back of his eyes. Maybe he could brandish a quote from Descartes to patch that three-foot gap in the south roof, Cathlin thought bitterly. She pushed past him and shoved open Seacliffe's massive, rose-covered door. "It's been nice to know you, Mr. Montserrat. Walk carefully."

The door wedged open beneath the firm force of his foot. "I happen to be great with roofs, O'Neill, and it sounds like you're going to need an expert."

"This is a bad dream," she said, closing her eyes. "I'm going to wake up and you'll be gone, I know it." She opened her eyes and sighed.

"Still here. Tell me why you haven't returned any of my calls."

"Because I don't want to talk to you," Cathlin said very clearly, the way one would speak to a sulky child.

"What is it with you Americans?"

"Ask Ben Franklin. He didn't like you aristocrats much either."

"Can we stop the warfare and get back to business?"

"What business? You were milling around trying to convince me you're seriously interested in my roof and I was trying to convince you that I don't believe a word you say."

Dominic frowned as he stood angled in the doorway. Over his shoulder he had seen a glint of metal down the hill.

Coincidence, or something more?

"What's wrong?"

"There's something moving out there."

"Of course there is. With white fur and four legs. They're called sheep."

"What I saw was no sheep."

"Then it was probably a hiker. We get them down here occasionally. It's certainly nothing to worry about."

His eyes swept the reed-filled pools along the coast. "A strange time for a hiker to be enjoying the scenery, considering the wind that's kicking up. Still, you might be right."

"Of course, I'm right. And now I have a roof to look at before it starts to rain."

Dominic Montserrat, however, was one step ahead of her. He pushed the door wide and strode past her, moving easily down the polished corridor. "Where are the stairs?"

"*What* stairs?"

"To the roof, of course." He moved in utter silence, and something about that silence made Cathlin's neck prickle. "I'm going to need a ladder and some kind of light."

"You're not going to need anything, because you're not taking another step inside my house!"

He turned. His shoulder brushed hers. "A deal, all right? I check your roof and you listen to what I have to tell you. How about it?"

"Then you leave?"

"If you still want me to."

Cathlin felt his anger but even deeper she felt his raw determination. He was a man who would always get what he wanted, she sensed. There was strength in every move he made, iron control in every word and look. He was a man comfortable in his power and comfortable using it over others.

But not on *her.* Because she wasn't going to listen to one word more. "The answer's no. I've got to go. The door's right back there."

A muscle tensed at his jaw. So Lord Ashton didn't like losing, did he? His eyes locked on her face and Cathlin felt the full force of his will directed over her, searching for her deepest strengths and secret weaknesses, like a hunter assessing his prey. And Cathlin found herself attracted to that basic power in some deep, elemental way.

Raw physical power.

Raw confidence.

Raw skill.

Cathlin hated to admit it, but those things struck a chord in her, subtly stirring her senses until she wanted to offer a counterchallenge, female to male, and find out what it would take to break that iron control. Instinct whispered that this man would be a warrior in bed as in all else. He would possess ruthlessly and demand total honesty from the woman he loved. There would be no secrets and no holding back. And that same instinct told Cathlin that he would offer all of himself in turn, body and soul.

She swallowed, trying to break the spell of her swift fantasies, trying to fight the dark, wordless current of sensation that bound them as they stood silent, shoulder to shoulder, in Seacliffe's quiet halls. What would it feel like to be loved that way? What would it take for a woman to claim such a man in turn, strength to strength, heat to heat, challenging his granite control until he felt the same blind, wild need that she did?

Dangerous, O'Neill. Very dangerous.

A wedge of plaster peeled away from the ceiling and struck her head.

"Maybe you'd better not take too long to make up your mind, O'Neill."

An abrupt fragment of memory stole over Cathlin. Something about a dark room. Low voices. *Fear.*

She was fighting a shudder when a pair of hard hands settled on her shoulders. "Let me go."

"You're covered with plaster. You can't just—"

"Can't I?" Cathlin's heart was pounding as she shoved past him. Why in heaven's name did this man affect her so? And what was it about him that had just triggered those dim memories of the day her mother had died?

She wasn't going to wait around to find out. She took the last few feet in a rush, following the narrow staircase up to a dim attic, illuminated by three large oriel windows. *Steady O'Neill.* It was just one of the old memories, the kind that skittered through her mind late at night when the doors were locked and the moon inched over the horizon.

"You all right?" Somehow he was right behind her, as silent as a cat.

"I'm fine."

"You don't look fine."

Cathlin swallowed, uncomfortable beneath that intent green gaze that seemed to miss nothing. "Oh, very well. Have a look at the roof. Then I'll hear you out." *But don't expect me to believe a word,* she thought grimly. *And definitely don't expect to be staying on afterward.*

Dominic swung a heavy wooden ladder over his back as if it were no more than cardboard, then carried it to the far wall, which was speckled with damp rot. A blizzard of fallen plaster covered the floor at his feet.

He shook his head. "Not good. Exactly how old is this place?"

"Nearly four hundred years. I'd say the structure has held up exceedingly well for that kind of age."

"Sorry, Ms. O'Neill, but I've seen buildings demolished when they were in better shape than this."

"You probably enjoyed it, too," Cathlin said angrily. Damn the man! This was all a game to him, like his wine dabbling and his womanizing. "Look, don't let me keep you. This was a mistake from the start. I'll take my chances with the structural engineer from Hastings."

Dominic's eyes didn't leave her face as he opened the ladder. Casually he stripped off his leather jacket. "What's wrong? Do you want someone older? Someone more polite?" One hand rose to the neck of his tailored denim shirt. "Or do you just want someone who'll agree with whatever you say?"

The soft blue cloth hiked up over his flat stomach. Cathlin's breath hissed free. "Just what do you think you're doing now?"

"Taking off a few clothes. You don't mind, do you, Ms. O'Neill?" His eyes held hers, shining with challenge. His chest was lean, deeply indented with muscle. And his shoulders... sweet heaven, they were a perfect fantasy, full and beautifully hard.

Warrior's chest. Warrior's body.

One look was enough to tell Cathlin that he'd earned those muscles anywhere except in a gym.

Cathlin took a steadying breath. He *wasn't* going to get to her. So the man had nice shoulders. Okay, so they were *phenomenal* shoulders. It would take a lot more than that to worm through her reserve, Cathlin told herself sternly. "I *do* mind, as a matter of fact."

"Sorry, but it can't be helped." He shrugged off his shirt and tossed it to the floor. The movement made the deeply sculpted muscles flex and curve.

Cathlin couldn't pull her eyes away.

"Do you have a problem with that, Ms. O'Neill?"

Cathlin swallowed. "No. No problem at all."

With a shrug, she swung the flashlight beam up toward the roof, intent on ignoring him. *He'll look, you'll listen, then he'll give up and go away,* she told herself. *It's not exactly World War Three, after all.*

"Are there any alarm systems up here I should be worrying about?"

"There's never been a need."

"It's the twentieth century. Nowhere is safe anymore." It sounded as if he'd had personal experience with the fact, but that was absurd. He didn't look like a man who thought about anything more serious than where he'd find the next night's bed partner.

Cathlin sniffed. She ignored the way his chest glinted, misted with sweat as he climbed the ladder and stretched up to feel the exposed beams in the ceiling.

That was when she decided it could be closer to World War Three than she'd thought.

"This house must hold a lot of memories for you."

"Enough." She wasn't about to discuss her past with him or anyone else.

His eyes narrowed at the chill in her voice. "Growing up in a place like this can be wonderful, even with the leaking roofs and ancient plumbing."

"Don't tell me, you just happen to have a drafty old castle of your own back in Sussex."

He smiled faintly. "Near Tunbridge, actually." He leaned back and braced an arm against the ladder. "Something wrong, Ms. O'Neill?"

"Wrong?"

"You're staring."

"No, I'm not." But she had been, Cathlin knew. No matter what she said, this was a different man from the one she'd met in London. This man was competent and cool and very intent. And there was something seductive about that kind of intensity, about the way he ran his hands through his hair, leaving it a rumpled mess when he was thinking. Or maybe it was the way he studied her, as if he were looking past the words, probing all the way inside her.

Suddenly she remembered Serita's description: *It's his eyes, I think. He looks at you and really sees you. There's something seductive, but dangerous about that kind of total focus in a man.*

Not for *her,* Cathlin vowed.

"Look, just finish checking the roof, if you don't mind."

Dominic shrugged and pulled a knife from his pocket. It looked comfortable in the palm of his hand. He gave the damaged ceiling an experimental jab. Instantly, plaster rained down over his neck and chest. He backed down the ladder, coughing all the way, then surveyed the roof in silence. "Not good," he said finally. "Not good at all."

"Can it be fixed?"

He rubbed his jaw and Cathlin tried not to notice the play of muscles across his chest. "We're probably looking at a new beam structure and a new tin alloy undersurfacing. Maybe even a whole new slate exterior. It's damp rot all right, and it's gone all the way through. It's going to take lots of money to repair it."

"How much money?"

His eyes darkened. For a fleeting moment Cathlin saw something like reluctance there. He hiked one powerful shoulder against a rung. "Two hundred thousand, give or take."

"Give or take *what,* the Crown jewels?" Cathlin moved to the window and gripped the sill. She'd never be able to put together that kind of money. And expensive or not, this old house was the only real connection she had left to her mother. How could she bear to lose it? "You're sure about that? Maybe it's not as bad as you think."

He laughed harshly. "Ms. O'Neill, I also happen to own an old château in the Garonne Valley in France. It was beautiful, too, right down to the rotten beams and crumbling foundation. Even the mice nesting in the walls were kind of cute. But the place was derelict. We had to rip out two complete walls and most of the top floor before we could even start on the roof. Believe me, I've waded through enough wood dust and ruined plaster to know damp rot when I see it."

Every word was a physical blow. The man clearly knew what he was talking about.

Cathlin's heart fell. Two hundred thousand pounds! Even if she signed up a hundred new clients, she couldn't scrape together that kind of money.

Which meant she would lose Seacliffe.

She sank down in the rickety armchair at the window, her visitor forgotten. She felt the dim press of images, of sounds and colors too faint to be real memories. Long ago Cathlin and her mother had come up to these attics. Seacliffe had belonged to Cathlin's grandmother then, and the house had been a happy place, ringing with laughter.

When Cathlin's mother had been alive. When they'd been a family, and she'd seen her father smile.

"What am I going to do?" she whispered.

More plaster exploded beside her foot. Cathlin didn't move, staring down at the white mound, her eyes haunted.

"Maybe it's time you listened to me. I think I can help you."

Cathlin shoved at the plaster with her toe. "How?"

"There might be a way." Dominic gave an experimental tap on the wall.

"Do you mean I could manage it for less? If I helped out with the work perhaps."

"It's too dangerous to allow amateurs up here once the beams are removed and the construction's under way. No, I was thinking of something else. All it will take is a week of your time."

Anger replaced the empty ache in Cathlin's chest. "I see. How very imaginative," she said acidly. "But I'm afraid it would take a whole lot more than two hundred thousand pounds to tempt me to do that."

"Damn it, will you listen to me?" Dominic frowned and ran a hand through his long hair. As he did, flecks of plaster skittered over his chest. "It's not what you think. I'm talking about seven days together under one roof, nothing more."

"Right. And I'm an emissary from the Martian base hidden on the far side of the moon."

There was a sudden curve to his lips. "Are you always this prickly, O'Neill?"

"Depends on my company. After all, I'm not a complete idiot. Who would pay that kind of money for a week of my time? I'm not exactly centerfold material."

Dominic's green eyes narrowed. "Who told you that?"

"Two hundred thousand pounds for the pleasure of my company, in bed or otherwise?" Cathlin laughed rather unsteadily. "I rather think not."

"You rate yourself far too low in that case." His eyes were hard, his voice deadly serious.

Goose bumps rose along Cathlin's neck. He *wanted* her. She could almost taste the force of his desire, so attuned were they at that moment. And Cathlin discovered what a potent aphrodisiac that kind of hunger could be.

But she forced herself out of her sensual haze. What was happening to her? She was a competent professional who dealt with powerful people every day. She was responsible for rare objects worth thousands of dollars. She was capable and intelligent and utterly in control of her life.

Up until the moment you met this man, you were.

"I don't believe anything you've told me, Lord Ashton, but I'll listen anyway. As you see I'm rather desperate. So now maybe you'll be specific. How exactly are you proposing I make that vast sum of money you mentioned?" Cathlin spoke tightly, not wanting to believe he could be telling the truth.

"Actually, it's a little difficult to explain. Hell, it's more than a *little* difficult."

"Try me." Behind Cathlin another clump of plaster struck the floor. She muttered something graphic and slid her hands into her pockets.

"If you'd answered my messages, I could have told you all this a week ago," Dominic said irritably. "What it comes down to is this. You and I are the beneficiaries of a two-hundred-year-old will that stipulates the ownership of a very precious old case of wine. A Château d'Yquem, to be exact. Vintage 1792," he added, in the coup de grace.

"Château d'Yquem?" Cathlin's eyes widened. "But a wine of that age and quality would be worth about…"

"A million pounds at least. I know the figures too," Dominic said tightly.

"But why? And how?"

Dominic turned to pace the dusty attic. "It has to do with one of my ancestors. Mad Uncle Gabriel, we always called him, though he wasn't an uncle and I have no idea if he was mad. But he was reckless, mysterious and a bit of a firebrand. And then, about a week ago…"

He stopped, rubbing the back of his neck irritably. Cathlin tried to focus on what he was saying, but she kept seeing the soft hair that swirled over his chest. "What happened then?"

"We found out when he died—and where. His skeleton was

discovered hidden inside a walled-in cellar with his wine. And with it was his last will and testament, stipulating the way the wine should be handled."

"Good heaven above."

"I was a little surprised too," Dominic said wryly. "But there's more, I'm afraid. According to the will you, as the descendant of one Geneva Russell, and I, as Gabriel Ashton's oldest living descendant, must spend seven days together at the site of the buried wine. Otherwise, the will is negated."

"Is that legal?"

Dominic smiled faintly. "Hell if I know. I'm told it is. The point is that the man who found the wine considers himself honor bound to comply with Gabriel's last request. I expect you would, too, if you found a two-hundred-year-old skeleton buried in your cellar."

Cathlin took an unsteady breath. "But it all seems so...so odd."

Dominic shrugged. "Don't look at me. I'm not exactly thrilled about taking a week away from my own work right now."

Cathlin looked out the window, listening to the wind rise. "One million pounds," she repeated softly. Then she looked up. "Is this some kind of joke? If it is, so help me I'm going to—"

"It's no joke. I've got the documents to prove it. I can even arrange for you to see the will, which was signed in Gabriel's blood," Dominic said grimly.

"You're kidding, surely."

His hard look told her just the opposite.

"My God, you're telling the truth, aren't you?" Cathlin watched a cloud of plaster swirl up, carried by a gust of wind from one of the holes in the roof. "But why us? What was the connection between our ancestors? They weren't married, by the sound of things. What happened to them?"

"That's part of the puzzle, I'm afraid. I've done some checking into the Ashton family records, but came up with nothing. I was hoping that you might be able to supply some answers about this Geneva Russell."

Cathlin frowned. "I don't know much about that side of the family. My mother was an only child, you see. And then, after she…" Cathlin cleared her throat. "After she died, my father and I moved to Philadelphia. He had scads of relatives there and it simply seemed the best thing to do." She glanced around the attic. "I suppose there might be some kinds of records around here. I haven't had much time to go through things." She looked at Dominic and gnawed at her lip. "Not that I'm agreeing, mind you, but where would this hypothetical week be spent?"

"Here in England."

"*Where* here in England?"

He seemed very concerned with closing the catch on the ladder all of a sudden. Cathlin's eyes narrowed. "I'm waiting."

"Someplace north of here. Nice grounds. A moat and a beautiful granite abbey."

A gust of air swirled down from the roof, ruffling the fine hairs at Cathlin's neck.

Moat. Granite. Abbey.

She shivered slightly. "Just give me the name."

Slowly her visitor wrapped one broad hand around the ladder. "Draycott," he said finally. "Draycott Abbey."

"*No.*" Cathlin's face had gone very pale. "That's impossible. Draycott is where my mother was…murdered."

CHAPTER FIVE

DOMINIC SHOVED A HAND IN his pocket and cursed softly. It wasn't going to work, he could feel it already. Still, something kept him from walking out. Maybe it was the pain Cathlin O'Neill was trying valiantly to keep from filling her eyes.

"I'm sorry." He ran a hand through his hair. "I can imagine how painful this is for you." He frowned at how that sounded. "Hell, probably I can't begin to imagine. But this is a chance for *you,* for your future. Your mother would want that kind of chance for you."

Cathlin turned and rested her head against the windowpane. The movement sent her hair sliding over her cheeks.

Dominic felt the force of that single gesture through his whole body. Even now there was a grace to her, a vitality that pulled him like a magnet. He'd felt aware of her as a woman since the first second he'd seen her, but the awareness had soon turned to something more. It was dark and elemental, like this beautiful wild landscape around them.

That's crazy, Montserrat. You're strangers with a business deal to consider, and nothing more.

He shoved a hand against the ladder, reminding himself that he was a man who prided himself on being in control. It was part of him by nature and profession. He couldn't think of one other woman who had managed to shake his control like this one, and he damned well didn't like the feeling? "Well?" he said.

He saw her brush at her eye, then study the six-inch crack of sky showing through the broken roof. "I can't. Not…*there.*" She started toward the stairs.

Her foot was on the threshold when Dominic caught up with her. As his fingers wrapped around her wrist, he could feel her anger and uncertainty pulsing through every bone in his body.

How did he tap into her feelings like this? They were two strangers, after all. They didn't even *like* each other, for God's sake.

Scowling, he looked down at his fingers circling her wrist. The sight of their locked hands was like being kicked in the stomach by a horse.

By a very *angry* horse.

Dominic went stock-still, feeling sweat bead his brow. He had to fight an urge to pull her against him and find out how she tasted, how she would fit, molded hot and naked against him. "Give me an answer," he said harshly.

"The answer's no!"

Dominic felt her trembling and bit back a curse. Was she remembering Draycott and her mother? No matter what happened, she'd have to face those memories some day, he told himself. Maybe the best time was right now. "Not even for a million pounds?"

"Didn't you *hear* me? My mother died there! I never even found out why," she said bitterly.

"Maybe this is your chance to find out. Maybe—"

"And maybe there's a tooth fairy," she said in a low, hard voice. "No, don't." She raised her hand, almost as if to ward off a physical blow. "No more, please." Dominic had a glimpse of the depth of her pain then. He knew that on some level he had just stumbled across some of those buried memories of hers.

But burying wouldn't work. He could have told her that from personal experience. The memories always came back to haunt you.

"You'll have to leave." Her voice was tight with anger, but beneath it was an edge of panic.

"You'd be crazy to turn this down. I'd have to be crazy to *let* you. This house is beautiful, but it isn't going to last another five years in this condition. Maybe not another five months."

"Why do you care?"

"Because I don't like to lose, Ms. O'Neill. Not in life, not in business." Some angry force made him add, "Not in love. And I'm not giving up. I'm going down to check on my car, then I'll be back."

"The answer will be just the same. I'm never setting foot on Draycott land again." She raised her head and Dominic saw pain seep through her eyes. He hated being the one to cause anyone that kind of pain. But something drew him, something made it impossible for him to turn his back and walk away from her the way he wanted.

"You love wine. I heard it in your voice at the auction in London. And this involves a wine of the very rarest sort. Just think of owning a wine like that, touching and holding it in your hands. It would be something beyond imagining."

Why was he making this harder for her? Dominic wondered. Why couldn't he just accept her answer and be done with it? Or had it already gone too far for that?

"I don't want to hear this! Not for any amount of money! I don't care who you are or what you're offering, the answer's still no."

"Cathlin, wait—"

She shoved past him, one hand locked to her mouth. The hammering of her feet down the stairs sent another slab of plaster hurtling to the attic floor.

Dominic didn't try to stop her. Something told him that once he touched her, once he felt her body shiver and then yield to his, all his years of careful experience at control would be swept away in a second.

Impossible, of course. And yet somehow he already knew exactly how she would feel wrapped against him.

Almost as clearly as if it had already happened.

CATHLIN WATCHED HIM stride down the long gravel drive toward the coast road. Gravel and dust flew up around him, driven by the wind.

The tears didn't come, just as they hadn't come after that day fifteen years ago. She had never found out what had led to her mother's fall from the roof at Draycott Abbey, though she had spent years wondering.

Suicide? Cathlin shivered. It couldn't possibly be. Her mother had always seemed so happy, ready with laughter and a hug. But perhaps a child couldn't see the pain that a grownup learned to hide.

When she was older, Cathlin's father had explained what he knew of the events of that night. Somehow Elizabeth Russell O'Neill had fallen or been pushed to her death from the roof. But Donnell O'Neill had steadfastly refused to believe that what had happened had been an act of suicide. He had gone on searching for clues for months, but neither he nor the investigating officers had ever solved the mystery of what had occurred up on that dark and silent roof.

Though she had no conscious memory of that night, Cathlin had been the one who found her mother's body, motionless and silent against the soft green grass by the moat. Yet the night remained one great blank. Over the years Cathlin came to consider it a blessing that her memories were locked away where they couldn't torment her.

And now in a matter of minutes this hard-faced stranger came striding into her life, touching those dark places in ways that Cathlin couldn't begin to imagine.

Or to bear.

Overhead a curlew shrieked and darted over a tidal pool. Cathlin looked down at her hands, angry when she saw the fine tremor that shook them.

She had to accept the hard truth then. It wasn't going to go away. Even though the memories were buried, they were still very much alive.

Cathlin watched angry clouds race in from the channel. Just like the storm, dark and gathering speed, there were things that couldn't be put off any longer. The doctors had told her one day everything would come back to her. As an adult, Cathlin finally had to consider methods of remembering, things like drugs and deep hypnosis. Maybe it was time she had an answer to those years of shadows. If so, the whole process would have to begin at Draycott Abbey.

Maybe she owed it to her mother to find out what no one else could.

SHE WAS WAITING, FISTS tight, when Dominic strode back up the drive. "There's one other thing you'd better understand, O'Neill." His hair was raked back by the wind and a fine sheen of sand covered his face. "Like it or not, we're in this together. You're not the *only* one who stands to gain from that will."

Abruptly Dominic stopped. Over Cathlin's shoulder he studied the eerie sweep of reeds and silver water. "Come inside."

"Why."

He bit off a curse. "*Now,* O'Neill. There's someone out there."

"It's not exactly a crime. As I told you, we get lots of lost hikers this time of year."

Dominic's eyes were cold and hard. "In this kind of weather? I doubt it. But if they're just hikers, they won't mind answering a few questions." He pulled her around, shielding her with his body. "Keep walking, slowly and very casually." He draped an arm around Cathlin's shoulder and began moving her toward the house.

As they neared her old Jeep, he bent low and pulled a backpack from the car. Turning quickly, he moved his body between Cathlin and whoever was out there on the marsh.

"What are you doing?"

Dominic ignored her, pushing her along toward the house. "Is there a door that will let me out on the north side of the property?"

Cathlin nodded. The confusion in her eyes began to be replaced by fear. "If you're trying to frighten me, you're succeeding."

"I'm not trying to frighten you," he said harshly. "I'm trying to protect you."

"From what?"

His mouth hardened. "That's always the question, isn't it? Now show me how to get to the north side of the house."

It was soft but it was an order, and they both knew it.

Cathlin led him wordlessly through high, wood-beamed rooms full of Georgian furniture, along a corridor that had once been lined with portraits but now held only a few proud faces. Even now the house contained a fragile beauty and a vast dignity, offering comparisons with its beautiful, stubborn owner.

When they emerged onto the lawn at the far side of Seacliffe a few moments later, Dominic's face was unreadable. "Stay here."

And then he sprinted off into the trees.

Cathlin started to stop him, but the memory of his eyes kept her still. In an instant the friendliness had slid out of them, leaving them wintry and hard.

Warrior's eyes.

A stranger's eyes.

Cathlin shivered slightly as his tall figure vanished into the dense woods above the house. She found herself wondering what Dominic Montserrat's real business was here at Seacliffe.

Because if his proposal was as simple as it sounded, then she was a lost Romanov princess named Anastasia.

CHAPTER SIX

STAY LOW.

Aim where they'll least expect you.

Always keep them guessing.

As Dominic entered the woods, all the old habits slammed into play.

Close protection work wasn't like in the movies, all speed and gleam and the slam of pumped-up bodies. In real life it was usually a test of patience, of agonizing minutes spent squatting in utter stillness, waiting to see who would get bored or careless or just plain hungry and give away their position first.

Dominic's jaw hardened. Memories…

He crawled into a canal ringed by waist-high reeds, and there he waited.

Five minutes.

Ten. Twenty.

A bird skimmed toward the channel. Wind whined through the reeds. And then he heard the faint growl of a car motor, gunned and abruptly silenced.

Across the reeds, across the quiet tidal pools, Dominic felt something waiting. There was no mistaking the prickling in his neck. When there was no noticeable movement, he worked down the slope. Soundless, he dropped to the ground and began to belly his way along the winding canal, the same way he'd moved in jungles from Asia to Colombia.

He'd gone nearly a mile and darkness was closing in over the marsh when he saw the dusty Saab with a deflated front tire and a broken jack tossed beside it on the ground. So this was what he'd seen from Seacliffe. Patient scrutiny told him no one was in the area. Probably the owner had gone off to the coast road for help.

He looked up the hill. Seacliffe's roofs were not visible from here, hidden entirely by the trees and the slope of the hill.

Even then, Dominic was taking no chances. He waited by the narrow stone bridge to see if anyone appeared. After fifteen more minutes of silence, Dominic decided that all was as it seemed, a simple auto malfunction. He emerged from the water wearing a layer of mud, slipping as he crawled up the wet bank. He was just heading back up the hill to Cathlin when the soil he was standing on gave way. He cursed, swaying wildly as his ankle struck something in the dark. Thrown off-balance, he fell sideways and rolled downhill.

He only had time to curse his stupidity once before his head slammed down against the unforgiving granite of the bridge.

CATHLIN PACED THE LIVING room, her eyes locked on the marsh. She had long since gone through the nail-biting stage and was now muttering a stream of graphic oaths about the moral fiber and questionable parentage of one Dominic Montserrat.

Where *was* the bloody man? He'd been gone two hours already. Outside lights were winking in the channel, but the winding gravel drive that ran past the seawall was a sheer wall of black. Those pools could be deceiving and the ground unstable.

Cathlin made her mind up in that moment. Something was desperately wrong.

CATHLIN TOOK THE GRAVEL road far too fast, squinting out into thirty miles of fog-swept tidal pools lapped by the cold sea. Suddenly something moved, out in the darkness.

Out in the lonely silence where no one should be moving.

Wind-driven sand pelted the windshield. Cursing, Cathlin flipped on the wipers and looked again, but whatever had been there was gone.

She sighed, rubbing her shoulders. Just nerves from too much caffeine and too little sleep, she told herself. Muttering, she jammed the gear into third and shoved her hair out of her eyes. From here it was only a mile to the coast road. Three turns, through the narrow fringe of yew trees, then over the little stone bridge. He *had* to be there somewhere.

She was talking to herself, repeating the words like a litany while her hands clutched the wheel, nursing the sturdy old Jeep over the pitted road. Gravel and dust flew up as she downshifted, passed the skeletal oak, now ringed with a ghostly drapery of fog, and swung onto the tidal flats that hugged the seawall.

Then she saw him, a black blotch against the night. Any faster and she'd have plowed right into him. As Cathlin threw open the door, fog coiled around her ankles.

He was upright but swaying tiredly.

"Dominic, what happened to you?"

Around them the wind hissed and whined, rippling the quiet pools.

Dominic swayed forward, hands clenched on his dark jacket.

Cathlin caught him with an arm around his waist. His body was rigid and he seemed to be trying to tell her something.

"Come on, big guy, let's get you home." She worked one shoulder behind his back and began maneuvering him toward the car. "A little help might be nice about now, okay?"

No answer.

"Dominic?"

Still no answer.

It was hard going; he seemed to have become deadweight. And then Cathlin felt something warm slide over her fingers. Something thick and wet.

Blood. Sweet God, he was bleeding. No wonder he hadn't answered her.

"Oh, Lord, just hold on." Fighting for calm, Cathlin shoved Dominic into the passenger seat and slammed the door shut.

His eyes opened just as the moon broke from behind a fringe of clouds. Cathlin felt his desperate intensity of will as he tried to clear his mind. "Bank...out." His fingers tightened on her wrist. "Stupid...bloody bridge."

Then his eyes closed and he sprawled back against Cathlin's shoulder.

She fought to keep her hands from shaking as she swung the Jeep around, gravel flying. She slammed back up the road, taking the stone bridge too fast, and veered into a shortcut that skirted the fallen tree.

It took her nearly ten minutes to haul Dominic from the car and maneuver him into the house. The stairs would have been impossible to manage, so she stretched him out on a big chintz couch in the front study.

Unfortunately the storm had downed the power lines, and she couldn't reach a doctor for advice about his wound. He was still unconscious and very pale, but his only wound was a narrow gash over one temple, which she cleaned and bandaged. Then Cathlin found the lump at the base of his neck.

All her fears returned in a rush.

What could she do for him, stranded out here miles from a hospital? What if he didn't wake up? What if he *died?* What if he—

One smoky green eye opened. "F-found me." He searched for her hands. "Knew—you'd come." Then his eyes closed once more.

But his fingers stayed wrapped around hers.

DOMINIC AWOKE TO MOONLIGHT on his pillow.

He blinked and looked about him in confusion. Where was the huge armoire at the far side of his room? Where were the cut flowers his French housekeeper always kept in a careless profusion by the window?

Where were his *clothes?*

Dominic frowned and looked down. His shoulder was covered by something bulky and his throat felt like old shoe leather. He sat up dizzily and glanced around the dark room. His jaw locked.

In the moonlight, he saw a chair where a woman with black satin hair lay sleeping in a long white gown.

For some reason, Dominic thought of candlelit rooms. Of fine blue satin and soft kid gloves and rare pink pearls set in triple strands.

All of it far, far away.

Her dark hair gleamed, lit by flames and a bar of lambent moonlight. Her head was angled against the back of an old armchair and a book lay open on her lap.

Lord, she was beautiful. Her name was as wild and lovely as the rest of her. His eyes drank in the sight of her: strong hands, flashing eyes. Full, high breasts. Would they fill his fingers, all warmth and silk? Would her nipples tighten and peak as he caressed them?

Dominic cursed harshly. In spite of what she thought of him, he was no cool playboy. He was not a man who treated intimacy casually or women lightly. This woman had undoubtedly saved his hide out there on the marsh after his stupidity in cracking his head against the bridge. Spinning X-rated fantasies wasn't exactly the best way to repay her.

But once begun, the heated images wouldn't stop. Images of white skin tormented him, fantasies of Cathlin moaning beneath him, sheathing his heat. And all of them felt achingly *familiar.* He twisted angrily, seizing his pillow and fighting the hot, deadly tide of desire.

Finally the pain at his forehead accomplished what raw discipline had not. His head caught in a vise of pain and, clenching his fists, he sank back against the bed.

Clang-clang.

Tired. So bloody tired.

Clang-clang.

Sweat clung to his brow. Pain, regret, and something far darker mingled in the gray waves that filled his head.

Dark things. Pain and secrets that wouldn't stay buried.

And then it was so close he could taste it, a memory that hung rich as fruit, but always out of reach. And somehow Dominic knew he had to make himself remember. It was almost as if his life—and Cathlin's—depended upon it.

But how?

Clang-clang.

Sweat broke from his brow and skated down his neck. Close, so close.

And it had something to do with *her.*

GABRIEL'S HEAD WAS ACHING and his mood was dark as he turned up the steps to his town house. Somewhere in the night a church bell struck three times.

He scowled. A bottle of claret at White's had not soothed his memories of France, nor had three offers of companionship to share his bed.

All he found himself thinking of was a pair of burnished golden eyes.

As he came to the top step, the polished oak door was thrown open and his butler's long face appeared in the sudden light. "My lord, there's a person—a person in the study!"

Gabriel's dark brow crooked. "Then put the person out, Stanton."

"I tried, most decisively. But the person would not—that is, she—"

"A woman?" Gabriel's voice hardened. *"Not here. You know better than to allow her in, Stanton."*

The old servant wrung his hands. *"Of course, my lord. But this female was most persistent. And she said you knew she was coming. Indeed, she vowed that you were expecting her!"*

"Persistent?" Gabriel laughed grimly. So his defiant angel had come to track him down, had she? Ashton tossed his gloves and hat onto the mahogany side table and smiled darkly. *"Where is she?"*

"She insisted on waiting in your study, my lord. I tried to dissuade her, but—"

"Never mind, Stanton. I suspect it would take a cavalry regiment to dissuade this visitor from a goal. I shall deal with her, however." The grim smile played over his lips as he strode down the hall toward the rear of the house.

The study was in shadow, lit only by the three candles in a silver candelabrum. Gabriel stood motionless in the doorway, while his eyes grew accustomed to the shadows. *"Since you've taken the trouble of pushing your way in, you might as well show yourself,"* he said harshly.

There was a rustle of silk. The light, sweet fragrance of lilacs drifted toward him.

And then she was before him, even more beautiful than he remembered. In the darkness her pale features shimmered, and her eyes glinted like rare old Roman coins.

Gabriel refused to be enticed. *"What do you want of me?"* he demanded.

She wore a velvet cloak with a hood lined in satin. Beneath, her shoulders gleamed white and elegant. *"Your help."*

The earl of Ashton shrugged. *"Find someone else."*

"I can't. I need a man who knows the boulevards and byways

of France. A man who knows Jacobin and Girondist alike. And that man is the Rook."

"Never heard of the fellow."

Geneva studied his face thoughtfully. "Adrian Draycott told me you would continue to be difficult."

"My dear, I haven't even begun to be difficult." Gabriel strode to a lacquered chest and poured himself a glass of wine. Blast Adrian for his interfering ways, he thought grimly as he emptied the glass. She was the third person Draycott had referred to him this month. All of them had equally desperate stories of relatives or friends caught in the terrors of the revolution in France. But Ashton was not about to be pulled in again.

Not even for a good friend like Adrian Draycott.

Geneva's lips curved. "Is that your usual way of dealing with encroaching females?"

Ashton felt a strange tickling sensation in his chest, a blend of hot and cold and purest hunger. The truth was that no other female had ever been so rash as to bait him in his lair as this woman had done.

"On the contrary." Gabriel moved soundlessly through the room and tossed off her domino, then stood studying the perfect ivory sweep of her shoulders and her full breasts. As his hand brushed her chin, he watched color tinge her creamy cheeks.

Curiosity. Determination. But no fear. Not a trace of that.

Maybe it was time the woman began to see what danger she was courting. He touched a powdered curl that lay coiled on her bosom. As his fingers moved, he watched the curl tremble, rising and falling rapidly on the full breasts confined against low, lace-trimmed satin. "To be perfectly blunt, my dear, this is how I treat encroaching females."

He caught her with a hand to her slender waist, pulling her into the shadows, pulling her to his heat, to his fury. There was not even a hint of subtlety in his fingers circling her neck and holding her still beneath his exploration.

But he did not touch her red lips, not then. Instead he worked along her jaw, her neck, her shoulder. Slowly he caressed the soft powdered curl at her bosom.

Geneva's breath caught sharply. His was not a touch but a possession. Later, she would realize it was not so much a kiss as a conquest. But for the moment, she did not think or analyze, swept along on the dark power of his touch. She did not flinch, not even when Gabriel's mouth shifted the powdered strand aside and tasted the lush rise of her breast.

Her hands slid to his shoulders. Her blood was a storm in her veins. She hated the man for his arrogance and his harshness, but Adrian had told her this was the only person who could help her, and Geneva knew he was right. Only a man of utter ruthlessness would face the terrors of revolutionary France. Only a man of total callousness could snatch her sister and her sister's children from the looming shadow of the guillotine. And the darkness in Gabriel Montserrat's eyes told Geneva that he had witnessed the fury of the guillotine many times.

For that service she would pay any price he named.

But Geneva had not been prepared to like the task, to feel her pulse sing and her blood drum as an utter stranger bent her to his will.

Inches away, Gabriel cursed harshly. She was even more sweet than he had imagined, a creature of silk and springtime. Her skin rose and fell, flushed and hot with her arousal.

She would be his, Gabriel knew. She did not even understand the significance of her fingers threading through his hair and the pebbling of her nipples beneath the tight satin.

But Gabriel did, only too well. The sight of her passion, so sweet and new and untried, was like a brand to his groin. He

traced the thrust of her breast with his lips and felt her shiver,
her fingers sliding deeper into his hair.

Right now, she could be his, all ivory skin and breathless
moans as he shoved up her skirts and brought them both to
reckless passion. Suddenly Gabriel was shocked by how much
he wanted that.

But he did not allow himself to pursue it by even one more
motion. It was Geneva's very response as she trembled against
him that made him curse and release her.

Because she was too young and he was vastly too old.

He looked down and cursed to see that his *fingers were*
shaking, while hers were perfectly steady. Grimly he caught up
her domino and tossed it over her pale shoulders. "Leave."

"I don't understand." Her voice was husky with passion.
"What you did—how it made me feel—"

"Was wrong. Damnably wrong. And unless you leave, it will
happen again. Along with something far worse."

"Worse?" Her eyes were dazed, confused. "It was very nearly
heaven, my lord. How can you call it wrong?"

"Damn it, have you no sense? My reputation is as black as
that domino you wear. People whisper that I consume innocent
virgins by the dozen. And if you are even glimpsed in my
company, then your *reputation will be blackened, too. What*
would your parents say then?"

"My parents and family are dead, swept away in one of the
cruel waves of cholera that ravaged the East India Company set-
tlement in Madras."

"And you are left alone in the world?"

"Except for my sister in France." Her chin rose. "But you needn't
worry about me. I have a substantial inheritance from my father."

"All the inheritance in the world won't protect your reputa-
tion as a woman alone here in London, you little fool. Leave now,
now while you still can."

Geneva did not move. "Is it true?" she asked softly. "Are you truly as black as everyone says?"

Gabriel laughed bitterly. "What does the truth matter? Either way you will still be ruined."

"It matters to me, my lord."

"In that case, you are a greater fool than you seem," Gabriel said harshly, striding across the room and drinking from the glass of fine Bordeaux that he'd poured, even though he knew it would taste like the cheapest vinegar to him.

Without a word Geneva slid her hand into the folds of her domino. Her eyes glinting, she held out a pistol, silver-etched and double-barreled. "Now, my lord, you will gratify me by sitting down and listening for once."

Gabriel did not betray his surprise by the slightest motion. "Is that weapon you are clutching supposed to frighten me?"

"Without question."

He threw back his head and laughed.

And as he did Geneva took an angry breath, leveled the sight, and shot the glass from between his fingers. "Does that? I am a crack shot, I assure you. The next bullet will land between your eyes!"

"Shoot away. I'll be of no use to you laid out in a coffin."

"I am serious. I will shoot."

"I am quaking in my boots, as you can see."

"As if you would ever quake," Geneva scoffed. "But you are far too practical a man not to do exactly as I say. As long as I hold this pistol, at least." She smiled grimly. "And I do not mean to let it go, I assure you."

At that moment Gabriel's butler appeared at the door, his face the color of raw dough. "My lord? I was certain that I heard a—" His voice trailed away as he saw the broken glass and crimson stain spreading over the fine Persian carpet. "Then I did hear it. You are wounded!"

"*Go away, Stanton. That is only a glass of Bordeaux down there, not my blood. There are those who say my blood is not red, but black, after all.*"

"*But my lord—*"

"*Begone! And close the door behind you.*"

As the servant fled, shaking his head, Gabriel settled his long length into a wing chair. Templing his fingers, he looked measuringly at Geneva. "*Well? You have me captive. My attention is all yours, Miss—*" His brow rose in a mocking question.

"*Miss Russell.*" Geneva felt the bite of his sarcasm, but raised her chin defiantly. "*It was necessary. I am sorry to spoil your wine and your carpet, but my sister's life is at stake.*"

"*How enormously affecting,*" Gabriel said with a yawn.

"*Only the man known as the Rook can save her.*"

"*As I said before, I've never heard of the fellow.*"

"*No?*" Smiling grimly, Geneva reached to the desk behind her. "*Then perhaps you will explain this black silk mask, which the Rook is well known to fancy.*"

Although Gabriel's mouth hardened, he merely shrugged. "*Left over from some masquerade, no doubt. I do not keep track of such things.*"

"*Indeed.*" Geneva tossed the mask onto his lap and held up a letter written in French and sealed with a bloodred crest in the shape of a rook. "*And this is from the same masquerade, I suppose?*"

Gabriel pushed to his feet, his body tense. "*Where did you get the key to my desk?*"

"*I had no need for a key. I merely picked the lock. One of our servants used to be an attic thief and he enjoyed teaching me his tricks. All it took was a corset stay, worked in exactly the right place,*" she explained.

Gabriel's eyes darkened as he moved toward her.

"*Stay back,*" Geneva ordered. "*I still have my pistol and there's a bullet in the second chamber.*"

Gabriel's pace did not slow.

"I'll shoot, I warn you."

"Be my guest."

His chest was before her. All she had to do was pull back the trigger. Geneva swallowed, focusing, preparing. Did the man know no fear? "Stop tempting me, blast you!"

The earl only laughed.

Her finger tightened. Sweat dotted her brow. She had to shoot, if that's what it took to make him listen. The situation was too desperate, and she had no one else to turn to.

Gabriel's hand circled her wrist. "Go on and shoot," he ordered, his chest level with the barrel of her pistol. "I fancy you couldn't miss at this distance."

"I would not miss at two hundred paces," she said irritably. "In this position, I would certainly blow away half of your chest."

"As I said, my dear, fire away."

"You're mad.*"*

"So I am told. But don't let that stop you."

She felt his heat and his utter indifference to her choice. Geneva knew then that there was no doubt he was the man who had time and again bested the finest officers of revolutionary France. "I will, I tell you!"

His eyes were coldest granite. "So you have said."

She meant to. She tried with every shred of her being. But her finger locked and would not close.

And then she let the barrel waver.

He moved in utter silence, shoving the pistol aside and wrapping his hand around her chin. His eyes glinted, gray and savage upon her face. "And now, my little hellion, you'll learn two lessons. Never make promises you can't keep. And never carry a weapon if you do not mean to fire it. Especially," he added grimly, "when it is leveled against your worst enemy."

"Are we enemies?"

He looked down at the naked sweep of her shoulders, and his eyes darkened. "Without a hint of a doubt."

"But why? I came here for your help, not as an enemy."

"Women and men are always enemies."

"Only because you think of them so. Indeed, you treat women most shabbily. You have had your pick of far too many, I think."

"So now you are a philosopher?" Gabriel pulled her hands to his chest, drawing her toward him. "I merely treat women as they wish to be treated, Miss Russell, as beautiful jeweled objects to be coveted, admired, and beautifully maintained. Never do I treat them more seriously than that." His eyes darkened. "Except in bed, of course. And there I treat them very seriously."

Geneva swallowed. A dark tendril of sensation coiled through her chest. "You are intolerable!"

He offered her a mocking smile. "One tries."

"Let me go."

"Not just yet, I think." He eased her backward until the mantel brushed her shoulder. "Not until I've had my fill of that honeyed mouth of yours."

"But I don't want to—"

"You will," he said silkily. And then his mouth hardened, fell, joined to hers. In conquest it began, but in silken exploration it grew. Geneva put one hand to his chest and shoved, but her strength was as nothing against his. She felt the cold metal at her fingers and remembered the pistol. She would use it, she swore. This time he would not escape her. But only if she had no other choice. Only if he continued to mock her, to tease her.

To run his lips so hotly, so sweetly across hers, until she wanted to cry out in wonder.

Heat spiraled through her. Inside her satin slippers her toes curled. Never before had she felt such a touch, such perfect skill that left her thoughts reeling. If only her head weren't suddenly so muddled, and her knees so weak.

On a sigh of breath, she rose to her toes and brought her fingers to his shoulders. Only for stability, she told herself.

Her forgotten pistol lay balanced precariously beside Gabriel's head.

He didn't even notice.

Geneva's eyes closed as his tongue touched the soft center of her lips and teased an entrance. She shivered beneath his heat and raw power, driven by a wild curiosity. What would he taste like? What would he do if she, too, tasted his heat?

Still holding the pistol, she brought her hand to his neck and ran her tongue gently over the hard curve of his lower lip. He muttered a curse and brought their bodies together, thigh to thigh, working her backward until her shoulders were crushed against the mantel.

His heat surprised her, as did the shudder that tore through his angry muscles. She had expected power and confidence and ease, but not that betraying moment of shock, nor the lash of his own desire. He wanted her, she realized. At that moment his body told her he wanted her very badly.

Geneva felt a wild surge of triumph. She had thought to tempt him, to yield to whatever price he wished to extract for his services in saving her sister. But never had she thought to taste such heaven in the process.

He muttered hoarsely, his fingers molding her soft hips, his lips pure velvet.

Geneva's hands trembled. Her pistol dropped forgotten from her fingers. An instant later the barrel discharged and a bullet cracked through the silence, sending a rain of plaster from the hole that now marred the damask-covered wall.

Somewhere a door creaked open. The butler's voice rose in panic from the corridor. "My lord! You cannot—the pistol—"

"Get out, Stanton. I'm busy."

"But the wall!"

Gabriel spun about. "Out!" he ordered.

"Yes, my lord." The door slammed shut.

The sound was like cold water hitting Geneva's face. She stared at Gabriel, her face pale, her eyes amber and gold in the firelight. "It meant nothing," she said hoarsely. "Nor did I feel anything."

"On the contrary," Gabriel said silkily. "You felt everything I did, and that was vastly more than I had expected."

She gave a calculated laugh, which broke slightly at the end. "La, my lord, how easy you are to fool." Her voice rose in a titter. "'Twas all an act, I vow, just to entrap you. And you have fallen for it."

His fingers bit into her shoulders. "It was no act, my sweet. And no pretense of passion. I felt it in the heat of your body pressed against me, and in the drum of your blood."

"A lie," Geneva gasped, shoving at his chest.

His fingers settled on the pale curve of her cheek. "A lie, you call it? No, by heaven, I'll have the truth."

"Does it matter?" she said bitterly. "You've had your sport with me, and now it's over. For myself, I don't choose to waste words on a man with no heart and no scruples."

Gabriel laughed grimly. "You're right in that, for I have neither. But I have a great curiosity about this mission you've been so busy tossing in my face."

He watched pride war with need in her face. She turned away. Picking up a poker, she nudged a log in the grate and watched sparks shoot up the chimney. "It's my sister, you see. She is married to the duc de Verney, whose estates run along the Garonne Valley in France. She assured me that she and the children were fine, but last month I received a letter written in desperate haste. She wrote that the villagers were in turmoil and she feared for her life."

Gabriel's jaw hardened. "Am I supposed to find this story interesting?" He lifted his glass and tossed down the fine wine as if it had no taste at all, wishing she would leave him, wishing he could forget the sight of the blood he'd seen darkening the

Place de la Concorde the week before. "Besides, I'm foxed. I'd like to enjoy my inebriation in peace."

"I do not believe that you are cup-shot," Geneva said softly. "I think that you are tired and very sad."

Ashton felt impaled on the clarity of those fine gold eyes. He cursed silently. How did she see so much, things that no one else even suspected? "Well, you're wrong," he said, pouring himself another glass. "I'm three sheets to the wind and I mean to stay that way till morning. If you have any sense of self-preservation, you'll get yourself gone while you still can."

"I'm not leaving. Not until you hear the whole tale. It is the children that my sister fears for most."

Always it was the children who suffered. Ashton frowned as he remembered three dark-eyed children he had lost in Paris. His coachman had been an accomplice of long standing, and Gabriel had never had reason to doubt his loyalty.

But he'd been wrong, and three innocent children had died because of it.

Never again.

He pulled the poker from her hand and raised her face to his. "It's no good, Miss Russell. The valley of the Garonne is impossible to enter. I know from personal experience that the peasants are rioting there. No foreigner would get a mile before they stopped him."

"But for you anything is possible."

Ashton tried to ignore the hope and admiration in her eyes but found he could not turn away. Suddenly he wished that he were all she thought him. He wished he could see the people she loved spirited away to freedom. But he had failed too often of late. He had been forced to watch the prisoners fall, one by one, as the new leaders in Paris offered a bitter example to all who offered any hint of opposition. Now even women and children were murdered under the ruthless tyranny begun by Marat.

No, he could not help her. The plan was impossible. He turned to the fireplace and stared down at the red embers. "Go home, Miss Russell," *he ordered.* "Go home to your balls and your beaux. You've come to the wrong place and you've found the wrong man to play at hero." *He was exhausted from three weeks of continual travel and the endless horrors he had endured on France's muddy roads. But Gabriel knew he was sick of life as well. Perhaps he'd seen too many things that no man should ever have to see.* "I want nothing to do with you and your schemes."

But even as he spoke, her scent assailed him, all sweetness and summer lilacs and the infinite innocence of youth. He knew she must be close behind him, for he heard the faint rustling of silk.

In the small, still room it was a damnably intimate sound and it sent a wild stirring through his blood.

"I fear I have not made myself plain enough, Lord Ashton. I do not ask you to risk your life for nothing. I would of course be beside you to help in every way I can. In addition I offer you anything among my possessions—or myself. All this I give freely and willingly, if only you will aid my sister and her children."

A muscle flashed at Gabriel's jaw. She was too damnably close, her scent a torment. The little fool could have no idea what she was saying.

Yet her offer lingered, haunting him. He wondered how it would feel to hold her and hear her breathless little sigh when he sank deep inside her. "Damn it, don't you understand English?" *he said harshly.* "Be gone."

"Then I shall simply find someone else," *she said flatly.*

"There is no one else. It is hopeless, and the sooner you accept it the better."

"I thought I'd found a hero. I thought I'd found a man who would risk all for honor. Instead I've found a man with no heart at all." *Her voice held a mix of fury and despair.*

Though Gabriel had thought his softer sentiments long since dead, her scorn cut deep. "You have found exactly what I warned you you would find, a man without principles or honor."

Her eyes shimmered gold with fury as she studied him. "So you did. But I thought it was simply a test of my determination. How you must have laughed at my worthless offer of my body."

The man beside her did not look up, keeping his gaze on the fire.

"Look at me," *she challenged.* "Or is even that task beyond you?"

Gabriel's hand tightened on the mantel. He didn't turn. It was dangerous to look at her when he was so susceptible. "Go away."

"One look. Can it be so very difficult?"

The man in Gabriel refused to ignore such a challenge.

As if in a dream he turned. And his breath fled.

She was haloed in the light of the candles. Her eyes were dark with shadows and some other unnameable emotion. "I would have given you anything you asked."

Ashton closed his eyes, trying not to see her vibrant face, trying not to smell that haunting scent of lilacs. "Damn it, begone."

He heard the rustle of lace. Her fichu slowly came free and slipped from her shoulders. "I would have been glad to come to you, glad to render any price you named." *The pale fabric slipped to the floor, bright against the shadows.*

Gabriel closed his eyes, trying not to see the curves suddenly revealed, pressing against the lustrous folds of blue satin. But he found that imagining them was even worse.

"It would have been my pleasure, in truth. When our parents died, Isabel raised me as a mother, putting every other interest behind mine. Now I must do the same for her." *She laughed bitterly.* "I am only glad that I discovered your true measure before it was too late."

Gabriel shrugged. "Consider yourself lucky." It took more effort than he would have imagined to keep his voice steady before her scorn. "And now that you've discovered my villainy, perhaps you'll leave me in peace."

"Peace?" She laughed grimly and Gabriel knew the sound would haunt him forever. "For such a man as you, there will be no peace, not in this world or the next."

She was right. He was honest enough to admit it. But her accuracy only fueled his fury. "My peace will begin the first moment I am rid of you."

She turned in a swirl of satin skirts and wrenched her domino about her shoulders.

"Haven't you forgotten something?" Gabriel said icily. A moment later her silver-mounted pistol went hurtling through the air.

She caught it deftly. "So it would seem. My only regret is that my bullet hit the wall instead of your black heart."

Gabriel was still standing before the fire when Stanton opened the door long minutes later. He did not turn. "Is she gone?"

"Yes, my lord."

Regret tightened his throat, but Gabriel ignored it. "Very good. She is not to be admitted again. Now you may go, Stanton. I shall need nothing else tonight." Nothing, at least, that he had any hope of obtaining.

"Very good, my lord."

As the door closed, Gabriel stared deep into the dancing fire-light, trying to forget the smell of lilacs, trying to ignore the heat that still washed through his blood from the nearness of a woman who would hold him in scorn for the rest of her days.

Below him the amber sparks snapped and hissed.

And every one left behind a bitter memory of haunting golden eyes.

As NIGHT CLOSED AROUND the marsh and lightning lit the distant sky, Dominic Montserrat shifted on the couch, gray-faced and sweating.

The dreams clawed at him. He heard the echo of shouted curses and the pounding of feet. And always there was the banging of a shutter, somewhere in the distance. He fought on through the pain, through the storm of dark images, knowing some part of that was dreadfully important.

But he had no idea what.

And as he fought, the bandage at his head tore open and his wound began to bleed anew.

But the fallen blood Dominic saw in his dreams was hundreds of years old.

And he could have sworn that he caught the faint, drifting scent of white lilacs carried on the still air.

CHAPTER SEVEN

THUNDER BOOMED OVERHEAD, angry against the roar of the wind. The sound wrenched Dominic Montserrat from restless sleep.

He stared about him in confusion.

Stone fireplace. Old Peking carpets. Fine etchings of English wildflowers on the walls.

Rain hammered at the window, and as he sat up, Dominic discovered his head felt roughly the size of Outer Mongolia.

Grimacing, he focused on the woman bent before the fire, prodding the dying embers to life.

Cathlin.

"What day is it?"

She whirled around. "Welcome back. It's either very late Saturday night or very early Sunday morning. The clocks have stopped because of the storm. I'm glad to see you've rejoined the living."

"I'm not entirely sure I have." Dominic scowled as pain slammed through his head. "What truck ran over me?"

"No truck, just a bridge. You hit your head and I found you wandering on the road just this side of the tidal plain."

"Grand." Dominic frowned as he felt the white bandage around his head. He shoved back the covers and tried to sit up, only to feel the blood flow summarily from his head.

Cathlin caught his shoulders. "You're not going anywhere, you fool. You're bleeding again and your neck's the color of ripe eggplant."

He pushed her hands away. "I'll be fine." He pushed back the bedding, oblivious to his near nakedness.

Cathlin flushed and looked away. "So go ahead and bleed to death. But before you do, I'd like to know just what happened out there."

"So would I." Dominic ran his hands over the painful lump at his neck. It was a fight to remember much of anything. There had been the roar of the wind, then the sickening jolt of the bank giving way. And then—nothing. "Still storming?"

"Straight through till morning, no doubt."

Dominic frowned. The ache in his head made him curse, the sounds all but swallowed up by the howl of the storm outside. Grimly, he focused on trying to stand up.

"Are you crazy? You can't—"

"Just watch me, O'Neill." As he rose carefully to his feet, his head felt as if it had been kicked several times around a soccer field.

"Oh, that's very smart. Who do I call to pick up your body?"

"Beats me. Try the pope. I'm going to need someone with lots of clout."

"He won't have any clout," Cathlin snapped. "Not where *you're* going."

Dominic pulled himself forward. Something warm oozed down his forehead.

"You're *bleeding*."

What was a little blood compared to the pain in his forehead, Dominic thought grimly. Even that was better than the strange dream he'd had, something to do with pistols and blue satin.

And amber eyes. The same eyes he'd seen as he walked along the marsh in the rising wind.

A dream? Dominic thought. Or something more than a dream? "Where are my clothes?" he demanded irritably, pushing away a question he wasn't prepared to face.

"Why? It's the middle of the night. Besides, you won't even make the door."

The problem was that she might be right, but he still had to try. There were things he had to tell her about Gabriel Montserrat's will, and he wasn't about to hold the discussion half-naked and flat on his back, no matter how much his head hurt.

He took another awkward step. "See, I'm fine. I'm fabulous, in fact. The reports of my death have been greatly exaggerated." He wavered and caught himself with a hand on the back of a wing chair. "Hand me my clothes."

"Forget it. You're not going *anywhere*." Cathlin blocked his way, her hands crossed over her chest.

They glared at each other as the angry seconds crawled past. Outside, lights dotted the hills. In the distance the streets of Rye gleamed faintly, a crown of color atop the gray blur of the marsh.

"Did you see anyone else out there? Tire tracks, or any sign of a hiker?" he asked.

"As I told you, there was only you and me and a heck of a lot of blood."

"How vastly romantic."

"Listen, this is an incredibly entertaining conversation, but it would be even more entertaining if you weren't about to pass out."

"I'm just bloody fine." Dominic stood back from the chair and raised his hands over his head. "See, no hands."

"Well, if the phone weren't out, I'd ask you to call a doctor for *me,* because I'm getting weak just looking at you."

"Look, we have to talk and I'd like to be on a little more equal terms when we do it. After that, we need to start going through whatever family records you can find around here. Gabriel Montserrat was murdered and I want to know why."

"So now you're blaming someone in my family?"

"No, I just want some answers."

"Be my guest. Get dressed and go look. At least you'll be fully dressed when you succumb to blood loss and complications from a cranial concussion."

Dominic cursed. "Just tell me where my clothes are, will you? I've got a letter in the pocket of my shirt that I'd like you to read."

"Get back on that couch and I'll consider it."

He swayed slightly. "First we talk."

"Now." Her eyes were fierce. "No couch, no deal."

Dominic gave her a crooked smile. "From anyone else, O'Neill, that statement might be promising." With a sigh, he turned and made his way back to the sofa. "I doubt if I could manage a serious response right at the moment, anyway."

His eyes were closed before his head met the pillow.

DAMNED STUBBORN FOOL.

Cathlin glared down at the man filling her faded chintz settee. At least his color was good and his breathing steady. Yes, Dominic Montserrat would be fine. He just needed some rest. It was *herself* she was worried about, especially if there were any more shocks like this in store.

She was supposed to be here for a quiet weekend, but nothing had gone right since that wretched wine auction. Richard Severance had already called her three times, persistent as usual, and now *this* man showed up on her doorstep with this wild talk about a two-hundred-year-old wine.

Cathlin frowned. What had he said about a letter that he wanted her to read? Feeling slightly guilty, she pulled his shirt from the wing chair and went through the pockets.

Nothing.

And that was probably how much truth there was to this whole ridiculous story. So much for Lord Ashton's honesty!

She sank down in a chair across from Dominic, listening to sand and pebbles clatter against the window. Suddenly Cathlin remembered how Seacliffe used to be, full of joy and laughter when her mother was alive. Every morning her father had risen early and dressed in an oilcloth jacket, red tartan scarf, and battered Wellies. He had liked nothing more than to tramp the marsh as the first mists drifted up from the sea, reminding him of the Galway Coast where he'd been born.

She looked out into the darkness, imagining the green reeds and tidal pools her father had loved so well. But he'd been a stubborn man in a dangerous profession, and that profession had finally caught up with him. When an old colleague had called him back for one last job, Donnell O'Neill had reluctantly agreed.

He'd never come back, felled by a sniper's bullet in a country whose name Cathlin couldn't even pronounce. She hadn't forgiven the men who'd pulled him back in, not then and not ever. She had never understood what made a man take that kind of risk, and she would never stop feeling bitter toward the country that had stolen him from her.

But all the anger in the world wouldn't bring him back.

She brushed a tear from her cheek, staring out into the night. Yes, her father had loved this old house and the deserted marsh, whose fierce storms and blustery moods were so much like his own. Perhaps it came from the memories of the five years in his youth when he'd appeared on every police blotter in Europe. Paintings by the old masters, Fabergé eggs, or uncut emeralds, none of them had been safe from the quick, clever fingers of Donnell O'Neill.

Or Patrick McKee, as he had called himself then.

But he had seen the error of his ways in time. One night a bossy female art student from Oxford had caught him rifling her jewelry chest.

Donnell had been lost before he'd gotten one full look at the striking, ebony-haired beauty. They'd spent the next twelve hours arguing over the morality of theft—and the following twelve making passionate love in Elizabeth Russell's lavender-filled room overlooking the canal.

Afterward Donnell joked that he'd stolen Oxford's brightest jewel that night, and there was always a trace of seriousness in his voice when he said it.

Soon Cathlin had come howling into the world, the product of an irrepressible Irish love and an adoring English heart. She'd thrived on that love and over the years she had learned to expect the occasional shouting and broken dishes, knowing that afterward would come the sudden, abrupt silences, when they did some unknown thing called "making up."

Under Elizabeth's pressure, Donnell had turned his back on crime and begun working for the English government, which always had jobs for a man with light fingers like his.

Jobs like planting a false set of documents at the Russian Embassy, replacing the attaché case of Tito's private courier to Albania, and filching a set of incriminating negatives from an East German who was blackmailing a very high-level English cabinet minister had come in quick order.

The big Irishman had come and gone like a shadow in the night, and with every success his handlers had grown more greedy. Just one more job, they'd swear. And he had agreed, because it was the only career he knew.

So the months had stretched into years. Cathlin grew to a fine girl of ten and began fretting to be out of London and into a cottage where she could have her own pony and a half dozen cats.

But it had never come to pass.

The week before Cathlin's eleventh Christmas, Elizabeth had taken Cathlin with her to Draycott Abbey, where she was to examine some Elizabethan textile samples at the request of the old viscount. And sometime during that night, while the servants slept and Cathlin lay lost in childish dreams, Elizabeth Russell O'Neill had been murdered, by whom it was never discovered.

No words could assuage Donnell's grief. Only little Cathlin kept him from crossing over the edge to madness. Together they had left England, settling in Philadelphia. There Donnell had established his private security business, among a grand extended family who had come over from Ireland years before. But even then, the painful memories of Elizabeth had persisted.

Three years ago Seacliffe had come into Donnell's hands with the death of Elizabeth's brother, and Cathlin and Donnell had moved back to England, to the old stone house perched on the rolling hills overlooking Romney Marsh and the silver sweep of the southern coast.

After twelve years in America, Cathlin had no ties to her mother's country and with the death of her father, her bitterness toward England had grown. But she had thrown herself into her work and stayed on, knowing her father would have wished it. And finally her wine business had prospered.

She smiled faintly, remembering how he had railed at her choice of career, saying she spent too much time in dark, cold cellars and too little with living, breathing people. "It's not healthy, a woman like you caught down there verifying humidity and cork conditions from morning to night. There's more to life than that— flesh and blood things. And if you don't reach out and take them, you'll wake up one morning and find it's too late, *macushla*."

Macushla. My dear. The sweet word still brought a tear to her eye. And her father had been right. One day Cathlin had awakened to find both her parents gone and this great old house hers to maintain.

But the cellars at Seacliffe had precious secrets, a vast cache of old wines and brandy laid down over a century ago. Undisturbed and perfectly preserved, those dusty old bottles had provided the capital to repair the house, and Cathlin had sold the old vintages judiciously. The business had grown swiftly, supported by her fine palate and ability to ferret out old bits of research and documentation. Soon she had commissions from around the world, and returned to America to set up shop in Philadelphia.

Staring out at the rainswept night, Cathlin frowned. She still didn't like England much. Its climate was dour, its food unremarkable. But the real reason she was uncomfortable here was because England represented too keenly the loss of those she'd loved most.

As Cathlin stood in the window, listening to the wind and the churning sea, she shivered, feeling a sudden premonition that she was about to lose something precious yet again. And then she heard a crack from high overhead. Dear God, not the roof, she prayed.

THE ROOF WAS EXACTLY the problem.

Cold wind and a hail of sand poured into the attic as Cathlin rounded the top of the stairs, candle in hand. It took her long moments to trace the source of the draft, a jagged hole in the south wall, where wind rushed in from the outside, fraying the rapidly eroding layer of plaster.

Muttering words that wouldn't bear overhearing, Cathlin dragged hammer, nails, and a roll of heavy plastic from a corner storage closet and set about sealing the hole.

When she had pounded in the last nail through plaster that felt as though it might pull away at any second, she sank down against the wet wooden floor. And there, strangely enough, she began to laugh, caught by the utter absurdity of trying to hold out a sky full of rain and a marsh full of sand. It wouldn't work, of course. Cathlin was far too practical not to see that. But she laughed on, clutching her sodden sides until tears rolled down her cheeks and the candle guttered beside her.

And as she laughed, she seemed to feel a presence beside her, almost as if someone were laughing with her—maybe the moody old house itself. Or maybe it was some dimly remembered ancestor who'd long ago walked these attics and played games under the old eaves.

She sprawled backward and kicked off her wet slippers, wriggling her toes. When the laughter vanished, there wasn't much reason to live, so her father used to say. Maybe it was even that rakish Irishman Donnell O'Neill himself whom Cathlin felt hovering about the attic. If so, she hoped he liked what he saw.

Still smiling, Cathlin reached for the slipper which she'd kicked off into the corner. In the process she snagged a loose floorboard jutting up near the base of the wall. *Probably warped by the rain,* she thought. She had found one shoe and was looking for the other, when she heard a hollow crack.

Without warning the old wood gave way and she was tossed painfully onto her side. When Cathlin raised her candle, she found not one but four panels of wood rotted through. Beneath them lay a recess long hidden under the old floor.

Cathlin's hands trembled with excitement as she probed the dark hole, wincing when something skittered lightly across her fingers. Pushing through dust and cobwebs and heaven knew what else, she reached deeper until she touched something shoved into the recess.

Cathlin worked the heavy object toward her, then eased its smooth bulk up onto the floor. In the candlelight she saw it was a large chest of etched leather with brass fittings.

Her breath caught when she opened it. Did it hold letters from some long-forgotten relative? A treasure hidden from the days when Seacliffe had been a haven for smugglers?

A hint of lilacs teased the air as Cathlin pulled back a layer of velvet. Inside, snuggled against the chest's silk-covered walls, lay neat tiers of costly silk clothing wrapped in fine paper. But whose?

Item after item she pulled from the chest, delighting in the glint of figured damasks and lustrous satins. Full-skirted and tightly fitted at the waist, the gowns were sewn in the grand style of the period paintings of Gainsborough and Constable. Cathlin ran loving fingers over the elegant garments. Pulling aside another layer of velvet, she found a pair of navy slippers with diamond buckles. Nestled between the slippers was a blue velvet ribbon with a cameo worked in precious amber and outlined with tiny diamonds.

Cathlin's breath caught as the diamonds burned in the candlelight, giving the cameo a warm golden glow. For a moment she did not move, awed by the sense that she had somehow stepped back into time, caught in the drama of a stranger's life, which she had opened with the discovery of this trunk. And something called to her, urging her to run her hands over the soft satin and stroke the velvet ribbon.

She could not resist. She was too much a woman to ignore such a temptation. She caught up the candle and ran to fetch the wobbly old mirror leaning against the top of the stairs. With the blotchy glass settled firmly in place, she stripped off her nightgown and slid on the most beautiful of the gowns, an elaborate creation of navy satin stiff with lace and rosettes and seed pearls.

It might have been sewn just for her, Cathlin thought, as the last soft fold fell into place. Its long sleeves ran full to her elbows, then spilled into clouds of creamy lace. The same lace decorated the low bodice, over full skirts in a bright satin cascade. *In for a penny, in for a pound,* she thought as she pulled on the satin slippers with their tiny heels. She watched, entranced. The diamond buckles caught the light, making her feel like an entirely different person.

Her fingers trembled on the cameo. The delicate features made something tighten in her chest. She lifted the heavy stone to her neck.

Instantly the stone warmed beneath her touch.

The diamonds burned and the mirror seemed to shimmer, light-ringed. In that extraordinary instant, while the moon rose over the marsh and a kestrel called in lonely splendor, Cathlin felt beautiful, admired, loved in every atom of her being. It was almost as if this dress, hidden safely away for centuries, was meant only for her, a message of love and protection.

Who had owned these things? Were they keepsakes of a very special evening, a night when two lovers had danced beneath crystal chandeliers and exchanged whispered vows by candlelight?

She would never know.

Hypnotized, Cathlin studied her image in the old, cracked mirror, watching the diamonds glitter. So absorbed was she that the creak of the stairs went unnoticed, as did the low, checked breath from the doorway.

"How did you get here?" came a low, harsh voice. "I warned you not to come. Now it's too late."

CHAPTER EIGHT

CATHLIN LOOKED UP, STARTLED.

Dominic's angry face was reflected in the mirror.

"Dominic? What are you doing up here?" She crossed her arms, feeling enormously silly pirouetting in the majestic gown before a cracked mirror.

There was a hint of madness in his eyes. He was acting very oddly, almost as if he didn't hear her, his whole attention focused on the dress.

"You have no right to be here." Sweat beaded his brow and he swayed slightly.

"Dominic, you're not well. Go back down to bed."

This was getting crazier by the second, Cathlin thought. The man was obviously delirious, and she would have to talk him back to the sofa before he passed out cold.

"You should never have come," he said hoarsely. "I warned you what would happen if you came back."

Warned me? Cathlin went very still. "You did?"

"I told you it was hopeless, but you wouldn't give up. And I told you what would happen if you returned."

"Tell me again."

He ran a hand through his hair, frowning. He frowned, as if he had to concentrate to speak. "I told you if you returned, I'd accept your bargain and there'd be no turning back. Not for either of us." His eyes were feverish.

He put out his hand, as if mesmerized by the sight of her in the candlelight. "You look even more beautiful than I remember. But your hair is all wrong." He caught her glowing black hair, letting it flow through his fingers like sand. "How odd it looks cut so short. And you've left off your powder."

"You're wrong. I—"

Dominic—who didn't seem like Dominic at all—went very still. He studied her face with fierce intensity. "Why didn't you stay away?" With a groan, he pulled her to him. His hands trembled as he kissed the creamy curve of her neck.

Cathlin shivered, hearing the voice of a stranger, feeling the hands of a stranger. What had happened to him? Who was this woman he took her for? And who in heaven's name was *he?*

He was simply delirious after falling down the hill, she told herself sternly. But the explanation didn't make her feel any better. It certainly didn't explain Dominic's strange behavior or the dark glitter in his eyes.

"Why didn't you put on my cameo?" he demanded.

"Cameo?" For a moment Cathlin had trouble breathing. She felt him pull the jeweled ornament from her fingers and fasten it at her neck. She shivered as the heavy piece of amber settled onto the fragile bones at her throat. "You mean…it's yours?"

"Have you forgotten so soon?"

"But you didn't—" Cathlin broke off, swallowing sharply as his mouth brushed her shoulder. He touched her with the cool certainty of a man who has touched many women—and has brought all of them pleasure.

Well, he wouldn't pleasure *her,* Cathlin vowed irritably. But she couldn't seem to think straight, not with his hands tracing the curve of her throat and his mouth doing slow, carnal things to the lobe of her ear. "St-stop," she said huskily. "I can't think when you do that."

"Then don't," he growled. "Just close your eyes and let me

love you. I've thought of nothing else since you came to me at the Crown and Dragon."

At the Crown and Dragon? "Mr., er—exactly *who* did you say you were?"

"Have you forgotten already?" A muscle flashed at his jaw.

"No, of course not." Cathlin thought wildly. "I just like to hear you say it."

His dark brow rose. "I am the fifth earl of Ashton, of course."

The *fifth* earl? Dominic was the tenth earl. That would make him…

Gabriel.

A tremor went through her. He was delirious. He had had an accident and this business of the will had made him hallucinate that he was his ancestor. There was no other possible answer. "Don't you mean you're the tenth earl?"

"I am the fifth, woman. And in case you've forgotten, let me remind you that exactly three days ago you offered me the pleasures of your body if I would agree to a desperate effort to rescue your sister from France."

"I did *what?*"

"Do you pretend to have forgotten?" he demanded.

Just great, Cathlin thought wildly. *Put on a pair of diamond-buckled shoes and find yourself caught in a deserted house with a madman.*

Correction. A madman who had been dead for something like two hundred years, if her peerage math was correct. She held up a warning hand. "Now I'm not saying that I disagree with anything you've told me, Lord Ashton. It's just that I have a tiny problem with, well, promising my body to anyone. It's nothing personal, you understand."

His lips brushed her ear and Cathlin suddenly found it hard to breathe. "It will be. It will be exquisitely personal when I take you. I can't get you out of my blood, and I mean to see that you want this as much as I do."

"You're not listening." Cathlin felt the sensual slide of satin atop her naked skin and the cameo pressed against her throat. She had to get Dominic back downstairs before he collapsed. Then she was probably going to collapse herself. "No matter what you say, I think it's time you got some rest."

"No," he said hoarsely. With a groan, he pulled the lace kerchief from the bodice of her gown. Cathlin watched, dazed, as satin and lace parted cleanly. How had he known the two were unattached? In fact, how had he known about the cameo? When he'd come in, the ornament had still been hidden in her hand.

She took a steadying breath. *Get a grip, O'Neill.* It's just a coincidence. "Look, we've got a little problem here."

"No, you look," he commanded, turning her to face the mirror. "Look at us together."

Cathlin did. He stood behind her now, his hands in her hair, his head bent as he planted little kisses over her neck. She shivered at his exquisite touch, watching their images dance as the candle sputtered behind them.

An odd dry ache gathered in her throat.

Suddenly she found she wanted him to touch her. "Stop this. We can't—" Her breath caught. "I don't want—"

"I've fought this with every shred of my being," he whispered. "But you've won, woman. You'll have your way."

Cathlin watched his bronzed hands slide over the creamy skin at her chest and felt her breasts tighten and ache as a man who looked like Dominic but was not Dominic brushed his lips gently across them. "Th-this is crazy."

His lips nudged the high swell of her breast. She caught back a breathless sigh and found her fingers buried in his midnight hair. "Dominic, this isn't what you think."

"Dominic? So now you confuse me for another. Have you made your wanton offer to so many men?"

"No! That is—"

"Gabriel," he said harshly. "Gabriel is the name of the man who is kissing you now, and, I'll see you don't forget it."

Cathlin caught a shaky breath. Through the smooth satin she felt the press of his callused fingers. They stroked and pulled, until her nipples hardened. His desire was a tangible wave as she stared at their joined images in the old mirror.

She had to stop him. She had to get out of this beautiful old dress and back to her old, everyday self.

But somehow Cathlin couldn't take her eyes from the lustrous folds of satin where Dominic's hands lay clenched. She couldn't ignore the jolt of her heart as his mouth brushed the velvet ribbon at her neck. All unbidden, her neck arched and she curved into the hardness of his body.

"Yes. Like that, my love. Let me feel your passion."

Cathlin shuddered. What was happening to her?

"You have won, I confess it freely. You have but to command me." His hands were hot and not quite steady as they burned over her sensitive skin.

"No. That wasn't me. This—this is all unreal."

Smothering a curse, he pressed his mouth to the rise of her breast. "Does this feel unreal? Or this?"

Cathlin saw his hands taut at her shoulders. She saw her own face, wearing a mix of shock and desire. And as the candlelight played over their images, she felt the tug of the cameo, warm and heavy at her neck. With it came the brush of a phantom curl at her shoulder.

She had a sudden sense of voices and distant laughter, along with faint lilting notes of music. She blinked, watching the mirror dance, feeling her mind open until the shadows fled. Before her she saw a beautiful room with frescoed ceilings and candles caught in golden wall sconces.

She struggled, caught in the nightmare, acutely aware of the tug of the cameo at her neck and the cool weight of the satin gown on her naked skin.

And then the mirror shivered and swayed, and there was only darkness.

"CATHLIN?" SOMETHING WAS striking her cheeks. "Cathlin, wake up."

"No!" She struggled blindly. "I won't do it!"

"You won't do what?"

"I can't. I won't betray him."

Cool liquid brushed her eyes and face, trickling into her mouth. "Look at me, Cathlin." It was a different voice, a voice that carried the soft hint of French vowels. "You are safe."

Safe? Cathlin cracked open one eye. No curtains, no wall sconces, thank God. Only Seacliffe's damp old floorboards and a trunk lying open at her feet.

And a man. A man whose eyes blazed with urgency.

Cathlin let out a long, low breath, fighting a wave of nausea. What in heaven's name had happened to her?

"Are you all right?"

"I'm getting there."

Dominic eased her back against this chest. "What happened up here? And where did you find all this?"

Cathlin hadn't a clue. Was it something to do with these old clothes and the cameo she'd found in the trunk? An hallucination perhaps?

She tried vainly to pull away. "I'm fine. I'd also like to get up."

"Not yet."

Cathlin glared at him. "Maybe you should be explaining what happened to *you*. You were the one who came charging up here like a man possessed. In fact, you acted like—" Cathlin started to tell him about the fragmented images she'd had, and her suspicion that Dominic in some way had assumed the identity of his ancestor Gabriel.

Right, O'Neill. Then he'll really be convinced you've had a major cerebral concussion. "Like a complete stranger," she finished.

Dominic frowned. "I did? All I remember was being caught in a hellish sort of dream, something with music and laughter and blurred lights. Then I found myself up here. And you were lying on the floor, dressed like that."

"It's not exactly a crime to dress in old clothes."

"I didn't say it was. I'm just trying to figure out how I got up here."

Cathlin ran shaky fingers through her hair. "Okay, I'm sorry. I'm still a little shaken." Abruptly she sat forward. "Where's the cameo?"

"What cameo?"

"The one I was wearing. A velvet ribbon with a carved amber stone. I had it on before I—" She swallowed. "Before I woke up."

Dominic frowned, looking at the floor around them. "Maybe it slipped off. It won't be easy to find. Some of the floorboards have broken right through."

"I know. That's where I found the chest with all these things."

Dominic gave a silent whistle. "Good work."

Cathlin wasn't so sure. Something about that gown and cameo left her distinctly uneasy. "That cameo has to be here somewhere."

"You're staying put," Dominic said tautly. "You must have fainted a few minutes ago and knocked over that old mirror against the wall."

Cathlin noticed the frame that lay on the floor, candlelight caught in a thousand shattered shards of glass.

It doesn't matter, she told herself sternly. It was just a mirror. "Can you see that cameo anywhere?"

"Maybe it's in the chest. I'll look, if you're sure you can—"

"Breathe without your assistance? I think I *might* be able to manage it." She caught a breath. "Look, I'm sorry. I suppose I should thank you. It's just—"

Just what? That I feel as if I've been tossed into a nightmare. That this gown feels somehow familiar. That I keep trying to hate you and I don't succeed. "Oh, forget it."

"No, let's not forget it." Dominic's voice hardened. "I didn't mean to upset you, Cathlin. Not from the first. It just seems everything I do rubs you the wrong way."

"It's not you. Coming back here always brings back a lot of memories."

"This is one beautiful house. You must have been very happy here."

Had she? A very long time ago, maybe, when she'd visited her mother and her family. But not in the last years. Then Seacliffe had been full of ghosts, reminding her of the parents she'd lost too soon.

Dominic watched her face intently. "What else happened up here just now?"

"Nothing." Too swiftly.

"I find you passed out on the floor, dead to the world, wearing a dress probably two hundred years old and you tell me *nothing?*"

"That's right."

Dominic shook his head. "O'Neill, when are you going to start trusting me?"

Rather than lie, Cathlin stayed silent.

"Great," he said grimly. After a moment he moved over to the chest and dug inside. His brow arched as he held up a fine cambric chemise with a white embroidered border. "Sure you wouldn't care to model this one for me?"

"Forget it."

Dominic's head disappeared back into the trunk. "Another

pair of shoes. A mask of silk and feathers. An enamel box of some sort. And—damnation!"

"What did you find?"

Dominic sat up, frowning at his hand. "Some kind of pin. Bloody sharp, too. It's cut me." Carefully, he lifted a scrap of yellowing linen from the dark interior of the chest. Attached to the fabric was a diamond stickpin that shot cold fire into the attic shadows.

Cathlin's breath caught. "It's…beautiful."

"Thirty carats at least." Dominic ran his finger slowly over the fine silver mounting, watching the facets gleam. "I've seen this before."

"How could you? This chest has been hidden here for years. My mother and her parents didn't even know about it."

"It's familiar." Dominic's eyes narrowed. "My God, it's Mad Uncle Gabriel's."

"Your ancestor's? The one who…"

"That's the one."

Cathlin's mind rebelled. She sat forward awkwardly, her fingers tense. "It can't be."

"It is. There's a full-length portrait of the man back at our estate and he's wearing that exact pin." Dominic looked at Cathlin oddly. "A pin, if I may add, that we have never been able to find. We always assumed that he'd run into bad luck at the gaming tables and been forced to pawn it. Apparently not."

Cathlin surged to her feet. "Are you accusing someone in *my* family of stealing it?"

"I'm not accusing anyone. I'm just curious."

"There could be dozens of pins like that. Who says that it belonged to this ancestor of yours?"

Dominic's fingers closed around the beautiful old ornament. He stared down at his closed fist, thinking about the dark legends he had heard about the Ashton diamond ever since he was a boy. They had given him more than a few bad nights. As he'd grown up, it hadn't helped that he bore the same brooding, dark good looks of the fifth earl. Only their eye color was different. "Look, it's—rather a long story, and you're shivering already. You'd better change and then get some sleep."

"But—" Cathlin sighed, knowing he was right. Half of the wind in Sussex had to be gusting through that hole in the roof, in spite of her efforts with the plastic. Staying here any longer might be distinctly unhealthy.

On the other hand, Cathlin wasn't taking another step in this beautiful, disturbing gown. "First I want to change."

"Fine. I'll go down and get a fire going while you—"

"No." Cathlin caught his hand, her eyes very wide. "I—I don't want to be up here alone."

Dominic's eyes narrowed. "Still not going to tell me what happened?"

Cathlin ignored him, reaching for her clothes.

"We'll never get anything done this way. Damn it, O'Neill, you're going to have to trust me."

"I'll keep that in mind. Now turn your head, if you please."

A glint went through Dominic's eyes. "What if I don't please?"

Color filled Cathlin's cheeks. "Don't," she whispered. "Not now."

Dominic cursed. "It wouldn't be any good anyway, would it? Not if you couldn't look me in the face. Not if you couldn't trust me." He strode to the chair at the far wall, his shoulders tense with anger.

Maybe she did trust him, Cathlin thought. Maybe it was herself she didn't have much confidence in.

She worked awkwardly at the laces at the back of the dress, freeing it slowly. As the satin slid away, a great weight seemed to lift. After a quick glance at Dominic, she eased out of the billowing satin skirts and tugged on her nightgown, relieved to feel the thick, practical cotton instead of rich satin.

She was buttoning up the front when she heard a hiss behind her. Without warning, one end of the plastic tore free, slapping across her cheek so hard that Cathlin bit back a cry of pain.

Dominic caught the flapping sheet and shoved it away from her face. "Are you okay?"

"It just frightened me, that's all."

"Hardly. You're shaking like a leaf and you've got a nasty welt on your cheek." Cathlin winced at even the gentle brush of his finger.

She looked up. His hair was unruly where the wind gusted over it. His eyes were flecked with gold by the candlelight. She wanted to hate him. She hated everything he stood for: men with easy fortunes, grand birthrights, and too much charm for a woman's safety. In spite of all that, Cathlin couldn't close herself off from him. He was too near, too overpowering. She'd never had a problem putting men in their place in the past, but with this man she didn't know where to begin.

Or if she even wanted to.

"Cathlin…" His fingers opened, eased across her cheek. They were trembling slightly.

Something sharp and sweet passed between them.

Dear God, he's going to kiss me, Cathlin thought dimly. *He's going to pull me to him and touch me as I've never been touched before. If I don't want it, I've got to stop him now, before it's too late.*

If I don't want it…

But the words wouldn't come.

Their eyes held, a universe of emotion slamming between them while their bodies stood frozen and the sea air gusted around them.

Dominic swallowed, his eyes hard. *God help me, I'm going to kiss her. How can I help it, when she looks at me with that crazy blend of innocence and passion, with eyes that go right through me and make me feel I've known her forever?*

Even then he fought it, telling himself he was a fool and worse, but she touched some deep corner of his heart, calling out to him, seducing him in ways that went far beyond the physical. He shouldn't touch her. He couldn't.

But he did.

Even the faintest brush of skin hit him like a jolt, made heat ripple through Dominic's body. He caught a low breath and eased her closer. When he heard her sigh, he covered her mouth completely.

She was all softness and need, all hunger and woman, and she fired his blood as it had never been fired before. He pulled her against his body, sliding his hands along her hips.

"Cathlin." It was a wave of need, of protest, of wild discovery. "God help me…"

Her lips opened beneath his. Somehow her fingers were in his hair. He felt her ease against him, her breath feathering against his mouth.

Her response made him harden with agonizing rapidity. Breathing heavily, he ran his fingers beneath the thick cotton and met cool silken skin. Her ragged little moan was loud in the taut silence between them and had the effect of gas poured on an open fire. Dominic told himself he was crazy to want her like this, but all the cold reasoning in the world didn't change the way she made him feel.

Hungry. Possessive. Like a man who'd found something precious that he didn't even know he'd lost.

What the hell was happening here? He drew a ragged breath and eased away.

He wondered if she even heard. Her hips moved restlessly. Her head fell back as she offered him the cool arch of her throat and the thrust of her breasts.

Dominic fought for sanity when all he wanted was to throw her down on the bare wood floor and bury himself inside her. And some crazy voice whispered that if he did, it would be unforgettable. And also somehow familiar.

He cursed. "Let's go."

"Go?" She looked dazed.

"You need food." He took a tight step backward and smoothed down her nightgown, cursing when he saw the tight jut of her aroused nipples against the soft cotton.

"Food?"

"Food," he repeated hoarsely. "Then a fire."

"Fire," she muttered dimly.

"And then we talk, Cathlin. Really talk."

She blinked, as if having trouble focusing. "Talk. Yes—have to talk." But her eyes were dark with desire.

Dominic cursed. Any more looks like that and they would end up naked on the floor. Maybe talking wasn't such a good idea either. Dominic wanted nothing more than to pull Cathlin against him and kiss her back into blissful insensibility.

But he didn't. He couldn't, not with all the questions hanging over them. He caught a ragged breath, wondering how much more torture he could take. She was looking at him, just looking, her eyes wide and haunted. And the sight of her eyes was like getting a roundhouse kick to the groin.

"What's...happening, Dominic?"

"You're asking me, the man you love to hate? Why start trusting me now?"

Cathlin ran shaky fingers through her hair. "Because like it or not, we're both involved. You knew about that pin. And something about that gown...affected you. Can't you feel it?"

In Dominic's hand the Ashton diamond felt cold and sharp. Frowning, he caught up the old shoes and satin dress and stowed them back in the chest, along with the diamond ornament. "Damned if I know *what* I feel right now, except tired." After a moment he shoved the lid down on the chest.

Somehow it left him feeling a hell of a lot better.

"It's probably just the effects of sleep deprivation. We'll talk in the morning, O'Neill. Tomorrow everything will look a whole lot better."

Dominic didn't believe it, but he hoped it sounded good to Cathlin.

CHAPTER NINE

THE MOON HUNG OVER THE marsh, veiled in clouds. It was a night such as smugglers might have plied their desperate trade and excise officers made their equally desperate pursuit. But now the sea was quiet. In the wake of the storm, only the night birds cried, winging low over the lonely curve of sand and cold canal.

While Dominic Montserrat twisted restlessly in dreams, the scent of lilacs filled the sleeping house.

"HELP ME."

"No one can help you, Geneva." A tall man with pale, hard features stood before Geneva Russell in the candlelit study of one of London's most prominent hostesses. Henry Devere was clad in black satin that was not half as cold as his eyes. He smiled mirthlessly as he toyed with an enameled watch on a silver chain. "Your sister's life is in your hands now. Find me the Rook and she lives. Refuse me and she dies." He smiled darkly. "And her children will die along with her."

"Monster! You can't do such a thing!"

"Oh, but I can, my sweet Geneva. And so I shall, unless you find me the Rook tonight. There is a reward of one thousand gold guineas on his head, and by God it shall be mine."

"But I don't know the man. I cannot do as you ask."

"Ah, but you can. With your sister's life in danger, you went straight to the Rook. I have had your movements watched, my

dear. You spoke to the man and you can identify him tonight. I want no question in my mind when he is taken."

Geneva's breath caught. *"Tonight?"*

"Of course. My informers say he will be here among the guests at the masquerade, dressed as Marc Antony. A most appropriate jest, don't you think, since he is soon to fall before your charms just as Anthony did before his Cleopatra?"

Geneva felt her flesh crawl as she studied the heavy-lidded eyes and fleshy lips. She had known Henry Devere slightly in India, where he had been a merchant like her father. After her parents' death, she had come back to England to find her sister, only to discover she had gone back to France with her husband.

Henry Devere had been only too kind, only too glad to help her communicate with her sister.

At first.

Then he had begun to press her with more personal attentions. When Geneva had repelled his advances, Devere's manner had changed. Instead of the condescending advisor, he had become a cold-blooded bully. When he threatened harm to her sister, Geneva knew it was within his power, since his business contacts with the new, revolutionary government in France were extensive.

She wanted to scream, to turn, to flee, but she could not. Not while her sister's life hung in the balance. *"There could be dozens of such costumes,"* she said desperately. *"How shall I know which one is the Rook?"*

"That, my sweet Geneva, is your problem." The man in black ran a finger down her shoulder. *"I suggest that you use your very lush charms to entrap him."*

Geneva shivered as the diamonds glinted on her shoes, reflected in the dancing light of a dozen wall sconces. *"Don't touch me,"* she hissed, feeling bile fill her throat.

His nail bit into her skin. *"Oh, but I shall touch you, my little beauty. And you'll fulfill my every command gladly, or you'll watch your sister die."*

Fear tore through her. She was trapped, horribly trapped. Only one man could help her, but she knew that to ask him would amount to betraying him. "Go away."

"Not just yet, I think." Cold hands slid over her neck. "You will kiss me first."

Fury filled her. Such a beast deserved only one response. She lashed out with her knee, catching him full in the groin. Instantly, he bent double, his face tight with agony.

But her hopes were dashed as he came upright, the triumph in his eyes replaced with blind fury.

"Bitch. I'll see you pay for that. I'll make you beg for my forgiveness before I'm done with you." He swept up a heavy silver candlestick from the lacquered table beside him.

"I think not, Devere." A shadowed figure stepped from the heavy curtains of the French doors to her left. "The lady does not seem to care for your presence. In view of that, I insist you leave."

"Who are you to order me about? By God, I'll teach you to interfere."

"Take another step and I rather think you'll die." Candlelight glinted off a pistol as Geneva's rescuer moved from the shadows of the window.

Her breath caught as she saw the draping folds of linen that stretched across his powerful chest. Above his masked face was set a garland of olive leaves.

"Marc Antony," she whispered.

"Of course." His voice was smooth, silken. It was a voice to sway men and entice women, she thought. A voice born to bear the weight of command. "But why are you not in costume?"

She did not speak, her hands clenched in the folds of satin. "I—I had no time," she heard her voice answer, as if from a great distance. It was a stranger's voice, full of fear. "I did not plan to attend."

"A pity." His eyes darkened. "You would have been magnificent as my Cleopatra." He turned to the man in black. "Goodbye, Devere." There was a hard note of warning in his tone.

For a moment Henry Devere stood motionless, his body stiff with fury. Then a cold, sly smile eased across his lips. "As you wish. All Rome must bow to Antony, after all." He looked at Geneva. "Be certain that you do not succumb as easily as Cleopatra did, my dear. You know what happened to her." Still smiling, he made his way back out into the hallway.

Geneva shuddered, clasping her hands to her waist. Evil clung to the man and filled the room even after his departure.

"You're shivering and you've dropped your shawl." A length of lace slid gently around her shoulders. "And you are bleeding." Carefully, her rescuer caught the bead of blood left by Devere's nail. Raising her arm, he ran his tongue lightly over the tiny prick.

Geneva shivered at the shocking intimacy of his touch. "It— it's nothing," she whispered.

"He was importuning you?"

She nodded, unable to speak, still repelled by the memory.

"The man is an animal. But perhaps you do not wish to speak of it."

Words came finally. "How...much did you hear?"

The silver eyes were unreadable. "How much should I have heard?"

She gave a careless shrug. "It is of no importance."

"You would do well not to find yourself alone with him in the future."

"And what of you, my lord? Need a woman fear if she finds herself alone with you?"

His low laugh seduced her flushed skin. "Perhaps. Does that make you want to run, Geneva of the golden eyes?"

YOUR OPINION POLL
THANK-YOU FREE GIFTS INCLUDE

▶ **2 ROMANCE OR 2 SUSPENSE BOOKS**

▶ **2 LOVELY SURPRISE GIFTS**

DETACH AND MAIL CARD TODAY!

OFFICIAL OPINION POLL

YOUR OPINION COUNTS!
Please check TRUE or FALSE below to express your opinion about the following statements:

Q1 Do you believe in "true love"?

"TRUE LOVE HAPPENS ONLY ONCE IN A LIFETIME."
○ TRUE
○ FALSE

Q2 Do you think marriage has any value in today's world?

"YOU CAN BE TOTALLY COMMITTED TO SOMEONE WITHOUT BEING MARRIED."
○ TRUE
○ FALSE

Q3 What kind of books do you enjoy?

"A GREAT NOVEL MUST HAVE A HAPPY ENDING."
○ TRUE
○ FALSE

Place the sticker next to one of the selections below to receive your 2 FREE BOOKS and 2 FREE GIFTS. I understand that I am under no obligation to purchase anything as explained on the back of this card.

Romance
193 MDL ELSZ
393 MDL ELVZ

Suspense
192 MDL ELRC
392 MDL ELUD

0074823 |||▮|||▮|||||| |||▮||||| ||||▮||| **FREE GIFT CLAIM #** 3622

FIRST NAME

LAST NAME

ADDRESS

APT.#

CITY

STATE/PROV.

ZIP/POSTAL CODE

(TF-RS-07)

Offer limited to one per household and not valid to current subscribers of Romance, Suspense or the Romance/Suspense combo. **Your Privacy** - The Reader Service is committed to protecting your privacy. Our Privacy Policy is available online at www.eHarlequin.com or upon request from the Reader Service. From time to time we make our lists of customers available to reputable firms who may have a product or service of interest to you. If you would prefer for us not to share your name and address, please check here☐.

© 2003 HARLEQUIN ENTERPRISES LTD. ® and ™ are trademarks owned and used by the trademark owner and/or its licensee.

The Reader Service — Here's How It Works:

"I can defend myself."

He did not laugh as other men would have, but only nodded gravely. "Against some, yes. But not against such a man as Devere." His hand slid over a powdered curl of her hair. "And perhaps not against a man like myself." His jaw hardened. "I think it best that I leave you now."

"No." She spoke quickly, remembering Devere's threat. "Not yet. I...I do not care to join the others."

He dark brow rose. "You play a dangerous game."

Dear heaven, how much had he heard?

Just then voices came from the hallway. A drunken couple swayed into the room, arms entwined.

Her rescuer cursed. Pressing a finger to his lips, he pulled her back behind the heavy damask curtains. Molded against him, with his faint scent of lemon and tobacco in her throat, Geneva felt cut off from the world, cut off from herself, cut off from all she'd been and known and felt before.

By some spell of night and candlelight she had become a stranger in a satin gown, a woman falling inch by inch under this man's potent spell. She turned slightly, feeling her hip nudge his hard thigh.

Heat burned out from those inches of contact, heat that left her pulse hammering.

Outside she heard the rustle of silk and a woman's soft moan of pleasure. Her own heartbeat quickened at the sound. She thought of what it would be like if this man took her into his arms. Would she know the same pleasure and moan softly?

"Look at your image," he whispered, pointing to the glass pane behind them. His fingers moved to her neck. Something cool and hard slid over her skin.

She turned, as if in a dream. A beautiful cameo of carved amber hung about her neck, strung from a velvet ribbon. "It's...beautiful. But I cannot—"

"Hush, beauty," he said with a trace of his habitual arrogance. "It pleases me to please you." He stood behind her now, his hands in her hair, his head bent as he planted little kisses along her ear. "Wear it always, and think of me."

Geneva shivered at his exquisite touch, watching their images meld and dance in the candlelight. She would wear it. Just as she would always think of him. Even after she betrayed him?

She shuddered.

"You are cold?"

"No, not cold."

"Then this is fear, fear of me?" His voice was suddenly taut.

"No, not fear. But surely, we cannot." Her breath caught. "Not here. I don't want—"

"You will," he whispered. "I have fought you with every shred of my being and failed." His voice hardened. "May God help us both."

Geneva watched his hands slide over the creamy skin at her chest. She closed her eyes, her breasts grown tight and aching beneath his touch.

As if in a dream, she felt his mouth tease one crest of crimson. She caught back a breathless sigh, and sank trembling fingers into the blackness of his hair. "This isn't what you think."

Outside their curtained bower came a low, choked moan and the indrawn breaths of cresting passion. Geneva flushed, horrified.

But the man beside her barely noticed. "Gabriel," he said harshly. "Say my name, and let me know you think of me."

"You," she whispered. Then, more huskily, "Gabriel."

"Yes, my love. That is the name of the man who is kissing you, the man whose cameo you wear. I mean to see you don't forget it."

His fingers brushed against her hardened nipples. She shivered, filled with heat as she stared at their images in the long glass window.

She had to stop this. She had to make him understand.

But her body mocked her. She could not deny him what she had long ago determined to give freely, in order to save her sister's life. Her neck arched. The cameo swayed, cool and heavy as she curved into the hardness of his body.

"Yes. Like that, my love. Come to me. Let me feel your passion."

Geneva shuddered, fighting the dark pull of his sensuality. Even if he left now, could he be swifter than Henry Devere, who would use every connection he had in France to see her sister brought to harm? Geneva knew she could not risk her sister's death. She would have to be clever and cool, using both men to her own ends.

With a low curse Gabriel caught her shoulders, his eyes burning over her face. "I have thought of nothing else since I saw you at the Crown and Dragon. You have but to command me, for whatever I have is yours. But in return you must fulfill your part of the bargain."

Geneva felt her throat tighten. A choked sigh emerged instead of words as his lips met the swell of her breast.

Outside there came a low hum of voices and the rustle of clothing. Then only silence. Geneva gave a silent sigh of thanks that they were finally alone.

"No more tricks. God help me, I'm not up to them. You have beaten me."

Dimly she saw Gabriel ease her dress from her shoulders and free her straining skin.

"Was any woman ever so beautiful?" he said hoarsely.

Geneva choked back a moan.

He wanted her.

And dear God, she wanted him, with a passion equal to his own. When had it happened? And how was she ever to escape this nightmare choice that Henry Devere had forced upon her?

The cameo dug into her neck, dense stone and cold diamonds. A jolting tension crept along her spine. But Geneva knew she must say the words that would spell his ruin. "Are you truly the man called the Rook?"

A powdered curl brushed against her shoulder. She felt the tension of his hard arms braced at her shoulders and was achingly aware of his fingers as they eased beneath the warm satin to cup the weight of her full breasts.

"Yes," he said hoarsely. "I am the man you seek. Now you hold my secret and my very life in your hands. Do not betray me."

Geneva knew with a vast and terrible clarity that she would do just that. She had no choice. She could not let her sister die.

"No," she whispered, her throat dry.

He took her answer for assurance, instead of the protest that it was. He smiled darkly, studying her sweet, upthrust nipples. "Your body shows its passion most eloquently. But I must see all of you."

"Someone might come. That monster Devere—"

"There is no need to fear. I'll keep you safe. At a masquerade such as this, nearly everyone has similar ideas," he said darkly.

Beneath the brush of his hands the satin folds moved. As they did, the heavy cameo swayed and came free. With a low hiss the ornament slid over the yards of satin and landed on the carpet.

The movement caught Geneva from her sensual haze. "No," she said wildly. "Not here. You must go. Find a place where we will be undisturbed." Her eyes were dark with entreaty.

After a moment he nodded. "My carriage is outside. I will send a man round to fetch it. Wait for me." He planted a slow, goading kiss upon her lips and Geneva felt her body stiffen, answering his passion. But he put her from him, laughing softly. "Soon, my lady."

Then he opened the curtain and disappeared.

JAGGED IMAGES FILLED Dominic's head, images of sadness and anger and a woman's soft sigh. Snatches of dreams played through his mind like distant music, familiar and yet not quite familiar.

Or were they memories?

GENEVA WAS STANDING BY THE window, pale and determined, when Henry Devere returned.

"He was the one?"

For a moment Geneva did not move. A man's honor and his very life flashed before her. "What will you do with the information if I tell you?"

"Do?" *Devere smiled coldly and motioned into the corridor. Six men appeared, all burly and unsmiling.* "Why, I shall see him transported to Paris, to those who will pay most dearly for his person. And then I fear we will see our Rook plucked publicly by Madame Guillotine."

"No," *Geneva whispered, her hands on the amber cameo she had recovered from the floor.*

"Don't think to trick me, my dear." *Devere caught her arm and glared down at her.* "If you lie, I will soon know it—and your sister's life will be forfeit." *His fingers tightened.* "Now the truth, was it he?"

Betrayal. A man's death delivered in a single terrible stroke. But what was her choice? If she was not very careful, her sister would die the same way.

Geneva nodded slowly, her face sheet white.

"Excellent. Your assistance has been most valuable." *Devere gestured curtly to his crew, who moved into hiding behind the curtains while he settled upon a large settee.* "Now we must wait for our hero to return."

THEIR PREY WAS NOT LONG about it. Less than ten minutes had passed before his tall shadow fell over Geneva's shoulder as she stood, still and unsmiling, by the fireplace.

The man known as the Rook halted on the threshold, seeing Henry Devere seated in a wing chair beside Geneva. "Was this man bothering you?"

Geneva shook her head.

"It is as well, or his life would be gone."

"Nonsense," Devere said easily. "Miss Russell and I were merely discussing—" He looked at the woman motionless beside the fireplace. "Why, we were discussing Roman history, I believe. And she was regaling me with stories of Julius Caesar." His colorless eyes swept Gabriel's tall form. "Dear me, why have you changed your attire, Lord Ashton? That toga rather suited you."

"Not where I'm going," Gabriel said curtly. For a moment he surveyed the room, frowning. Then he moved to Geneva's side. A diamond stickpin gleamed among the lace at his neck. "But the lady grows tired. We shall bid you adieu, Devere." He pointedly took Geneva's palm and raised it to his lips, turning his back on Devere.

Geneva's throat tightened. Don't kiss me, her heart screamed. Don't trust me. Run. Run while you can. Run before I must betray you.

But she didn't speak. Isabel's image swam before her, holding her to aching silence.

She watched Devere raise a questioning brow.

And although she knew the memory would torment her forever, taking away all joy and happiness and hope, she nodded her terrible betrayal.

One gesture was all Devere required. With a growl, he pulled forth a silver pistol and called to his crew, who charged toward Gabriel.

"Run," Geneva gasped, her hand rising to shove at his chest. "Run, before it's too late!"

Gabriel's eyes burned in fury. His fingers tightened on the fragile bones at her wrist. "Jezebel," he said hoarsely, the word hurled through her heart, killing her dreams as surely as a bullet would have ended her life.

And then he plunged through the door, with Devere's men yapping at his heels like a pack of unruly dogs.

"Damn you, you'll pay for this trickery," Devere hissed. "And *your fine sister will pay also, when her head flies bloody onto the French cobblestones."*

Geneva didn't move as Devere ran out. She did not even breathe in that moment.

She felt nothing, saw nothing, heard nothing, for she was totally dead inside.

A single tear glistened on her cheek, the crystallized loss of all her dreams. And in her palm the Ashton diamond torn from the Rook's neck gleamed cold and cruel, locked between her bleeding fingers.

CHAPTER TEN

DOMINIC TWISTED TO HIS side and pommeled his pillow. Cursing softly, he tried the other side, but with no greater success.

He sat up, groggy as if he'd been drugged, with fragments of dreams still drifting in his head. He remembered angry voices, stamping feet.

And a vow betrayed.

Sunlight fell through the window as he shoved to his feet. The sunlight made him think of Cathlin's eyes. Damn it, how had she worked her way under his skin like this? His lower body tightened with a jolt of desire.

But that feeling, like all others, would have to be denied. Over his long years of professional service, three unshakable rules had kept Dominic alive in the shadow world that had taken him from one hot spot of the globe to another, and he was counting on those rules to get him through now.

The rules were the same as always.

Don't let it get personal. Don't let them see you sweat. And when you leave, don't ever look back.

Dominic scowled off at the distant gleam of the channel. He'd already broken two of those rules with Cathlin.

He didn't even want to think about the third one.

THEY SPENT THE DAY APART, by mutual consent.

Cathlin searched Seacliffe from attic to cellar, looking for any old documents that might shed some light on Geneva Russell. Dominic spent the morning sawing through the fallen tree and dragging it from the drive. When he came back, dirty and wind-blown later in the day, Cathlin still had found nothing.

"Forget it. Go sit down while I clean up and then I'll make something to eat."

"You?" Her tone was decidedly suspicious.

"Don't be such a chauvinist, O'Neill." Dominic's eyes glinted. "You might just be surprised."

SHE WAS.

The man could cook.

He sorted through the meager contents of the refrigerator and lined up ingredients neatly on the old pine table. Then he went to work, silent and intent, competent in this as he was in every-thing else.

Cathlin watched, amazed. First a handful of crushed mint leaves and the juice of two crushed limes went into a bowl. Next came a trace of garlic, a single piece of rosemary, and freshly ground pepper.

The man could *really* cook. What's more, he actually seemed to like it.

Dominic smiled, enjoying her shock. He'd learned at his mother's knee all the arcane mysteries of stockpot, roux and foie gras and was utterly comfortable in the kitchen. Some of his warmest childhood memories, in fact, were of her big, window-lined kitchen filled with sun and wonderful smells, fresh eggs in handmade baskets and a hundred different copper pans.

But Dominic shuddered to think what Danielle Ronsard Mont-serrat, *nouvelle cuisine* virtuoso and sister to one of the best known chefs in all France, would have thought of *this* particular meal.

It certainly didn't help that the electricity was still out and he had to work by the light of four candles shoved onto cracked porcelain saucers in the dark kitchen. He cursed as he nearly set his cuff afire wrestling a plate of grilled salmon with lime sauce out of the old gas stove. He was even less happy with the thought that Nicholas's letter to Cathlin was missing from his jacket. Most likely he had lost it out on the marsh, when he'd fallen by the bridge. But he couldn't be certain, and that thought bothered Dominic. If the letter fell into the wrong hands, the news of Gabriel's will would soon become public.

And that would put Cathlin in real danger.

As these thoughts churned through Dominic's head, Cathlin sat silent at the end of an eighteenth-century pine table. Chin in hands, she watched his swift, efficient movements, utterly hypnotized. The fish was perfect, crisp on top, crowned with a light sauce and freshly cut lime slices. She had brought the fillet from London, but had been too tired even to think of cooking since she'd come to Seacliffe. Not that her efforts could have come anywhere near this.

But the amazing thing was how different Dominic looked here in the kitchen wrestling pans and juggling spatulas. He seemed quieter, self-sufficient. Entirely self-absorbed, in fact.

Happy.

Cathlin didn't know what made that word come into her head. Or what made her think he wasn't usually happy.

Uneasy at the increasingly personal direction of her thoughts, she turned to pour two glasses of the French vintage La Trouvaille which she'd also brought from London.

It was her only contribution to their lunch, in fact, since Dominic had insisted she rest while he worked.

Now he turned, two steaming plates in hand. "Lunch, such as it is, is served."

Cathlin studied the grilled fish, golden slices of pan-fried French bread and bananas cooked in brown sugar with walnuts and whipped cream. "Amazing. It smells absolutely wonderful."

"There wasn't much to work with. Two limes, a handful of crushed mint leaves, a banana, and a single salmon fillet don't exactly made a full larder." He set the dishes on the table, raising a brow as he saw Cathlin's contribution. "Chateau Climens '71?" There was a gleam in his eyes. "You shouldn't have, Ms. O'Neill."

"I *didn't*. Not on my salary. We can't all be born with a silver spoon, you know. But this La Trouvaille will do very nicely. In fact, I've always thought red wines make a perfect complement to full-flavored fish, and rules be damned."

Dominic set her plate before her, his face unreadable. He raised his glass. "Here's to good wine and rules be damned."

Their glasses glinted in the candlelight. Outside the wind whispered through the elm trees along Seacliffe's south front. The etched crystal touched, clinking softly.

Dominic's hair glistened from the shower he'd taken after his efforts with the fallen tree. A few drops still clung to the dark strands at the neck of his opened shirt, of faded but beautifully tailored blue on blue herringbone cotton.

His damp skin smelled slightly of lemon and cloves. Cathlin wanted to inch closer and see if he felt as good as he smelled.

She caught a ragged breath at the unruly path her thoughts were taking and looked away, busying herself with the salmon. "I'm impressed. You didn't tell me you were a cook."

Dominic shrugged. "I've picked up a few things here and there."

A few things? This was world-class cuisine and Cathlin knew it. What other secrets was the man hiding from her?

"So tell me about this great wine you've discovered." He held up the glass and studied the rich crimson liquid. "Looks pretty ordinary to me."

"Hardly. It's got a unique nose—a mix of raspberries and smoke. Great tannin."

Dominic sniffed. "Passable," he said.

"Better than passable. Try it."

He did, his eyes on her face.

"Well?"

"Good body. Deep color. A rather pleasant little mix of fruit and moss."

"Pleasant? It's extraordinary," Cathlin protested. "And it's got wonderful staying power."

Dominic smiled slightly. "Do you happen to hold shares in this vineyard, Ms. O'Neill?"

"Of course not. It's simply my job to recognize a good wine when I find one." She swirled the liquid thoughtfully. "My prediction is that this will be one of the very best. If it's handled properly, maybe even a legend."

Dominic made a muffled sound that might have been a cough and set his glass down sharply on the table. "A legend. You mean that?"

"It *is* my job to know wines, Lord—"

"Dominic, please. I think your saving my life entitles us to progress to first names."

"Very well, Dominic. You sounded happy at my assessment. Maybe *you* have shares in the vineyard," she said teasingly. "But I happen to know that the reclusive owner of La Trouvaille is very old and very bad tempered. He sees no one, and he's a perfectionist when it comes to his wine." She frowned. "Come to think of it, Serita mentioned something about your owning a vineyard."

Dominic's eyes darkened. He started to speak, then looked down at the wine in his glass. "Would it change anything if I were someone else, if my vineyard were as exceptional as La Trouvaille, perhaps?"

"I judge my friends by who they are, not what they own."

"I expected something like that." Dominic laughed grimly. "No, my acres are nothing extraordinary. I'm just one more playboy earl trying to make ends meet in this day of a shrinking British economy and crippling death duties."

"Your idea of economy is probably giving up the second pastry chef and the twelfth gardener."

Dominic gave a tight smile. "Just remember, O'Neill, I can always take away that food you're devouring at roughly the speed of light."

"Okay, I give in. You have perfect notions of economy." Cathlin made a protective movement with her hands. "And this salmon isn't going anywhere except into my mouth, I warn you." She studied Dominic. "By the way, where *did* you learn to cook like this?"

"My mother. She was wonderful in the kitchen, always with bread rising somewhere and a bit of candy fruit tucked away in one of her big pockets to reward curious fingers. She believed in having children learn right along with everyone else. I could make a soufflé before I could ride a bicycle, I think. A most un-English childhood, believe me."

"She sounds wonderful."

Dominic heard the question in Cathlin's voice. "She died four years ago," he said. "Swift but painless. It was very hard on my father, for they were very much in love even after all those years." A muscle flashed at his jaw. "My sister, Alexis, bore the worst of it, because I was—away."

"I'm sure they understood if your work kept you from them."

"They might have understood, but I'm not sure I did. At least I got to see her, before…" His voice drifted away as he ran his finger along the rim of his glass. When he looked up, his voice was steady. "And what about you, Cathlin O'Neill? What secrets are you hiding behind that brash American exterior?"

"Nothing very exciting, I'm afraid. My father was…in the English government."

"Someone I'd know?" Dominic asked casually.

"No. Just one of the nameless, thankless drones," Cathlin said bitterly. "My mother died when I was ten. Donnell was a wonderful father. He taught me all the important things."

"Oh? I'm afraid to ask."

Cathlin gave Dominic a challenging smile. "How to palm a card. How to spot a counterfeit bill. How to tell diamonds from Diamonique. It was rather important in his line of work, you see."

"He was a government jeweler?"

Cathlin laughed softly. "No, he was a jewel thief, among other things. Then he went straight. If you can call government security work going straight," she added grimly.

"Not interesting? You've beaten my tale to shreds, O'Neill. Tell me more."

"There's not very much." Not much that Cathlin knew, at least. There had been long months in the Far East and Arabia, but Donnell never spoke of them when he returned and Cathlin knew not to ask. It seemed that the tension had just begun to leave his eyes, and he started to laugh again, when the call would come dragging him off. "He worked for the government and was away a great deal of the time." Her voice hardened. "No son of mine will ever have that kind of life," she said flatly. "It destroys too many lives. That's assuming I ever have a son, of course."

Their eyes met. Heat flared. Cathlin cleared her throat and took a bite of the salmon she'd been pushing around her plate.

"What if your son *wants* a job of that sort? Wouldn't the choice be up to him? Just hypothetically, of course."

"No." Cathlin toyed with the last piece of banana. "Not if I could help it. I've seen too closely the kind of pain it brings."

"I see."

"Do you? I had a father I never knew. And when I finally had the chance, when we both needed each other most, they still wouldn't let him go. They called him out again, always just one more time. Only one time he didn't come back." Her voice wavered, then grew strong once more. "Sorry. Maybe we should talk about something else."

A muscle flashed at Dominic's jaw. "Maybe we should. Tell me what you found today?"

"The short version? Nothing. The long version? Dust and dirt and then a whole lot of nothing." She sighed and ran her hand through her hair. "I've searched everything but one small closet of my father's and found nothing. If there are any records in this house, then they must have been hidden by an expert."

Dominic frowned. "I'll call someone in London to look into the official records. Marriage licenses, wills, property transfers, that sort of thing."

"Isn't that rather a long shot?"

"Do you have any better ideas?"

Cathlin gnawed at her lip. "If your Mad Uncle Gabriel and Geneva Russell were truly close, maybe we should spend more time looking into his life. Maybe you can trace his friends and acquaintances from their letters or one of the family diaries."

"You're right, of course. I have an aunt who has whole trunks full of that kind of thing. I'll have to put her on it." He smiled wryly. "Of course, Great-Aunt Agatha would love nothing better. You're brilliant, O'Neill."

Laughing softly, he bent forward to brush a strand of hair from her cheek. Cathlin stopped, fork midair, her eyes very wide and very dazed.

And Dominic knew why. Years of experience had taught him to recognize that the arrested look he saw there, the look that shocked her just as much as it did him, was pulse-slamming desire.

He pulled away as if burned. When had a simple touch become such a complicated prelude to utter disaster? "I'm sorry."

"Don't be." Cathlin looked down. "It's not your fault that I'm acting like a fool. It's just that I don't usually—what I mean is, it's been a long time since—" Muttering, she tossed down her napkin and stood up quickly. Her hands tightened on the carved back of the pine chair.

Dominic was around the table in a second. "Sit down, damn it. This is enough to drive any sane person crazy. I wouldn't be surprised if Mad Uncle Gabriel arranged all of this just to poke his nose at his family when they finally thought they were rid of him. In fact, maybe he and Geneva ran away and eloped, then died in blissful obscurity in some little hamlet in the Cotswolds."

Cathlin gave him a pained look.

"No? Then perhaps they just fell out of love. People do, you know. Perhaps your Geneva married another man and had ten children and lived happily ever after. Gabriel might have continued his reckless, dissolute life, only to discover that he had no one else he cared for enough to leave his wine to."

"But what *was* his end?"

Dominic frowned and rubbed his temple, which was aching slightly. "I haven't a bloody clue. But I'll tell you one thing. Something happened to you when you put on that gown. And something happened to me when I saw you in it. We've got to find out what, and the only place left to try is Draycott."

Cathlin stiffened. "I'm not sure I want to think about this. I came down here to rest and deal with Seacliffe, not with Draycott Abbey."

"Maybe you've got no choice," Dominic said grimly.

There was a hiss and pop as the electricity returned. The refrigerator gurgled and then whined back into activity.

A moment later the phone near the door began an incessant peal.

"Let it ring, Cathlin. We have to talk."

But Cathlin pushed away. "It might be Serita. I have to take it."

Dominic glared at her as she lifted the phone. After a moment she smiled sweetly. "Richard? How nice to hear from you. Oh, nothing major. A storm knocked out the power here. No, everything's fine."

Dominic's hands tightened.

"No, it wouldn't be a bother. I have the cases here anyway. Three o'clock? Fine. Of course, I remember. See you then."

She'd barely put down the phone when Dominic was beside her, his shoulders braced and determined. "You're not going."

Cathlin's brow climbed. "Oh? Since when are you telling me what to do?"

"This is important, Cathlin."

"And my business isn't?" Her foot tapped angrily against the polished wooden floor.

"Be quiet."

"Who are you to—"

"Be quiet." Dominic's fingers clamped down on her shoulder. Outside the window the lavender bushes rustled.

"Get down and stay down." Dominic moved, pinning Cathlin to the floor.

"But—"

His palm lodged over her lips. "There's someone out there."

Cathlin stiffened. She had just seen what Dominic had seen.

A man was standing outside the kitchen. He was dressed in a hunting jacket and boots and looked like the usual country gentleman out for an outing.

Then Cathlin saw the revolver in the man's fingers.

She swallowed, watching Dominic inch along the wall toward the door. He slipped out into the corridor, knees to his chest and body low to the floor.

As she watched, Cathlin went very still. Her father had taught her just such a movement a year after her mother's death. "Keep low," he'd ordered. "Focus your weight forward so you're ready to run if necessary. Try to make the smallest target in case of an attack."

Oh, yes, Cathlin remembered. Now she watched the man she'd rescued from the marsh moving exactly the same way, a professional in every sense of the word.

The realization left her cold.

Dominic Montserrat was one of *them*, the men who had stolen her father from her and held him captive in their nasty shadow world.

And that meant she couldn't trust a single damned thing he'd told her.

LATER DOMINIC WOULD WONDER about the raw instinct that made him turn and shove Cathlin to the floor.

Even after three years in France, some deep part of him had registered the cues and responded instantly. He didn't even like to think about that fact. But now, with adrenaline racing through his veins and anger tightening his throat, he didn't think, he only *moved*.

When the man outside the window disappeared, Dominic waited for instinct to kick in. Almost immediately it did.

Around to the back.

He headed for the front, meaning to circle back through the dense woods bordering Seacliffe. In the process he'd also have to verify if the intruder was armed, if he had backup, and what kind of transport he had hidden.

Dominic went very still as all the old reflexes went into play. His fingers dug into a polished chair leg as one part of him watched and analyzed, calling on the long years of grim experience that had kept him alive in too many back streets and parade grounds and government cavalcades.

The other part, the saner part that had struggled to be free of that dangerous life, stood away, sickened by what he'd become.

His superiors in Whitehall would have been delighted at how easily he slid back into the old patterns. It seemed that the years in France had made no difference. Maybe his retirement had come too late, or maybe the pattern was part of his nature. He didn't have the answers to explain it, and God knows he'd spent three years trying.

The truth was that he would never be free of this world. He'd been in too deep for too long.

Silently, Dominic eased the front door open, his fingers itching for a gun he didn't have and a holster he couldn't even remember. Following the dictates of dark memories, he worked his way outside and then sprinted soundlessly toward the woods.

Knowing already that some part of him had gone dead inside.

TEN MINUTES LATER, hidden within a tangle of hew trees, Dominic stared down at the set of fresh prints left in the soft earth. Whoever had been outside the kitchen window was gone. But it had been a professional, that Dominic knew. The man had been dressed casually, like a tourist who'd lost his way upon the marsh and stopped to ask directions.

Except for the Smith & Wesson in his right hand. Something chambered for .357 cartridges, which stayed accurate even at long distances.

Dominic's jaw hardened as he felt the old adrenaline high begin again. He'd been slow in the kitchen. He'd lost more precious time at the door, thinking about a past he had tried hard to bury.

And because of it the man had gotten away.

Nicholas had been only too right. The news of the wine discovery had gotten out, possibly from someone who'd been watching him when he'd fallen by the bridge and gone through his pockets to find Nicholas's letter explaining the discovery of the wine and the terms of the will. Now Cathlin would be in danger every second of every day.

And it would be his job to keep her safe, whether she liked it or not.

HE WALKED IN, TIRED, disappointed, and very angry. If he thought he was going to be thanked for his interference, he soon realized he was wrong.

"You lied to me." Cathlin's hands were stiff at her sides and her face was white. "You lied to me all along. You're one of *them,* aren't you? One of the men from my father's world."

"Cathlin, listen."

"No, I don't want to listen! I saw how you went after him, your whole body a weapon, your mind cold and hard as a computer. You have all the same moves that Donnell had. All along, you sat there and listened, nodding. Lying. How much more is lies, Dominic? *How much?*"

"None. I meant to tell you, Cathlin. Then you mentioned about your father and I decided you weren't ready to hear the truth."

"Ready? Who are *you* to make that kind of decision?"

"It was necessary, Cathlin."

"You bet it was. You had to lie to me, to manipulate and steer me just where you wanted." Her fingers locked. It had all been a lie, the story of his mother and his playboy life. Yet he'd made it all seem so believable, shredding her careful defenses. "When were you going to tell me, Dominic? Or maybe I should say *Officer* Montserrat."

"Officer will be fine," Dominic said grimly. "Because from now on I'll be giving the orders. We each stand to gain at least half a million pounds when the terms of that legacy are fulfilled, Cathlin. I was carrying a letter of explanation from Nicholas Draycott and I'm afraid it's been stolen. That means that the news of the will has gotten out, and the danger is now very real."

She laughed tightly. "Because of one case of old wine?"

"How many men do you know who would kill for a 1792 Château d'Yquem?"

Cathlin did a rough estimate and felt a sickening jolt in her stomach. Wine collectors were a fanatic lot. It was part of the reason Cathlin liked them. Yes, she could think of quite a few who would go to any lengths to possess such a treasure. "So I might be in danger. Do you want me to apologize? Very well, I'm sorry, Officer Montserrat. I only fell for part of your lies, not the whole lot."

"Cathlin, listen. I made a decision. It might have been the wrong one, but I never meant it to hurt you."

"Tell that to my father." She spun around, tears glinting on her cheeks. "No and no and no! I hated that world then and I hate it now. I don't want anything to do with it."

Dominic looked at her hands, locked on her soft floral blouse. At her eyes, blazing and gold and haunted.

"I don't need you here and I don't need that wine, not if it involves going back to Draycott. So just stay out of my way and let me do my work."

"I can't," Dominic growled, his eyes on the satin skin exposed at the neck of her flowing blouse. "You see, you *are* my work right now. Where you go, I go. What you do, I do. And no matter what I tell you, you do it, since it could be the one thing that saves our lives until this business is finished. By God, I'm going to keep you safe, whether you like it or not."

"What gives you the right to—"

He cut her off harshly, pulling his gaze from the creamy skin that left a hot pulse pounding at his groin. "That letter from Nicholas Draycott gave me the right. Either you go with me and do things my way or you don't go at all. And then we're both out half a million pounds." He shoved to his feet, muscles tense. "So what's your answer?"

"What choice do I have?"

"None at all," came the flat answer.

"I don't like you, Officer Montserrat. I'm inclined to say that I hate you right at this moment. Which doesn't make much of a basis for a week's stay anywhere in close quarters." In her anger, Cathlin sat forward, shoulders stiff. Her blouse moved, revealing a satin curve of skin and the shadow of one perfect, dusky nipple.

A muscle flashed at Dominic's jaw. "I'll survive, O'Neill. But maybe you'd better remember that I've got perfect eyesight."

Cathlin looked down, saw the gaping fabric, and sat back abruptly, hot color in her cheeks.

"Don't let it worry you," Dominic said coldly. "I've guarded more women than I can count, and none of them has ever gotten through to me. The sex can be great when you're in that kind of life, don't get me wrong. The danger and adrenaline push everything to the edge and make even a kiss explosive. But when I'm in bed with a woman I want to know it's not just adrenaline that's making the high between us. So you can relax, O'Neill. You might as well be dressed in a habit and a crucifix, because from now on it's business, just cold-blooded business between us."

"Oh? And what's the good news?"

"That *is* the good news."

Again the swift flare of color, this time sweeping down to Cathlin's chest. "I'm delighted to hear it, Officer Montserrat. Now maybe you'll get the bloody hell out of my kitchen."

"One more thing. You're not going to see Severance. Not alone, anyway. Not after what just happened."

"Any other orders?"

"If there are, I'll tell you, O'Neill. And you'll obey them." His voice was cold. One hundred percent professional. "Because that's the only way we're going to get out of this whole bloody mess."

Cathlin watched him stride from the room. "Like hell I will."

DOWN THE HILL, HIDDEN beyond the ragged line of trees at the edge of the marsh, a man eased back into the shadows. Carefully he flipped out a transmitter. Then he began to speak softly.

CHAPTER ELEVEN

DOMINIC SAT DOWN ON THE old rosewood desk and frowned at the sunny study filled with pictures. Pictures of Donnell O'Neill, looking happy but as if he were thinking of something else. Pictures of a beautiful woman with golden eyes. Cathlin's mother, no doubt.

And then there were the pictures of Cathlin, riding her first pony, climbing her first tree, going to her first tea dance in high-heeled satin pumps.

Something twisted in his gut.

Muttering darkly, he picked up the phone and jabbed out a number. "Nicholas?"

"Right here. Any luck with Cathlin?"

"I'm working on it. Things have been a little chaotic here, I'm afraid."

"The same on this end," his friend said grimly. "We've had a call from my solicitor in London. Someone has been asking about the reports we had to file locally after the discovery of Gabriel's remains. We've asked the people here to keep it quiet as best they can, but I'm afraid someone's gotten wind of the story. It was only a matter of time, I guess."

"I'm not surprised to hear it. We had a visitor today, too. An unexpected visitor," Dominic said flatly. "And that letter you wrote to Cathlin has disappeared. How long do we have until the newspapers get hold of this, Nicholas?"

"Who knows? I'll do what I can. I still have a few friends on

Fleet Street I can trust. But I think you'd better get Cathlin down here now, so you start fulfilling that week of residence. Meanwhile, Kacey and I have begun looking into the documents here, trying to track down anything about the elusive Gabriel Montserrat. So far, no luck, however."

"Ditto here. The whole thing's damned strange. Cathlin's attitude isn't going to help either."

"Attitude?"

"She hates anything to do with the work that killed her father. And unfortunately, that means me."

"You'll bring her around," Nicholas said confidently. "You always do."

Maybe not this time, Dominic thought. And maybe this was the only time that really counted.

"Dominic, are you still there?"

"Right here, Nicholas. By the way, there's nothing you aren't telling me, is there? No other crazy stipulations that Gabriel put on this bequest."

There was a tiny pause. "What makes you ask that?"

"You haven't answered me, Nicholas."

His friend cleared his throat. "Look, I've got to go. Kacey's just come in with Genevieve. I'll talk to you when you get here, Dominic. And make it soon."

SHE'D BLOODY SHOW DOMINIC Montserrat, Cathlin thought.

She would be pampered, perfect, and beautiful when she left this room. And just let him *try* to stop her from conducting her business. Serita had friends, after all, friends in the very highest places. They would dispose of a nasty little insect named Dominic Montserrat in a second.

Frowning, Cathlin dumped a packet of expensive French bath powder into the big old tub and turned the faucets on high, letting the fragrance rise in rich clouds around her.

Angrily, she settled into a froth of bubbles and forced her mind to business, something she'd woefully forgotten in the last twenty-four hours since Dominic had come charging into her well-ordered life. Cathlin sat back and began a mental tally of her current inventory against the desires—and ruthless dictates—of her well-heeled clients.

No Sauternes for Alexandra, the banker's wife. Her third husband had recently absconded to parts unknown, taking the family diamonds along with him. And since *he* had adored Sauternes, now *she* couldn't abide the sight of them.

Next was her German diplomat. No more vintage champagne there. Poor Herr Schmidt had recently been involved in a scandal with a hot-blooded but underaged heir to a French champagne dynasty. As a result, he'd had to pay a cool two million to buy his way out of the nasty legal proceedings the family threatened him with. Yes, only fine robust burgundies for Herr Schmidt from now on. Cathlin decided that an elegant Clos St. Denis 1969, silky and rich with fruit, would make a perfect offering for the fastidious Herr Schmidt.

That left only the Château Lafite. A very upscale restauranteur in Brighton had been pestering her for a new shipment of first growth burgundy. After lunch she'd place a call and see if Marcel still wanted—

Abruptly, all thought stopped as Cathlin watched the bathroom door inch open. Maybe it was the intruder. Or maybe it was—

Dominic eased into the room, silent and cool. Only his glittering eyes showed his fury. "Just what the hell do you think you're doing?"

Cathlin made a lunge for a towel, missed, then sank low into the now-churning water. "It's bloody obvious, I should think. Get out!"

A muscle flashed at his jaw. "I didn't know where you were. I called a dozen times, but you didn't answer."

"Next time I'll post a schedule." Cathlin slid lower, bubbles frothing around her. "I'm fine, as you can see. So now you can get out."

But Dominic merely angled one broad shoulder against the doorframe. He was naked from the waist up, his bronze chest dusted with dark hair. Cathlin felt her cheeks flame as he studied her from the end of her toes emerging from a froth of bubbles to the damp black hair curling at her neck. "I got worried when you didn't answer. Didn't you hear me calling?"

"No. Now are you satisfied?" Foam sloshed across Cathlin's shoulder, skimming the curve of one breast.

"Not in the least."

Cathlin felt her face burn.

Dominic said a raw word and grabbed the towel hanging over the edge of the door. "Get dressed, damn it. I need your help. I've found something up in the attic."

"What?"

"You'll see." The towel flew toward her and landed in the scented foam with a soft hiss.

Cathlin lurched up, bubbles sculpting her breasts and thighs as she dived to rescue the now sodden towel.

Dominic's gaze followed her every inch of the way.

"Get *out!*" Cathlin stormed, her cheeks crimson, the wet towel clamped protectively to her chest and thighs. "Unless you want a broken neck to go along with those bruises on your head!"

"It might just be worth it," he said softly. His eyes flowed over the towel. Her every wet curve lay molded in its damp, seductive drape. Then his gaze moved lower, to the creamy legs that ran up to—

Dominic bit back a curse and turned away. "Hurry up. Unless you want me to come in after you and bleed on all those nice bubbles."

Somewhere down the hall the phone began an incessant clamor.

"Damned bloody phone." Jamming his hands into his pockets,

Dominic strode off, muttering a stream of curses that left Cathlin red-faced. But worst of all was the way her heart was slamming as she clutched the damp, entirely useless towel to her chest.

Because even though she wanted to hate him, even though she was struggling desperately hard, she still wasn't able to manage it.

DOMINIC SLAMMED DOWN THE phone. Wrong bloody number. It didn't help that his head was pounding and his shoulder ached from crawling around that bloody attic searching for her cameo.

Then, when Cathlin hadn't answered—

He frowned, not wanting to remember the fear that had kicked in at her silence. He'd plunged up the stairs, head down and shoulders low, in a textbook stance as he braced for a concealed attacker. Even now, his nerves were screaming, and he was riding a wave of adrenaline. He'd crouched just outside her door, then reached for his shoulder, just at the spot where a revolver would have been holstered.

Only there was no gun. Dominic had sworn there'd never be a gun there again.

But here he was, making all the old moves. And there had been no one better at those moves than Dominic Montserrat.

Right up to that day in Rome when four kidnappers had moved in on the car where Dominic was escorting the twin children of one of the queen's lesser-known cousins to a horse show. Dominic had shoved the towheaded eight-year-olds behind him and dropped to one knee, then squeezed off six quick shots.

It had all happened before he'd known it.

When he'd turned the bodies over, he'd discovered that three of the men were still in their teens. And the fourth "man" was really a girl of barely sixteen.

He'd gotten through the rest of the tour, then gone back home and fallen apart. He'd gotten stinking drunk and stayed that way for nearly a week.

After that he'd turned in his resignation. And he'd never worn a gun again, nor wanted to.

Until now.

He jabbed shaky fingers through his hair, sick at the old memories. Outside the window, wind shook the trees that bordered the tidal plain. Seacliffe was a desolate place, but it had its own kind of beauty. It was a place where a man could find himself. A place whose solitude forced a man to face his private demons.

The only question was if the man *liked* what he saw.

Dominic was wondering how he'd gotten pulled into this mess when he caught the faint scent of flowers behind him. Something subtle. Lilacs, he decided.

And then she was behind him, fast and utterly furious. "Let's get one thing straight right now, Macho Man." Cathlin poked his chest and the cold, wet towel, newly rescued from her bubble bath, slapped him in the face.

"Nice aim, Irish. Almost as nice as those long legs of yours. But come to think of it, I prefer the sight of your high, full—"

"I don't care what you like!"

His hands rose in surrender. "I'm all ears. Well maybe not all ears. I'm a flesh and blood male, after all. There are some parts that are—"

"Shut up!"

Dominic complied, crossing his arms and watching more of that damnably enchanting color sweep Cathlin's cheeks. It left him thinking about what it would take to make her blush like that again.

In soft, hidden places.

Places he'd graze and stroke until—

Forget it, Montserrat. It's all business now, remember? "Whatever you say, Cathlin. I put myself entirely into your hands."

Again the color, rising through her cheeks. "If you did that, you'd be sorry, because right now I'd consider it a great pleasure to snap several bones into neat little pieces. And *that's* just for starters."

His eyebrow rose. "Sounds painful."

"Blast it, you—"

His eyes slid over her robed body. "Hadn't you better get ready? You're seeing your debonair friend in an hour."

Cathlin tossed the wet towel right in his face. "You're right, I am. And I'm going alone. And that's one order you're *not* going to worm your way around, *Officer* Montserrat."

WHEN CATHLIN WALKED OUT the front door, she was tugging on a jacket of Harris tweed. Dominic noticed how the smoky golden plaid brought out the turbulence in her eyes. He also noticed the pallor in her face and the set to her jaw. Attitude.

"Let's go," he said curtly.

"This is business. You're *not* coming."

"From now on, where you go, I go, O'Neill."

"What gives you the right to interfere?"

"Interfering is my job," Dominic growled. It was only too true. Interfering was the heart of close protection, because protecting someone meant being unpleasant. It meant pointing out problems. It meant being nosy and curious and meddlesome while you were busy suspecting anyone and everyone.

And Dominic had been damned good at that part of his job. Before it had nearly eaten a hole through his soul, that is.

"Your job? You mean along with repairing roofs?"

"Taking care of a woman has always been a man's job."

She pushed past him. "Maybe this woman doesn't need protecting."

"Too bloody bad." Dominic strode after her. "You're forgetting something else, Irish. Half of that money is mine, and I need *you* to get it."

Cathlin swept her hair from her face and called back over her shoulder. "I'm loading Richard's wine. If you're not in the car when I get back, I leave without you."

Dominic watched her stride off toward the Jeep. Until he had something more concrete, he was going to keep Cathlin O'Neill close. It was only logical, given the amount of money involved in Gabriel Ashton's will.

Good try, Dominic thought. *But we both know that it's already gone a whole lot further than the money.*

CATHLIN HAD JUST SHOVED the last case of wine into the back of her Jeep when Dominic strode down the drive. His long legs ate up the distance, and his casual elegance in an old leather jacket gave him the look of a movie star traveling light. Mirrored aviator sunglasses gleamed silver beneath his wild, dark hair.

Cathlin barely allowed him time to sit down before slamming the car into gear and roaring down the drive.

"Tell me about Severance."

"There's nothing to tell. He tried something once, but I wasn't interested. Now it's strictly business."

"Let's hope *he* knows that."

"Oh, he does. We have an understanding, Richard and I. I understand that he's an irresponsible, arrogant jerk, but I need his business. He understands that if he tries anything out of line, he's going to lose a few teeth."

Dominic laughed. "Very well, enough about Severance. Tell me about this wine you're taking to him. No doubt it's going to cost him a lot."

"A shocking amount." Cathlin smiled faintly. "The case comes from Bordeaux."

"I believe I've heard of it," Dominic said dryly. "I've also heard that half the Bordeaux vintages are worth little more than the bottles they're housed in." It wasn't quite true, but Dominic wanted to hear her talk, even if it was only to refute him.

"Sometimes they're overvalued. In 1972 an exceptionally poor vintage was foisted on the world at record prices. Buying a name-brand château that year was a major mistake. It's a question of land and continuity, you see."

Dominic sat back and listened to Cathlin slide into her subject. She thought she was being boring and obnoxious, but Dominic was intrigued by her passionate knowledge of all things related to wine.

"The old houses, or châteaux, usually have the best soil and ideal growing conditions. Because of that, over a long period of time their wines will be consistently better than any others."

The lady was good, all right. It seemed that anything she didn't know wasn't worth knowing. But her concern spread beyond crop yields and pesticides and harvesting schedules. Clearly Cathlin O'Neill had a heart for wine and a love for the land. Both came through even in this bland description of vintage controversies and vineyard soil conditions.

Dominic sat back and let her deluge him with facts and figures. As she described the fields of Bordeaux, he pictured green vines climbing over a rolling hillside. He saw the low mists that clung to the valleys, shielding the grapes until they reached perfect maturity.

Yes, Cathlin O'Neill was damned good. And she was good because it came from her heart, not her head, which was where too many well-heeled vintners and arrogant wine connoisseurs failed. Dominic had learned all this from his French mother.

Danielle Montserrat had taught him that a very fine wine should not be coddled, worshiped, or bartered as a simple commodity. Wine, she had always insisted, should be treated like a fine old friend. It should be savored and appreciated, enjoyed in the heat of a fine summer afternoon and in the last cool slide of velvet evening.

Dominic had always made that his credo at La Trouvaille. He wanted to create wines that were rich but subtle, with a power and elegance that lingered. And apparently he'd succeeded. Cathlin herself had pronounced La Trouvaille a success. He didn't suppose it was because of trends either. Cathlin O'Neill would never be a slave to fads. She would judge a Château Lafite with the same honesty that she accorded the most anonymous French *vin de pays*.

And a part of Dominic Monsterrat honored her for her cussed independence. That kind of stubbornness had no doubt created any number of problems for her, given the conservatism of the wine world. But she'd survived.

Dominic knew he could learn a great deal from that kind of tenacity.

As they drove on through bars of golden sunlight and a haze of bright spring wildflowers, Dominic found himself wishing he didn't know her name or her past or anything about her. Then he could simply pull her into his arms and kiss her the way his hardening body urged him to do.

But that was impossible.

She was business and nothing else, right up until the will was honored. Somehow he was going to have to remember that.

An hour later they turned up an oak-fringed drive that overlooked the sea. A pink granite palace squatted at the top of the hill, its banks of modern windows ablaze in the setting sun. The beautifully manicured lawns were marred by two tennis courts and a garish black flagstone swimming pool.

Money, Dominic thought. Lots of it. Money that was screaming to be seen. "Remind me not to look up *this* guy's decorator."

Dominic saw Cathlin frown and run her hand absently over her neck, as if it ached.

A uniformed guard met them just beside the gatehouse. Obviously, Mr. Millionaire didn't like to have his privacy threatened.

"Name?" the guard said, trying to eye Cathlin's legs.

Dominic had to restrain the urge to give him a savage right uppercut.

"Cathlin O'Neill to see Mr. Severance."

"I'll have to phone up to the house." The man frowned, scanning Dominic. "Who's he?"

"My assistant," Cathlin said silkily. "He'll help me with the wine cases."

The guard shrugged, then turned away to his radio. A moment later he gestured over the trees. "Drive to the top of the hill. Park at the servants' entrance," he added maliciously.

As the ornate wrought-iron gates slid open, Cathlin pulled in and started up the drive. "You stay in the Jeep. You'd never pass for a workman, not in that jacket and those glasses. Definitely not with that attitude."

"What's wrong with my attitude?"

"You're too arrogant."

Dominic shrugged. "We bodyguards have an image to keep up after all." Cathlin pulled into the parking area, but made no move to get out. "We're here, O'Neill. Or hadn't you noticed?"

"I noticed."

"Then you'd better get going. Mr. Lifestyles of the Rich and Famous isn't going to like that pricey Bordeaux throwing phosphates from the heat."

Cathlin muttered and reached for the door.

"Damn it, O'Neill." Cursing softly, Dominic caught her cheeks in his hands and pulled her against him.

God, but she fit his arms perfectly. And her scent...

Slowly, he ran his hand through her silky cap of black hair. It danced against his fingers, warm and electric. Then he reached beneath and slid something around her neck.

Cathlin didn't speak. She seemed to be struggling with a wave of conflicting emotions. Hell, Dominic knew that *he* was.

"I found your cameo. I thought you should wear it, as a reminder of that old house you love—and of the way you can save it." It was playing dirty, but Dominic didn't care. He was going to get through to her any way he could.

"Dominic, I don't—"

He didn't give her time to be angry. He just pulled her head back and then crushed his mouth over hers in one hard motion.

This had to be what summer tasted like, he thought dimly. Hot and endlessly sweet. His fingers tightened. He wanted and wanted and wanted.

But Dominic knew he couldn't have what he wanted. This was as far as it was going to go. When he pulled away, her face was flushed and her hands were fists.

"What was *that* for?"

It took Dominic a few heartbeats to recover enough control to answer. "It's for the man who's staring at us through those windows. I want him to know exactly what we were doing out here."

CHAPTER TWELVE

CATHLIN TRIED TO FORCE her heart back between her ribs.

Who was she kidding? She wasn't even *close* to normalcy. Her mouth was still tingling from the burn of Dominic's lips, and the cameo hung cold and heavy at her neck.

Cathlin shoved open the door of the Jeep and tugged her satchel over her arm. Once again the man had outflanked her and left her speechless.

Forget him, O'Neill. You've got work to do.

She tugged her satchel higher and ran a hand over her hair, but she needn't have bothered. She did not look like the cool professional as she hoped, nor the level-headed wine expert.

At that moment Cathlin O'Neill looked like a dewy-eyed beauty, like a woman lost in love after being kissed by the man she adored. The fragile cameo at her neck above her soft blouse subtly complemented that image.

Dominic had planned it that way, of course.

RICHARD SEVERANCE WAS A picture of casual elegance in raw silk trousers and an Armani jacket carefully selected to exaggerate the width of his unimpressive shoulders. He received Cathlin warmly, all smiles and curiosity to see this case of Bordeaux she wanted to sell him. But as Cathlin cradled the sample bottle, Severance's hard eyes settled on the smooth curves beneath her blouse. From there, they ran to the long, slim thighs and rounded calves beneath her blue jeans.

His lips curved in a smile.

His cordiality lasted ten minutes. By the time Cathlin began tendering bills of sale and import documents, the London merchant banker and socialite prince had waited long enough. He cornered her by the Louis XIV writing desk as she was working a cork out of her first sample bottle.

"I thought you'd like a taste before you made your decision."

"How true. I always sample anything I consider buying." His eyes narrowed as he moved toward her. "You really do have the most beautiful mouth, Cathlin. I wonder if it tastes the same as last time." He caught her waist and pulled her into his arms.

"This is not amusing, Richard!"

"Simply part of the sampling." His tongue thrust between her lips. His hand flattened over her breast.

Cathlin shoved at his hands. "Stop this, Richard. I told you last time, it was strictly business and you agreed."

"I'm afraid I lied," Severance said coolly. "Dear, sweet Cathlin, why else would you have come back? I knew that little scene last time was just to get me crazy. And it worked, love. I haven't been able to get you out of my mind."

"I came for the wine, Richard. Nothing else."

"For Christ's sake, I saw how you came on to your young stud out there in the car. You two looked like you were going to make it in the front seat. So don't tell me you're not interested."

"What you saw was—a mistake."

"Good. I'll please you more than he did. Besides, it always pays to keep your clients happy."

Cathlin's face paled. So it had all been a game. She was part of the package—otherwise, no deal. "I don't have time for these antics."

"Of course you do, Cathlin. You know you want it. Judging by the way you kissed your friend in the car, you were primed, loaded, and ready to fire." His fingers pushed under her blouse, working at the delicate layers of lace beneath.

Cathlin felt a memory stir deep in her mind, an image of hard hands shoving her into a dark room. She closed her eyes, fighting to stay calm, fighting to remember. But there was nothing more.

She shook her head as Severance pulled her closer. "Let me go, Richard."

"Damn it, Cathlin, I haven't been able to think straight since I met you. It's long past time that we—"

Cathlin sent her fist into his stomach. Severance bent over, gasping in pain. "You'll be sorry for that. I've got friends, damn it."

Suddenly Dominic charged through the doorway. "Cathlin, are you—" He stopped when he saw Severance doubled over, his suit awry.

Cathlin put a restraining hand on his arm. "Go away, Dominic. Things are fine here."

"Fine? Your blouse is up to your chin and your cheeks are bright red and you say you're *fine?* What in the hell was he doing?"

"Nothing that matters. Now if you will please leave, I'd like to finish here."

"Finish what?" Dominic glared at Severance. "The man was muscling you over. He wasn't interested in any bloody wine."

"I know that," Cathlin said calmly.

Dominic crossed his arms at his chest. "Go ahead and finish. I'm not leaving without you."

"This is my fight, Dominic."

"Not anymore, it isn't. The second that bastard laid a finger on you all bets were off."

Severance tugged his coat straight and scowled at Cathlin. "Get this person out of here so we can talk, Cathlin. Otherwise I—"

"Otherwise what, Richard? You'll warn off all your friends? Serita and I will survive, I assure you." Smiling grimly, Cathlin ripped her bill of sale into tiny pieces and tossed them over Severance's head. Then she very carefully overturned the vintage Bordeaux across Severance's beautiful carpet. "There's your wine sample, Richard. It was an excellent year, by the way, fruity and quite intense. I hope you enjoy it, because that's the last one you'll be getting from us."

"You bloody little—"

Severance never finished. Dominic's hand smashed into his jaw, and sent him staggering backward onto the floor.

CATHLIN SLID BEHIND THE wheel, her hands trembling. "I told you not to interfere."

"Too bad," Dominic said tightly.

"I don't want anything from Richard Severance. Nor do I want anything from *you*. I can manage by myself."

"Sure you can." Dominic's fingers tightened on her door. He took in her stiff shoulders and pale face. She was prickly and stubborn and grade-A impossible.

And he still wanted to pull her against his chest and kiss her breathless.

No mistake about it, Montserrat, he thought grimly. *You've really blown it this time.* So much for all that impartial body-guard routine.

He glared down at Cathlin, angry at the desire still battering his body. "Slide over," he ordered. "I'm driving."

Cathlin's hands tightened. "I told you, I'm fine."

"Like hell you are."

Cathlin couldn't ignore him, no matter how hard she tried. His eyes were smoky and his body was rigid. He looked angry and frustrated and determined to protect her—even from herself. And his strength was seductive, tempting her to give in, tempting her to let him take charge and smooth her way, like the professional he was.

Only Cathlin knew one other thing. This was all just temporary. She'd let down her defenses and learn to rely on him, and then one day she'd wake up and find him gone, off to Tashkent or Bogotà or Timbuktu, just like her father had gone.

And she'd be the one left behind, drying her tears and fighting her pain, trying to pick up the thousand shattered pieces of her life.

No. Not ever again. "Forget it, Macho Man. I'm just fine."

"Fine? Your hands are shaking and you can barely see straight, O'Neill. I don't intend to die from your reckless driving. Now move over."

Cathlin thought about arguing with him, but the cold light of reason told her he was right. Her hands were shaking so hard that she'd probably have them wrapped around a tree inside of two minutes.

So she'd do it. Just this once. But she didn't have to like it.

Scowling, she slid into the passenger seat, trying not to notice how his shoulders filled the seat, how his strong fingers worked themselves around the steering wheel.

Blasted, competent male. "You didn't need to come barging in. I was managing just fine. And I certainly didn't need you decking one of my best clients."

"One of your ex-best clients. If that snake gets near you again, he'll spend some serious, quality time getting to know the traction equipment in an intensive care ward."

"Stay out of my life, Montserrat. If I do decide to go to Draycott and listen to Nicholas Draycott's explanation, you'll be the first to know. But that's all you're entitled to, understand? Everything else is mine, my business, my house, my life. I can take care of myself. I've had a lot of practice, you see, and I don't need any lessons now." Now that the adrenaline rush was fading, Cathlin felt a wave of numbness begin to climb up her legs. Seconds later a tear inched down her cheek, but she shoved it away.

"Damn it, Cathlin." Cursing, Dominic pulled the car onto the shoulder and pulled Cathlin against his chest. One tear worked into two and then more, but she made no sound. He held her anyway, feeling the heat of her tears on his shirt, feeling her soft breasts wedged against his chest, feeling her stiffness and her fury. He fought back the intense desire he felt and only held her, one hand buried beneath the warm shadow of her hair. When she finally pulled away he found a tissue and held it out to her.

She gave a defiant sniff and blew her nose. "Drive. I'll be fine."

When Dominic saw there would be no more tears and certainly no explanations, he shoved the Jeep into gear and roared away from Richard Severance's monstrous palace.

As he did, he caught the faint scent of lilacs.

Another trick of his imagination? There was a logical explanation, of course, but right then it was beyond him. All he could think of was Cathlin. The way she'd forced her chin up. The way she'd tossed the contents of that bottle over Severance's carpet. The way she left him hungry and hard and crazy to kiss her.

But in doing that, he violated the first and oldest rule of his profession: Never, ever let it get personal.

He moved away from her and closed his hands around the wheel. To his fury he saw they were trembling slightly.

THEY DIDN'T TALK. BOTH OF them knew they had too much to say and too little hope of ever saying it.

After fifteen minutes, Cathlin insisted on taking the wheel and Dominic finally agreed.

She drove the Jeep along the narrow roads by instinct rather than sight. She drove too fast and she knew it, but the shadows moving down into the valleys left her with a sudden uneasiness and an urgency to be back at Seacliffe—and away from the man beside her. The man Cathlin couldn't seem to stop thinking about.

As they rounded a bend, two sheep lumbered out of the gathering shadows and Cathlin jerked the wheel to avoid them.

"Slow down," Dominic said harshly.

"Go to hell," she snapped back.

His hands clenched. "Are you trying to kill yourself?"

"I'm simply trying to get home. And to get as far away from you as possible."

Dominic's eyes went hard. "Cathlin, don't. Not like this." He caught her shoulder.

She shook his hand away, frightened by the hundred wild emotions even that single touch conveyed.

It had all happened, just as she feared. He had gotten too close, and he was making her remember, making her feel things she didn't want to feel. Not ever.

And somewhere deep inside her, Cathlin O'Neill knew that to feel again, real and deeply, she would have to brave the dark gates of her childhood memories. She could feel them there sometimes in her dreams, but nothing ever remained the next morning when she awoke. It was safer that way, she told herself firmly.

So she would keep things just as they were. No strings, no emotions, no attachments. And needing Dominic Montserrat was just not going to happen.

She scowled into the rearview mirror and saw two headlights loom up out of the twilight. She eased to the left of the narrow lane, hoping whoever it was would slow down, in case there were any more sheep wandering past. The ditch at the edge of the road was bordered by a high stone wall which left little room to maneuver. No matter that she was born and raised in England, she'd learned to drive in Philadelphia, and being on the left still made her uncomfortable.

Behind her the lights kept coming, and they were coming faster. Cathlin frowned.

"I see it, O'Neill. Ease into second and get ready to turn."

Cathlin swallowed, hearing the iron in Dominic's voice. This couldn't be happening. He was overreacting again, just trying to frighten her, hoping to find a reason to interfere in her life. "You're joking, right?"

"Eighty percent of all professional kidnappings take place from cars, O'Neill. This is no bloody joke."

Cathlin heard the roar of a motor and knew that slowing down was the last thing on the mind of the driver behind them. "What if there's no place to turn?" she said hoarsely.

"There will be. Just hold it steady. If we have to ram them, we will."

"*Ram* them?"

"I added some reinforcement to your front and rear bumpers, just in case. It will hold, don't worry."

Ram them. Cathlin swallowed. "Great."

Dominic scanned the wall to their left. "There's a sharp left up ahead, as I remember. Just after that, you'll make a quick right down a lane between two cottages."

He *remembered?* "Tell me when." Behind them the lights loomed closer. Cathlin blinked, sliding out of the line of reflection, concentrating on the road. Beside her, she heard Dominic search under the seat. "What are you doing?"

"Evening the odds."

Cathlin heard a click, but didn't dare take her eyes from the road.

"Steady, Irish. We're almost there. Just a few seconds. And—*now.*"

The same second Cathlin jerked left, he pulled a canister from the seat and leveled a high-intensity beam of light straight back into their pursuers' eyes. Desperately Cathlin braked and then skidded to the right, praying Dominic's memory was as sharp as the rest of him.

The road was there, right where he said it would be. Gritting her teeth, she floored the Jeep and shot between the darkened cottages.

"Good. Now get ready to pull over and cut your lights."

Cathlin's fingers were trembling on the wheel. Dimly she felt

Dominic's hand grip her knee for a moment. "You're doing fine, Cathlin. Remember, they need us in one piece. That's the only way they'll get that wine."

She swallowed, nodding but not feeling very much better.

"Now."

She pulled left just behind an ancient overhanging oak, braked sharply, and then cut the lights. The car settled with a hiss of gravel and the pop of cooling metal.

Darkness closed in. In the sudden silence Cathlin heard the sigh of the wind and the rush of oak leaves overhead.

But no sound of a car.

She looked questioningly at Dominic, barely able to make out his hard features in the darkness.

"Give it a few seconds. If it stays quiet, then take this road straight on into the village."

"But how—"

"It's my business to know, Cathlin."

Business. Of course it was. She looked away, her fingers clenched on the wheel. Just business. She had to remember that.

The seconds ticked past. No lights. No shouts. No noise.

"Let her rip."

The engine answered her movement, thundering back to life, but it didn't match the thunder of Cathlin's heart. Then she heard the sound of a door opening. "Dominic? What—"

"Drive straight ahead and stop just past the church. Lock your doors and wait for me there. I'll meet you in ten minutes, after I take a look around."

TEN MINUTES COULD BE A very long time.

Cathlin found it was time enough to be born and die and be born again, not a dozen but a thousand times. She learned it was ample time to taste your own fear, feel your sweat, and force yourself to desperate decisions. It was also time enough to see just how dangerously entangled her life had become with Dominic Montserrat's.

She was beyond fear, beyond feeling much at all, when the light tap finally came on the far window.

Dominic's face loomed up from the darkness and she shoved open the door.

"Drive," he said, noncommittal. Impassive.

"What happened? Were they—"

"Later."

She knew he was right, but it only made her angrier. She didn't want to drive; she didn't want to sit here in her own sweat. She certainly didn't want to be in this crazy situation.

But she started the Jeep in silence, knowing there was nothing else she could do.

He didn't talk until they were well beyond the coast road and Seacliffe loomed dark up the hill. "There was one car. You lost them in the village. They doubled back, looked around, then turned north and I lost them." He sounded angry.

"Who were they? What did they want?"

"My best guess is that someone heard about the wine and wanted to assess how well protected you are. Once the news of the discovery leaked out, and you were identified as the inheritor, it wouldn't take them long to track you down. After all, there must have been a few thousand people at that auction at the British Museum. Your picture was in several newspapers the next day. Anyone there could be behind this, and now they all know your face," he finished grimly.

"I'm not running," Cathlin said flatly. "I'm not hiding."

"You'll do whatever I tell you has to be done."

"Dream on, Ace." Cathlin swung into the graveled circle beneath Seacliffe's darkened windows and yanked open her door. "Right now I'm going up to bed. If you want to argue, fine. Stay out here and argue with the wind."

DOMINIC MADE NO MOVE TO stop her. He had enough demons of his own to fight without adding her to the list. He'd been slow and stupid and missed things no beginner should have missed.

But as he went over the night's events, frame by frame, thoroughly analyzing every detail, he couldn't get one thought out of his mind.

It had all been too bloody easy.

CHAPTER THIRTEEN

"IN THE TRUNKS? THAT'S wonderful." Dominic was on the phone with his Great-Aunt Agatha the next morning explaining what kind of documents he needed when he heard Cathlin's light step on the stairs. "Just a minute, Aggy." He covered the phone. "We're in luck. Aggy says she remembers an old packet of letters that might be from Gabriel. They're stored away in one of her trunks. She was just going to—" His voice fell as he took in Cathlin's pallor and the dark shadows under her eyes. "What's wrong?"

"I'm going back to London, Dominic." Her voice was tense and determined. "I'm done with this cloak-and-dagger business. I'll stop on the way and talk to Viscount Draycott out of respect for a woman I've never met and never heard of before, but don't expect anything more of me."

"Not alone. Remember what happened yesterday."

"Yesterday was a bad dream. Today is—reality."

"Damn it, Cathlin, listen to me."

"No, *you* listen. I don't want to hear the explanations and the excuses. No doubt they're all brilliant, but I've heard them too many times before. My father never told me exactly what he did, but I'll tell you this, he was exactly what you'll be in twenty years, Officer Montserrat. Cool and smart and fatally charming. In fact, there was only one problem with my father. He was always off on some fantastically important business on the other side of the globe and never here, where we needed him. And even when he *was* here, his mind was a thousand miles away." She looked at the walls lined with framed family photographs, her eyes resting on a picture of her father caught in a smile that didn't reach his eyes. "So I'm not interested. Not in you, not in your wine, and not in this crazy mess you've steered me into. I'll go to Draycott Abbey because I owe it to myself and to my mother. Then I'm renouncing any claim that I or my family holds over that wine. Forever."

"You can't do that. It's your past, Cathlin. It's also your future. You don't walk away from something like that."

"No? Just watch me."

From the receiver in his hand, Dominic heard his aunt's voice rise in quavering questions. "Yes, Aggy, I'm still here. Yes, that's wonderful about those letters. I know it will be a load of work and your arthritis is devilish these days, but we're really counting on you. Now I'm afraid I really must run. What? A woman?" He cleared his throat. "No, afraid not, Aggy."

By the time he put down the phone, the study was empty. So was the hall. When Dominic ran outside, he cursed darkly.

It was already too late. Cathlin's Jeep was hurtling off down the gravel drive.

CATHLIN SLAMMED THE OLD Jeep over the rutted coast road. She coaxed and nurtured her anger, even as she felt the pain choke her. Anger was the only safe thing, because she was free inside her anger as she never could be in affection.

But Cathlin found that she was draining the well dry. What she'd find beyond, where the shadows began, she didn't want to think about.

As she drove over the little stone bridge where Dominic had been wounded, she wondered just for a moment what things might have been like if they were two different people with two different pasts.

If only...

No use. No bloody use, O'Neill.

She brushed at her cheek, jabbing the gears and grinding them angrily. She knew that she was bolting, running away from fifteen years of shadows.

Seacliffe no longer held any protection for her. A jade-eyed man had brought the holes in with him, pulling up the questions and unveiling the shadows she'd managed to plug up every night with work and lists and fine, detailed dreams.

Now there were shadows everywhere. An old mystery had forced her to face a more recent one. What had really happened that day fifteen years before? Her father had never found any answers, which meant that Cathlin was the only one left who could find out the truth.

In that instant, with the ocean glinting before her and the wind rippling the canals behind her, Cathlin realized something else.

She was looking for the child, the grieving child who had lost her mother too soon and been left with a father she'd never really known. No matter the pain, Cathlin knew she had to become that child again. Without opening up to that ache, she'd never be whole again. The woman stood just beyond that door of shadows, waiting for the child to open it; only through the child could the woman come truly alive.

Her hands were trembling as she headed north, the wind whipping at her hair and cutting the salt tears into her cheeks. She listened to the thunder of the motor, the whine of the wind, the fury of her heart.

As she did, she felt the child reach around that big rusty knob and slowly, slowly push open a door that had been closed far too long.

A door of shadows that led to a bridge of dreams.

PART II

A Bridge of Dreams

CHAPTER FOURTEEN

CATHLIN DIDN'T KNOW WHAT she had expected. After fifteen years the abbey was bound to look different, and her memories had been brief.

Stone, probably. Dampness and crumbling age everywhere. A marshy pool, trees and untended grass, and the terror of irreparable loss.

But she didn't find that, not on this day in the sunlight of a spring morning.

Instead she found...

Eternity.

Seacliffe had prepared her for age and grace, but not for great gray walls, flower-hung and vast. Not for swans sliding through a shimmering moat. Not for mullioned windows twinkling in the sheer sweep of the long gallery.

Draycott Abbey, she thought wonderingly. She was fully prepared to hate this place and, looking around her, she tried very hard. But it was hard to hate something that was so beautiful.

The weathered gray walls floated above the Wealden hills like a summer dream, playing on all her senses with almost tangible fingers. She blinked, caught by the rose-rich air, mesmerized by the gentle swirl and lob of the moat.

And then Cathlin saw the small stone bridge, banks of lush white lilacs teeming over its granite foot. For an instant memory shivered through her mind—heavy, dark and formless, like thorns hidden by the petals of a rose.

Just as swiftly, the image vanished, burned away by the sunlight and the flare of the moat.

Cathlin remembered something her mother had once told her. One could live many years in a place of such age and beauty, but it would take lifetimes to understand.

Cathlin frowned. She didn't *have* lifetimes. All she was prepared to spend here was one day. She would walk and watch and listen, hoping that she found the answers she wanted. But if nothing came, she would turn her back on Draycott Abbey and never come back.

That, too, she owed to her mother.

A movement pulled her eyes to the ground. There among the blooms, drowsing against the warm gray blocks, lay a cat, great and gray, at ease, as if this bridge and all else were his realm and his alone.

Standing in the magic of a bar of sunlight with the wind soft in her hair, Cathlin could almost believe it was so.

She set her single bag on the car and sank down on the soft grass, listening to a bird sing over the ancient trees, listening to her heart.

And there she heard again the dim strains of old memories.

Here. It was all here. What Dominic had said was true, then. She would finally have her answers.

If she wanted them…

A door of shadows, she thought, looking through the vast oak door that opened into the gatehouse.

A bridge of dreams.

Did she truly want those answers?

She was tugging hard at the grass, her eyes half-blinded by the glint of the sun on the moat when she felt something warm and soft slide past her leg.

The cat ghosted next to her, amber eyes keen and clear, giving Cathlin the oddest idea that he was waiting for something. And that he might have waited here forever.

She ran a hand uncertainly over the sleek fur, smiling when the creature turned imperiously and shoved against her opened palm. "You are one real beauty, aren't you?"

A quick, sharp hiss of sound. Protest.

"Oh, I see. Handsome, I should have said."

A quick flick of the tail. The keen eyes blinked.

"I am sorry. Truly."

The creature settled back on velvet paws, one eye on the moat. Cathlin could have sworn his other eye stayed on the tiny path that ran through banks of lilacs and roses twisting down from the bridge above.

She shook her head. Coffee, that's what *she* needed. Not daydreams. Lord, anything besides these odd, fanciful sensations. The wild idea that—

"Were you looking for someone in particular?"

"Oh, heaven!" She jumped to her feet, hand to heart. "You—you frightened me!"

He was a tall man, dressed all in black. A certifiable English eccentric, Cathlin thought. With a home like this, she supposed a man could afford to be eccentric. His face was all hard planes and unforgiving angles, not handsome in any usual sense of the word.

But it was an utterly compelling face just the same.

He bent to his knees and ran his fingers through the big cat's sun-warmed fur. "Did I? I'm vastly sorry for it."

"You were so quiet. It sounds mad, but, well, you seemed to come from nowhere."

A smile, faintly sad. "Maybe I did at that."

Cathlin felt a lump in her throat. "Strange."

"Strange?" he murmured, picking up her conversation as if they had known each other for years.

"I know someone else who has that particular trick of silence."

Sharp eyes the color of cold gray walls probed her face. "And it bothers you, does it?"

Cathlin shrugged. "It might. If I let it, which I won't." She looked up. "Do you own all this?"

The hard lips curved. "You might say that."

Might? Either he did or he didn't. Definitely eccentric, in the best English tradition.

"You like it." Oddly, it wasn't a question.

Cathlin frowned. For a moment she'd had the strangest feeling that those granite eyes were looking right through her. Seeing things that she couldn't see herself.

Memories.

Dreams.

Thoughts buried so deep she didn't even know they were there.

The cat at her leg purred softly.

"Yes, I do. More than like it."

"And that frightens you." Again, it was no question.

"No." Something about the keen eyes called for honesty. Cathlin sighed. "Well, perhaps a little. Maybe even a lot. Because I can see the shadows behind all this beauty. Sometimes they even keep me awake at night. I…lost someone here, you see, a long time ago."

The gray eyes narrowed. "Your mother."

Cathlin nodded. It was hardly a secret.

"And still you can find it beautiful?"

"I didn't want to," she said frankly. "I expected to hate this place."

"And you don't. Very interesting." He nodded. "My abbey does seem to have that effect on people. Especially my roses."

"They are lovely. You must be very proud of such—" She searched for the word. Something about the man demanded she get the word right. "Power. And beauty. Beauty that will last an eternity."

He looked down at the cat. "Ah, this one is good, Gideon. She sees much more than one would expect."

The cat's tail flicked slowly, a study in elegant geometry, all smooth arcs of gray.

"No? I don't agree at all, you know."

Cathlin found herself smiling in spite of the rank improbability of it all. A granite abbey? A man in solid black who spoke to a cat who looked intelligent enough to talk back?

Definitely, coffee is needed here, O'Neill. And fast.

"You will be here long?"

"Long enough to poke around in your cellar and see if that wine you discovered is authentic." Cathlin looked out over the haze of green hills. *And to find out if this wretched story about a murdered man and two lost lovers has any truth to it.* "I only wish I knew more about the man who left the wine there."

"Gabriel? Yes, he was a most complex man."

"Do you know very much about him?"

The expressive hands stilled for an instant, pale against the cat's sleek fur. "What would you like to know?"

"Everything. Dominic—that is, Lord Ashton—led me to believe no one knew anything at all about his Mad Uncle Gabriel."

"Is that what he calls him? How amusing. And how very much Gabriel would dislike that term."

Cathlin was growing impatient with this vagueness. "Can you tell me how he died?"

"I'm afraid not."

"Then why was he interested in the wine and why did he end up in the cellar?"

"These are useful questions." Her companion nodded slowly. "The why is always the most important thing."

"I was hoping for some answers." Cathlin frowned. "After all, you must know this place better than anyone."

"Much better," he affirmed.

"So what's your guess? Why would a man do something like that?"

The dark eyes narrowed. For a moment Cathlin felt their force through every molecule and atom of her being. Divining. Assessing.

"Love. Hatred. Jealousy. Revenge." He smiled bitterly. "All the usual reasons."

"We know who he loved. She was my ancestor, Geneva Russell. But her life is just as sketchy as his. Did they fall in love, only to fall out again? Or did something come between them?" Each question seemed to leave things more tangled.

"I expect there must be records of some sort," her companion said absently, stroking the great cat. "There usually are. Damned nuisance, too, don't you agree, Gideon?"

The cat popped open one keen eye and blinked at Cathlin.

"Ah, well, *you* would."

Did the man always speak in riddles? "Do you know where I might look? For the records, I mean."

"There are many treasures in this ancient house, Miss O'Neill. And the greatest treasures of all are those that cannot be seen. I suggest you remember that."

Unseen? Oh, that was going to be *really* useful, Cathlin thought irritably. Couldn't the man give a single straight answer?

"Beyond that, I'm afraid I can't help you," he said, somehow answering the question she had not asked. "Ask the right questions and you'll find the right answers," he added cryptically. "But all the answers—and all the questions—must come from you." He smiled faintly. "And from *him.*"

"Him?"

Again the smile. "The one with that trick of silence you're not going to let bother you."

"Dominic? But how did you know—"

"We are remote here but not entirely out of contact with the rest of the world, my dear. Besides, you have a most expressive face. I suggest that you forgo prevarication."

Cathlin swallowed. The wind trailed over her hair, enveloping her in a cloudlike scent of roses and lilacs. Maybe he was right. Maybe she hadn't been asking the right questions at all—about this wine or about her own past. As a bee droned from one heavy bloom to the next, she considered that possibility.

And the seconds stretched out, full and silent and companionable in the warm sunlight.

After a long while her companion nodded to the cat. "Yes."

Cathlin hadn't any idea what he had said yes to. It might have been to her or to the day, or even in some strange way to the keen, imperious cat who seemed so comfortable here.

It might even have been a yes to something much, much more.

But before she could ask, the cat stirred and uttered a low cry. "I must go."

She felt a sudden tug of disappointment. "Must you?" There was power in his company. A strange comfort.

He laughed, a sound as soft and fluid as the moat's swirl. "I'm afraid so. But there is one thing you might do for me, if you will."

"Of course." She studied the hard face, the face of a man who had tasted far more than his share of pain and pleasure, anger and despair. "Anything."

"Anything?" The hard lips curved. "I suggest you be rather more careful with your promises, my dear."

"Why? Should I be afraid of you?"

"Perhaps. Perhaps not. For now at least, you are quite safe. As it happens, my request is harmless."

"I'm listening."

His eyes narrowed. Again that faint tug of lip that seemed to send light into every corner of his hard face. "Tell him I send my greetings. And my blessings." At his feet the cat stirred, suddenly restless. "Yes, I know, my dear Gideon. But blessings, I send nevertheless. Such good as they are. I have every confidence that this mystery, too, will be solved, just as all the others were. And you will be part of its solving, my dear."

"But how? And whom should I tell—"

The cat ghosted past her ankles and vanished into the tossing lilacs, silver-white against the weathered stone. Something about those movements was lulling, effortless, almost...hypnotic.

"Who..." She tried to speak, had to swallow first, fighting a pull of sleep such as she had never felt before. It was only the sun, of course, bounced a hundredfold back across the moat. Only the high, sweet trill of a bird somewhere in the high hills.

Only her heart, full of peace in this odd, beautiful place.

"I can't just—" She spun around.

He was gone.

As the roses tossed in the wind, Cathlin caught a glimpse of black through the tangle of leaf and bud. And she could have sworn she saw white lace flutter at his dark wrists.

A MAN IN A BLACK SUIT AND lime green running shoes was clipping crimson roses from a hedge as Cathlin carried her single bag toward the weathered gatehouse. He stopped when he saw Cathlin. "Miss O'Neill?" He tugged off his gloves and held out his hand. "I beg your pardon, but I should have introduced myself at once. I am Marston, Lord Draycott's butler. Let me take that for you, please."

Butler? Cathlin had to repress an urge to pinch herself. Butler. Of course. "Shall I trade you for the roses? The bag's not heavy, since I won't be staying for the night. I'm only here to look at the wine Lord Draycott discovered."

The butler frowned as she handed over the bag. "But his lordship is definitely expecting you to stay. He and his wife will be very disappointed otherwise."

Cathlin shrugged as waves of glorious scent filled her lungs. "The viscount seems to be an unusual man."

"Ah, you've met him, have you?"

Cathlin nodded. "I ran into him by the moat as I came in. He is a most…interesting man."

"Indeed he is." Marston led the way across the forecourt toward a wall of rose-covered granite. "I have prepared a room overlooking the courtyard. I thought you might like the roses. Will veal with strawberries and asparagus vinaigrette be satisfactory for luncheon?"

Satisfactory? Was the man serious? "It sounds wonderful. But I'd like to wash up and take a look at the wine cellar first."

"Ah, yes, the wine." Marston shot her an assessing look.

"Is something wrong?"

"Pardon me, but you seem so very young to possess the amount of expertise that you have."

"Not all wines need age to develop body or character." Cathlin had used the phrase often in her first tough years carving out a consulting business in London.

"You're right, of course. Forgive me."

His sincerity made Cathlin feel a little small. "Only if you let me carry some of these lovely roses."

That won her an answering smile. "Very well. We'll call it even. And perhaps you would be so kind as to have a look at our cellar conditions. There are two or three old clarets that I fear may be showing signs of damaged corks. Perhaps there is a problem with the humidity."

Cathlin looked sideways. She had a fair idea of this man's character and doubted that he cared to ask advice from anyone. Either he was trying to compliment her or he was treating her as an equal.

Both sounded good to her.

"I'm rather looking forward to poking around down there. Draycott's wine cellar has quite a reputation, you know."

"Indeed." Marston looked pleased. "It was largely the work of the eighth viscount, you know. So were all these roses. According to legend, he led an unhappy life and devoted his rather considerable skills to building up Draycott for his heirs. There are a number of Sauternes and champagnes that he personally selected, along with some particularly fine vintages of Lafite. There is even an 1825, I believe."

Cathlin's brow rose. "You'll have to watch for cracking of the glass there. Those old commemorative bottles are the devil to protect."

Marston nodded thoughtfully. "I shall relay your instructions to the viscount. He's just been out riding, so he will wish to change before he greets you himself."

Riding? Dressed in formal black? Another mark of eccentricity, Cathlin decided. If so, it was no business of hers. "You needn't trouble him to show me around. We can talk later, after I've looked through the cellars."

Marston looked genuinely horrified. "Not show you the abbey personally? His lordship would not dream of it."

Protocol, O'Neill. Cathlin thought of the man in black, a man with eyes like granite. He would be the sort to live by all sorts of ritual and formality, she decided. And he probably had an ironclad sense of honor to go with them.

She decided there was a lot she had to learn about the Draycotts and their abbey.

"Does that great cat go everywhere with him, by the way?"

Marston faltered for a moment. "I beg your pardon."

"The cat," Cathlin prompted. "The one with the gray fur and black paws. I found him dozing beside the moat."

Something came and went in Marston's eyes. "I couldn't say, miss."

Couldn't say? Either the cat did or he didn't. Cathlin sighed. No good getting upset. Good butlers were notoriously tight-lipped, after all.

"You say you met—the viscount? With his, er, cat?"

Cathlin nodded. "They seemed great friends, although I know that will sound odd."

A frown worked between Marston's eyes. "Did you happen to note what the, er, viscount was wearing?"

"All black, actually. He looked very—rugged."

Marston looked off in the distance, his eyes narrowed. "About ten minutes ago, would you say?"

"More or less."

"I see."

You see what?

But he didn't say anything more. By then they were at the great oak doors covered with trailing roses and Cathlin felt her heart tighten.

Memories. Or were they simply shadows?

She turned her head, forcing herself to look at the abbey and really see it, not as a place of shadows and dread, not as the image of childhood memories, but as it truly was.

From here she could see every cleft and fissure of the sun-warmed stones, their ancient faces speaking in a language she could not hear but only feel. And it felt like peace, like abiding age. Like a vast will that had walked every foot of Draycott's ground and left an indelible mark there.

Oh, it was definitely time for coffee, Cathlin told herself, shaking her head. But memories teased her as she followed Marston over the small granite bridge, through the sunny courtyard, and into the rich darkness of the abbey. Her pulse only quickened as she walked past walls hung with priceless Tintorettos and Whistler *Nocturnes,* past rooms bright with costly old tapestries. It was the antique fabrics which had drawn Cathlin's mother here fifteen years before, and Cathlin had never forgotten their fragile beauty.

But there were also differences. Now there were roses everywhere, arranged in old porcelain jars and crystal bowls that filled the house with fragrance. Tapestry pillows brightened fragile gilt wing chairs. Sunlight spilled through opened curtains, bouncing off polished wood and casting a mellow glow over the ancient rooms.

Peace.

Again the thought came to her, playing over her senses like summer sunshine, like a sweet and very heady wine.

Steady, O'Neill. There are shadows, too. And memories. Don't forget those. Frowning, she shoved a strand of hair from her cheek and looked at Marston. "I've changed my mind, Marston. I'd like to go straight down to the wine cellars, if you don't mind."

The butler smiled faintly. "Lord Ashton predicted that you would," he murmured.

Lord Ashton. Cathlin's eyes narrowed. "Lord Ashton might be wonderful at stalking around dark alleys and snapping off assassins' heads, but he doesn't know me as well as he imagines."

Marston gave her a sidelong look.

"I'm sorry Marston. It's been a long day and I'm—" *Thinking about shadows. Thinking about dreams and a mother I barely had a chance to know.* She swallowed. "I'm anxious to see that wine."

"I quite understand. The stairs to the wine cellars are right over here." Marston pushed open an oak door that had to be at least six feet tall and flipped on a light.

Cathlin stared in disbelief. A passage of solid granite stretched before her, hacked out along with the abbey's original foundation hundreds of years before. The structure had been built to withstand the attacks of raiders, invading armies and rival political factions, and it had certainly succeeded.

Cathlin shook her head. "This is some building you've got here."

"So it is," the butler said proudly, "and if I may say so, you haven't seen anything yet."

"HOLY, HOLY HEAVEN."

Cathlin stood at the bottom of the stone steps and studied the shadowed recess stretching before her. Like everything else about Draycott Abbey, the cellars had been built on a vast scale, in an age when high rank commanded huge amounts of manpower. Cathlin tried to conceive how many men must have been needed to hew these stone walls, but her imagination failed her.

"I suppose you've heard how the wine was discovered? About...the body?"

Cathlin nodded, fighting a stab of uneasiness as she looked down and wondered exactly where the remains had been found. "And there's been no other information? Nothing that explains how Gabriel Montserrat came to be buried behind that wall?"

"I'm afraid not."

Cathlin thought of a dying man writing his will by candlelight, while shadows closed in around him. As Marston led her past rows of neatly stacked bottles that ran twice her height, she found herself praying she would find an answer here amid the wine that had been his only companion for two centuries.

Assuming this was not some kind of hoax.

Around her lay the treasures collected by proud generations of Draycotts. First growth claret. Château Petrus. Clos du Mesnil champagne, from a walled vineyard in existence since 1698. Neaby ran the old Krugs themselves—the superbly sweet 1928 and the big, textured 1945.

And on and on.

Beyond the champagnes came the clarets, housed in graceful, wide bottles that themselves had become collector's items. Another long wall held eighty prime vintages of Lafite, the *pièce de résistance* a commemorative bottle of 1825 with a handmade ground glass stopper. Cathlin could think of two dozen men who would kill to possess that treasure alone.

Perhaps her mother had been right. A person might truly spend a lifetime here and still not understand this vast, beautiful abbey.

"Is something wrong, Ms. O'Neill?" Marston was staring at her oddly.

"I think I'm in shock, Marston."

"There are several more rooms to the left. But you will wish to see the Château d'Yquem, I imagine."

"I don't think I can wait another second," Cathlin confessed unsteadily.

"Of course. Come right this way."

As Cathlin followed Marston through the semi-darkness, trying to ignore the priceless wines stretching away on each side of her, she noticed a dozen wires snaking over the old granite to terminate in digital thermometers. She smiled. Though the cellars might look like a medieval set piece, the current viscount had gone to a good deal of expense to upgrade them to current standards. A good thing, too, since he was probably sitting on several million dollars worth of wine down here.

At the end of the room the stone walls narrowed and the ceiling dropped until it was almost within Cathlin's reach. "How was the hidden room discovered?"

"It was all most extraordinary, miss." Marston's voice was low, in unspoken awareness of the body that had been found here. "Recently we've had a number of problems with the water pipes that feed the south end of the house. When they were tracked to this segment of the cellars, the viscount called in a specialist."

"And he got rather more than he bargained for?"

The butler nodded. "As he was working, a section of the wall simply crumbled and he was left staring into darkness—into a grave that had been sealed for nearly two hundred years. I've never seen a grown man look more frightened in my life," Marston said quietly. "He kept talking about feeling as if something were down here with him." Marston shook his head.

"Absurd, of course. Not that there aren't a host of odd stories about his old place."

"And no one knows how or why it happened?"

"I'm afraid not."

Just like my mother, Cathlin thought, suddenly aware of the shadows and the heavy, looming silence of the damp cold walls.

"Watch your step, miss." They were moving lower now, and much of the floor lay in total darkness. "There's a particularly bad stretch here where the floor dips. One of the workmen took a nasty tumble here on the day of the discovery."

But Cathlin seemed to have no trouble negotiating the passage. It was almost as if she could sense where the stone floor would dip in front of her. As if she had been here before.

Crazy, O'Neill. No doubt all old houses affect people this way.

A click. Suddenly light covered the damp stone walls that loomed up out of the shadows. Close to the ground Cathlin saw a jagged opening in the stone. She looked questioningly at Marston. "Here?"

The butler nodded. "The skeleton has been removed, of course. The remains were interred at the Ashton estate near Tunbridge with full church rites."

Dominic hadn't mentioned that. Somehow the news didn't make Cathlin feel any better. The shadows felt oppressive, and a nearby palpable sadness brushed at her neck. A sound beside her made her turn. "Yes, Marston?"

"I'm afraid I did not say anything, miss."

"No?" Cathlin frowned. She *had* heard something. It had come in that moment while she'd studied the jagged hole at the far end of the cellar. And it had been a single word.

Gabriel.

She took a steadying breath. Time to stop dodging ghosts and get to work. "May I?" She pointed to Marston's flashlight.

"Of course."

"Is there an alarm working?" She balanced one leg on the stone ledge, flashlight in hand.

"Only a simple electronic affair." Marston moved off to the wall and flicked a switch on a matte gray box.

Cathlin moved deeper into the shadows, shining light over the uneven stones. Dust skittered around her feet as she bent close to the cold granite floor.

And there she froze, her body rigid.

Rising from the shadows was a mold- and dust-encrusted wooden case filled with eight bottles cushioned lovingly in a nest of straw.

She was staring down at Gabriel Montserrat's legacy.

CHAPTER FIFTEEN

CATHLIN'S PALMS BEGAN TO sweat.

Château d'Yquem 1792. She knew it instantly. Her heart told her all that her scientific analysis would take days to resolve.

The wine was real; she could feel it in every screaming pore of her body.

She raised the flashlight, forcing her mind to its work. The wine looked authentic enough. The glass was of the proper texture and weight for that period. The bottle lips were full, another sign of authenticity. Her heart hammered, loud in her ears. Had Gabriel Montserrat truly died to bring this case here two hundred years before? And if so, how was her own ancestor involved in the mystery?

Chewing on her lip, she crouched over the priceless find. If the wine was indeed authentic, as all her senses screamed, then the demanding work of conservation would begin. She would have to check the bottles for hairline cracks, pitting and corrosion before moving to a delicate scrutiny of the corks. Even in the cool damp air of the abbey cellars the corks would have turned brittle. Old wines needed to be recorked every quarter century as standard practice, and these had had no such care.

Yes it would be the greatest challenge of her career.

If she stayed, of course.

Cathlin ran her finger carefully over the case, touching the dust that had accumulated for decades, probably for centuries.

How could she possibly leave until she'd had a chance to verify scientifically that the wine was genuine? And how could she ignore the tragic mystery of Gabriel Montserrat's death in this place of cold shadows?

Dominic was right. It was too rare an opportunity for her to turn her back. There was no doubt that the intensely sweet white wines of the Garonne had been prized for centuries, and no less a figure than Thomas Jefferson had visited the area and sung their praises. She recalled a letter she had once seen. "I have persuaded our president, George Washington, to try a sample. He asks for thirty dozen [bottles], sir, and I ask you for ten dozen for myself." Cathlin knew that there was no record of either American receiving his shipment that year. Was it just possible that this case came from the order commissioned long ago by Jefferson?

Trying to control her excitement, she pulled out a fine brush and cleaned the dust from the closest bottle. As her fingers touched the cold glass, a tiny, electric jolt ran through her. Heaviness seemed to gather at her heart, like the French valleys she had seen filling up with mist. She shivered, fingering the cameo at her neck, which had grown suddenly cold.

Nonsense, Cathlin told herself sharply. It was just a hidden tunnel that sent cold air slashing against her face.

But she was intensely aware of the shadows pressing around her. And she found herself wondering which shadows belonged to her and which were Draycott's.

HE WATCHED HER FROM THE shadows. Even in the dim half-light of the narrow tunnel, her hair had a glow of vitality. As she bent protectively over the old wine, using a fine brush to remove two centuries of dust, Dominic Montserrat understood just how vast was Cathlin O'Neill's love of fine wine.

Yes, this was the perfect opportunity for her, if only she could be persuaded to take it. Suddenly Dominic found himself praying that the case was authentic, because he wanted to see the excitement blaze in Cathlin's eyes when she astounded the wine world with her discovery. She deserved that joy. The abbey owed her that much, after taking her mother from her.

Without warning, tension stirred along Dominic's neck. Crouching low, he spun about, prepared for an attack.

But none came. There was no movement around him, nor sound of any sort. He was alone here beneath the damp stones, ringed by shadows. And something about those gray walls with their leaden darkness made sweat touch his face.

Something was wrong.

Habits too deeply ingrained to deny screamed out that he was not alone, that someone was watching him. Only his imagination, Dominic tried to tell himself as he eased upright.

TWENTY MINUTES LATER Nicholas Draycott tracked Dominic down in the middle of the gently sloping lawns that led away from the moat. The viscount smiled wryly as he watched his friend go through sharp jabs and impossibly high whipkicks, covered with sweat and looking mean.

The man was a master and no mistake, Nicholas thought.

And just as well.

They all were going to need that expertise to survive when the news of this discovery got out.

"You're looking damnably fit, Dominic."

Dominic wiped his forehead with a towel and held out a hand. "Not too bad for an old playboy vintner. You look lean and mean yourself."

"Oh, my Thailand days are over, I assure you. The most exercise I get these days is chasing that scapegrace young daughter of mine around the abbey grounds."

"There could be worse ways of getting exercise."

Nicholas nodded. "You ought to try it. Kacey has little Genevieve in town, while she does some research on the local records, but you'll see them tonight."

Dominic looked off over the hills. "I'm glad for you, Nicholas. For this. And for how well everything has worked out."

For a moment the silence stretched out. Then Dominic bent over the wooden fence and lowered his body into a thigh-stretching warm-up. "And it's about time you showed up, considering that you finally have me where you wanted me."

"Not alone, I hope."

"No, Cathlin's here, too. She got in an hour before I did, but I'm not sure how long she'll stay. She's down in your cellars right now nursemaiding that bloody case of wine." Dominic broke into a series of dancelike high kicks coupled with shadowboxing jabs. Fists raised, body moving, he jabbed, then lunged into the *chassé* kicks that made French kickboxing, or *savate*, so lethal. "Nothing could tear her away, in fact."

"Is that irritation I hear?"

Dominic glared at his friend, as sweat ran in beads down his broad chest. "You're damned right it is. The woman's impossible. Not time nor prayer nor divine intercession is going to change that. She hates me, she hates my profession, and she hates Draycott."

"She's here. That's a start."

"Against her every wish, she's here. Even after what happened at Seacliffe, she refuses to believe she might be in danger."

"Something happened down there, did it?"

Dominic pounded at an invisible opponent, dipping and bobbing, his face grim. "Which incident are you referring to, the time I lost the prowler with the semiautomatic revolver or the time that someone nearly ran us off the road on the way back to Seacliffe?"

Nicholas whistled soundlessly. "That bad already? I'd hoped we'd have a little more time."

"Well we don't. I discovered that your letter to Cathlin was missing my second day at Seacliffe. Whoever took it knows every detail of the discovery and Gabriel's will. Someone wants that wine and my guess is they're willing to kill to get it."

"Instinct?"

"Like a kick to the gut." Dominic's eyes hardened. "You remember that last winter in Thailand? How I was sent out alone?"

Nicholas wouldn't ever forget. It had preceded his own captivity by mere months. "I remember."

"Well, I'm feeling that same way right now, and I don't like it." Dominic stabbed at an imaginary opponent and frowned. "I never wanted back into this life, Nicholas. There are too many shadows. And now, on top of that, there are the dreams..." He cursed and turned away.

"What dreams?"

"Something—nothing. Blast it, I don't know, Nicholas. Maybe I'm just too rusty. But my dreams aren't your problem. I don't know why I even mentioned them."

"Maybe because we're friends. By listening, I also ensure a continuing supply of that wonderful wine of yours. If you'd put more fields into production, I wouldn't have to bribe half of the Garonne Valley to save a few cases for me."

Dominic looked shocked. "Bribe? I never knew. The volume is low to keep my quality high until I can expand in an orderly fashion. But you could have called me anytime, Nicky, and I would gladly have—"

"Not a bit of it. You've made a wonderful success of La Trouvaille in three years, and I'm perfectly willing to grease a few palms if it will make the French functionaries look on you more indulgently." Nicholas's smile faded as he looked at the old Jeep parked near the stables. "And now I think it's time I spoke with Ms. O'Neill. Marston tells me she has every look of intending to stay in the cellars for hours. I want to see that she is given every

courtesy here, Dominic. It's the least I can do, considering…"
His voice hardened. "Considering all she lost here."

"I understand." Dominic spun a sharp right hook at an
opponent only he could see. "I just don't want you surprised if
she doesn't stay around very long."

Nicholas stared at the roses dancing beside the moat. "Then
I suppose we'll have to find a way to change Ms. O'Neill's
mind, won't we?"

There was a marked firmness to his jaw as he strode off toward
the abbey a few moments later.

DOMINIC WAS FINISHING another series of flying high kicks,
oblivious to the world, when a slender form homed in on him
with the ferocity of a Scud missile.

"Dominic Montserrat, I want to talk to you!"

"You want to pull out my nails slowly, one by one, more
like," he muttered, giving his chest a swipe with the towel
hanging on the fence nearby.

Cathlin puffed up, arms akimbo, black hair waving in the
wind. "Just what do you think you're doing?"

"I believe I'm exercising," her quarry said calmly.

Cathlin caught a breath, pulling her eyes away from the broad
expanse of Dominic's bare chest. "Are you trying to deny it?"

"I might, if I knew what you were talking about."

"I *knew* you'd deny it!"

"If you'll just calm down, Cathlin—"

"That's *Ms. O'Neill* to you, Officer Montserrat. Or have you
already forgotten your riveting little speech about everything
being business between us from now on?"

"I've forgotten nothing," Dominic said. Softly.

"Don't you threaten *me*."

Dominic reached past her for his shirt. "What's got you so
furious?"

"*This.*"

Tossing his towel over his shoulder, Dominic picked up the tabloid pages Cathlin was waving in the air.

The headline was brutal and bold. "Dead lord comes back from grave to uphold family curse." Below the blazing headline was a very out-of-focus photo of Nicholas Draycott, hollow-eyed and gaunt after his return seven years before from a hellish captivity in Thailand. Next to Nicholas was overlaid a grainy shot of an oil painting in the National Gallery.

The hair was long, the eyes were hard. Discounting the black satin and the diamond stickpin, the man might have been Dominic Montserrat's twin.

"Mad Uncle Gabriel, I presume?"

Dominic nodded. "This one is by a lesser artist than the portrait at home, but the likeness is accurate."

"You two could be twins," Cathlin said accusingly.

"I'm a regular throwback, all right, demons and all. Where did you find this?"

"Under your seat in the Triumph."

"Searching my car now, Irish?"

Cathlin colored. "I had to get something from the Jeep. Your car is parked right next to mine and I happened to notice the headline. When were you going to tell me about this?"

"When it became important."

"Dead lord comes back to uphold family curse? I'd say that was fairly important."

Dominic sighed. "It's just nonsense. Some bright person got the idea that Mad Uncle Gabriel had lost the Ashton diamond through treachery and had cursed whoever possessed it. It's just family legend, Cathlin."

"And I found the Ashton diamond at Seacliffe." Her eyes darkened to burnished gold. "Do you think he gave it to Geneva?"

"We're here to look for facts and records, Cathlin, something that makes sense. Not family legends."

"Maybe legends are all we're going to find. Maybe that's all you have to go on when the facts are lost over time. Or when they're hidden," she added bitterly.

Dominic fingered the towel slung over his shoulder. "Are you talking about Gabriel or your own past now?"

Cathlin frowned out at the shimmering waters of the moat. "Both. I need to know what really happened here, Dominic. Without that piece of my past I'll never have a real future."

"What if it gets dangerous, Irish? When news of the will leaks out, a lot of people are going to be interested in your whereabouts. A fanatic collector might consider trying to steal the wine from the abbey, but it would be much easier to get the wine through you."

"Kidnapping?"

"Possibly. Or some nasty coercion. Even a barter, if one of us gets taken. What I'm saying is that things are going to get rocky."

"Then do your job. You're a bodyguard, aren't you?" Cathlin's voice was cold.

"Even bodyguards make mistakes. And when that will becomes public knowledge, every two-bit criminal and out-of-luck thief in England will be trying to get his hands on that wine. Or on *us*."

"Like the men in that car?"

"Maybe." Dominic cursed softly, tired of having to field questions he couldn't answer. "But the conditions are still the same, Cathlin. If you stay, you do what I say, when I say. Nicholas will back me up on this."

"Don't count on it," Cathlin said flatly.

Dominic's eyes hardened. "You know that Gabriel's murderer was never found, don't you? No one knows what happened that last night down in the cellar. And Aunt Aggy tells me—" He stopped.

Something about the hardness in his eyes made Cathlin frown. "What, Dominic? What did she tell you?"

"You're not going to like it."

"Tell me."

"She found some letters in an old hatbox in the back of her armoire. It appears that all London was abuzz with gossip in the spring of 1794."

"So?"

"So the story circulating was that Gabriel Montserrat had finally gone past the line by kidnapping a respectable young woman from the safety of her own house." Dominic looked out over the moat, past the tangle of old roses. "And then he murdered her."

"No," Cathlin whispered. "Why would he murder her, then mention her in his will? It doesn't make sense."

"Maybe it does. Maybe guilt drove him to make up in death for what he'd done to her in life."

"You can't believe that."

Dominic shrugged. "I don't know what I believe. And I don't know if we'll ever have the answers." When he turned, his face was hard. "Nicholas said to tell you we're dining at eight in the Yellow Salon." His eyes glinted for a moment. "Wear something special."

CHAPTER SIXTEEN

"DAMNED, STUBBORN WOMAN."

Dominic watched Cathlin stride over the gravel path along the moat.

A dozen tasks awaited him. He needed to go over the inside security arrangements, then discuss them with Nicholas. After that he wanted to take a look at the cellar and see if anything had been overlooked down there.

Yet here he stood, thinking about the past, thinking about a woman with haunted amber eyes.

Dominic's shoulder began to throb. Too much boxing. But someone who came up from behind wasn't going to care if his shoulder hurt or not.

He reached into his pocket and pulled out a fragile piece of fabric. Light broke over the Ashton diamond glinting on his palm, cold and beautiful.

Dominic twisted it thoughtfully, wondering why such a precious gem was attached to a piece of simple white cambric. He had taken it from Cathlin's chest at Seacliffe, sensing he might find answers somewhere in those cold facets.

He stared down now, watching the diamond sparkle, thinking about this hard-faced ancestor and his strange bequest.

Feeling the images form into memories…

GENEVA RUSSELL CROSSED THE polished floor and sank down on the gilt chair before her dressing table.

Her face was pale, her eyes haunted as she slid off her gown and tugged on a cambric wrapper.

Though a week had passed, she could not forget the fury in Gabriel's eyes, nor the fierce disgust in his voice.

Jezebel. How right he had been.

Listlessly she pulled the pins from her hair and brushed out the rich black curls, barely aware of her movements. Devere had come to see her twice already, braying and blustering that he would have Isabel de Verney carried to the guillotine.

But not yet. Devere needed Geneva's sister alive, as a means to threaten Geneva. It was the Rook he wanted, and he needed Geneva to lure the shadowy hero of a hundred forays out of hiding.

It was for that reason that Geneva was leaving London tomorrow for Seacliffe, the family's estate near the southeast coast. The grand old house overlooked the barren sands and tidal pools of Romney Marsh and not even Henry Devere would bother her there.

She stared down at the exquisite leather trunk neatly packed beside her bed. Inside were the jeweled shoes and satin gown she had worn at the masquerade. With them was the cameo that Gabriel had given her. Geneva would never wear any of them again. There was too much pain in her memories of that night.

"Will you be wanting anything else, miss?"

Geneva smiled at her maidservant, hired along with this furnished house in a very elegant part of London. "No, that's all, Amelia. I shall close the trunk and you can see it loaded onto the carriage to go with us to Seacliffe tomorrow."

The young woman nodded. "Very well, miss." She dropped a quick curtsy and went out as silently as she had come.

Geneva barely noticed. Carelessly she pulled off her wrapper and studied her reflection in the mirror. Her face was as pale as the white cambric nightgown she wore. The only light and ani-

mation about her came from the diamond stickpin she wore at her neck. Geneva would wear it always to remind herself of her perfidy and the grim look in the eyes of the man she had betrayed.

A shadow slid into her vision, captured in the mirror. A shadow with glinting eyes and a hard jaw.

She spun around, her hand at her lips. "You!"

It was the only word she uttered before Gabriel Montserrat pulled a snow-white cravat from his pocket and bound her mouth. His eyes moved over the curves hinted at beneath the fragile cambric. "So you think to mock me, do you? You even wear my own jewel. But I shall see you repaid for your treachery, my sweet, in ways you can't imagine." He ignored the burning desperation in her eyes, ignored the way her face paled to white. In tight silence, he found her gown, tugged it over her shoulders, and drew the laces up the back. "We are going on a trip you see, my love. We have a great deal of business to finish, you and I."

He looked at her one last time, saw the hint of the diamond at the edge of her gown, and with a curse he tore it free. "I'll have that back now, my dear."

But Geneva kicked him wildly, every movement filled with desperation. Cursing, Gabriel dodged the blow.

And in the process the Ashton diamond dropped unnoticed from his fingers, landing in the chest beside Geneva's bed.

Grim-faced, Gabriel caught his captive over his shoulder and strode down the stairs. "No more tricks, my love. We've a long coach ride before us, so I suggest you cool your anger." Through the quiet house he stalked, Geneva draped over his shoulder like a sack of flour, her bare feet kicking. At the bottom of the stairs he was met by a wide-eyed servant, his clothing all awry.

"Miss Russell! My lord! What are you—"

Gabriel slid a pistol from his pocket and leveled it at the man's chest.

"But you can't—" The butler looked at the pistol and swallowed. "That is, you really shouldn't—"

"But I am," Gabriel said flatly. Then he strode out into the London night, his kicking hostage held tightly in his arms.

GABRIEL'S COACHMAN HAD been waiting for his signal. Immediately a high-stepping team raced around the darkened square. Gabriel bolted down the steps and slid Geneva to the ground.

His eyes burned silver as he removed the gag from her mouth. "There is no use screaming, my dear. I am taking you where you cannot betray me."

"But you can't!" Geneva's eyes were wild as she studied the darkened square behind them. "Devere has been watching the house all week, hoping that you would come after me. That's why I was leaving for the coast."

"An unsuccessful lie, my dear."

Geneva pounded his chest, her small hands fisted. "He'll come, I tell you! The French have put too high a price on your head for him to resist."

Gabriel's eyes narrowed. Was this another of her tricks? He studied the darkness around them, watching for any sign of movement.

None came. So much for that, he thought grimly.

Not that it mattered. An hour's ride would see the dust of London's streets long behind them. Soon they would be beyond the reach of Devere or his minions.

Gabriel was just on the verge of telling Geneva to save her breath when he heard an old wooden shop sign hammer across the square.

Clang-clang, it cried, creaking in the wind. The noise reminded Gabriel of the windmill in Dunkirk, sails straining in a channel gale. He had heard the sound just before he discovered the three dead children. He knew the sound would haunt him always.

Suddenly a crack split the night. Gabriel shoved Geneva inside the carriage, while the coachman fought to control the team.

Another shot exploded past as Gabriel leaped within and wrenched the door closed behind him.

He tried to ignore the press of Geneva's soft breast where she lay beneath him. He tried to ignore her lilac fragrance and the way her hip rode against his thigh.

"I tried to tell you," she said raggedly. "He knew that you would come."

Gabriel smiled coldly. "I have naught to fear from Henry Devere. He'll never find us where we're going."

As they took another jolt, he saw Geneva wince. Cursing, Gabriel pulled her onto his lap and wrenched back her cloak.

He stared down in horror at the trail of blood on her gown. "They hit you."

Geneva's hands were white where she gripped the folds of her cloak. "He will never give you up. The French have promised him a fortune for your capture."

Gabriel pulled her against his chest, cursing softly. He couldn't go all the way out to his estates near Tunbridge with Geneva bleeding. He had already closed up his London town house, in preparation for his departure.

Which left only Draycott House.

Gabriel sat forward and called curt direction to the coachman as Geneva twisted restlessly in his arms.

GENEVA RUSSELL'S SHOCKED servant watched the carriage race from the square and shook his head disapprovingly.

He had thought it most peculiar when the woman had called upon his services as a butler. No respectable female lived alone in a house without family or a single chaperone. He supposed that's what came of her growing up in the heathen climates where her father had been a high official in the East India Company.

Yes, Edward Wilson hadn't like it then and he didn't like it now. There had been something very peculiar about Miss Geneva Russell. Respectable ladies simply did not set up housekeeping by themselves in London.

His muddy eyes narrowed. This was just the sort of information that gentleman Mr. Devere had asked him to report. The servant straightened his collar and pulled on his cloak. Yes, he would see that Henry Devere learned the news of this outrageous affair from his own lips. No doubt there would be several gold guineas in it for him.

His thoughts were full of greed as he set off for the address that Henry Devere had been careful to leave with him two weeks before.

THE WINDOWS AT DRAYCOTT House were ablaze with light as Gabriel's coach lurched up to the front door. Gabriel prayed that his reprobate friend, the viscount, was not holding one of his wild parties. As he pounded up the front steps with Geneva in his arms, the door of Draycott House was thrown open. A dour figure in black appeared.

"Let me down," Geneva protested raggedly. "I can walk."

"No, you can't."

Templeton, the old butler, gave a sniff of disapproval, eyeing the woman in Gabriel's arms. "I shall fetch Lord Draycott."

Frowning, Gabriel crossed the beautiful marble foyer and made his way to Adrian Draycott's study. After lighting a candle, he pulled back Geneva's cloak.

"It is nothing, I tell you. But you must leave. Henry Devere will follow you here."

Gabriel snorted. "Let him try. Meanwhile, stop fighting me, woman." In the light he made out a jagged line of blood, the path of a shallow bullet.

He was muttering a stream of graphic curses when the door

opened behind him. "My dearest, Gabriel, what an unexpected pleasure. Templeton tells me that you have now taken to kidnapping gently bred females from the London streets." Adrian came to a halt as he saw the white-faced woman on his settee.

"It's a shoulder wound from a ball meant for me."

"I am quite well," Geneva said faintly. "And I pray you will not speak of me as if I were not here."

Adrian smiled. "So you have the same sharp tongue as ever, Miss Russell."

At the doorway Templeton cleared his throat anxiously. "Will your lordship be desiring brandy?"

"No, hot water and fresh linens, Templeton." Adrian looked down at Gabriel. "What happened?"

"Henry Devere decided to let Miss Russell act as his bait to trap the Rook. Unfortunately it worked." Gabriel's breath caught as a scrap of blood-soaked lace came into view.

"Let me alone," Geneva protested.

"Another word and I'll bind your mouth again, hellion."

Adrian smiled slightly at this byplay, watching Gabriel turn Geneva against his chest and strip away the lace of her chemise to bare her shoulder.

But she didn't complain, not by a single word. In fact, Gabriel looked worse than she did, sweat covering his brow as he studied the wound.

"It's jagged but shallow, thank God," he announced finally. "I'll have some of that brandy, Adrian."

Adrian Draycott, rake and hardened cynic, looked rather pale himself as he held out a glass decanter with the Draycott crest of interlocked dragons.

Gabriel splashed some of the brandy on Geneva's shoulder, then pressed the linen tight. As he worked, she began to struggle in his arms.

"Steady now," he murmured. "It's almost over." After binding

fresh linen over the wound, he sat back, with Geneva still cradled against his chest.

After draining the rest of the brandy, Gabriel carried Geneva upstairs to rest.

When he returned, Adrian's eyes were thoughtful. "I'm afraid this isn't the best time for your identity to come out, Gabriel. Not after that last pamphlet bearing the Rook's name. One can't go around calling for the arrest of most of the members of Parliament without expecting a nasty reaction. I agree with you that something needs to be done to stop the bloodshed in France, but it won't happen that way."

"Then what way? How many more children have to die before something's done?"

"You're doing all you can, Gabriel. I've stopped keeping track of the times you've nearly lost your life over there. Isn't that enough?"

It should have been, but it wasn't, Gabriel thought grimly. Not after walking the bloody streets of Paris and seeing the horrors committed daily in the name of equality and liberty. "I shall have to go and search for her sister, of course. But what am I going to do about Geneva?"

Adrian toyed with the lace at his cuff. "Take her to Draycott Abbey. She'll be safe there. I'll send word ahead to let them know you're coming."

"No," Gabriel said sharply. "Only you and I are to know our final destination."

Adrian's brow rose. "You suspect a traitor here?"

"I was betrayed once, Adrian, and three children died because of it. I'll never make such a mistake again. From now on I trust no one."

"Not even me, Lord Ashton?" The fluid, cultured male voice had something foreign about it as it drifted from the doorway.

The speaker was a tall man with a high, arched nose and eyes of keen, cutting blue.

Gabriel stared at the American statesman who had already made a name for himself in England and France. "Is that you, Jefferson? Lord, it seems an age."

"Too long. Templeton tells me you've charmed another woman off her feet."

"She wasn't swept away by charm," Ashton said grimly. "A ball did that to her. A ball meant for me."

"A ball meant for the Rook, you mean."

A hard look passed between them.

"We must leave London tonight. Now that Geneva knows my identity, she won't be safe here."

Adrian nodded. "Of course."

"But what brings you back to London, Jefferson?"

The American looked thoughtful for a moment. "As it happens, I'm here to track down some wine as a gift for our president. Of course, it must be something very special and I have a partiality for some Château d'Yquem I found in the Garonne Valley some years back." He accepted a glass of sherry from Adrian and sat down on a leather settee by the window.

"Perhaps I can help you. As it happens, I have other business that will take me to the area."

"I don't suppose that this business of yours has anything to do with rescuing emigrés from the guillotine, does it?"

"I can't imagine why you would think that." Gabriel's voice was full of calculated boredom.

"Because I've heard nothing else since my arrival in England but stories about this man who defies death time and time again, a man who speaks French like a Parisian. It's said that the Rook could pass for a sans culottes even if he were stopped by Marat himself."

Gabriel's eyes darkened. "As it happens, he has been stopped by Marat himself."

"Now there's an encounter I would like to have seen," Jefferson said intently.

Gabriel poured himself a glass of Madeira and settled one broad shoulder against the mantel. *"Tell me exactly what you require from the Garonne, Jefferson."*

"Six cases of Château d'Yquem, since my friend particularly enjoys the Sauternes. But it is no place for an Englishman, Gabriel." Jefferson frowned. *"Even a Frenchman may find his welcome uncertain in these trying days."*

Gabriel's jaws hardened. *"You need harbor no concerns for me. I know my way about."*

After a moment, Jefferson nodded. *"I shall, of course, leave you a draft on my Paris bank. I am more than happy to pay you a fee for discharging this business, of course."*

"Just consider it my small repayment for the enjoyable hours we've spent discussing the ideals of freedom and equality." There was a cynicism in Gabriel's voice that had never been there before.

Jefferson and Draycott exchanged a look.

At that moment there was a whisper of silk from the doorway and the soft scent of lilacs drifted on the cool, still air.

Gabriel's jaw hardened as he looked up.

Geneva stood in the doorway, silhouetted in the golden light of the hall lantern. Her hair was a black cloud against her shoulders and her white hands were clasped against her waist. But it was her eyes that held him, eyes that were filled with pain, eyes that were a thousand miles away.

"I must go—I must find her before it's too late."

He was beside her in a second, his arm circling her shoulders. Geneva's slender hands shoved blindly at his chest. *"Must go."*

Cursing, Gabriel caught her as she swayed. The bandage at her shoulder was dotted with fresh blood. With infinite gentleness, he lifted her into his arms and brushed a lock of hair from her face. *"Stubborn little fool,"* he said in a tone of vast tenderness.

Jefferson's eyes hardened. "I think I will have a talk with this man Devere tomorrow. Do you care to join me, Adrian?"

"Without a doubt. It will be a decided pleasure."

At that moment Templeton appeared, livery awry. "There's a man below demanding to see you, my lord. I told him you were not receiving, but he insisted he would not go away until he'd seen you himself. He said his name is Devere," the butler said tightly, as angry footsteps exploded across the marble entry.

"He'll be looking for Geneva," Gabriel said grimly. "I'll take her upstairs."

Adrian smiled coldly. "What do you say, Jefferson?"

"I've seen nothing of any woman. Nor have I heard of anyone called the Rook."

Adrian laughed lazily. "No doubt Devere will be far too busy to concern himself with questioning an upstart American."

"You English persist in your mistakes, don't you?" came the American's utterly confident reply.

"No doubt in time you Americans will teach us to rectify our behavior."

Then Templeton was at the door. "Mr. Devere," he announced, his voice stiff with disapproval.

A big man with small, hard eyes stood in the doorway, fingering a long silver cane. "Who is the owner of this house?"

Two pairs of eyes looked him up and down with lazy disdain.

"I demand an answer."

Adrian stared haughtily at the intruder. "I am Viscount Draycott, although I can't image what business it is of yours."

"I'll tell you what business it is. A woman was seen being carried into this house less than an hour ago. I demand that she be released."

Adrian toyed idly with the lace at his cuff. "Into this house, you say?" He looked at the butler. "Templeton, don't tell me you've taken to prowling the High Road for bed partners again."

The old servant broke into startled coughing.

"No? Then you must be mistaken, Mr...." Adrian let the word linger in a question.

"Devere, damn your hide. And I won't be fobbed off with fine stories. I have witnesses, I warn you. I'll have a warrant, so I will."

"Next you'll be demanding satisfaction in a duel, I suppose."

Devere's face darkened with anger. "I wouldn't spill my precious blood for a wastrel like you."

Draycott's brow rose. "It is just as well, since I only duel with gentlemen."

The barb hit home. Devere's hands clenched to fists. "Do you give her up or not?"

"There are no women in my house, more's the pity. It's been damnably lonely of late."

"I warn you, I mean to make a thorough search before I leave." Devere peered sharply around the room and gave a crow of triumph, "There! Blood, if I ever saw it. She was brought here, just as I said."

"Are you in the habit of shooting women, Mr. Devere?" Adrian's voice was elegant in its mockery.

"I merely protect my own. The woman tried to escape after robbing my house and I mean to see justice done."

"You're lying, Devere," Adrian snapped.

Gabriel now appeared in the far doorway. "Devere," he said. "I don't suppose you happen to be of the Hampshire Deveres?"

"I have no relations in that area."

Gabriel eyed the cut of Devere's jacket. Although the garment was made of the highest quality materials, it hung awkwardly over his protruding stomach. "Then perhaps you are one of the Oxfordshire Deveres?"

"Never heard of them," Devere snapped. "And I'll play no more of these games." Scowling, he grabbed up the scrap of bloody linen and waved it angrily. "She is here, I know it. I'll have the law down upon you, see if I don't!"

"You quite mistake the matter," Gabriel said icily. "The wound is mine." He held out his hand, revealing a bloody palm.

"This is your blood?" Devere's eyes were full of suspicion.

"A mere scratch. I was enjoying the merits of my friend's Château d'Yquem far too much to bestir myself."

"Scratch?" Devere looked down at the blood on Gabriel's cuff. "You're mad, the lot of you! But don't think your lordly and arrogant tricks can hide her for long. I'll be back, you may be sure. And I'll see that Miss Russell is made to pay for flouting my authority in this manner! I'll also find out all that she knows about this man called the Rook," he hissed, glaring straight at Gabriel. "There will be no questions as to his identity."

AROUND DOMINIC, THE ABBEY lay quiet, drowsy in the late afternoon sun. Only the roses swayed on the warm granite walls as a great gray cat slid through the lilacs by the little bridge.

He looked down. Blood covered his palm where the Ashton stickpin had torn his skin.

But he had no memory of the pain. He was aware only of a fleeting trail of images and the angry hum of distant voices.

And a network of danger that felt close enough to touch.

BEYOND THE MOAT, BEYOND the Witch's Pool and the rows of dancing roses, shadows gathered. Overhead the sky darkened to crimson and then to deepest indigo.

And as the last fleeting rays of daylight fled before the night a single bell began to chime across the distant hills.

Ten times. Eleven. Twelve.

And then once more.

High in an abbey bedroom Cathlin stopped to listen, brush in hand as she changed for dinner.

Stepping out of the shower, Dominic heard and scowled, telling himself he was imagining things.

And Nicholas Draycott, standing before the opened French doors with the curtains drifting around him like mist, looked out at the darkness, a frown etched upon his brow.

For on this matter the abbey legends were only too clear. When the church bells rang twelve times—and then once more—the ghost of Draycott Abbey was called forth to walk the grounds.

Not out of love.

Not in search of joy.

But because some new danger threatened his beloved ancestral home. As it did now.

THE WIND WHISPERED.

Shadows trembled.

Somewhere in the night, darkness gave way to black satin cuffs and pristine white lace.

As the last bell faded, the abbey's guardian ghost stepped out of nothingness onto the cool stones of the parapets. Eyes agleam, he turned his head and studied the first stars, just glinting upon the velvet sky. "Again it begins, my old friend."

A great gray cat ghosted over the roof, purring.

"Yes, I must agree. What we seek is not new but very old, something hidden but never quite forgotten." Frowning, he looked out over the abbey's stark walls, his eyes as impenetrable as night itself. "They are strong, these two. But their strength makes them weak. In their strength they are content to see with their eyes, and not with their hearts."

The cat moved, rubbing against his master's booted foot.

"Too late? It is never too late, my old friend. But your concern is real. With every day lost, every hour wasted, this danger grows."

The cat's tail arched.

"Gray?" Adrian Draycott thought of the woman he loved, a woman who had shown no fear before a madman's treachery. As she had shown no fear in death.

His jaw hardened. "She says we must *make* them see. Alas, it is not so simple, is it, Gideon?" Adrian ran his hand over the cat's sleek fur. "There are some things that cannot be given and some choices that must not be rushed. Even when time crowds close." He looked out over the wooded hills, formless in the gathering darkness. A shooting star flashed and left a trail of silver through the silent night. "No, not even by such creatures as we are, my friend."

With a sigh, the black-clad figure turned and paced the cold stones. Beside him the great cat flicked his tail and waited, eyes agleam, sharp with intelligence. A cat and yet far more.

Overhead the moon pulled free of the clutching black fingers of the woods and rose in chill splendor, its beauty mocked by a racing curtain of clouds.

SOMEWHERE IN THE GREAT, restless beast that was modern London, a figure sat hunched in darkness, listening to the quiet voices.

It always began with the voices.

So it did this night. They were never much at first, just a whisper in the shadows or a sigh in the chill light of dawn. But they never stopped there.

The figure in the darkness frowned, trying to hold back the light and the memories.

And the voices.

But it never worked. The pictures were too sharp, the voices too shrill. In a wild dance they rose, racing ever closer till they broke in a feverish rush. Only then would the blessed silence return. The nothingness, once more. The peace.

Until it began all over again, with a whisper or a hiss.

Just as it had tonight.

Just as it always would, until the traitors were made to bleed, to weep, to pay for all the pain they had caused.

Now—and two hundred years before.

CHAPTER SEVENTEEN

CATHLIN CAUGHT A HARD breath. She didn't want to be here. The abbey was lovely, the will an unbelievable godsend, but Draycott Abbey left her throat raw and her pulse lurching.

It wasn't because of the portraits glaring down in cool arrogance from the silk-covered walls. It wasn't because of the scattered roses or the fragile tapestries that her mother had loved so well.

It was the past and its memories that Cathlin couldn't bear. Every room, every corner carried shadows that reminded her of the mother who had died here.

She looked at herself in the cheval glass, seeing the pale cheeks, the stormy eyes. Seeing a face full of shadows.

Just one night, she told herself.

The sun had melted over the western hills and reddish gold light poured over the old Aubusson carpets and gilt chairs. The Yellow Salon was lit by a massive crystal chandelier and candles set in silver candelabra. Four people stood gathered by the opened French doors as Cathlin entered.

The chandelier flashed. The crystal gleamed. All was peace and order.

Except for the spot where pain was eating a hole through Cathlin's heart.

She tugged uneasily at her dress, a fitted shimmer of amber silk that perfectly matched her eyes. Modest and demure in front, the dress turned dangerous at the back where it plunged straight to Cathlin's slender waist.

It was the sort of dress you didn't wear much under. Cathlin had meant it as a challenge to a man who had challenged her too often lately. Now, looking at Dominic, who was looking dangerous himself in a black turtleneck, smoky tweed jacket, and black trousers, she decided she might have made a slight miscalculation.

She shrugged. She could handle one arrogant bodyguard just fine.

About Viscount Draycott, she wasn't so sure. She tried to force away a wave of uneasiness. He was a tall man with thoughtful eyes and hair that showed the faintest sprinkling of gray. His young daughter was tugging at his hand, and he caught her up on his shoulders, heedless of protocol or the very expensive Hermès tie he wore. As he turned, Cathlin realized this was not the man she had seen by the moat, accompanied by his gray cat.

So the man liked his anonymity. Probably he let some member of his staff play at being viscount when there were visitors about. Very clever.

She looked around her, aware of the abbey's golden glow of age and wealth and unerring good taste. And though she hadn't meant to, Cathlin smiled softly. There was love here, love that whispered in the corners and gathered around her heart and clung tightly. Maybe something about this beautiful old house would accept nothing less than love.

As the blond-haired viscountess stood up and tickled her daughter's toes, Cathlin felt a burning in her eyes. She had had that kind of happiness once, only to lose it.

Here at Draycott Abbey.

Her hands tightened. She shouldn't be here. She couldn't face this. She was turning to leave when she felt Dominic's hand on her shoulder.

"Don't run, Cathlin. They won't bite." He took in her pale face and the glistening in her eyes. "Besides, you look spectacular in amber satin. Let me introduce you."

"I can't," Cathlin said flatly. "It was an abstraction before, just a name and a place. But seeing the three of them here, so happy, and knowing this is where it all happened..." She swallowed. "I'm not up to this."

"You would hurt Nicholas unbearably if you left now."

Cathlin brushed at her eyes. "Maybe I would hurt myself unbearably if I stayed."

"It never pays to run from shadows." Dominic pulled her hand under his arm and tugged her forward. "Another one of Ashton's laws."

"TWO WERE GRAY AND TWO WERE black with white spots. They were squirmy and soft and all covered with straw."

Cathlin sat by the windows an hour later, Genevieve Draycott beside her describing the nine baby kittens they had just discovered mewing in the old stables. The viscountess sat nearby, radiant in a simple Thai satin sheath as she watched her five-year-old daughter charm the room.

"I think it's time we put Archibald to bed, don't you think, my love? He looks very sleepy."

Genevieve looked down at her battered stuffed turtle. "Archibald doesn't look sleepy to me." She frowned. "I think he would like to stay up and have dinner with the grown-ups tonight."

The viscountess ruffled her daughter's curls. "Did he tell you that? But what about the nice bed we've made for him in Uncle Michael's old fishing basket? I'm sure Archibald will want to try that out."

Genevieve brightened. "Oh, I forgot. Let's go right now." She took her mother's hand and smiled at Cathlin. "Maybe I can show you the kittens tomorrow." Her brow furrowed. "If you're still here, that is. Papa said you might not stay for long."

Cathlin felt a pang of regret. "I'd love to see them, Genevieve."

The little girl's head cocked. "I like your eyes. They remind me of a ring Papa gave me. He told me you can see all kinds of wonderful things frozen inside it, and that if I look very hard, I can look right back into the past. Archibald and I do hope that you'll stay to see our kittens." With that, the girl skipped from the room, Archibald dragged carefully behind her.

Cathlin's throat tightened, burning with tears shed long ago. She had to go. She had to leave this beautiful, unbearable room before—"

"Ms. O'Neill, a toast." Nicholas Draycott was holding out a fragile Murano glass goblet. The rippled design, spun diagonally, shimmered in the candlelight. "It's not a Château Climens '71, but I think you'll enjoy this particular champagne."

Cathlin gave a jerky smile and accepted the fragile vessel.

"To the return of old friends," Nicholas said, raising his glass. "And to the welcome of those who will become new ones. While you are here, my home and everything in it will be at your disposal."

Crystal clinked. Candles glowed. The champagne slid down Cathlin's throat, velvet and fruity and flawless. A Roederer Cristal '77, intense, full and sweet.

It might as well have been vinegar.

The pain in her chest grew and grew. As if from a distance she heard Nicholas Draycott clear his throat. "And now, I have something I must tell you both. I'm afraid that Gabriel left another condition in his bequest."

Dim, so dim, Dominic's muttered surprise. A tight, sharp question. Cathlin didn't hear, walls heavy and looming, her head hammered by memories still formless.

"Seven days…abbey…"

Dominic's voice, louder this time. Sharper.

She could barely hear. Her throat was burning and Cathlin was afraid she was going to be sick. Get away—had to get away. *Mother, where are you? I'm alone and afraid and you're not here. Where are you? Why is everything so quiet?*

Her fist pressed at her mouth, holding back tears, holding back pain, holding back fifteen years of stark shadows.

"Together...very specific. You must pass one week here in the manner of husband and wife..."

Dominic's voice rose to a harsh curse. "...should have told us...utterly ridiculous..."

Cathlin heard no more. Pushing unsteadily to her feet, she shoved past the drifting curtains, past the rose petals strewn over the flagstones by the wind, and out into the blessed darkness.

"Cathlin."

She turned away, her legs curled on the damp lawn, her cheeks slick with tears. "Go away."

"We've got to talk. Then I'll go away."

"It's too late to talk. You knew. You *knew* about that stipulation of Gabriel's, damn you!"

Dominic's voice tightened. "I didn't know. Turn around and look at me, Cathlin."

"Go away. Go away forever."

"No."

Cathlin stumbled to her feet and shoved past him. He caught her at the cool weathered granite of the abbey's south wall. Near their feet the moat gurgled softly and a pair of swans left tracks of silver in their wake.

"It's not too late. Talk to me now."

"You want a peek, is that it? You want to see the tears and touch the pain. You want the full spectacle, blood and all." Her cheeks glistened, silvered and wet in the moonlight. "Well, you can't. No one can, not even me. It's all locked away somewhere, deep in a place where even I can't find it. All that's left is a hole,

Dominic, a great jagged hole that tells me something's missing. Only God help me, I don't remember what."

She twisted, her face to the cold stone. Dominic turned her slowly, his fingers gentle at her waist.

"Let me go."

But he didn't release her, and Cathlin shoved at him wildly. Her fists tightened, hammering at his chest.

And he let her. Silent. Thoughtful. Unmoving. His eyes full of an emotion Cathlin didn't want to see.

After a long while she caught a ragged sob. Her hands slowed, then sank to her sides. "I miss her. Oh, God, I miss her every second, every hour." She took a ragged breath. "I'm an adult. I have charge cards. I know about balloon rates and term insurance. I handle wines worth hundreds of thousands of dollars, and here I am crying like a fool over something that happened fifteen years ago. Something I can't even remember."

Dominic's fingers wound through her hair. "She was your mother, Cathlin. Bone and blood memories like that don't go away. Maybe they just get buried."

"Why, Dominic? Why did he plan all this in that will of his? Why does he want us here together for a week?" She shivered. "Sometimes I almost think he's here, watching us."

"Because the tragedy never really ended, Cathlin. Gabriel knew that better than anyone. Maybe it's up to us to end it by finding out the truth. That could be why he wanted us here." He brushed her cheek. "The bottles are authentic, aren't they?"

"A complete chemical analysis and corroborative research will take weeks, but I can tell you the answer already. Oh, yes, they're real and they're nearly priceless."

Dominic let out his breath slowly. "If we don't agree to go along with the stipulations of the will, Cathlin, Nicholas has to dump that wine into the moat."

"He can't!"

"But he will. He's absolutely serious about all this. It was the last expressed wish of a dying man—possibly a murdered man. Nicholas is dead set on honoring every single word."

"But then—" Cathlin closed her eyes. "I still can't."

Dominic eased a damp strand of hair from her lips. As his fingers brushed her mouth, he cursed softly. "Cathlin," he whispered.

"Yes?"

"Heaven help me, I want to…"

Kiss me. Cathlin's heart did a funny lurch in her chest. *Please. Now. Before I can think.*

His fingers slid around her neck. His eyes burned, all smoke and jade, but he gave her time to move away, to pound his chest, to curse him for a blasted fool.

None of which Cathlin did. Somehow her hands were wrapped around his lapels and she was easing him closer.

"Cathlin?"

"No. Don't talk."

Their lips hovered, brushed, fitted lightly. It was like coming home, only a thousand times better, deep and sweet and full.

"I'm…sorry." Her words melted over his open mouth. "About hitting you."

"I'm not. I think that particular storm—" a pause to lick the ridge of her lip with his warm tongue "—has been too long coming." He slid his legs between hers, pulling her into his heat. "And I'm very, very glad that it broke over me."

"I won't do it." Cathlin's voice was husky, lost in arousal as he moved against her, smooth and slow and perfect. "Not here. Not for a week. I can't, Dominic."

"Then you can't. Finished. End of lot, end of category."

"Why aren't you shouting at me?"

"Because I'm far too busy kissing you, Irish. And damn, but you're good to kiss."

Her fingers eased into his hair. "I…am?"

"Wonderful."

"Dominic?"

"Hmm?"

"I tried to hate the abbey. I tried so hard, but I couldn't. It's too beautiful and there's too much love here. But there are shadows, too. I try to tell myself it's just me, and then I see something flicker out of the corner of my eye. I catch the hum of a voice or a hint of fragrance and I wonder is it her, is it some memory, or am I simply losing my mind."

"Irish, one of us here is losing his mind, and it isn't you." Dominic eased away, his body too hard, his eyes too hot. "You're not losing anything. It's coming back, don't you see? That's bound to hurt at first. Maybe you don't have any more choice about how or when it comes."

"Maybe not." She studied his features, stern, beautiful, awash with silver in the moonlight. "What are we doing here, Dominic? What happened to the nun and the rosary?"

"You want me to stop?"

A universe of thinking. Asking. Taking time to be honest. "No."

"Good." A low groan. "Very good. Because I think I might go on kissing you forever, O'Neill. And when I'm not kissing you, I plan on being busy touching you in the most amazing ways." His hand eased over the naked skin at her back and he fitted her to his awesome arousal.

"I bet you tell all your clients that."

"No." Dead serious, his hands rigid. "Not one. Not ever, Cathlin. It's important you know that."

"I do." Her fingers traced his lips. Her sigh was loud in the silence of the night. "Meanwhile, I suppose we'd better get back inside or Nicholas Draycott will think we've fallen into the moat."

"Maybe I feel like I have. But you're right. Any longer out here and I might do something monumentally stupid. Fantastic, but very stupid." Smiling softly, Dominic smoothed Cathlin's hair and straightened the neck of her dress. "Let's go."

NICHOLAS WAS TOYING WITH a row of jeweled Fabergé miniatures when Dominic and Cathlin came inside. His eyes narrowed as he saw the hardness at Dominic's jaw. "I'm sorry I didn't tell you sooner, Dominic, but I was afraid you wouldn't come if you knew."

"I wouldn't have."

The viscount's steady glance took in both of them. "What about now?"

Dominic looked at Cathlin and took a deep breath.

"Yes," she said.

"No," Dominic snapped.

Their eyes met, startled.

Nicholas smiled faintly, noting Cathlin's disordered hair and swollen lips, along with Dominic's rumpled lapels and the hint of lipstick at his cheek. "I'm delighted you're in agreement, just as I'm certain that Gabriel Montserrat would be, were he here." The lights in the hall flickered for a moment. "Sorry. That happens sometimes when the wiring gets damp. Now I suggest that we move things along as fast as possible, before the value of this wine is made public. Meanwhile, my wife, Kacey, will continue to go through the county archives along with church records of marriages and deaths." He refilled their glasses with a flourish and turned, smiling broadly. "And now, to a toast to your upcoming wedding."

Dominic's eyes darkened.

"I have checked with the vicar and he is free to marry you tomorrow. Whatever happens after that will be..." He cleared his throat. "That is, I leave the practical details of your marriage up to you."

Wind gusted through the study and the abbey's lights flickered. A moment later the room was plunged into darkness.

CHAPTER EIGHTEEN

DOMINIC CURSED.

Long and fluently. In English, then in back-alley Thai, then in very eloquent French. He couldn't see a thing.

Cathlin's fingers slid to his arm. "Is this another idea of Marston's? I hope he's not going to wheel in crêpes flambées."

"I doubt that Marston had anything to do with this." As he spoke, Dominic inched toward the wall. "Nicholas?"

"Right here. What's going on?"

"I don't know yet, but I soon will."

"Good. In the meanwhile, I'm going up to check on Kacey and Genevieve."

Cathlin reached out blindly. "Dominic, wait. I'm coming with you." Silence. "Dominic?"

But Dominic Montserrat had already disappeared into the darkness.

DOMINIC INCHED DOWN THE rear stairs, his mind racing. Swift and methodical, he ran through all the permutations of exits, entrances, and electrical sources. He was at the last step, easing alongside the first row of shelves, when he heard a low whisper at his ear.

"Dominic?"

"Cathlin? Why in God's name—"

Her voice was a wisp of sound. "Because something's wrong

and you're going to need my help. I know this place better than you ever will."

"After only one afternoon?"

"One long and very thorough afternoon spent in the cellar. And I remember every detail, believe me. Right now we're standing beside a row of claret bottles. That means there's a power source just a little over four feet to the left on the south wall."

A creaking sound came somewhere to their right. Instantly Dominic's fingers tightened on Cathlin's shoulder, motioning her to silence.

He bent close, lips to her ear. "Stay here."

"But you can't just—"

"*Stay.*"

She didn't hear him slip away. As always, he moved in utter silence. All Cathlin felt was a whisper of wind against her skin.

Her heart pounded as she crouched in the darkness of the ancient cellars, thinking about death and betrayal, about nightmares that wouldn't stay buried.

Thinking about ghosts past and present and a sad and lonely man named Gabriel.

Her senses were screaming and her nerves stretched to the breaking point when she finally heard the hiss of a match being struck. Through the neatly stacked rows of bottles Cathlin made out a shadowed figure bent over one of the wine racks. She was inching closer when she heard bone strike flesh. The wine racks shivered with the impact of a blow. But there were no words, no voices at all. Only later would Cathlin realize the significance of that silence, the mark of two professionals who gave nothing away even in the direst circumstances.

Cathlin didn't stop to think about what she was doing next. She reached deep, calling up her memory of the cellars. Before her were three rows of claret and a row of Madeira.

The muffled thud of bodies grew louder as Cathlin worked

through the darkness. She felt a ridge of wood at her feet, a small wooden step stool pushed out of reach.

Her hands closed around the rough wooden legs. It would be heavy enough to deal a stunning blow, if only she could figure out where Dominic was.

She took a breath and then repeated one of Dominic's French curses, one of the few she had understood. She heard a quick gasp. Close by, a harsh voice, raw with pain, grated out an answering curse.

Dominic was slightly to her right, next to a rack full of priceless claret. Cathlin waited, praying, then she hurled the footstool with all her strength.

After a satisfying crack, Cathlin heard a sharp curse, followed by footsteps. Glass shattered and a shoulder rammed into her chest. She gasped as a hard body shoved her to the ground and charged off into the darkness.

"Cathlin, are you there? Talk to me, damn it!"

"I—I'm fine, Dominic." Cathlin clenched her teeth against the pain in her side. "I think he's gone."

Nearby a match flared. Cathlin frowned as she saw Dominic propped up against one of the wine racks. His jacket was gone and his cuff was splashed with blood.

"You idiot," Cathlin sputtered. "You complete and utter idiot."

"Don't get upset, Irish. Some of this blood is *his.*" Dominic's fingers tightened. "Though maybe not so much as I'd like. I see you inflicted a little damage yourself." He frowned down at the glass splinters spread over the floor.

"Who was he?"

"I don't know, but he was good. *Too* bloody good for any amateur thief." Grimacing, he headed for the stairs.

"What are you doing?"

"Going after him. It's my job, remember?"

NICHOLAS WAS PACING THE drawing room, looking grim, when Dominic returned. "Did you find anything?"

"Footprints leading to tire tracks. Not much help, I'm afraid. At least you managed to get the electricity working again."

Nicholas rubbed his neck. "Someone had thrown the circuit breaker. Obviously, the news is out, and we're going to have to take some precautions. What do you suggest?"

"You need a new alarm system up and running by tomorrow. I know a man in London who can handle it. We'll also have to establish some other procedures. I want to know where everyone is at all times." He looked at Cathlin, who was sitting pale but composed next to Marston. "That means at *all* times, understood? I'll arrange to have radio transmitters for each of us." He turned to Marston. "Nothing goes in or out without my seeing it first. Not books, not groceries, not a single matchstick."

"Understood, Lord Ashton."

"I have a question," Cathlin said tightly. "When are you going to do something about that blood on your cuff?"

"Later." Dominic's voice was hard. "Any more questions? No? Then go up and rest. Nicholas and I will take watch down here until I can get someone to help in the morning."

"YOU'RE BLEEDING AGAIN."

Cathlin frowned as she followed Dominic out into the hallway. No answer.

"Dominic, you can't just go around *bleeding* on everything." Still no answer.

Cathlin grabbed his uninjured arm and pulled him to a halt. There were lines of tension at his mouth and forehead, lines he couldn't hope to conceal. Her eyes widened with disbelief as she ran her fingers over the front of his jacket.

It was wet with blood. "So when were you planning to do something about this?"

Dominic shrugged. "You'll be the first to know."

"It's all a game to you, isn't it? All about seeing who's faster or smarter or braver. Well, I'm not playing. Not now. Not ever." Her eyes were dark and haunted. "I've already lost one man I loved that way, you see."

RESTLESS AND UNABLE TO sleep, Dominic stood on the middle of the stone bridge, rubbing his neck. All the entries and exits were in good shape. Only two windows needed new locks and rewiring for the upgraded laser security system.

Now he had to try the places that weren't so obvious. He looked out over the darkened hills, trying to think with the mind of a man who would do anything to possess the wine in the abbey cellars.

A thief would automatically assume electronic protection was in place and look for a way to cut it. Next he'd go for backup generators—which Draycott didn't have. After that, he'd go for the bodyguard.

Dominic's eyes hardened. Being a target didn't frighten him. He'd done it too often before to be afraid of a bullet he couldn't prepare for. But the thought that he might fail and allow Cathlin to be hurt scared the living hell out of him.

Abruptly he turned. "Nicholas?" he called, scanning the darkness behind him.

No answer. Nothing moved amid the shadows.

Dominic inched toward the gatehouse. But the doorway, too, was empty.

"Of course no one's out there, Montserrat. You're losing your mind, that's your only problem. And all because of a woman as changeable as quicksilver, a woman who's smart and irritating and has suffered too much pain in her life already."

Muttering, he made his way over the bridge. Everything was peaceful. Not a shadow moved on those manicured green slopes. So why didn't he feel safe?

High overhead Vega flashed sharply against the deep velvet of the sky. To the north the Big Dipper dangled in a perfect silver chain, pointing to some long-forgotten mystery that only primitive man had understood. Dominic thought about newer mysteries, about white dwarfs and red giants and black holes so dense not a single speck of matter could ever escape their vast intractable pull.

Right now he felt drawn that way to the woman upstairs.

Around him the soft night sounds of wind and water drifted and ebbed. Dominic took a slow breath and told himself to relax.

Cathlin had gone up to bed hours ago. From the bridge he had watched her shadow move back and forth against the curtains. Her slim body had been silhouetted against white lace, a tantalizing sweep of curves and hollows, before the light had gone out.

He tried not to think about her undressing, then sliding down against the quilt, her hair loose and glossy around her face.

Roses tossed beside the moat, filling the air with perfume. The moon burned, unblinking over the wooded hills.

Only night. Only silence. Only the darting silver images of moon and stars, reflected in the ever-changing currents of the moat.

Suddenly something made the back of Dominic's neck tighten. "Marston?"

But it wasn't Draycott's eccentric butler who stood in the stone courtyard before the abbey's huge front gate. It was Cathlin O'Neill, wearing some damned jersey that barely covered her thighs. It wasn't feminine. It wasn't fetching or flirty or seductively silken.

But it might as well have been, because Dominic took one look and felt something burst into hot, furious life inside him. He envisioned her in white lace and peach satin. In a long gown that swept the floor and a navy velvet cloak with a soft hood.

Just like the sad-eyed woman in his dreams.

And then he imagined her in absolutely nothing at all.

"Sweet God above, Montserrat, get up off all fours and start trying to be reasonably human, will you?" Frowning, he pushed away from the stone railing.

And then he froze. Cathlin was moving toward him. He whispered her name, but she didn't answer. She moved haltingly over the arch of the bridge, then cocked her head, listening to the silence.

Dominic felt a chill at his heart as she sank to her knees at the top of the bridge and inched protectively against one of the stone columns. And there she sat, huddled in the shadows, her eyes huge, her hands twisting.

It took several moments to realize exactly what those white fingers were doing. They were scraping desperately, trying to wash off a stain that only she could see.

Dominic knelt slowly beside her. When she didn't look up, he touched her shoulder softly, waiting for some hint of recognition.

"Is it time?" she asked, in a voice that was hers but softer. Younger. "Can I go yet? I want to go."

Dominic felt something cold and sharp go in just beneath his ribs and twist hard. She was caught in the past, caught in the nightmares of her mother's death. Had she held a killer's identity trapped in her mind all these years? "You can go, Cathlin. Anytime you want. It's all over now, I promise."

Her hands twisted sharply. "You said that before. You told me I could go, and then you locked me in."

Dominic tasted a rage that threatened to overwhelm him. What kind of sick mind would torment an innocent child?

Somehow he bit back his fury. "Not now. There's nothing to hold you now, Cathlin. Look around you. All you have to do is walk over that bridge and you'll be free."

"But I can't. If I do, they'll know. And then—oh God, then—" Her hands slid to her mouth as she tried to hold in a muffled sob.

Had they threatened her? Had she been afraid to make a noise? "I'll take you wherever you want. I'll take you home,

Cathlin. I'll take you back to yesterday or on to tomorrow. No one will ever stop you again, I swear it."

After an agonizing silence, she pushed to her feet. When she walked back across the bridge, there was no recognition at all in her face.

Dominic's throat tightened as he watched her climb the stairs and make her way back to bed. There she curled into a ball and pulled the covers protectively around her.

As if they could hold out a lifetime of shadows.

Dominic slumped in a chair beside her bed. When dawn finally broke over the Wealden hills, he had decided two things. He was going to keep out those shadows for Cathlin O'Neill, whether she liked it or not. Nothing was going to stop her from being free ever again.

And if it took a wedding performed at the order of a man who had been dead for two hundred years to accomplish that, then the abbey was damned well going to have a wedding that no one ever forgot.

CHAPTER NINETEEN

IT TOOK DOMINIC TWO HOURS on the phone and Nicholas another three, but by eleven o'clock, everything was arranged.

The vicar was on his way. Serita was coming from London and several of Nicholas's friends had been invited. The wedding plans were set.

Cathlin had protested when Nicholas told her the ceremony was all arranged. She wanted to help solve the mystery of the will, but refused to believe an actual wedding ceremony was necessary. But Nicholas held firm. This was Gabriel's last wish, and he would see it carried out or the wine would indeed go into the moat.

When Cathlin had looked at Dominic, she'd seen a similar determination on his face. His reason was more practical: he wanted Cathlin cooped up at the abbey where he could keep an eye on her. His final words had been unequivocal.

It might be the wedding from hell, but it was going to take place whether she liked it or not.

IT WAS A LOVELY WEDDING. The bride wore black and the groom was bleeding.

The study was bright with centifolia roses arranged in cut crystal bowls. Marston looked upon the proceedings with patent pride beside Nicholas and Kacey Draycott.

First to arrive was Michael Burke, one of Nicholas Draycott's closest friends and his neighbor to the north. With Michael came his wife, who was looking rather pale after a bout with the flu. Soon after, Serita McCall made a grand entrance in a jumpsuit of gold lurex and seed pearls.

Introductions were completed and sherry passed by the discreet but ubiquitous butler. Nicholas was just helping himself to a glass when the vicar rushed in. "So sorry to be late," he apologized haltingly. "There was an accident on the A28, and I'm afraid it's rather upset me. The fellow wasn't hurt, thank the Blessed Father, but the poor man's truck was left in most distressing condition. If I'm running on, do forgive me."

Nicholas hid a smile. "Quite understandable under the circumstances."

The vicar passed his hat and coat to Marston, then rubbed his hands and looked about him. "Now then, where is the bride?"

Draycott and Marston exchanged a quick look and Nicholas cleared his throat. "I expect she'll be down shortly, Vicar. Last-minute affairs to be taken care of and all that. Why don't you have a sherry while you wait?"

Right on cue, Marston passed a goblet to the vicar. The polite flow of conversation ensued.

Only someone looking very closely would have noticed the faint frown working down Nicholas's forehead.

CATHLIN PULLED OPEN THE door to the closet and glared at the clothes inside. Muttering, she ran over her choices, on loan from Kacey. A simple but very elegant cocktail dress of ivory satin?

Too formal.

An off-the-shoulder designer knock-off from Paris, made in a clingy knit of striking amber that perfectly matched her eyes?

Too slinky. Cathlin wasn't about to give Dominic any reason to think she *liked* this idea of his.

Next came to simple suits in dark fabrics.

Possibly.

And then Cathlin's lips curved up in a smile. She'd marry Officer Montserrat all right, and it would be in clothes from her own bag.

And when she did, it would be a ceremony he *never* forgot.

A HALF HOUR LATER THE clock was chiming as Cathlin started down the stairs. Through the doors to the study she saw a dozen or so people talking quietly, trying to pretend it was the most normal thing in the world for a man to marry a woman he barely knew because of the will of an ancestor he'd never met.

An ancestor two hundred years dead.

The sun poured golden through the abbey's great mullioned windows as Cathlin looked down and smoothed her black silk blouse. Her black flowing trousers. Her black silk scarf.

She smiled faintly. The message should be clear enough even for a hard case like Dominic Montserrat.

DOMINIC WAS ALONE IN THE front hall when he looked up and saw Cathlin at the top of the stairs. The chandelier cast glints of gold, red, and amber through her hair as she moved down the steps, smiling.

Dominic blinked. Silky hair. Satin blouse. Flowing trousers. All black.

A muscle twitched at his jaw. Even as he registered the solid black of her attire, Dominic felt a jab of admiration. No shy, awe-filled bride here, he thought ruefully.

Somewhere in the house a clock began to chime.

Dominic's arms tensed beneath his perfectly tailored jacket. Motionless, wary, he stared at Cathlin, dressed in black. At the jeweled satin rose in her hair, also black.

He found himself torn between fury and disbelief.

Very well, my dear, if it's war you want, it's war you'll get. He took a step forward, poised for battle, a hard-faced warrior clad in impeccable evening dress that played up the rich bronze hue of his skin.

Cathlin studied him coldly from head to toe. "Heavens, I seem to have made a terrible mistake. I'm dressed all wrong for the occasion."

"I'm sure it was no mistake," Dominic murmured, taking her arm. "Rather an unusual way to dress for a wedding, isn't it?"

"Is it, Officer Montserrat? I wouldn't know, having never been married before."

"I'm not exactly a veteran myself. However, the guests have arrived, the vicar is waiting, and Marston is positively on the verge of a crisis of nerves. So let's just get the damn business over with, shall we?"

"Of course," Cathlin said tightly, trying to pull free of his hand. But he slid his arm under hers and guided her inexorably toward the noise and lights of the study.

Dominic was attuned to her every emotion now. He felt her slight tremor and knew the moment that her step faltered. His fingers tightened, firm but gentle, as he guided her forward.

"Is—is Serita here yet?"

"Offering healths to anyone who'll listen. She's already got Nicholas's promise to tour the wine cellars later. And Nicholas's friend, Lord Burke, has asked her over for a consultation next week."

"That sounds like Serita." As Cathlin spoke, the flower above her ear swayed and slid to the floor. Dominic went for it at the same instant she did, and their shoulders butted beneath the five-hundred-year-old chandelier casting warm sparks over the oak floor.

Pain streaked through Dominic's shoulder, his memento of yesterday's scuffle in the wine cellar. He winced as his fingers closed on the satin flower. Already he could feel blood seeping beneath the bandage on his arm, but he'd be damned if anybody got the slightest hint that he was uncomfortable.

"Turn around," he ordered.

"Why?"

"So I can put this damn bow back in your hair. Since you seem so intent on wearing the bloody thing, it's the least I can do to see that it stays put." He caught her shoulders and spun her around, and his long fingers smoothed the hair back from her cheek and slid the anchoring pin deep into her hair. It felt like satin in his fingers and left his blood on fire. "Stop moving, damn it."

"I'm *not* moving!"

"Then stop breathing. Since you've gone to all this trouble to tell the world exactly what you think of this wedding, dressed like some sacrificial virgin going off to be beheaded and deflowered, the least you can do is stand still until this ugly flower is back in place."

Cathlin's shoulders tightened. "It's not a wedding. At least not a real and proper one. I just wanted to make my opinions clear on that."

"Oh, you've made yourself crystal clear, O'Neill. I expect everyone will be thinking you're a widow rather than a bride-to-be."

Her eyes glittered. Color slashed over her high cheekbones. Oh, yes, it would be a lovely ceremony all right.

Dominic scowled, wanting to shake her, wanting to order her to be careful. Wanting to kiss her, until she gripped his shoulders and poured over him like slow, still water and he had his fill of her.

Except something told Dominic he'd *never* get his fill of this woman.

He bit back a curse as Marston came through the study doors, magnificent in a black coat and new orange running shoes. "It appears as if we are ready, my lord. You will be wishing for the ring, of course."

Dominic opened the case Marston gave him. Inside lay a square-cut emerald, outlined in tiny pavé diamonds. "Thank you, Marston."

The ring had been passed down through his family for centuries, maybe even back as far as Gabriel's time. Family legend said the emerald had come from somewhere in the Sri Lanka hill country and that the stone changed hands a dozen times within the first two hours of its discovery.

Dominic looked down, remembering how it had flashed on his mother's strong, capable hand. She had given it to him, smiling tenderly, only an hour before her death.

"My stubborn, serious son, take this and believe. Believe that you'll find her, the one who is the other piece of your heart. You'll know who she is because she'll fit into your soul, completing something you didn't even know was missing until that moment." She had waved her hand, dismissing his protests. "Hush, my love. Let me finish, for my time is nearly gone." Dominic could still remember how the ring's sharp corners had cut into his skin. He had been repulsed at the thought that the only way the ring could be his was with his mother's death.

"When you find her and your heart whispers that she is the one, listen, my love. And give her this. When you do, I'll know it. Somehow you'll feel it, too, my dearest Dominic. Somewhere you'll know I'm smiling."

As her fingers had closed over his, her eyes had flickered shut. An hour later she was dead.

Dominic wondered if she was watching now. If so, what would that calm, practical Frenchwoman make of this bizarre ceremony performed at the wish of a man dead for two centuries.

He wasn't sure he wanted to know.

"Shall we begin, my lord?" The balding vicar moved from foot to foot, clearly ill at ease. Nicholas had explained the whole odd story to him, and in the end he had given way before Nicholas's persuasion, contenting himself with a single, muttered, "most extraordinary."

The heady scent of roses filled the air where the French doors stood open to the golden valleys.

Dominic felt a sudden pressure in his chest. He ignored it, just as he had been trained to ignore anything without relevance to his job. "Your hand, my dear."

Only Dominic saw the swift burst of color that filled Cathlin's cheeks. Only Dominic felt the tremor that shook her fingers, then was quickly suppressed as his hand closed over hers.

"Dearly beloved, we are gathered together here in the sight of God…"

Dominic's jaw hardened as the vicar began to speak. A will was a will, after all, and a million pounds was a million bloody pounds. Oh, yes, it would be a lovely ceremony, he thought grimly.

Especially if the bride and groom managed to keep from murdering each other before it was over.

"…TO BE JOINED TOGETHER…"

Cathlin's knees felt like Seacliffe's disintegrating roof beams.

"…in holy matrimony…"

She was really here. She was really consenting. This was *really* happening.

"…an honorable estate, instituted of God in paradise…"

The air was full of the scent of roses. She could feel the cool slide of her satin blouse, heavy against her sensitized skin. She caught every smell, registered every noise and movement around her, however small.

"…not to be enterprised, nor taken in hand unadvisedly…"

She took a quick, steadying breath, ignoring the strong hand on hers, ignoring the urge to look sideways, toward the man whose startling eyes reminded her of a pine forest at dawn, full of secrets.

But Cathlin discovered that she didn't have to look to see Dominic.

Every detail of his face was already burned into her memory.

FIFTEEN MINUTES LATER IT was done. The vows were said, the oaths exchanged. Dominic's elegant emerald ring now sat gleaming upon Cathlin's slender finger.

The whole ceremony had gone smoothly, in fact, if one discounted the tension between the bridal pair so thick it could be cut with a knife.

Nicholas and his wife looked on in high good humor, delighted by Cathlin's unusual style of dress. The vicar, downright uncomfortable, limited himself to a few uncertain smiles.

As soon as the service was done, Dominic had given her a firm but very swift kiss. Almost immediately she turned away and moved to greet Serita.

After a hug, Serita studied her friend intently. "I hope you'll be happy, Cathlin. I know this wedding is just a formality, part of that crazy will, but your eyes are sparkling and your cheeks are flushed. And don't tell me it's just from anger, because I won't believe it." Her voice fell. "You're entitled to be happy, you know. Both of you are." She squeezed Cathlin's hand, then offered her a glass of Dom Ruinart champagne.

Cathlin emptied her glass, determined not to think about vintage or acidity or carbonation levels, only to enjoy how the champagne tickled all the way down the back of her throat.

When Nicholas and his wife walked up two glasses later, Cathlin gave the viscount a blinding smile. "A lovely ceremony, wasn't it, Lord Draycott?"

"Call me Nicholas, please," the viscount said with a smile. "And yes, so it was, Lady Ashton."

Lady Ashton. Cathlin met Dominic's eyes and felt color flare through her cheeks.

Nicholas's wife smiled. "Just yesterday I had it from the head of Harrods Wine Department that you are the best source of information on old Sauternes in England."

Cathlin caught up another glass of champagne from

Marston's tray and drained it rather wildly. "I'm afraid Mr. Grandville-Jones is in my debt because I saved him from wasting a great deal of money on a consignment of what was supposedly fifty-year-old Sauternes." A smile played around her lips. "I tracked him down mere seconds before the auctioneer's hammer fell."

"And in the end who purchased this overrated and overpriced grape juice?" Dominic asked.

"It was a corporate purchase by a rather dour group of financiers from Osaka. But I doubt they will have noticed the problem with the wine. They were buying strictly for investment purposes." Cathlin's tone conveyed exactly how little she thought of such transactions.

"You don't like the idea?" Dominic found he enjoyed watching Cathlin leap in to defend the things she believed in.

"With wine, really good wine, becoming more expensive by the day, I can see the necessity of investment acquisitions, but I don't have to like it."

Serita laughed. "Oh, Lord, now you've got her talking about wine. No one will be able to get a word in the rest of the night. Never mind, I'll rescue you all. Here's a toast." She held up a beautiful goblet of handspun glass whose stem was worked in gold. Marston had told Cathlin the set had been in Dominic's family for generations, and he'd sent for it specially for the ceremony. "I offer a toast to two friends." Her eyes gleamed with mischief. "May their wine be sweet and their nights be long."

A storm of color swirled through Cathlin's cheeks. She refused to meet Dominic's eyes as she raised her glass. Crystal tinkled amid a murmur of salutes.

Then another voice cut through the pleasurable stillness. "Dominic Montserrat? My dear boy, it has been far too long since I've seen you."

Dominic turned, his eyes hard. The new arrival sported a perfectly cut tweed jacket and a smile that did not quite reach his eyes. It had been three years since Dominic had last seen him, but James Harcliffe looked exactly the same. "What are you doing here, Harcliffe?"

"Oh my, things really haven't changed, have they?" James Harcliffe, thin and balding, clicked his tongue. "As you guessed, I'm here for business, not pleasure." He gestured toward the man beside him. "Have you met Jeffrey Hayes? He's a particularly good chap in our department."

Dominic looked over the powerfully built man whose eyes were the color of muddy ice. "I've heard the name," he said coldly.

"Jeffrey, do be helpful and fetch me a glass of champagne, won't you?" Harcliffe's cool voice held the edge of command that had allowed him to rise high in the government security apparatus. Hayes nodded and disappeared.

"You haven't changed a bit have you?"

"I expect not." Harcliffe smoothed his lapel. "Nor have you, my dear old friend."

"Friend? We were *never* friends," Dominic snapped. "Now tell me what you're doing here."

"I have some papers for you. I think you'll find they make enjoyable reading." Harcliffe's eyes were full of malice. "I left them in the viscount's study."

The others had moved away.

"I don't want files, I want answers," Dominic growled. "That's why I called you last night. Who was in that car? I gave you a license number and now I want a name."

"We're working on it."

"Working's not good enough, Harcliffe. Someone was after Cathlin, someone clever. I want to know who."

"What makes you assume that the attackers were after Cathlin? Perhaps, my dear Dominic, they were after *you*." Harcliffe's eyes narrowed. "After all, you've left a great many enemies in your wake."

"Why would they come all this way when they could track me down in France? No, there's a knot in my gut that tells me this has to do with the wine."

"Ah, yes, that much vaunted instinct of yours. It has proved extremely valuable on occasion, I admit. It has also given you some very influential admirers, people in very high places who are interested in acquiring that priceless wine in Draycott's cellars. So listen to me and listen well," Harcliffe commanded. "This is out of your hands. The palace wants that wine, and that makes this a government operation. Are you following me?"

Dominic bit back a curse. Was there anything that James Harcliffe didn't know? "I'm following."

"Then I expect you to go by the book. Keep that wine safe and see that Cathlin completes the authentication that the palace wants." Harcliffe smiled thinly. "Otherwise, I'll see that Hayes replaces you in charge of security here at the abbey."

"Hayes? The man is totally unreliable and you know it. He bungled that last case in Manchester and nearly got a whole airport blown up in the process."

"Too bloody bad. Mr. Hayes is all we have available right now." There was smug triumph in Harcliffe's voice.

"What about those three harassment suits lodged against Hayes by women he was protecting? You and I both know they had total validity. Pulling the full force of the branch was the only way you got them dropped."

Harcliffe clicked his tongue. "Pure hearsay. Like any other man involved in a dangerous job, our Mr. Hayes feels the need for an occasional release of stress."

"You call it a release of stress when he forced that nurse from Brighton into his car and kept her bound and gagged for six hours?" Dominic growled a curse. "By God, there was hospital testimony to support physical evidence of assault."

"Nonsense, Dominic. It was all amicably resolved out of court. Now I really must insist that you stop dredging up unpleasant aspects of Mr. Hayes's past. It's either him or you."

"Then it's me and only me. Meanwhile, I need backup here. Men, equipment and anything else I happen to think of."

"It can be arranged."

"Tonight, Harcliffe. Not in two weeks."

"I suppose you're right. The press will soon have all the details of that wine. By the way, how is your wife holding up?"

"As well as can be expected."

"What's the problem? All our records say that Cathlin O'Neill has permanently repressed those memories of her mother's death."

"And just what else do those records say? Do they tell you how it felt to be ten years old and see your mother lying dead in front of you? Maybe you even got a sample of the woman's blood for the files."

"Don't let it get personal." It was a cold, flat order. "You know the rules as well as I do, Dominic."

"It *is* personal. I'm the one who brought her back here. How would *you* like to take responsibility for her sanity, Harcliffe?"

"I wouldn't. But then I don't have to. You have always been the favorite with the Royals. You racked up highest scores in every class. Firearms, threat analysis, close escort and evasive driving—you were always the best and they took you in as one of their own, didn't they?" For a moment there was hatred in Harcliffe's voice, hatred born of jealousy that he himself had never been able to break into that royal and rarefied world. "But it won't help you one damned bit now. You're back and you're going to stay back, Montserrat. And while you're here, you're mine to control."

"You've waited a long time for this, haven't you, Harcliffe?"

. "Longer than you know," came the flat answer. "So shut your mouth and get back to your duties, Officer Montserrat. Unless you want to see Hayes replace you."

"What if Cathlin blows from stress? Then you've got no bequest and no one to carry out the verification work for the palace."

"She won't. We've got her complete psychological profile, and I've already gone through the debriefing notes made after the death of her mother. At the time there was some suspicion it might have been a political killing in retaliation against her father's government activities. Donnell O'Neill was very useful to us, you see. But that idea was scrapped. In the end, the conclusion of a panel of experts was that Ms. O'Neill knew nothing of importance—and anything she might have observed at the abbey was permanently blocked in her subconscious as a result of the trauma. Don't you think we looked into every possibility? As a matter of fact, my wife was the expert of record in the case and she did nothing else for weeks. If there was a chance, even the slightest chance, that Cathlin O'Neill could remember something of use, you can be bloody certain that we would have pursued the possibility."

"And then what would you have done, Harcliffe? Pumped her full of hallucinogens? Given her pentathol? Sweet God, to a ten-year-old child?"

"If it would have resulted in useful ends, that's exactly what we would have done." Harcliffe's eyes were utterly cold.

"By God, sometimes I think you're mad. Sometimes I think *all* of us are."

CATHLIN WATCHED DOMINIC stride away from the balding man who'd just arrived from London. Was it something about the wine? She was going after Dominic when she felt a hand on her arm.

"Don't go yet."

Cathlin looked up into soft brown eyes. There was something

sad about the woman's faint stoop and the strand of gray hair trying to escape from her prim chignon.

"You do remember me, don't you?" The woman frowned. "I see you don't remember at all. I am Joanna Harcliffe. Dr. Joanna Harcliffe." She looked at Cathlin, her head cocked, as her husband moved off in search of more champagne and new prey. "I'm afraid my husband has managed to irritate Dominic Montserrat yet again."

"Again? I don't understand."

"You didn't know? My dear, they worked together for years."

Cathlin stiffened at the reference to a world she continued to hate. "I see."

"Good heavens, you *do* have the look of your mother, especially when you're angry. I would have thought it was impossible."

"You *knew* her?"

"Oh, yes, I knew Elizabeth O'Neill." Joanna Harcliffe said the words slowly, as if they held a host of memories.

Cathlin's face paled. "You knew her well?"

"Oh goodness, yes. We were up at St. Hilda's together—Oxford, you know. We read English before she developed an interest in art. Then she leaped right ahead of me. She was quite brilliant, your mother." The older woman's voice tightened. "Don't let anyone tell you anything different."

"But I don't—"

"No, of course you don't. How could you?" Joanna Harcliffe's eyes softened. "It's been fifteen years, after all. And perhaps it's far better this way, with your having no memory."

Cathlin felt a heaviness in her chest. "You know about that? About how she—she died?"

"I'm afraid I do, my dear." The woman hesitated.

"No, don't stop."

"You see, I'm a doctor. A psychiatrist. The—police called me in afterward."

"And you were called in for me." This time, it was a statement, not a question. "My God, I talked to you about it." Cathlin's eyes darkened, locked on the elegant Baume et Mercier silver-link watch on Joanna Harcliffe's wrist. As if in a dream, she watched the second hand sweep toward the top of the silver face.

Eight.

Nine.

Ten.

Cathlin swallowed. "For a moment it was all there, so close. Oh, God, I almost had it."

Eleven.

Twelve.

Cathlin felt darkness settle over her with light, scraping fingers. Memories drifted, then faded. "How can I make it come back? How can I remember?"

The psychiatrist shook her head. "I'm afraid it isn't that easy my dear, no matter what the television serials imply. It takes hours and hours. It takes hard work and complete commitment and *wanting* to remember."

"But I do want to remember!"

After a moment the woman smiled. "I believe that you do, Ms. O'Neill. But forgive me, I should be saying Lady Ashton."

"Why?" Cathlin said flatly. "It's just for the will. In a week this marriage will be over and I'll be Ms. O'Neill again."

"You sound wistful."

"You're wrong about that!"

"Am I?" Again the faintly sad smile. "As you will. But I fear I must be going now. My husband and that intense Mr. Hayes are returning. For some reason, I can never feel entirely comfortable around that young man."

James Harcliffe cocked his head as he strode up, with the young man in question a careful pace behind him. "So sorry if I'm interrupting anything, my dear."

"No, nothing. I was simply telling Lady Ashton how lovely she looked. So very refreshing to see someone take charge of her own wedding, dressing just as she likes without all this folderol and expense." She smiled and Cathlin felt as if they were sharing a private joke.

"Yes, quite lovely," James Harcliffe agreed indifferently. "Rather unorthodox however."

"Nonsense, James. She looks wonderful." Joanna Harcliffe took her husband's arm, effectively cutting him off in midsentence. "But we really should be off. It would be nice if we could make your sister's party without being disgracefully late for a change."

After a stiff farewell, Harcliffe moved toward the door, only to halt and turn back. "Your gloves? How the devil should I know? You never lose things, Joanna."

His wife came back toward Cathlin. "Here they are, just as I thought. I'm afraid it's all true, my dear," she said, patting Cathlin's hand. "The memory really is the first thing to go."

Cathlin watched the unlikely couple move off, Harcliffe doing all the talking and his wife doing all the listening. Suddenly she felt something prick her palm. Looking down, she saw that Elizabeth Harcliffe had pressed a business card between her fingers listing her office number and a twenty-four-hour answering service.

It takes hard work and complete commitment. It also takes wanting to remember.

Cathlin felt something pull at the pit of her stomach. Did she have that kind of commitment? Did she really want to remember, no matter how painful the result?

She wasn't certain, not even now.

"You look a thousand miles away." Silent as usual, Dominic had come to her side.

She shrugged. "I suppose I was."

"Want to talk about it?"

Cathlin looked at his long, tanned fingers wrapped around an etched crystal champagne flute. How could he always look so strong, so handsome, so damned competent? "No," she said flatly. "But I will take some of *this*." She reached for his glass and emptied it.

"Delighted to be of use," Dominic said dryly.

"Oh, you're bound to have any number of uses. Carrying wine cases and chasing away intruders is just a start." Cathlin snared another glass of champagne. "Cheers," she said, raising her glass. "And here's to the departure of that terrible man."

Their eyes locked. A wave of hunger flooded Dominic's face.

The force of it let Cathlin reeling. "Why are you looking at me that way?"

"What way?"

"Like you can't decide whether to kiss me or deck me or drag me away somewhere?"

"Maybe because I can't decide whether to kiss you or deck you or drag you away somewhere."

Too smart. Too fast. Definitely too *dangerous,* Cathlin thought. "Forget it, Officer Montserrat." She was determined to remind him this was business.

"Dominic," he said huskily. "Barring that, try 'husband,' or 'my dear.'"

"Don't count on it anytime this century."

Again the hungry gaze. Cathlin blinked and gulped her champagne.

"More champagne, my lady?" Ghostlike, Marston appeared, carrying a bottle of nicely misted Dom Ruinart Blanc de Blancs.

"That would be lovely, Marston."

Dominic arched a brow as Cathlin tipped the pale, creamy froth to her mouth. "Going a little heavy, aren't you, Irish?"

"Nonsense. Drinking is my job. Well, tasting at least," she said scrupulously. Her head cocked. "Are those two people friends of yours or Lord Draycott?"

"Both, actually. Michael Burke is a good man. But I should call them the marquess and marchioness of Sefton, to be precise, even though Michael prefers his old naval title. His wife's an archaeologist by trade and a magician by birth, if half of Michael's stories are true."

Cathlin looked at the softly laughing couple. They were standing very close, their hands entwined. "They look very much in love." Her voice was wistful.

"So they are. And they deserve it. They've both had a rough time."

Cathlin shrugged. She wasn't going to think of shadows. She definitely wasn't going to think about a man with bottomless green eyes, on whom she was coming to rely entirely too much. What she was going to do was snare another glass of that wonderful champagne.

"Are you sure you want that, Irish?"

"Absolutely." She waved her hand, narrowly avoiding Marston's shoulder.

Dominic frowned. "Have you eaten anything today?"

"Of course," his new wife said grandly. "Huge amounts of food."

Marston edged past, tray in hand. "Half of a croissant for breakfast, my lord. Two strawberries for lunch," he said helpfully.

"I see," Dominic said slowly, watching a very becoming flush slip over Cathlin's neck and chest.

"Quite, my lord," Marston murmured.

"What?" Cathlin frowned and steadied herself with a hand on a nearby chair. "*What* do you see?"

"Everything, I should think." Dominic took the empty goblet from her fingers and set it on Marston's tray. "No more, thank you, Marston."

"What, had enough, have you?" Cathlin studied Dominic smugly.

"I believe I have."

"Well, I haven't." Cathlin threw her hands wide, narrowly missing a priceless Tang ceramic horse. "I could go on drinking Dom Ruinart all night."

"Not tonight." Dominic's eyes darkened. "Not on our wedding night."

Cathlin frowned and reached for another glass. As she did, Dominic turned, managing to jostle her arm so that the champagne landed in a potted orange shrub.

"Really, Dominic," Cathlin said crossly. "If you can't tolerate alcohol, you shouldn't drink."

"How right you are, my dear." A smile ghosted over Dominic's face as he took her hand. "Maybe you'll be kind enough to give me a steadying hand."

"Of course. No reason I shouldn't—" Cathlin stopped abruptly. "Where are we going?"

"It *is* our wedding night. People are rather expecting us to leave," Dominic said gently.

"*Can't* leave with all these guests still here." Again she gestured broadly.

Dominic eased a priceless Sèvres figurine out of her striking range. "Rude, is it?"

"Absitively." She blinked, then cleared her throat. "Rude, I mean. Couldn't possibly leave. Not yet."

"And just how long are we supposed to stay?" There was a glitter in Dominic's eye.

"Don't ask me. Never been married before." Cathlin eyed him uncertainly. "Have *you?*"

"Not that I recall," Dominic said dryly.

By now he had a secure grip on her arm and was guiding her through the room.

She sniffed.

"Try some of this lovely champagne," she advised Serita as they moved past. "It's doing wonders for me."

Serita frowned. "Cathlin, have you eaten today?"

Marston ghosted past. "Half a croissant for breakfast. Two strawberries for lunch," he murmured.

"Why does everyone keep talking about food? Where's the champagne, that's what *I* want to know." Cathlin took a step, frowned, then put a hand on Marston's arm for support. "Could you find me another glass of that divine Dom Ruinart?"

"Er, the champagne, my lady?" The butler looked at Dominic, who gave a tiny shake of his head. "Alas, my lady, I fear it is— all gone. Yes, it was a great hit. A very good suggestion of yours to serve it. May I compliment you on your taste?"

"Don't know why. It was *your* idea, though you were amazingly clever about making me *think* it was mine." Cathlin peered at him. "Are all butlers like you? If so, I can't imagine how anyone in England manages without you."

Marston's cheeks went bright pink. He murmured something incomprehensible and strode off, glasses rattling audibly on his silver tray.

"Come on," Dominic muttered. "Marston has something he wants us to see in the kitchen."

"But why did he leave? Did I say something wrong?"

"I expect he's not used to compliments from beautiful women," Dominic said smoothly. "Meanwhile, no more champagne for you."

"I'll have whatever I want. Don't think this ridiculous ceremony entitles you to order me around."

"The wedding doesn't, but my job here does." Dominic's voice was grim. "Until this is over I need you one hundred percent sober."

They were still arguing when they made their way back into the kitchens, where rows of copper pots gleamed from hooks above a pristine white marble counter.

"Marston's domain, I take it."

Dominic nodded. "He won't thank us for disturbing anything. I warn you, he's a true dictator in his realm."

At that moment the butler appeared, his face impassive. "I believe you informed me I should beware of anything unusual, my lord. Boxes, bags, packages and things of that sort. If you'd care to come this way, there's one particular item that's had me more than a little curious." He pulled open the door to a massive sixteenth century French armoire at the end of the kitchen and lifted out a cardboard box. "I found this on the counter just before the wedding ceremony today. I was curious because there were no deliveries expected."

Dominic's eyes narrowed. "What did the card say?"

"That's just it, my lord. There wasn't any card."

"You were right to alert me, Marston."

The butler started to open the box, but Dominic caught his hand. "Don't."

"But why—"

"Not yet." Dominic reached into his pocket and pulled out a metal box which he ran carefully around the outsides of the box, watching the dial.

"A possible electronic triggering device?"

"It never hurts to be prepared," Dominic said grimly. When his search revealed nothing, he pocketed the electronic sensor and pried open the top flap. Inside was a mass of folded white tissue paper. Dominic frowned. "You two had better move back."

Then he began to unroll the white tissue, every motion slow and controlled.

"You're wrong, you know. It's probably something totally ordinary like a cake." Cathlin smiled crookedly. "Or a bottle of merciless zinfandel."

Dominic frowned, remembering other seemingly innocent packages that had escaped detection only to blow up in their recipients' faces twenty minutes after their arrival. He happened to know that one small briefcase could hold enough *plastique* to blow up the whole abbey. "I'm not taking any chances."

Layer by layer the tissue parted. He felt sweat beading his forehead as he ran through the various devices that could be used to trigger a detonation from a remote location. None of them took up much space or weight.

The last layer of tissue slid free.

And then Dominic stood, staring speechless at the bottom of the box as a wave of heat climbed to his face.

"Dominic, what is it?" Cathlin moved closer, trying to see into the box.

"Nothing important." He shoved the box out of reach. "Just forget it."

But Marston outmaneuvered him, sliding past Dominic and lifting out the box's contents, his expression deadpan. "Excessively dangerous, my lord. Most lethal indeed."

From Marston's fingers dangled a nearly transparent froth of black lace and satin ribbons. It was the sort of nightwear bought by sinfully elegant women in sinfully expensive Parisian boutiques. Marston's eyebrow rose as he lifted another item from the box, this one a single piece of black nylon meant to cover the male anatomy—but just barely. "An anonymous wedding gift, my lord?"

Cathlin pulled the smaller garment from Marston and tugged it between her fingers, frowning at its size. "But how would you, that is, how could this *possibly*—"

"Never mind," Dominic growled, snatching away the two items and tossing them back into the box. He glared at Marston. "And if I ever hear one word said about this, Marston. One single, bloody word…"

The butler looked affronted by the mere suggestion that he would ever breach a confidence.

"Come on, Cathlin," Dominic said harshly. "Let's say goodbye to the guests. Then there are some security arrangements for the wine that I want to discuss with you."

"But what about these lovely gifts?" There was a wicked gleam in Cathlin's eyes. "I adore black, and something tells me you'll look positively unforgettable in—whatever that bit of nylon is called."

Dominic muttered something sharp and unrepeatable. "*Now,* damn it."

As MARSTON WATCHED THE pair storm out, a smile crept over his lips. "Yes, altogether a most satisfactory day." Marston was still smiling a few moments later when Nicholas and his wife strode into the kitchen.

"Mission accomplished?"

"Quite satisfactorily, I would say, your lordship."

"Wonderful." A smile softened the viscount's angular features.

"Nicholas, you didn't! What a beastly thing to do to them."

"I am afraid, your ladyship, that he did." Marston smiled broadly at the viscountess. "It was most interesting to watch a grown man blush, by the way."

Nicholas gave a bark of laughter, while his wife managed to look disapproving. "You two are impossible, you know. Just like two children."

"Yes, I expect so," the viscount said happily. "Perhaps this will make up for what Dominic did to me the last time we were in Bangkok."

His wife's eyes widened. "What is that supposed to mean, Nicholas Draycott?"

"I couldn't possibly repeat it," her husband said coolly. "It would be a violation of A-level state secrets."

"I'll violate a great deal more than state secrets if you don't tell me all about it this minute."

"I suppose I might be persuaded to talk," Nicholas murmured.

"Under great duress, of course. Seduced by the wiles and intrigues of a trained enemy agent." Heat filled his eyes as he looked down into his wife's smiling face.

Kacey inched closer. She slid up onto tiptoes and whispered something in Nicholas's ear. The viscount looked skyward and shook his head. "Some torture is definitely beyond a man's capacity for resisting." He took his wife's arm and guided her toward the corridor. "Very well, Mata Hari, it all began some time ago…"

"Is Michael Burke in this story?" his wife asked eagerly.

"As it happens, he was there too."

Kacey clapped her hands in glee. "Perfect. I want every single detail. And I am prepared to pay well, of course," she added wickedly.

Nicholas slanted a pleading look skyward. "Definitely more torture than any red-blooded man could bear. Maybe we'll have to leave for London sooner than I planned," he murmured, as his wife pulled him out of the room.

CHAPTER TWENTY

DARKNESS GATHERED IN THE valleys and slipped over the silent hills. Somewhere in the night an owl cried, long and shrill.

"I'll rest easier now that there's a backup generator in place." Dominic and Nicholas stared at the dark hills. Dominic's old associate from London had worked through the day, and the system was now complete. "At least we won't be having any more unexpected visitors."

Nicholas studied his friend. "You're sure you want me to leave, Dominic? I could change my plans, if you think—"

"No, I'll handle things here. Now that the power is guaranteed, we'll be fine. Harcliffe has promised to send some more men down in the morning, along with whatever equipment I need. So shove off, Nicky. Take your wife and daughter off to London, as planned, and stop fretting."

The viscount sighed. "Very well. I just hope you know what you're doing."

"I do."

"But what about—"

"Good-bye, Nicholas." This time it was a flat order.

"WHAT AN EXTRAORDINARY wedding."

All the other guests had left, and now Cathlin and Serita stood in the rose-filled courtyard before the gatehouse. Cathlin watched a swan part the sleek waters of the moat. "Too bad it wasn't real," she muttered.

"It could be, you know. That's up to you and Dominic. There's something else you should know. La Trouvaille is his."

Cathlin's eyes widened. "I don't believe it. What about all the stories?"

"Just a smoke screen. He wants total privacy and no interference until he's convinced the wine is as good as he can make it."

"But it's wonderful!"

"Try telling Dominic that. My guess is he's still feeling shaky about whether he can pull off such a huge change in his life." Serita frowned. "He's a good man, Cathlin. Not at all like the image he projects. That was all part of his work, to allow him to mingle among high-profile celebrities and Royals, with no one the wiser. Underneath the flash, he's very kind—and very careful."

Cathlin sniffed. "He would be. He likes to be in control of every detail. I suppose that's what makes him such a good bodyguard."

"*Made* him," her friend corrected. "He's out of that life for good, from all I hear. It took this wretched will to force him out of retirement."

Cathlin frowned. "There's something else, isn't there, Serita? Something you haven't told me."

"Dominic carries around a lot of ghosts, Cathlin. On his last job in Royal Protection duty I understand that the car he was in came under attack. When the bullets started flying, he did what he was trained to do—shoot first and ask questions later."

Cathlin swallowed. "And?"

"I don't know the details. They're classified. But I know people died that day and…Dominic considered himself responsible. He left the profession he was very good at."

Cathlin closed her eyes and shivered.

"He turned in his resignation after that. I understand that Harcliffe has come after him again and again—he's never gone back."

"Why won't they leave him alone?" Cathlin asked bitterly.

"That's James Harcliffe as much as government policy, I

expect. I have heard that once Harcliffe has his claws in someone, he never pulls them out. It's a matter of principle with him." A shadow fell across the weathered flagstones. "But I expect I'd better be going. Just you remember what I told you, Cathlin."

"I will."

Dominic was framed in the broad oak doorway, his face cast in shadow. He looked at Cathlin for long moments. "You'd better come in now. The alarms are all triggered."

Cathlin nodded. But still she did not move.

Are you carrying around the memories? she wanted to ask. You gave up your gun but did you give up everything that goes along with it?

But Cathlin said nothing. She wanted nothing more to do with the shadow world that had stolen her father, because it had brought her far too much pain already. And as Dominic stood unmoving, his face hidden by the shadows of the cloud-veiled moon, Cathlin decided he would hardly be likely to entrust her with any confidences.

She turned away. "I'm going down to have a last look at the wine."

"Fine."

STANDING IN THE COURTYARD with his hand on weathered stone ten centuries old and the wind in his face rich with the scent of a thousand roses, Dominic wished he was someone different, someone without ghosts and a past, someone who could be anything it took to make Cathlin O'Neill smile and laugh and feel whole again.

Someone who wasn't plagued by memories.

But there was a job to be done and Dominic meant to see it through. Until it was completed, there was no time for dreams or carelessness or emotion—not if he hoped to protect Cathlin's life.

He scowled down at a section of flagstone, nudging it with

his toe. A section of rope lay half-hidden in the shadow of a stone. Small, cleanly sliced at both ends, it was twisted into a rough loop handle.

Dominic picked the rope up and turned it idly. The loop was like those used by French farm workers to carry cases of wine.

Frowning, he turned the rope to and fro in the moonlight. Then he saw the dark blotch of blood near one end.

Blood from their recent intruder?

Cursing, Dominic turned and ran for the cellars.

"CATHLIN?"

She wasn't in the cellar. She wasn't in the foyer. She wasn't in Nicholas's study. Fighting down his fear, Dominic hammered up the stairs to her room.

No sign of her.

A wild instinct brought him around with a start. "Cathlin, answer me!"

He raced along the hall to the kitchen and pounded down the stairs. She was standing before the broad rear windows, watching moonlight spill over a bank of white lilacs. There was a box on the table beside her and a glass in her hand.

Dominic knocked the elegant crystal goblet from her lips just as she was about to drink.

"Are you *crazy*?" Cathlin gaped down at the shattered glass.

"Did you drink any?"

Cathlin just stared at him.

"Did you *drink* any, damn it?"

She shook her head. "What's wrong with you? That was exceptionally old and rare—"

"Poison, unless I miss my guess." Dominic's mouth set in an angry line.

"Poison? I don't believe it."

"It's my job to be right, Irish. To spot things that are wrong, even when they look entirely unimportant. And it's always in the little things." Grimly, he shoved open the wooden case and studied the bottles inside. "Where was it from?"

"The card was from the Wine Department at Harrods."

"Was it addressed to you by name?"

Cathlin nodded. "The gift of an old colleague of mine who works there now."

"You're absolutely sure of that?"

"I know his stationery, if that's what you mean. We've worked together several times in the past. Dominic, this is ridiculous. You can't really believe that a perfectly respectable wine expert from Harrods would try to poison me."

"Someone tried to drive us off the road two days ago, remember? Nothing is impossible, O'Neill. You'd better remember that." He lifted the cork and studied it carefully. "No cracks or needle marks." He sniffed the rim. "But there's a slight excess of acidity that shouldn't be there, even in a markedly dry vintage like this. A few minutes longer and the aroma of any contaminants will have entirely dispersed."

Cathlin frowned. "For an amateur, you know an awful lot about wine." *But then he wasn't really an amateur, was he?*

"Maybe." Dominic shrugged as he wrapped the cork in cellophane. "Meanwhile, this goes up to London for testing."

"Who, Dominic? Who would want to poison me?"

"Just about anyone. You're the heart of this whole business, Cathlin. Without you, that wine doesn't get certified and it loses its importance as auction material—or as the political football it might soon become. To bring in another expert with your credentials would take a fair amount of time, and by then, the wine would probably be gone."

"Dear God." Cathlin caught a sharp breath. "Was it…someone here today? Someone at the wedding?"

Dominic wasn't about to share his worries with Cathlin, not

when her face was sheet white and her fingers were trembling where she'd locked them at her waist. "I doubt it. Direct involvement like that is far too dangerous. Whoever did this was probably careful to put a dozen steps between this wine and himself."

He ached to run his hands through that vibrant black hair, to pull her against his chest and hold her until he felt the tension slide away.

But he didn't trust himself to do either. He had already gotten far more emotionally involved than was safe for either of them. "There's no sense brooding, Irish. Tomorrow we'll know more." Jade eyes burning, he took in Cathlin's pallor and her faint edge of fear. "Steady Irish." His hand cupped her chin.

"Then someone tried—tried to poison me. It's true." She caught a ragged breath. "I'm frightened, Dominic. And I hate being frightened almost as much as I hate owing people—and I owe you for saving my life yet again." She caught a tight breath. "Was it the same men who were in the car near Seacliffe?"

Dominic thought of lying, but gave up. She'd see through a lie anyway. "I can't be sure. Not until James Harcliffe gets back to me with some answers. Now it's time you were in bed."

"What about you?"

"Not yet." His face was grim. "I've still got a few things to clear up down here."

"By that you mean calls you don't want me to hear."

He didn't deny it. "Get some rest, Irish. Something tells me you're going to need it tomorrow."

Yes, it had been one hell of a wedding day, Dominic decided grimly.

SITTING IN THE ABBEY'S dark kitchens, Dominic made three calls. Each was to an old friend, each a man whose life he had saved over the years during his career as a bodyguard. And each man was delighted to repay an old debt by coming to the abbey and helping Dominic keep the vast grounds secure, no questions asked.

But when he was done, Dominic didn't go upstairs. Instead he pulled out the folders Harcliffe had given him, folders that laid bare the inside of Cathlin O'Neill's young mind, as recorded just after her mother's death.

The reports were chilling, and made even more chilling by the cold, precise, and utterly impersonal language they used.

…deep trauma…unpredictable formation…uncertain prognosis…

Dominic read through page after page of clinical reports that recorded everything, but explained absolutely nothing.

The conclusion? Cathlin O'Neill's memory of that night was clean, swept bare by a trauma that a ten-year-old mind was beyond enduring. The prognosis, couched in five pages of extremely technical language, was that any answers the police hoped for would have to be gotten elsewhere. The girl would never remember what had happened that day at Draycott Abbey.

Except in one unlikely condition.

Dominic sat forward, frowning as he read the sentence over and over again. One condition might trigger Cathlin's memory, and that was if she experienced another trauma of equal and similar severity.

Dominic leaned back and let his breath out slowly. Was that the purpose of these threats to Cathlin? Had someone learned of her past and hoped to trigger those lost memories? Severance, perhaps, as a perverted form of revenge? Or had it been one of the smug, tanned faces who had smiled at Cathlin in London at the charity auction, then gone home to arrange for her murder?

Too many bloody questions.

Grimly, Dominic checked the entrances once more and then the alarms, though he knew they were all in perfect order. After that he made his way upstairs, drawn inexorably to a room with red roses, where moonlight played over the polished floor.

She was sleeping, her hands flung out, her hair a dark veil against the white pillow. He moved closer, feeling faintly guilty, yet unable to take his eyes away. She twisted as he watched, shoved at the sheet, tugged at the pillow.

Staring down, he heard Cathlin's soft breathing and the wind in the branches outside the window.

Memories, again. How strange that he should have too many memories and she too few. And Dominic wondered what she was seeing in those restless dreams.

SILENCE. PANIC THAT RAN *through the darkness on sharp little feet. Her heart, pounding like knives in her chest.*

The little girl sat up, fingers clenched on the strange sheets in the strange bed in the strange, beautiful old house.

No one there. No one but shadows.

She pushed out of her bed and ran to the door, with the wind from an opened window blowing her hair like cobweb strands across her eyes.

Fingers tight, she ran past the hard-faced portraits, past the tapestries her mother had come to study, past all the pretty rooms with all their pretty things.

At the great oak door she stopped.

It lay open, open to darkness, open to shadows and the murmur of the moat.

She ran into the night, calling for her mother, calling wildly. And then she saw.

A dark shadow was spread against the lawns. Beneath the folds of her favorite amber plaid lay her mother's body. Unmoving. Arms twisted, legs bent.

All wrong. Wrong, wrong, wrong...

And then ten-year-old Cathlin O'Neill began to scream.

Afterward all she could remember was the blood.

THE WINDOW WAS OPEN AGAIN, curtains drifting. Just as before, her hair played over her face, faint as cobwebs. She ran out of her room, drawn to the faint glow of light, her eyes wide, full of shadows.

"Dominic?"

No answer. Dimly she heard the hammer of water. She shoved open the bathroom door. "D-Dominic."

The water stilled. "Damn it, Cathlin, what are you—" His anger died as he saw her face, her rigid stance. "Hold on, Irish." His eyes never left her face as he tugged a towel around his lean body and strode through the drifting steam. "I'm here, love. What's happened?"

She moved against him, oblivious to the beads of water that ran against her chin and seeped through her gown. "A dream. Just another stupid, silly dream." She caught a ragged breath, hearing her heart pound.

Hearing his heart pound.

Feeling his muscles, tight and damp beneath her cheek.

Wanting him. Oh, God, wanting him more than she'd ever wanted anything.

But there was something wrong. Ever since she'd met this man, he'd drawn upon the shadowed part of her mind, pulling images out of the vacuum of her past. And every day she spent in his company the pull grew worse, until Cathlin knew one day she'd shatter.

"It's okay, Irish. You're safe now."

"Am I?" Cathlin gave a shaky laugh, her eyes locked on the drifting mist, on a blur of blood she could never quite forget—even when she remembered nothing else. "And if I'm safe, it's only because you're *not*. And, I—I don't think I could stand it if any more blood were spilled here. Do you understand? It's gone too deep."

Dominic's fingers slid into her hair, cradling her head. "Does this mean you've remembered something?"

Cathlin shook her head. "Only the old dream. The blood, just like always. And then—nothing. But now it's worse, because the memories are only inches away. Waiting. Hanging."

Callused fingers smoothed over her lips. "Take it easy. They'll just keep coming, Cathlin. That's part of remembering."

"I thought I wanted this, but I didn't expect it to hurt so much. I didn't expect to feel like I was a child again."

"Shhh." He eased his arms around her waist, his long damp body warm against hers.

Cathlin took a ragged breath. Her head rose. "Could I make you forget if I tried, Dominic? Could I make us be two strangers, just for one night?"

A muscle beat at his temple. "You don't know what you're saying, O'Neill. It's late, and you're exhausted."

"I know, Dominic. I know exactly what I'm asking. So do you."

The air shimmered between them, heavy, slow, electric.

As if compelled, his hands slid lower, trapping the pulse that throbbed at her neck. "The timing's wrong. Damn it, all wrong."

"I don't care."

Slowly, slowly his head bent over hers.

And she leaned into him, leaned into the unbowing strength of his body, into the mystery of his arms and the unbearable pleasure he was making her feel.

All the denials crumbled. All the protests fled.

All that was left was heat and hunger and a hundred kinds of needing. Lips, light and hot, feathering her skin. Her heart racing.

"Dominic, I can't—breathe. It's not supposed to—to feel like this."

"Like what?"

Trembling, her fingers inched into his hair. "Like...forever."

"Who said?"

She made a low uncertain sound. Her hands slid deeper into his hair. Dimly, she realized she was pulling him closer.

And Cathlin didn't care. She wanted him close. She wanted their bodied meshed, with only sweat and skin between them.

She wanted *him*.

With all his demons and his fears. With all his flash and his careful brand of honor hidden beneath.

Warrior's honor. Warrior's heart.

She raised her hand, smoothing the crease at his brow. She saw the face of a man who'd looked into his heart and found his strengths and weaknesses. Each cold memory had left another line etched on that face. But the victories were there too, each set into the proud, sensual flare of his mouth.

And her skin was aflame as he caught her mouth with his. Lips hard, he slid across her, shaped her to his passion.

No fear. No room for fear. Too much need.

He made a low, rough sound. A sound of pain that left her utterly possessed.

"Please, hurry. Don't let me think. Don't let the dreams get through. Just once. Just tonight."

Silent like the warrior he was, he moved behind her. Hands across her waist, he pulled her against him. "Sorry, Irish," he whispered huskily. "Tonight hurrying's the last thing on my mind." He found the hungry little hollow behind her ear and planted slow kisses down to the bend of her shoulder. There he nudged aside the soft gown.

"Can't you...go a little faster?"

His low chuckle drifted over her naked skin. "Not a chance. Hell, Irish, I've got whole continents to discover." His voice darkened. "And paradise to claim."

"Dominic, something else. Serita told me."

Silence.

"About your last job in Royal Protection. She also told me about La Trouvaille."

More silence.

"What I'm trying to say is I'm sorry. You're doing wonderful things over there, and I'm just making all this harder for you."

Her hands tightened. "I'm sorry you had to come back to a world you hated."

More silence. Thicker now.

"Dominic?"

A raspy breath. "Not now, golden eyes. Only this now." He turned her face and his tongue swept hers. "Only the heat to stop the nightmares." Lace shifted. Linen rose.

Then only her heat, melted against his. Only her soft, muffled breath as he carried her to her room and laid her on the chintz settee beside the window. Moonlight pooled against her skin below curtains that drifted like ghostly fingers. The air carried the perfume of a thousand roses mixed with the warmth of lilacs.

He was confident in this as in all else, his hands sure in their possession. Cathlin watched his face, one side silver with moonlight and the other cast into darkness. She wanted then to be the one who pulled him from those shadowed memories. She wanted to be the one who made the laughter brighten his eyes and smiles crinkle his hard mouth.

She wanted. Oh, how she wanted. But he was moving too fast, spinning his dark enchantment over a body that was fast turning into a stranger's. Wanting struck her and a hot, sweet melting.

"Dominic, I—"

"Not now, Irish. I'm…busy." He bent his mouth to her throat, to her collarbone, to the high, sweet arch of her breast.

"Dominic, why—"

"Do you always talk this much?"

Only when I'm frightened. Only when my heart is about to slam right out of my chest. Because it feels like I've wanted you this way forever and nothing has ever felt more natural than your skin touching mine.

"Sometimes," she lied, wondering why his scent was somehow familiar. Why his eyes shone with a brilliance Cathlin seemed to have known somewhere before.

Or sometime before.

The sheer impossibility of it left her chilled for a moment. What was happening to them here in this lovely, dangerous place with too many secrets and too many shadows?

Then Dominic's mouth coaxed the warm skin at her shoulder and Cathlin forgot about secrets and shadows.

The only mystery she cared about was the mystery of skin brushing naked skin, of fingers twining and thighs caught in silken discovery.

Dominic seemed to have the same idea. His palm opened over her waist, drawing her back against him.

And he felt like forever. Like all the questions she'd ever had, answered in one hot, jerky breath.

With a strangled sound she raised her hands to the hard planes of his face. Her linen gown parted with a low hiss. Cathlin went utterly still, breath jammed in her throat as Dominic feathered tiny kisses over the high, full swell of her breast.

Desire slammed through her, finely edged, shining like a blade. Dominic nudged aside lace and linen, easing his way down to one swollen crest.

Champagne bubbles raced up her spine. "I don't think—this is anywhere in the rule book, Officer Montserrat."

"To hell with the rule book," her bodyguard said hoarsely. "Damn it, you taste fine." Slowly he kissed his way up the curve of her throat. "Let me have all of you, Cathlin. Let me have your taste in my mouth. I want you to be part of me."

Heat again. Delicious and amazing. Utterly tormenting. How could she possibly resist? "Dominic, I've never—that is, it's never felt so—"

Like forever. Like coming home.

Like we've done this a hundred times before. "Good," she finished lamely.

"No, perfect," he growled.

"But you, haven't you ever felt—"

"No." He frowned, studying the perfect crimson thrust of her, rising hungry to his lips. "Not like this." His voice fell. "Not the way it feels with you. But I'm going to feel it now." His breath caught. "With you, Cathlin."

The old house slept, silence in the corridors, silence in the rose-filled courtyard. Only two shadows moved in the moonlight.

The wind played over her through the opened window, sweet and light as Dominic's fingers. Sweet as the dreams that pressed, full of heated memories.

Of yesterday and a hundred other yesterdays.

Cathlin caught a ragged breath as he kissed the hollows of her spine, then turned her slowly in his arms.

"Cathlin. Sweet God, you're so…"

So perfect for him, perfect against him as he found the curve of her and then her hidden heat. Pleasure welled through her heart, coursed through her veins, and she unfolded to him like a flower.

Forever.

That's what he gave her in his touch, in his hot, dark words poured against her yearning skin.

And forever was the place she struggled to find, anchored in his arms. But fighting wouldn't take her there, not when the memories followed, chill and leaden and all the more frightening because they had no form and no face.

Around her the curtains rose and fell, silent ghosts that mocked her for her fear.

Was he Gabriel, their spirits somehow linked, carried through time by laws older than simple human understanding? And was she the woman Gabriel had kissed, there in a candlelit drawing room on a smoky London night two centuries before?

Images lapped at the edges of Cathlin's mind, images of another warrior and another pair of strong, callused fingers that had bared her body to racing pleasure.

Forever.

"I can't. Dominic, please, this isn't—"

"You *can,* Irish. Because my love will take you there." She felt the silken slide of his fingers, firing her heat, wooing her silently until she arched in restless abandon. "Now, Cathlin. While the moonlight plays around you. Let me take you beyond dawns and darkness. Through that door of shadows you never dared to open."

A low groan. Maybe his, maybe hers, or maybe it belonged to them both. She tightened around him, head flung back, mind and spirit shimmering in a wave of breathless pleasure.

But it didn't end. He wouldn't let the pleasure end. Some instinct told him just how to move, where to skim until the light rocked her again and the last shadow fled, banished by his love, banished by his care and joy. Her breath swelled in a choked cry of discovery. Of love.

Forever.

No more shadows. Not in the still, silent house where the curtains drifted. Not in the slanting bar of moonlight, which crept across the floor and filled the room with beauty.

Not even in Dominic's eyes, which followed every inch of her wild journey with an urgency that signaled his own discoveries.

As the roses danced, as swans coursed the moat, Cathlin gave herself up to his wild pleasure, to his knowing touch and his dark, whispered praise, knowing that somehow she had loved this man forever, that somewhere she had vowed to find him and heal him and give him back his joy—even if it took uprooting his life and tearing his calm composure into tiny little shreds to do it.

Today.

Tomorrow.

And a thousand dawns to come.

"DOMINIC?"

He pulled her against his chest.

"Why—"

"Hush."

"But you—"

A husky laugh. A lopsided smile that shattered her heart in the quiet moonlight. "Sleep, Irish. There'll be time. A century of nights like this to come, I promise."

"But you didn't—"

He knew one way to silence her, and he used it, pressing his lips to hers, his body hard, his fingers even surer now. And when her pleasure came again, she cried his name in wonder.

She slept at last, curled against his chest. Their bodies were blocked by only a thin towel—and an ironclad code of honor that kept Dominic Montserrat motionless even when his mind screamed for him to take her, pounding and hard, until they both discovered the taste of forever.

But he didn't.

Though it was truly torture, he held her gently, unmoving.

Because at that instant it was the very best way this warrior knew to protect her when the shadows came back.

And as the moon slid toward the horizon, it wasn't Cathlin who twisted in dark dreams.

It was a man with eyes like jade and smoke.

A warrior with too many memories to fit inside one lifetime.

CHAPTER TWENTY-ONE

THE SKY WAS STILL DARK when a heavy coach moved out of the mews behind Adrian Draycott's London town house. Slowly it lumbered around the corner and came to a halt at the front of the house. Black lacquer doors bright with the Draycott crest were thrown open and a woman, heavily veiled, came down the stairs, leaning on her companion's arm.

"To the East India docks," the liveried footman called out crisply. "And make it sharp."

Across the street, hidden by a mass of ugly wrought-iron railing, a man in a dusty greatcoat smiled grimly. So they were making for the docks, were they?

Henry Devere would pay him well to see that they never completed their journey.

FOR LONG MOMENTS GABRIEL Montserrat stood in the darkness, listening for sounds of pursuit. Only when he was satisfied that he was alone did he motion into the shadows behind him.

Geneva Russell, swathed in a hooded gray cloak, moved into the cobblestone lane, assisted by the tall American from Virginia.

"We'll leave you now," Lord Ashton said. "I wish I could see Devere's face when he realizes his prey in the Draycott coach is an inebriated butler and a woman who is far from a lady."

"You're going to have to forgo that pleasure, Gabriel." Adrian motioned into the mews and a swift traveling chaise, without *identifying crest or insignia, pulled out of the shadows. He helped Geneva up the stairs.*

She pressed his hand for a moment. "How can I possibly thank you for your help? You have been kindness itself, Lord Draycott. You, also, Mr. Jefferson. But do not underestimate Henry Devere. He is more than a little mad and has never been bested in any goal."

The American patted her hand. "We are more than equipped to defend ourselves against a bounder like that, my dear. Now you had better go, for these spirited grays do not care to be kept standing." He raised his hand in farewell. "Godspeed," he whispered as the carriage rumbled into the night.

GABRIEL STARED DOWN AT the woman across from him, moonlight silver on her cheeks. She sat silently, her body cast into shadow.

Outside, the crowded thoroughfares gave way to quiet hamlets and then to long, rolling hills. Beyond the city the coach picked up its pace, jolting over the pitted road. At a particularly large rut, Geneva was tossed forward and Gabriel saw her face illuminated for a moment in the moonlight.

Her cheeks were pale. Her mouth was set in a thin line.

"He will come after me, I know it. He is ruthless and has powerful friends. I have brought my own ill fortune down upon all of you."

"Why, Geneva? Why did you betray me?"

"For my sister. As I fear I might betray you again, for every thought brings her face before me."

"I will bring her to England, Geneva. I make you this promise."

Gabriel gathered her against his chest. "And I will see you to safety before I go, in a place where Devere can do you no more harm."

"You don't understand. He is not sane." Geneva caught a jerky breath. Her face was a blur of light against the darkness.

A lock of her hair trailed over his hand, and he could feel her hips pressed against his hard thighs. With every jolt of the carriage her breast thrust against his chest.

Desire slammed through him. They were alone, far from prying eyes. She had already offered him the pleasure of her body in return for his assistance. His thighs tightened at the thought of pulling away her lace fichu, of loosening her stays until her creamy breasts sprang free and filled his hungry fingers.

He caught a sharp breath. What kind of blackguard had he become? She was innocent, completely in his care. Nothing could take place between them.

"Why do you frown?"

"Because it is time you rested." He pulled her head against his shoulder. "Don't argue," he growled as he felt her body tense in protest. "You didn't win before and you won't win now."

Slowly her hand relaxed its grip on the folds of her cloak and Gabriel heard her sigh. From the softening of her shoulders he knew that she had fallen asleep. But it was not that which left him reeling, shaken to his very core.

It was the way she curled close to him in her sleep, utterly trusting, then ran her hand along his chest and tucked it gently in the curve of his shoulder.

OVERHEAD THE SKY WAS FULL of stars. They were in open country now, level fields stretching out into silent forests. Gabriel estimated they had three hours of traveling before they reached Draycott Abbey. Careful not to awaken the woman asleep in his arms, he sat forward to get a better view of the countryside and the road behind them.

No vehicle was to be seen. The road was empty and they were safe.

For now, at least.

He looked down at Geneva's face and frowned. Soon Devere

would discover Templeton's masquerade and send his men in search of any other carriages which had left the mews.

If only they could make Draycott Abbey in time.

DOMINIC WAS SWEATING. HIS fingers clutched at dreams as he saw another place of moonlight and plunging horses and a shutter crashing somewhere in the night.

He tried to pull free, to gain a footing in the dark chaos of his dreams.

No good. Too many noises. Too many memories. Too many broken promises. And a danger that tracked him through time, even in his dreams....

THEY DIDN'T MAKE IT TO *Draycott Abbey.*

They didn't even make it to Tunbridge Wells.

A trio of riders clattered into the road behind them.

"What is it?" Geneva blinked and sat up, awakened by the sound of racing hoofbeats.

"Nothing."

"It's him, isn't it? He's found us." The color bled from her face.

"No one has found us yet, and no one will." Grimly Gabriel seized her arm and uttered a sharp command to the coachman.

The wind was rising and the smell of rain hung heavy in the air. Gabriel knew that the river lay less than half a mile away. He signaled to the coachman, who put them down where they were hidden by a bend in the road. When the coach lumbered forward, the riders followed, giving Gabriel and Geneva precious time to escape.

But in the face of a rising wind, every yard was a struggle for Geneva, even though Gabriel knew she was fighting to conceal it. "Let me carry you."

"I'll be fine." Her face was white and the rising wind tossed gravel and twigs in her face. "Is it much...farther?"

"Just beyond that line of trees."

Overhead a bolt of lightning cracked through the sky. A wall of wind tore at their clothes. Without a word, Gabriel caught Geneva up in his arms and carried her over the rocky slope to the river.

A quarter of an hour later the storm had raged past. In its wake a veil of fog crept over the river. Here and there a branch emerged from the drifting mist, black skeletons clutching at nothing. The dark figures broke, shouting, from the mist.

Gabriel pressed his pistol into Geneva's fingers. "Take this and use it. I'll try to lead them off into the mist." He shoved forward and then set off in a sharp angle, his footsteps purposely noisy as a lure to Devere.

Geneva watched in horror as his plan succeeded too well, and moments later he was facedown in the mud with Devere's pistol at his back.

"It is really a very simple question, Lord Ashton. I fail to understand why you refuse to answer it. Are you the man known as the Rook?"

FOG SWELLED UP AROUND THE men standing at the edge of the river. Gabriel lay facedown, his hands bound tight at his back. A jagged bruise mottled his forehead and the corner of his cheeks. "Rook? Never heard the name."

Henry Devere smiled coldly. "I fear your bravado is wasted on me." He made a sharp gesture with his hands. "Hold him down."

One minute passed. Then half again.

"Bring him up," Devere snapped. When Gabriel was pulled back onto the sand, he coughed harshly and strained at his bonds. His only reward was a sharp kick in the ribs.

"Now then, Lord Ashton, shall we try again? I repeat, are you the man known as the Rook?"

"And I repeat, you maggot, that I have no acquaintance with anyone by that name."

Devere shook his head. "I shall find out, you know. Someone will remember a voice, the set of a face. And then I'll have you."

Gabriel coughed and watched blood stain the muddy bank in front of him. "She's free, Devere. And I'll kill you for laying a hand on her."

Devere gestured sharply and Gabriel was shoved back into the muddy water.

"This time rather longer I think." His eyes flat and hard, Devere stood at the edge of the river as fog lapped around his beautifully polished boots. "One minute," he announced icily, watching with interest as Gabriel's submerged body flashed and twisted. "Two minutes." When the big body ceased to move, Devere smiled grimly. "Haul him in."

This time their victim gave no response.

"Rouse him," Devere hissed.

After three sharp kicks to his back, Gabriel shuddered and began to cough.

"You are truly stubborn, Ashton. But not half as stubborn as I am. I have had to be since whatever success I hoped to attain had to be earned with the strength of my fists and the cunning of my mind in the mud of the Whitechapel slums. And that is why it is particularly fitting that I relieve my poor French victims of all the gold that nature in its ignorance gave them in excess. Now for the final time, on pain of death, admit that you are the man known as the Rook. Miss Russell may have escaped me, but you have not. And you were what I really wanted anyway."

Gabriel spat up a mouthful of bloody water and laughed coldly. "You should have kept her when you had her, Devere. She'll suffer no more of your torment, even if I have to buy her safety with my life."

"A touching sentiment, but I fear that that is exactly what you will do." Devere stood for a moment, veiled in fog, smoothing the priceless lace at his cuffs.

"Kill him," he ordered.

He wasn't going to make it this time, Gabriel thought as the two men shoved him beneath the water.

Strange red lights played before his eyes and his throat burned, but he kept himself from moving, knowing that surprise was his only chance at escape.

But what happened next took him by surprise. Even underneath the water he heard the muffled shouts. There was a sharp tug on the rope at his wrists, and then the rope went slack.

Gabriel knew it was now or never.

With the last of his energy he pushed off the bottom. Fog lay everywhere and he gasped for breath, trying to make sense of the chaos around him. A bullet hissed past and then he heard Devere curse.

Suddenly, slender fingers seized his wrist and pulled him into the water.

"Geneva?"

"I've found a rowboat downstream. Can you swim out to it?"

"I'll manage." Gabriel followed her into the water, amazed at her resourcefulness and quiet courage. He watched her skirts drift up against the dark waters. She'd come storming into his life, overturning all his peace, but now he couldn't imagine what life would be like without her.

"What happened to Devere?"

"I shot him," she said grimly. "He was holding his arm when the others brought him his horse."

Moments later they reached the rowboat and Geneva climbed in, her hair tumbling in a wild cloud down her back, her satin dress molded to every curve.

Gabriel swallowed, fighting a desperate urge to take her right there, rocking in the fog.

He told himself this was just the ache of a man who had gone too long without the comfort of a woman's body.

But he knew it was something far deeper.

"I'll tend to the oars," he said, his voice harsher than he intended.

The slap of the water was the only sound as they drifted through mist and darkness, following the bends of the river. Eventually, Gabriel knew, it would lead them toward the abbey.

When his shoulders finally began to ache with strain, he pulled beneath an overhanging tree. Beyond was an old mill that looked long deserted. "We'll rest here and push on later."

Geneva gathered her sodden skirts and stepped onto the muddy bank. As she did, the boat lurched and she tumbled backward. Gabriel caught her clumsily, dropping an oar to keep both of them from being tossed overboard.

Her young body covered his. He felt the thrust of her breasts through the wet silk of her gown. She looked at him, a dark emotion in her eyes, her hair gusting black and rich around her shoulders.

Gabriel felt himself falling, falling into an ocean without any bottom, his heart spread high and wide like the sails of the swift ships that had carried him so often to France.

He wished he were a hero then, the kind of man she thought that he was. But he was no hero. A hero would have turned her away, and he could not. There was too much sweetness in her face, too much yearning in her eyes. Her hair blew about his face and all Gabriel could think of was the sweet smell of lilacs that filled his mouth, his lungs, his whole being.

He knew then that he had to have her, that all his honor could not save her, because it had gone far beyond heated thighs and rasping breath.

Now it was a thing of rushing spirit, of deepest yearning dreams, the sort of hunger that could not be denied because it went past bone and muscle to the very soul.

"I'll hurt you, damn it. I'll take you, my love, again and again, until you forget where you start and I begin. Once there's a

starting, there won't be an end, I warn you. Not today. Not tomorrow. Maybe not ever."

He had hoped to scare her away, but he might have known he could not succeed. Her hands whispered over his arrogant mouth. "I pray so, my lord."

"Fool." There was anger in his voice along with an infinite tenderness. "You don't know anything about me."

"Except what counts. That you are a hero and...I love you."

"I can give you nothing but pain, Geneva. Through my whole life, that's all I've done to those I love most."

Then her body blocked out the night, the river, the fog, and she kindled a joy he had thought long dead.

When she touched him, he was lost. Gabriel fought for sanity, for strength to deny her, but found neither. "Geneva, are you sure?" His voice was harsh as his fingers moved through her hair.

"Yes, now. There, in the mill beside this dark river." And if the words had not been clear enough, then the soft pressure of her body was.

"It's wrong. Wrong and I know it." His fingers tightened, locked deep in her hair.

"Maybe, my lord," she murmured, her hands achingly gentle on his face, "it's your knowing that's wrong."

THE MILL WAS FULL OF DUST, but Gabriel mounded clean straw and made a bed in the moonlight. When Geneva turned, her eyes were full of love.

Her fichu, gown and stays slid free. Beneath she wore only a chemise of finest cambric, now damp from the river and nearly translucent.

Gabriel feasted on the sight of her, on the full, rich sweep of her soft shadows beneath the moon. His throat constricted. "So fine. So bloody beautiful..."

She smiled a little sadly. "I am too tall for fashion and my mouth is too wide. I have no graces and I squint." She spoke with utter candor.

Gabriel would have laughed, could he have summoned up a single sound. He would have bellowed with laughter, for she was all that he'd ever hungered for—all that any man could ever hunger for.

"None of the graces?" he managed.

"Not a single one," she said defiantly.

"And surely not a squint."

"Just so." She demonstrated.

He thought to himself that it made her look enchanting, lending a lovely intensity to her fine, regular features. But he did not tell her so. He could not speak with any safety.

"Now you'll not want me."

It was all beyond his taking in, standing in the moonlight and talking calmly, as if she wasn't half-naked, straw at her feet.

"Besides, I smell."

"Smell?"

"I carried a bottle of perfume in my gown. It was my mother's. The bottle broke in the river." She sniffed. "I'm certain you must have smelled it."

Lilacs. Oh, yes, he'd smelled them. Like her they were fresh and full and everything young. They were spring come to the dark earth and joy to a hardened heart. They would help him remember this moment forever.

"Come closer and let me see."

She moved through a bar of moonlight, all whisper and heat, her shoulder extended. "Will this do?" Her voice was husky.

Did it do any better, he would die of her!

Gabriel nodded gravely. Bending slightly, he inhaled while the tantalizing sweep of one breast, barely veiled beneath white cambric, lay inches from his fingers.

So close. So sweet.

He found lilacs and more—courage and honesty and fierce loyalty. Lilacs would mean that to him from now on, Gabriel thought. "I can smell it now."

She nodded gravely. "You've wanted none of me, not from the start. And why should you? You're far too grand. You can have your pick of fine, grand women without a squint and with every sort of grace."

He swept her against him, his hands lost in her hair, his mouth raining hot kisses over her face.

Geneva gave a shaky laugh. "I am too tall."

"Which means I can see your face when I do this." He caught her lip gently between his teeth.

She swallowed, her hands at his shoulders. "But my mouth—"

"Is just perfect."

He filled himself with her, and his fingers were not quite steady as he slid her chemise from her shoulders, following the fine fabric with his mouth, kisses like a storm.

She sighed as he slid the cambric away and found the impudent coral thrust of her breast.

Lilac filled his senses. Geneva filled him, heart and soul. He'd take away her pain, and with it all her doubts.

"But you are dressed and I am not. Besides, I want to touch you too. If...that is allowed."

He laughed, could not help himself. "Most certainly it is allowed."

She frowned for a moment. "I've lost your stickpin. I had it to remind me of the night I betrayed you. It must have fallen."

He brushed her cheek. "I'll put a curse on whoever finds it."

"Do not jest, my lord." She sank onto the snug little bed of mounded straw. "Come here."

He did. Wondering.

She tugged away his cravat, shoved at his buttons, and freed his jacket, two buttons bursting in the process.

Gabriel knew a fierce urge to give her all her heart desired, to sweep down the very stars and give them to her on a platter of beaten gold.

But he had no gold nor stars. All he had was his touch and his joy in her.

"You—are beautiful," she said, her voice low with wonder. "I'm far too ordinary for you." Her fingers touched his muscled arms, brushed the fine hair across his chest.

"Geneva," he said warningly, heat climbing.

She traced the silver trail of an old scar, earned on his first foray to France. "You've been hurt too often," she said gravely. Her lips covered the skin, bringing a pleasure more fierce than any pain Gabriel had felt when the French cavalry saber had sliced through him.

Her tongue was magic, blinding as she came slowly upward. And then she met his mouth. Inexpert. Eager. Maddeningly fine.

Too soon. He had her body yet to taste.

But she pulled him down against her, suddenly demanding, cambric fallen aside and only burnished skin before him.

"Now," she whispered, her eyes grave. "Before I can remember, I pray you." Her thigh moved along his. "Unless you have changed your mind?"

He caught her, pulled her down atop him in a sprawl. "Never," he said grimly. He palmed her thigh and moved to higher glories. "Satin. Sweet." And wet, he saw, with sharp delight. Not that she yet understood the significance of that.

"But you—"

"Hush." Sliding to part her, pushing deeper. Ignoring her startled breath, he remained intent on his goal.

Which was her *pleasure.*

"Gabriel—"

No words. Nothing but the joy he could show her.

Nearly there, all clinging skin. All heat that welcomed.

"Gabriel." *This time her voice came in a rush of awareness. Her skin flushed warmest pink.*

"Yes, my stubborn love?"

"I feel—so strange. And I don't at all understand—"

"You will."

He taught her then, his hard hands carefully gentle against petals lush. She flowered in the heat of his care and love and opened her glorious amber eyes, shock warring with a final instant of fear.

But he swept her beyond both, into a dark storm of feeling, in a place where all memories stopped and all wounds were healed. He felt her arch against him, a single word on her lips.

And the word was his name.

It coiled around his heart, held him speechless, made him feel a thousand times young.

And truly the man she loved.

There was no more fighting then, not for either of them.

WITH A SOFT MOAN CATHLIN turned, shoving blindly at her pillow.

River.

Night.

A man whose face was hard with regret.

She fought her soft pillow, seeing trails of white fog, feeling the heat of a lover's hands and mouth and skin, understanding all her years of distance and regret and fear that came from a distant time when she had found love, only to have it stolen from her.

And in that moment of aching awareness, with one foot in dreams and the other in waking, she saw all the rare, remarkable things she had never had a chance to know as Cathlin O'Neill, but had never quite forgotten as Geneva Russell.

GABRIEL WAS SMILING WHEN *she opened her eyes, her body poured over his in a moonlit glow of breast and thigh.*

"You—knew? You have felt this?"

"Of course I knew."

She touched his chest, wondering. *"It is—quite extraordinary."*

"There is more."

Her head cocked. *"Truly? It seems beyond imagining."* A hesitation. *"You could be persuaded to…show me?"*

A dark smile. *"Very likely. With the right inducement."*

Her fingers moved along his chest and then lower. His eyes closed when she found him, fire a drumming in his blood.

"Persuaded like this?"

"Maybe faster than you like."

A soft laugh. Her hair a veil across his chest. Her kisses—heaven itself.

He caught her in her flight downward.

Her smile was a luscious invitation as she eased her legs around him, fitting herself to the awesome mark of his need.

He cursed. *"Geneva—"*

Deeper. Encasing him in satin. Taking him to a paradise beyond his dreams.

He tried to hold her, but she wriggled free. *"There will be pain, so I have heard. Yet I think it will be well worth the sight of your face now, my lord,"* she whispered huskily.

Gabriel frowned, trying to be sane for a few moments longer. *"It is true, there will be pain. I only wish—"*

She stilled his lips and moved against him, frowning when she could move no more.

Gabriel twisted, knowing it would be best finished in one swift stroke. He studied the glory of her beneath him, hair spread wild, eyes ablaze, a questioning smile on the beautiful mouth she assured him was far too wide for beauty. *"As little as I can make it, my love."*

She nodded, grave. Indescribably beloved.

He moved, filled her, met the barrier and then thrust beyond.

As he did, she swallowed, her eyes closed, her hands tensed. But even then she did not push him away or struggle against him, her body open to whatever he would offer her.

And that very openness was the greatest bravery Gabriel had ever known.

Bending, he claimed one nipple while his hands claimed a different bloom, sliding deeper and teasing her to maddening need.

She gasped and shoved hard against him.

He met her instantly, sliding deeper through honeyed skin where now no barrier stood. Only heat leaped up to meet him. Only blazing desire.

"Wrap your legs around me," he ordered hoarsely.

"Like this?"

"Good, sweet God!"

"No?" Immediately she tried to pull away.

"Yes. A thousand times yes, my beauty."

He showed her how right it was, how much he loved her, sliding deep and finding the still, hot core of her. Finding at the same time the still, hot core of himself.

There love lay coiled, a love he'd never thought to find.

She cried out, her back drawn tight like a bow, her nails to his chest. He smiled, with his last shred of sanity enjoying her soft, choked cry of delight, the hot sweet tremors that proclaimed her cresting pleasure.

Then Gabriel followed, cast up in the wave of night, swallowed and then made whole just as she had been reshaped in the hot, still crucible of love.

And as he fell, Gabriel swore he would never let her go again.

SLEEPY MINUTES PASSED IN *moonlight and drifting shadow.*

"You sleep, my dearest, like an army on the march."

A soft murmured sigh. "And what would you know of armies on the march, my lord?"

"*Too bloody much.*"

"*You've left me exhausted.*" A frown. "*Is that quite usual?*"

"*Only for those who are very lucky.*" He gently combed a curl back from her forehead. "*But I'm not offering a complaint, you understand, since all your marching was done over me.*"

A flush. An enchanting dimple. "*I am quite beyond redeeming, I fear.*"

"*I have no thought of redeeming you.*"

His hand found her breast. Instantly she was afire again, needy for this wondrous thing he'd made her feel.

There was a moment of sadness in her eyes, and something like regret. Then she smiled and inched closer. Her thigh rose, coaxing till it found a most enchanting hardness. "*Perhaps I am not so exhausted as I thought.*"

Gabriel slid the length of her. "*Are you quite certain?*"

"*Without a doubt.*"

"*In that case…*" He drove against her, filling her in one hard, perfect thrust, delight swirling through every muscle as she crested against him anew. "*How very, very glad I am to hear it,*" he managed, just before he followed her down into a swirling ring of pleasure.

Lulled by the soft rush of the river and the muffling veil of the fog, they finally fell back against the straw. Outside the mill an owl cried over the river and little animals curled warm and safe in their dens.

Somewhere, far in the distance, a church bell chimed.

Twelve times and then no more.

Hands entwined, breaths soft, Gabriel and Geneva finally slept.

HENRY DEVERE SAT UNMOVING in the darkness, listening to a church bell chime.

He liked the darkness. He could think in the darkness, plan in the darkness.

And he planned now, careful and thorough, while he nursed the wounds delivered at Geneva's hand. For that she would pay dearly, as would her arrogant lover. The Rook was almost within his grasp, along with the thousand-guinea reward the French had posted for the Englishman's capture.

His eyes glinted, hollow and cold.

He would have the Rook. Then he would begin teaching Geneva Russell how very stupid she had been to think she could escape him.

CHAPTER TWENTY-TWO

"THERE WERE THREE CALLS from France, two equipment deliveries, and two calls from London, my lord. In addition Lord Draycott has already called twice."

A notepad in hand, Marston stood in a beam of early morning sunlight beside the desk Dominic had commandeered in Nicholas's study. "Oh, yes, the vicar also called. He wished to offer his felicitations to you and the countess. He said that if any difficulties should arise, you must feel free to call him."

Dominic laughed. "Can he secure a frayed electric wire, do you think?"

"I could not say, my lord. However, I have always believed that with the help of the Almighty, all things are possible." With that enigmatic utterance, the butler laid a pile of parcels on the desk and turned to leave.

"And...the countess?" Dominic swallowed. The word brought back too many heated memories to face easily in the daylight. Things were still too uncertain between them. At least she had slept deeply. He had seen to that before he left her at the first light of dawn.

And his body still pained him for that celibate departure.

"I believe she has not come down yet, my lord. Shall I give her a message?"

"No need, Marston. I'll be cooped up rewiring this bloody security system for several hours and then I have to inspect that backup generator. It's already acting up." He frowned. "If I didn't know better, I'd almost think there *was* a ghost here playing havoc."

Marston cleared his throat, then moved off, astounding in black broadcloth and neon purple running shoes.

After he left, Dominic sat staring at the files Harcliffe had left him the day before, thinking about the stresses Cathlin must be feeling and wondering if these waking dreams of hers were a sign that she was skating near the edge of her endurance.

The phone cut short his reveries.

It was Nicholas, his voice grim. "I'm sorry to add any more pressure, Dominic, but I've had bad news. Already the heads of three European countries have expressed profound interest in at least one of the bottles of your wine—as a 'token of British goodwill.' In addition, two American senators have made discreet contact through the American embassy in London, each claiming a bottle to present to the president. Jefferson happens to be one of the man's heroes, it seems."

Dominic was uninterested in legends, living or dead. "What you're saying is that things are going to get even rockier, is that it?"

"I'm afraid so. With this kind of interest the ante has just shot up in one enormous leap. Be careful, Dominic. Be certain that Cathlin is careful, too."

Dominic frowned. He decided not to mention Cathlin's sleep-walking and the poisoned wine. Until he had answers, there was no use discussing his suspicions. "Anything new with Kacey's search of the church records?"

"Nothing yet. I'll let you know if we find anything though."

Dominic looked down and sighed as the lights flickered. "I'd better run. Problems with that backup generator already. Are you sure this place isn't truly haunted?"

Silence.

"Nicholas? Are you there?"

"Tell Harcliffe to send another one down from London."

"Oh, he's promised to help, but you know how the man is. Something might arrive tomorrow or next year."

"Blast him! Is he supporting this project or opposing it?"

"He plays his own game, as always. He has a rare, Machiavellian mind."

Nicholas said a few curt words that expressed exactly what he thought of James Harcliffe's mind, leaving Dominic laughing as he hung up.

BUT DOMINIC WASN'T laughing ten minutes later. He had just finished reading the last of the fifteen-year-old files Harcliffe had left him. Between the flat lines of cold, scientific details he saw the blood and bones of a wounded mind and a horror that no child should have to bear.

Maybe it was better if Cathlin never remembered, he thought. And maybe bringing her to Draycott had been more dangerous than he'd realized.

When the phone rang again, he answered with only half his attention, the rest still caught in that chilling day fifteen years before, a day that still held too many unanswered questions.

"Slept well, did you?"

Harcliffe. Dominic frowned. "Perfectly. But I'm sure this isn't a social call."

"Quite right. Two things. I've found a mention of this Geneva Russell of yours. According to the data our people uncovered, she was the daughter of a rich Suffolk East India Company merchant. It appears that she died in 1794. Interestingly enough, the nasty event appears to have taken place at Draycott Abbey."

Chills gathered along Dominic's neck. "How did it happen?"

"Unclear, I'm afraid. The whole affair seems to have been hushed up. Except for an odd village bookseller and an obscure researcher who has spend the last twenty-five years researching the unexplained deaths of women over twenty in the southern counties of England, we'd never have found anything."

Dominic cut him off coldly. "What about that cork I sent you last night?"

"We looked into the fragments. It's poison all right. Amazon curare alkaloids with an admixture of pepper to hasten blood absorption rate. A damned sophisticated mix."

"Did you check any deliveries made to Richard Severance's London town house?"

"Our people found a bill of sale for that particular vintage. Severance received the bottles yesterday, but there's still no way we can prove a connection. Frankly, I think the whole idea is preposterous."

"Try the delivery company. They keep records. With a little pressure someone's bound to talk."

"It's going to be damned hard. Luckily, Severance is in Brighton for the day. When he hears what we've done, he'll have a whole regiment of legal experts down on us. The man's got an impeccable reputation and all the lawyers that a million pounds can buy. I still don't understand what makes you think he's involved."

"Instinct," Dominic said flatly.

"Really, Dominic, without ironclad proof, this is going to result in one nasty scandal."

"It's a dirty job, but someone has to do it, Harcliffe. And get me those generator parts I ordered yesterday. You *are* interested in seeing that the government and royal family are entirely satisfied with the handling of this affair, aren't you?" *Especially since there might be a knighthood in it for you.*

"I suppose it can be arranged. But—"

Dominic hung up, tired of hearing protests and more bad news.

So there had been another, much earlier death at Draycott Abbey. He frowned, unable to get the thought out of his mind.

Looking down, he saw the opened files, page after page of

sterile details that provided absolutely no answers to his thousand, burning questions about Cathlin. He sighed and rubbed his shoulder, which was throbbing from his tussle in the cellars. But he decided hard physical work was just what he needed to clear his head.

First he'd take a look at the malfunctioning generator, and then he'd have a look at the new alarm system. After that he'd fill in the three men he'd asked to help him out with the abbey's security.

And then, if Cathlin still wasn't down, he'd think of an unusual way of waking her.

THE MOAT WAS SHIMMERING in the sunlight as Cathlin stood by the tall window overlooking the abbey's roses, dreams that were far too real for dreams chasing through her head. Her pulse raced as she thought of memories, heated memories. And then the brush of shadows.

She reached into her pocket and traced the corner of the crumpled card she had shoved there. There was no point in waiting. The intimate encounter she had shared with Dominic had pushed her beyond her normal defenses, leaving her prey to feelings and half-seen memories that threatened to tear her apart. She knew now that her questions would not go away. If she were truly going mad, then she wanted to know it now.

As she turned to make her way to the study, she saw an envelope shoved beneath the hall door. It bore her name and a London postmark, but no return address. She opened it slowly, then froze. Plaid. Amber plaid, the pattern that had been her mother's favorite. The same fabric that she had worn when she died.

Or when she had been murdered.

Fingers trembling, Cathlin pulled a sheet of paper from the envelope. It bore only one word, in bold block letters.

Remember?

CATHLIN'S HEART WAS RACING as she dialed the number on Joanna Harcliffe's card. A pleasant female voice answered.

"I'm afraid that Dr. Harcliffe is not available right now. Shall I have her phone you?"

Cathlin swallowed. "Of course." She left the abbey's number, frowning. "Do you know when she will be back?"

"Not long. Forgive me, but…is it an emergency? You sound rather upset."

Cathlin thought of her restless dreams. She thought of the memories jabbing at the edge of her consciousness. And now there was the unexplained scrap of plaid and its cruel message. Was the killer in the abbey right now, planning another deadly attack?

"Just have her call me," she said tightly.

Dominic had to be told next. Cathlin tried his room and the cellars, where a new laser security grid gleamed in the darkness. But Dominic wasn't there, either. No doubt he was in Nicholas's beautiful study making more of his covert calls.

But the study was empty. Only a pile of files and an old book lay on the rosewood desk, with a gilt bookmark in the center. Cathlin opened the book idly and then froze.

A tall woman in blue satin stared back at her. Nearby stood a young girl, her eyes a blaze of happiness.

The caption was most specific: EVANGELINE RUSSELL AND DAUGHTER GENEVA. INDIA, 1782.

Cathlin felt the blood rush from her face as she stared down at those two happy faces, wondering how everything had gone wrong. Then a piece of paper caught her eye. A paper that held her own name.

Frowning, she slid the sheet free.

It was dated fifteen years before, a neatly typed transcription of some sorts of interviews. As Cathlin read further, her eyes widened. First came confusion, then shock, then pure, blazing fury.

Muttering, she pulled out sheet after sheet from the files that

Dominic must have been reading. All of them held her name. All of them held the fragments of her past, recorded in dry, clinical sentences that speculated about trauma depth and recovery time and psychological prognosis.

Damn them! Damn them all!

She dropped the papers as if burned, hating to see herself pinned there like some dying insect caught beneath the scientist's knife.

What right did they have to dissect a child's mind this way? And what right did Dominic have to this kind of painfully private information, information even *she* had never seen!

She shoved the papers off the desk and watched them scatter in an angry cloud. Something about the sight made her think of fog and darkness and a danger that stalked her still. In her head, the slow ache became a savage drumming. Suddenly Cathlin felt stifled, choked.

Terrified.

Remember? the note had said. Was it her mother's killer watching her even now?

She turned, white-faced, desperate to escape from this strange old house, which held too much pain and too many secrets.

HIS HANDS BLACK WITH grease, Dominic turned away from the moat.

His eyes narrowed as he heard the sound of running feet.

A premonition of fear hit him as he saw Cathlin's slender form disappear into the dark boxwood copse to the north.

Her face had been bleak with pain.

CHAPTER TWENTY-THREE

THE FOG SEEMED TO COME from nowhere, drifting in little pools that hung in the hollows near the river. Cathlin ran blindly, uncaring where she stepped as the white layers grew thicker.

All the while, the cold words of the medical report danced before her eyes, along with the bold letters of the anonymous note.

Remember?

The river was below her now, a shining trail of green that ran along sloping banks of moss, streaked now with fog.

Fog.

Darkness.

The river...

She shook her head, shoving her hair from her face, trying to separate *now* from *then*. Mud clung to her shoes and branches scraped at her arms and face as she plunged blindly forward into the fog.

"Cathlin! Stop, damn it!"

It was Dominic's voice, but to Cathlin it was somehow unfamiliar, like the voice of a stranger. Wildly, she pushed through the thick bank of flowers, her pulse ragged in her ears.

"Cathlin, wait!"

She shoved past the lilacs, past ferns and anemones, until she came to a sheltered grove in the lee of a granite cliff. Roses danced crimson on stems that coiled all the way up the bank.

Her breath caught. Memories again—a lifetime of memories. Too many to hold inside her throbbing head.

Hard fingers gripped her shoulders. "Damn it, don't run from me, Cathlin!" She was shoved around, caught against a man's chest.

Her eyes were hazy, unfocused. Suddenly she was a thousand miles away. Or two hundred years away…

THE SHARP WHISTLE OF THE wind woke him.

He blinked, feeling a strange bed of straw beneath him. Memory dawned. He smiled, sated, happy. "Geneva?"

No answer. No welcoming warmth.

He sat up, frowning at the first gray light filtering through the mill's narrow windows.

She was gone.

GABRIEL FOUND HER TRACKS just beyond the bank, set into the soft mud. Grim-faced, vowing the worst of retribution, he stalked her past ferns and mossy stones and thickets still white with drifting fog.

The sun was just visible, burning red over the horizon as he strode over the hill, his eyes locked on the prints that showed her haste.

How could the woman think she could escape him?

Then Gabriel stopped. Here the prints were joined by a second pair.

Devere!

He muttered a curse and ran.

At the top of the next turning in the path he ran her down and pulled her around to face him. "Where is he?"

Her face was pale, determined. "I—I hid from him in the fog. They made their way on toward Stevington Ford. Devere was only wounded."

"You could have been killed!"

Her face was blurred with tears. "Let me go!"

"Damned if I will. Now answer me. Tell me why you ran away."

"Because I won't see you hurt. Devere will never give up.

He'll send a dozen men after me if that's what it takes. He wants you, Gabriel, and your love for me is your only vulnerability. I must go!" Her voice was raw with desperation.

"You're not going anywhere."

She shoved at him, her lilac scent intoxicating. "You don't understand. He'll never give up."

"When we're married, he will," Gabriel said grimly.

"But—" She swallowed, shook her head. "I cannot."

"You are married already?"

"No."

"Then you can," he said flatly, already decided. "And you will. I will see you safe from Devere."

"No! You must let me go!" She pulled away and ran into a bower heavy with roses, her hair whipping out around her. "I'll never be safe—nor will anyone who harbors me, not as long as Devere lives. He has killed men and now will exact his revenge against my sister, through his many friends in France who owe him favors."

"I will help her to safety and see that you are safe from that madman forever. I give you my promise, Geneva."

"And in the process I will only bring you more pain, you have known so much already!" She turned and ran, her skirts trapping her as they caught in the rose briars. "I cannot. I will not!" Gabriel pulled her against him, even as she rained angry fists across his chest. Her cheeks were streaked with tears, her eyes haunted.

"Stop fighting me, woman."

But she was wild, lost to his words.

And the storm of her brought an answer in him. He seized her twisting body and pinned her against the trunk of a towering oak. She was beyond words, beyond reason, gripped by fear and a terrible remorse for a betrayal she could never forget.

Words failed, reason lost, Gabriel touched her the only way he could, with a need that was as fierce as her regret. Satin pulled free and linen fell in a heap. Geneva fought him like currents in a spring flood, pummeling his chest and twisting until he buried his hands in her hair and ground his body against hers.

Heat met heat. Wild hunger called to its match.

"No. I won't have you hurt. I won't!"

"Hurt me," Gabriel said hoarsely. "Rip out my very heart. For you I would give it gladly, don't you see? Perhaps I already have." He shoved away her gown; she had dressed in haste and wore nothing beneath. Her body was flushed, the thrust of her breasts testimony to the desire that already gripped her.

He groaned, found the pulse that beat at her neck, stroked the silken skin that hid her heat. He did not stop until he heard her cry out and wrap her hands around him.

"Don't hold me, my love. Let me go."

"I must," he said hoarsely. "All my life. Perhaps far longer than this mortal life." As he spoke Gabriel felt a sharp chill at his neck. But he had no time for chills or warnings, not with Geneva in his arms. "And I'll set my brand on you to prove it, a brand of love that carries all the joy you've given me."

She stared at him, a universe of love in her eyes as he bent his head and measured the pulse at her neck, then caught the soft skin to his lips.

With a low moan she curved toward him, impossibly lost, feeling the hot brand of desire that would mark her as his forever.

And then they were thigh to thigh, sliding to the damp, dark earth. Both tugged at her tangled satin skirts; together they shredded his shirt and then pushed away his breeches.

He took her there, bowered by roses, cushioned by soft moss and spring ferns with the murmur of the river to lull them and the fog to veil their nakedness. She met him with wild delight, driven by a desire that followed his in equal measure. Control was beyond him and regret beyond her where they lay among the roses, among the fingers of drifting fog.

"Together," he swore hoarsely, driving home to heaven.

"Forever," she answered, following him there.

It was a promise whispered, shared and sealed with their joined bodies as they met in mad abandon. And if sheer force of will and human need could forge a bridge of time, then their promise would pass beyond the bounds of death itself.

"CATHLIN?" CALLUSED fingers traced the tears on Cathlin's cheeks. She shuddered, her mind on fire, her thoughts a tangled blur, past and present no longer separate.

"Sweet God, love, what's happened to you?"

Gabriel. How very much he had loved her. And the remembering made it far, far worse.

"Talk to me, Cathlin."

"Let me go!"

"No." Dominic's hands—*Gabriel's* hands—dug into her waist. "Not until you tell me what's wrong."

"Don't try to stop me. Not again, Gabriel." Then the sharp gasp, the horror of realization, the gray pain from deep in the mind that was somehow both Cathlin and Geneva. "No, I didn't mean—"

His eyes were grim. The jaw so hard, so beloved. She *had* to make him go.

"You're here now, here in the twentieth century, Cathlin. You're no eighteenth century heiress fleeing from a madman," Dominic growled.

She caught a wild breath, shoving at fragments of memory, fighting to hold apart the two worlds still crazily superimposed. "They're both here, caught inside my head."

"Fight it, Cathlin. Come back. I need you too much to lose you now," he said hoarsely.

Sweet words. Dangerous words.

"Why, so you can dissect my mind for that monster Harcliffe you work for?" She choked back a sob, hammering at his chest.

"You knew all about me. About the bridge and how my mother died. Damn you for knowing what even I couldn't see clearly."

"You saw the files." Dominic's voice was hard with regret.

"Oh, yes, I saw them, Officer Montserrat. Did you enjoy reading about me, about that silly little girl they found crying on the bridge, trying to scrub the blood from her hands?"

"You're a fool if you have to ask me that."

Ragged laughter. "Then I *am* a fool, a fool along with everything else. How did they phrase it? 'Vestigial amnesia, trauma syndrome of uncertain outcome and unpredictable prognosis.' Fool? Yes, I'd say the word fool fits me very well."

"Stop it, Cathlin. Stop fighting and listen to me."

But she didn't. She only fought him, twisting and furious, the empty place in her head suddenly too full, too heavy with memories, each more shattering than the last.

Around them the fog drifted higher.

Cathlin wrenched free of his hands and stood at the top of the slope, her skirts playing about her, her hair a wild cloud.

Just like another woman long years before.

She pressed her forehead, fighting the rush of images. "Do you want to gloat? Do you want to laugh at the little girl who is still as crazy as she always was?" Her shoulders slumped against an ancient overhanging oak. "Dear God, what's happening to me? Why do I see too much, when for years I couldn't see enough?" She felt him behind her. "Go ahead and laugh."

"I'm not laughing, Cathlin." Dominic's voice was raw.

Around him came the sigh of the wind and the whisper of the roses. Dominic staggered before a flood of memories, images of this same bower rich with green moss and veiled with fog.

Madness, he thought. He *couldn't* remember. And yet he did. "Look at me, Cathlin."

She backed up. "I hate you. You're one of them. You turned my mind into a neat little game in one of those files. My God, you've *always* been one of them." She took another step and felt a rock at her back. "Maybe you even sent the note pushed beneath my door, with a scrap of plaid from my mother's dress."

"When did this come?"

"This morning. Of course you were nowhere to be found," she said accusingly. Then her voice broke. "Just let me go."

"Too late, Irish. Maybe it was always too late," Dominic said hoarsely as the fog swirled up between them.

Cathlin turned and ran up the slope, stumbling as her entirely twentieth century skirt caught on a trailing vine of roses. "No, Dominic, no more. I should never have come back to the abbey."

"You can't keep this buried, Cathlin. It will kill you. And you can't possibly believe I had anything to do with that letter," he said grimly.

"I don't know what to believe anymore." She felt no strength at all, only anger and confusion, like the drifting fog. Memories were coming too fast now, images and emotions bound together, seen in two times and by two different women. "How did you know about Geneva?"

"The same way that you knew, Cathlin."

"Dreams?"

"Of us. Together. Yes to all of it, no matter how bizarre it sounds. I remembered the desire, Cathlin, and all the unbearable loneliness."

"No, you're lying. You're just like all the others. They told me to wait, that my memories would come back when I was ready. But God, they never told me about this second set of memories."

Dominic held out his hands, and Cathlin saw they were trembling. "Am I lying about *this?* Am I lying about wanting you so much I can't sleep or eat or breathe for the pain of it?" He cursed savagely. "You think I enjoy being ripped in two, feeling another man's thoughts hammering inside my head? Do you think I enjoy lying awake night after night and seeing you, cool, beautiful and naked, waiting for me? Wanting me. Dear God, wanting me so much that I can't ever be free of you."

Cathlin shivered. He couldn't lie, not in such a tone, not with eyes that blazed with such fury. She, too, had seen his body hotly naked, wanting her in a way she'd never been wanted before. She had felt the same wrenching loneliness, a dark emptiness that reached out beyond the years, across a bridge of dreams, tormenting her with a happiness she had known too briefly and then lost.

She tried to argue. The small, sane part of her mind shouted he was lying. But she was already beyond reason. It was a matter of blood now, of yearning blood and hot wanting muscle. While the fog drifted, coiling about her legs, Cathlin finally accepted that.

Past and present swam around her, inexorably entwined, kindled minute to minute, hour to hour, lifetime to lifetime.

Dominic caught her hand to his lips. "Tell me you can't feel it, Cathlin," he challenged her hoarsely. "Tell me you don't want this as much as I do."

She couldn't. Her eyes betrayed her dark secret. His touch left her skin hot, hungry, wounded by a thousand memories.

Of Cathlin O'Neill. And of Geneva Russell.

"No!" Cathlin closed her eyes, trying to tear herself from the past, from memories that tore at her sanity.

SHE WORE ONLY THE FINEST cambric chemise, now damp and nearly translucent. She was all soft shadows beneath the moon.

DOMINIC'S EYES WERE A blaze of green. "You remember. You're seeing it now, aren't you? God, just the way I am."

HIS FINGERS WERE NOT quite steady as he slid her chemise from her shoulders, following the fine fabric with his mouth, kisses like

*a dark storm. He had no gold nor stars to give her. All he had
was his touch and his wild joy in her.*

"TELL ME CATHLIN," Dominic said hoarsely, his fingers in her
hair, his lips pressed to her satin cheeks. "Tell me I'm not going
mad alone. Tell me that and I'll stop."

How could she when it was true? Too many memories bound
them and too many regrets.

Above them the roses danced. Fog swirled noiselessly as a
great gray cat flicked his ears and then slipped off through the
shrubs. A dim shimmering, the faintest trace of light, outlined
the edges of the little grove.

Cathlin tried to hate Dominic Montserrat but she couldn't. She
couldn't even distrust him. There was too much living, breathing past between them. And right now Cathlin's body was remembering every silken second of that past.

She felt him tense slightly. Because they were so closely
attuned, she could read every one of his gestures. "Your
shoulder's hurting you," she said accusingly, expecting him to lie.

Before the fog, before the river, he *would* have lied. But not
now. "It…does hurt, but not badly."

"Why didn't you tell me?"

"Because it's not my way, Cathlin. I've been trained not to
show pain—as far as possible not even to feel it. That was my
career, and it became my whole life." He laughed bitterly.
"Yes, that was at the very top of Ashton's rules—never let
them see you sweat. Never show a hint of weakness, because
there's no room for weakness when you're doing close protection at the top."

"But you gave it up, Dominic. The old rules are gone."

"I had to. It was that or lose everything I valued, everything
that kept me sane." His eyes closed. "What do you want from
me, Cathlin?"

"I want everything, Dominic. All that Geneva had—and lost."

"We can't go back, Cathlin. If there's anything I've learned, it's that."

"Maybe we don't have to. Maybe it's all here." She ran her hands over the warm skin atop his heart. "Deep in here. Maybe we're here to finish all that wasn't finished then." Her lips slid to his jaw.

"The timing's wrong, Cathlin. What if something happened to you now—"

"Officer?"

"What?"

She placed her hands on his shoulders and pushed him backward until he was cushioned by the mossy bank. *"Shut up."* She tugged open his shirt. Her lips grazed the warm skin at his neck. Her hand slid down his chest, exquisitely slow.

With a low curse he pulled her beneath him, a dark gleam of determination in his eyes.

"Dominic? What are you—"

"Be quiet, beauty." His fingers jabbed at the little buttons on her blouse. He watched her skin come free, warm and hungry and flushed. Inch by inch the cool silk slid back, while his eyes locked on her face.

The last button pulled free. "Sweet God, Cathlin," he said hoarsely. She was lush ivory skin capped with tight nipples of dusky coral. His head fell and he took one pouting crest, smiling when she moaned.

"Dominic, I—" She swallowed. "Oh, God, you—"

He circled her wrists and shoved them to the cool, soft moss. His body fit the perfect mold of hers as he explored her, stroking crest and hollow and every bit of velvet in between. He groaned to find a tiny beauty mark just above her breast. A smoky crescent, it inflamed him, bringing memories of another time, another pair of lovers.

HE SWEPT HER INTO A DARK storm of feeling, in a place where all memories stopped and all wounds were healed. He felt her arch against him, a single word on her lips.

And the word was his name.

HAD SHE WORN HIS mark into another time, a reminder of all they had once been to each other?

Dominic closed his eyes. Every muscle screamed out, urging him to take all that beauty revealed before him, to spread her wide and fill her. His fingers tightened on her wrists with the fury of his need.

Not yet, he swore fiercely. Not until he'd watched her climax in her pleasure, not until he heard her cry out his name in wonder and delight as she had the night before.

Her skirt was long and soft, covered with roses. It moved easily beneath his fingers, rising over her thighs to cluster at her waist. He pulled aside the delicate swath of lace.

And then looked upon her, long-legged, beautiful, with another smoky birthmark nearly hidden by the graceful inner curve of her thigh.

He cursed darkly, at the very edge of his control.

There were no more words as he found her heat, pleasure hanging upon them like a haze. Cathlin's breath caught and she gave a soft cry. Her back arched, taut like a bow as she drove upward against him.

He watched, enthralled by her beauty, enslaved by the wanting and her elemental sensuality. With her fire summoning him, he spread her and laid his mouth against the silken skin which wore the dark mark of her beauty.

She twisted, cast against him anew, her breath a wild cry that echoed through their silent, rose-covered bower. And Dominic held her, his hands playing lovingly over her flushed skin as she fell back from heaven into the wonder of his arms.

He watched her, heat in his eyes, heat in his heart.

"Dear God," she managed. "I haven't ever—" A ragged laugh. "That is, I didn't expect—"

"I'm delighted to hear it, my sweetest love." Smiling gently, he eased deeper inside her. Instantly she opened, yielding around him, all heat and silken skin. All flushed woman.

Deeper, gently deeper. Finding, learning.

Loving.

It was all that Dominic wanted, this joy, this fine delight reflected in Cathlin's love-hazed eyes.

Moving deeper, he molded her to his conquest.

Her hands opened, nails sharp at his shoulders. "Sweet God, Dominic, no! I—"

She arched against him and cried out wildly, Dominic's name on her lips as she was hurtled into another storm of pleasure.

Slow, breathless moments later she opened one eye.

A rose, broad-petaled and red, nestled at her neck, silver with dew. Dominic's smile told her he thought of different petals.

Her eyes widened. "I couldn't possibly, Dominic."

The rose brushed her lips, then slid to her neck, crimson petals scattered in its wake. Cathlin watched, breathless, as the bloom made its way lower, petals shedding with every inch.

Dominic's smile grew darker as the lush petals traced the hollow of her stomach and eased downward.

"Dominic, I'm not at all sure that—"

But *he* was. God, how he was. Years of uninvolved emotion gave him the ironclad certainty now, and he used every shred of it in his silken conquest.

Then petal met dewy petal, crimson met softer crimson.

Cathlin's breath caught, desire swiftly rekindling. She moved to meet him, rapt.

Then her eyes opened. "Stop," she said breathlessly, shoving at his chest. "I felt a rock."

He stopped instantly, concern in his face as he slid aside.

But Cathlin was quicker. She followed her advantage instantly, slipping over him and pulling his shirt free, popping buttons with ruthless disregard. His belt hissed free and then a new set of buttons challenged.

Dominic frowned and stilled her hand.

But Cathlin tackled the buttons and watched his tantalizing inches emerge.

She reached out awed by the heat of him, the extravagant thrust of him.

Dominic cursed low and pulled her closer. His voice was like gravel, one final question necessary before turning back grew impossible. "Are you sure, Cathlin? Any more and I won't be stopping."

Her eyes rose, smoke and amber. High above them a single beam of sunlight pierced the drifting fog and slanted down into their quiet corner of paradise.

"I'm not changing my mind, if that's what you're hoping for." Her soft hands clutched his shoulders and sunlight glinted off her glossy hair. She inched against him, her eyes hazy with passionate intent. "Is this the general idea?"

"God…"

Lower. Soft and yielding. Hot ache spreading, joy building. Then the sudden barrier. Her eyes opened, pleading.

Dominic took a harsh breath and cupped her hips. With a hard thrust he brought himself deep and Cathlin cried out with the shocking joy of feeling him tight inside her.

Pleasure trembled, shimmered, any discomfort burned away by the fire of his fingers where they joined. She gasped and let her body fall, poured over him like a rain of roses. "Please, Dominic. All I want—is this, this with you."

Her thighs slid warm against him. Dominic drove himself into her, gentle conquests forgotten, amusements irrevocably past.

Now his only need was to claim her, to possess her as completely as she had possessed him.

With every dark inch he came closer to that hot, still core, closer to the vow he had to pledge with body and soul.

Suddenly her body tensed and Dominic felt the pleasure rippling through her. His own followed, all dark fire and jagged fury, wilder than anything he'd ever known.

But in that moment he felt the mystery of a deeper joining, breaths and molecules fused, thoughts and memories and spirits bound together like sunlight amid the drifting fog.

And at that moment the scent of lilacs seemed to rise around them.

"TOGETHER," GABRIEL swore hoarsely, driving home to heaven.
"Forever," Geneva answered, following him there.

SLOWLY THE FOG LIFTED. A pair of otters glided through the green river and a thrush called from the roses.

Cathlin fitted herself to him, boneless and replete. She curled closer against him and sighed. "Eminent body," she murmured. "Excellent breed." She moved by a silken fraction. "And a potent finish, just as you promised, Officer Montserrat." She ran her foot gently along his thigh.

Dominic cleared his throat. "I don't actually think it's possible," he said hoarsely, half laughing, half accusing. More than half-sated.

"But I say it is," Cathlin demurred, voice muffled as she began her silken foray, taking exquisite care over all the hard places that had been intriguing her. "And I *am* the wine expert here."

"There are certain time frames, you know. I expect it was so those cavemen could find the strength to get up and go—" He swallowed suddenly as her lips moved downward. "Er, to go kill a woolly mammoth or two for dinner." A low curse. "To feed all those little cavemen and cavewomen they were making right and left."

Cathlin ignored him, smiling when she felt the hot rise of him inside her. "Extraordinary stamina, too." She stared down, one brow raised. "You were saying, my lord? Something about cavemen and time frames and impossibility?"

Dominic cursed and rolled her beneath him, her dominion abruptly ended. Closing his eyes, he brought himself down to her in a sharp, swift slide. "Forget whatever I just said, Lady Ashton."

ON THE HILL ABOVE THEM, beyond the circle of roses, beyond the mossy bank, a tall figure shimmered, then slid into being, all black silk and white, rippling lace.

He bent to stroke the great gray cat seated at his side. "Most satisfactory, don't you agree?"

The cat's tail flicked gracefully.

"No, I really can't agree with you there. Those two are meant to be right where they are. Just as they were meant to be together, all those years ago."

The cat meowed.

"I know that, my friend. But who would have expected Devere's resourcefulness?" Adrian sighed, his face lined, suddenly weary. "As it comes again."

Behind them a kestrel cried. The wind sighed over the boxwood and the dancing roses. Adrian's eyes softened as he heard his name called.

For a moment light outlined the graceful form of a woman in a dress of glimmering cloth of gold.

"Nosy? Not at all, my love. I am merely taking a well-deserved pleasure in the success of my little project."

Soft laughter drifted over the hill. Adrian's eyes darkened as the woman's shape shimmered away into the dark silence of the wood. "I rather think I must go, Gideon," he said shortly. "She captivates me as ever, even after all these years." His eyes narrowed and he thought of another time, of another world where the force of will and sheer human need had been put so cruelly to the test.

But he had won, he and the beautiful woman waiting for him on the hill.

And Adrian Draycott knew, as few other people possibly could, that some promises could truly bridge time, passing beyond life and even beyond the bounds of death itself.

The cat purred softly, pressing against his polished boot. Nearby the roses danced, bloodred against a wall of green.

And then abruptly both cat and master disappeared.

CHAPTER TWENTY-FOUR

THE SILENCE BESIDE THE river was broken by a shrill, mechanic beeping. Dominic sighed and rolled to his back, fishing a metal box from the chaos of their clothes as static filled the air. "Montserrat, are you there?" The voice at the other end was urgent. "There's just been a call from Harcliffe. Richard Severance has been taken into custody for questioning, but he insists he will only talk to you."

Dominic frowned. "To me?"

"That's the word. Harcliffe wants you to get right off to London. He's sent a car."

Dominic sighed. "I'll be there shortly." He punched a button, silencing the receiver, then sat up.

"What does it mean, Dominic?"

"I'm not sure." But in that moment Dominic had a flash of intuition that they, like the *Titanic* drifting in the foggy Atlantic night, were heading directly toward something from which they had no chance of escape.

IT TOOK DOMINIC ONLY minutes to pack a small bag. Then he turned and pulled Cathlin to him. "I'll be back tomorrow. At least I hope I will. There are three men working the grounds in shifts and one will always be in the house with you."

Cathlin brushed his cheek. "Take all the time you need. I'll be fine. Just as long as it isn't another two hundred years."

"You've got my promise on that, Lady Ashton."

Their fingers tightened. Their lips touched for long, aching moments. Then Dominic turned sharply and slid into the unmarked but very official car that James Harcliffe had sent to take him back to London.

"WERE THERE ANY MESSAGES for me, Mrs. Holt?" Joanna Harcliffe tipped her wet umbrella carefully into its ceramic container and hung up her raincoat neatly.

Her receptionist looked down at a stack of papers. "A half dozen, Dr. Harcliffe. The usual, all except for this one." The woman held out a sheet of paper. As the older woman studied the message, a frown worked between her calm brown eyes.

"YES, MRS. HARCLIFFE—Dr. Harcliffe, I should say. Thank you for returning my call." Cathlin was standing in the rose-filled study overlooking the abbey's moat. Marston had finally tracked her down in the cellars to tell her that she had a call. But now Cathlin felt a strange reluctance to talk about the flood of memories and the chaos of feelings that were still painfully new.

"I expect you want to know why I called." She straightened the beautiful Fabergé egg at the corner of Nicholas Draycott's desk. "Actually it has to do with my memory. I—I think that it's beginning to come back."

"This is a very significant development, my dear. I'm sure you must find it a little shocking," the woman said sympathetically. "When did this all begin?"

"Yesterday. Oh, it didn't come all in one rush, but in bits and pieces." Cathlin looked out at the silver waters of the moat, trying to explain. "But it's not just about what happened fifteen years ago. This concerns another person—and another time." She sighed. "I expect this sounds entirely mad."

Joanna Harcliffe laughed softly. "You'd be surprised at the behavior I see in the course of my day, Lady Ashton. The majority of it is far stranger than what you've just described, and yet each of those people functions quite normally. To all intents and purposes they are quite, quite sane."

Somehow this didn't reassure Cathlin as much as it ought to. "But I'm coming face-to-face with memories of myself—as a woman who died two hundred years ago. And on top of that, the memories about my mother have begun returning."

There was a moment of silence, then the sound of papers rustling. "I see." The psychiatrist sighed. "I believe it's finally begun."

"Begun? I don't understand."

"You've finally begun to remember, my dear. Something has triggered the images that have been blocked inside you all these years. Don't ask me why, because I can't tell you. The human mind is still far from being well understood, no matter what experts like me would have you believe. And as for your memories of another person and time, all I can say is that many famous people have consciously experienced lives as other people, some as illustrious as Aristotle and Plato or Thomas Edison and General Patton."

"But it's all happening so suddenly."

"I'm sure it must feel that way, but you really needn't feel you have to take it in all at once. It reminds me of a rhyme I once heard. Let me see if I can get it right.

"There is a hawke at my father's house,
By oak and ash and bonny deer."

The woman's voice became smooth and singsong as she continued.

"And though to me he sings full fair
No one else can hear, oh
No one else can hear."

Cathlin frowned, struggling with a thread of memory. "I've heard that, I think." Suddenly the next lines rushed into her mind.

"There is a dove on my mother's hill,
By oak and ash and bonny doe;
And though to me she sings full sweet,
No one else can know, oh,
No one else can know."

She rubbed at her forehead, wondering where that strange scrap of poetry had come from.

"I see you've heard it too." Another pause. "A silly bit of verse I suppose, but it's something I think of when I am faced with unanswerable questions. And I'm faced with them rather more often than I care to admit when dealing with the human mind. But my dear Lady Ashton, I could come to the abbey if you feel it is important."

Cathlin frowned. "No, I'll be fine. I—I'm sorry to have troubled you.'

After she hung up, Cathlin stood for a while, the sunlight on her shoulders entirely unnoticed. She thought about the call and about that odd bit of verse—and then she thought about nothing at all. It was long minutes later before she gave herself a shake and roused herself from her reverie.

JOANNA HARCLIFFE FROWNED at the receiver. The new Lady Ashton had been decisive enough in her assurances that she did not require any help, yet there had been something in her voice, a quiver, an edge of uncertainty that Joanna Harcliffe, experienced from years of professional practice, recognized as deep inner turmoil.

She sat back at her desk and looked at the framed diplomas that hid nearly every inch of the silk-covered walls. Steepling her fingers, she went over the conversation word by word. Outside a wave of automobiles screamed and snorted through Piccadilly Circus, but she barely heard.

A moment later she reached forward and pushed down the button for her receptionist. "Something has come up, Mrs. Holt. I'm afraid I'll cancel the rest of my appointments for the day."

CATHLIN FROWNED DOWN AT the dusty wine case. One of the precious bottles now stood on her worktable, where she had placed it after carefully freeing it from its case.

But as she stood in the cool shadows, the old glass bottle before her, Cathlin felt images surge, pressing at her consciousness with painful intensity. She rubbed her eyes, blinking. As she did, the bottle changed. No more was it dust-streaked and dirty, its cork brittle. Now its glass shone and its label was crisp.

As new as the day it was printed.

THEY ARRIVED AT THE ABBEY just as night was falling. Roses filled the courtyard and climbed the weathered granite walls.

Geneva lost her heart instantly to this place of wrenching beauty. They would be safe here; she felt it clearly. Even Henry Devere's madness could not reach Gabriel inside these moated walls.

For three days she explored every shadowed corner, every sunlit room. Even the cavernous wine cellars did not escape her curious eye. She marveled at the variety of the wines collected in those cool shadows and Gabriel encouraged her to choose a different bottle to sample every night with their dinner.

At last, Geneva saw some of the sadness eased from Gabriel's silver eyes. Amused by her boundless curiosity, he followed her everywhere, sharing information from his earlier visits with Adrian. With unflagging energy Geneva dragged him through the imposing portraits in the long gallery while she fired innumerable questions about the Draycott ancestors. When Gabriel could bear no more history lessons, he pulled her off to the moat, where Geneva dangled her toes and returned his teasing kisses.

But when night filled the valleys and stars shone in the shimmering moat, Gabriel fed a different kind of curiosity as he pulled Geneva against his hard body. Her breath caught when he carried her to the huge poster bed that overlooked the rose gardens, though neither noticed the view through the beautiful mullioned windows.

Their joy was in a different world, a place of endless discovery and boundless love where Gabriel taught Geneva pleasures beyond imagining.

And in their reckless joy, neither noticed the eyes that watched from the darkness.

"I COULD STAY ANOTHER day. I would just have time." Gabriel stood exquisite in navy silk and crimson damask on Draycott's gravel drive. Behind him a groom held the reins of his restive mount.

"No, you must go. We could have no peace, not while my sister's life hangs in the balance. And though it breaks my heart, I must let you go for you are the only one who can save her. Otherwise, I would hold you here forever, my love." Geneva straightened her shoulders and looked up at the man she loved. "But there will be time, endless time for us when you return from France." With a little choked cry she flung herself against him, her hands thrown around his neck. "Be careful, my love. They know you now and will be watching for you. Be watchful also for Henry Devere. He may well be a greater threat than any of the French Tribunal."

"No one will find me. I've put all my cleverness to use this time. I have every intention of returning, now that I know there's *an incorrigible hoyden with an unquenchable curiosity waiting in my bed."*

Caught in emotion, Geneva didn't think to scold him for his plain speaking in front of the groom, who turned away, careful to look as if he had not heard.

She caught a ragged breath and then her chin rose. "Go now, my love. Go quickly and Godspeed. I'll be waiting, waiting here in the shadow of the abbey's roses. Remember that and come back safe to me."

A dark, unnamed emotion crossed Gabriel's face. As the wind sighed through the roses, he pulled Geneva close and pressed a hard, desperate kiss upon her lips. Then he flung himself up into the saddle and galloped south to the coast, where a sleek cutter was waiting to run before the tide to France.

CATHLIN STOOD IN THE half-light, feeling the memories burn through her hand where she touched the old, dusty bottle. They tore at her with aching force, until it seemed she was reliving every agonizing moment of the past.

And as she stood she heard the faint sound of a woman's breathless sobbing.

GABRIEL DID NOT MAKE the next county, nor even make the next valley. They caught him as the sun burned over the horizon, twenty men with muskets ready.

He fought them long and well, sweat on his brow as he cut down one after another. But in the end he was no match for this cutthroat crew hired from London's cruelest slums.

As darkness fell, he was bound and gagged and shoved into a carriage bound for London. There Henry Devere waited in keenest expectation of his arrival, and of the look on Geneva Russell's face when she saw her lover lying dead at her feet.

DOMINIC SHOWED A BADGE to the bored officer sitting behind the desk in the cavernous office building he hadn't visited in years. "I'm looking for Richard Severance."

"Then you found him. He's right over there."

The international jet-setter and financier was being held in a narrow room with a single desk and chair. Dark lines of strain bit into his face. Even a few hours of questioning could do that to the toughest people, Dominic knew. And something told him Richard Severance was far from tough.

Severance came to his feet immediately. "There you are, Montserrat. It took you long enough to get here."

Dominic leaned back against the battered table. "What's the idea of dragging me into this? It's a simple enough case—attempted murder. We've found the company who delivered that wine to you before you added your poison. There's no reason for me to be involved."

"That's where you're wrong." Severance turned and paced the narrow room. "She's got the same hold over you, hasn't she? I know how it works. I saw her, and from that minute on I couldn't get her out of my mind either." Severance laughed grimly. "I've seen that same hunger in *your* eyes."

"So?"

"So I didn't give in without a fight. I made it my business to find out everything I could about Cathlin O'Neill. I studied her father, I studied her mother, and I studied her past. Oddly enough there wasn't that much to find, which made me curious. With the kind of access I have to people in high places, I'd expected to find more."

"Get to the point, Severance."

"I'm not certain *what* Cathlin has in her past." Severance frowned and pulled a hand through his now disordered hair. "Oh, there were a few fragments about her mother's murder at Draycott Abbey, but after that nothing. Stranger still, I found out that someone else had been along that same paper trail. Whoever it was made damn sure to sweep every detail clean after him."

"Which only made you more curious."

"You're bloody right it made me curious." Severance shrugged. "I won't say I loved her. I won't even say that I liked her all the time. But I couldn't seem to get Cathlin O'Neill out of my mind. Especially her eyes. All I could think of was seeing them hot with passion, just for me." He cursed softly. "Yes, I was damned curious. I've made a great deal of money by being curious, Officer Montserrat. Business is about information, after all. So I pushed and then I pushed some more and bit by bit the pieces of Cathlin's past finally began to emerge."

Dominic sat back, waiting to hear the rough outlines of the story Cathlin had already told him along with some of the details he had learned from Harcliffe's file. "Go ahead, Severance, astound me."

The other man studied Dominic. "Tough, aren't you? But you weren't so tough in Rome, not when those three teenagers died from your gun. And you weren't so tough when it turned out that one of them was a girl."

Dominic's jaw hardened. Less than half a dozen people knew about that bloody episode. It had been carefully covered up, not out of concern for Dominic's reputation but as a precaution in case other members of the royal family might be attacked. "Just how the hell do you know that, Severance? Not that I'm agreeing there's any truth to it, of course."

"I have access to the best sources, Montserrat. I'm not talking about receptionists or clerical staff here, but about highly placed cabinet-level contacts. These people owe me all kinds of favors. That's how I began to fit the clues about Cathlin together." He began to pace again, his expression growing more and more tense. "And finally those pieces began to make sense."

"Why did you go to so much trouble? Certainly not just because of a pair of remarkable eyes?"

"At first that's all it was. Then it changed. My instincts began screaming that there was more here than met the eye. Secrets are power, Montserrat, and power is what keeps me where I am." Severance laughed grimly. "Or where I *was*." He frowned at Dominic. "You still don't believe me, do you? You think this is all a scheme to work my way out of the charges. But this is absolutely true. Someone else was going to a great deal of trouble to destroy the details of Cathlin's past. Those psychological files of hers are not available even to fellow physicians. They're considered national secrets, don't you see? There's only one reason that would happen."

"Because Cathlin knew something important?"

"Exactly! Do you understand now? Somewhere in that jagged, tormented memory she holds a scrap of information that someone considers very, very deadly. That's why they want her past erased."

Dominic sat forward, his eyes narrowing. "Tell me who."

CATHLIN STOOD IN THE WINE cellar, her hands locked at her chest, images of past and present flooding her mind. Around her lay piles of rubble, remnants of the wall that had been Gabriel Ashton's lonely tomb.

A wall that reminded her of the jagged hole in her own mind.

Fragments. Images. So much of the past she could never get away from. As Cathlin moved over the floor, something glinted from the shadows. Bending down, she sifted through the dust and picked up a small metal link, the kind that came from a piece of expensive jewelry.

Cathlin studied the piece of silver, turning it in the light. Something about it nagged at her memory, but she couldn't decide what. After a moment she slipped the smooth link into her pocket, where her fingers continued to turn it over and over.

What had happened to Gabriel? And what had happened to this wistful amber-eyed woman that he'd left behind at the abbey?

Frowning, Cathlin touched the old bottle. The glass was cold, dust-streaked, heavy beneath her fingers, but now it held no answers, its secrets locked in the same tomb that had held Gabriel's bones.

Behind her the new generator popped sharply. She heard a faint hiss. A moment later the cellar was plunged into utter darkness.

CHAPTER TWENTY-FIVE

"A NICE STORY, SEVERANCE, but you're wasting my time. I need facts, not speculation."

The rumpled financier gestured irritably. "Get me some coffee, for God's sake. I've been cooped up in this place for six hours. The least you can do is get me something to drink."

A stalling tactic? Dominic shrugged and moved to the door, spoke softly with the man outside, then returned. "I need something specific if you want my help. This kind of empty speculation won't get you an extra blanket on your prison bed."

"It's far more than speculation, you fool! It's about secrets, damn it. The kind of secrets that keep governments afloat—or shatter them."

"I need a name or I can't help you," Dominic said flatly.

Severance rubbed his neck and cursed.

At that moment there was a tap at the door and a uniformed man brought in a paper cup. Dominic noticed he was a different guard from before. "Where did the other officer go?" he asked.

"Off duty," came the bored answer, coupled with a shrug.

Severance turned the cup nervously in his hands and took a quick drink. "Help me, Montserrat. That wine was just to scare Cathlin. When I saw her with you in the car I went a little crazy, I admit it. But I never meant to kill her. There wasn't supposed to be enough poison for that."

"Says you."

Severance stared into the steaming coffee, as if looking for hidden answers. "My God, you still don't understand!" He took another swallow and rubbed his throat. "It was all planned. *All* of it, don't you understand? Someone knew." His fingers tightened on the coffee, which sloshed over his wrists.

There was another tap at the door. The uniformed guard beckoned to Dominic. "Mr. Severance's lawyers are upstairs," he explained softly. "He is to be released in fifteen minutes. Mr. Harcliffe wanted you to know."

Dominic bit back a curse. Did Harcliffe expect him to get answers before Severance walked? He turned back, his face expressionless. "If there was someone involved, tell me how. Then maybe I can help you."

"That's just it, I never found out. And I should have been able to find out. Whoever buried Cathlin's records had access to the very highest levels. He *also* had the power to keep his involvement totally hidden." His eyes widened, desperate. "But I did learn one thing, Montserrat. The palace was never interested in that wine you're shepherding down at Draycott Abbey."

"What wine?" Dominic's tone was cool.

"That Château d'Yquem 1792, you fool! I told you, information's my business. When I found out, naturally I was interested as a collector. But no one at the palace was showing any interest and that bothered me, since it could mean the wine was a fake. When I looked into it, I found out the palace was told discreetly that the wine is only a modern copy."

Dominic's palms began to sweat as he felt a noose of betrayal slipping around him. "Why should I believe you're telling me the truth?"

"Because I need you too much to lie." Severance's fingers were trembling and his voice was agitated. "That man you caught the day before yesterday at the abbey was my man. I sent him for pictures of the wine. I wanted verification. Of course, he wasn't as good as you, Montserrat. He barely made it out, bleeding badly."

"Tell me about the palace. Where did you get this information? No one on their staff leaks information for long."

"You're right. But this time an old associate there called me. It seems a member of the royal family was searching for a fine wine to give as a family birthday gift. He knew I occasionally obtain unusual vintages and can be counted on to be discreet. I can assure you, he had *no idea* that the wine in the abbey's cellar was authentic. Which means, Montserrat, that someone is double-crossing you." Sweat covered Severance's brow and his face had gone pale. "So now will you help me?"

Dominic tried to hide his fury. Severance couldn't be lying, not when so many of his facts were correct. And that meant someone had betrayed him. Harcliffe? Or someone even higher? "What about the car that tried to run Cathlin off the road? Were you behind that, too?"

"Car?" Severance ran a hand clumsily over his brow. "I don't know anything about a car. The poison was just to scare Cathlin and make her leave the abbey. Something's wrong there, don't you believe that now?"

He did believe it, Dominic thought grimly. But who was the person who stayed one step ahead of him?

"Did you send Cathlin the letter with the scrap of plaid?"

"What plaid?"

Another dead end. Dominic rubbed his shoulder idly, feeling it burn. "Maybe you can be useful to me, Severance. When you're released from here, I want you to do something for me."

"Anything. Just get me out."

"I want you to start asking questions again. Pull in all your old debts and make it clear that answers will be well rewarded."

"You want me to be the bait, is that it? To make my interest clear and see who comes looking for me?" He nodded slowly.

"Risky, but I'll do it. Just give me your assurance that in return, you'll—" His hands lurched. A shudder ran through him.

"What's wrong?"

Severance's body tensed. He swayed toward the desk. His coffee cup fell to the floor and liquid ran in a brown stain across the dirty tiles.

"The woman," Severance muttered. "Harcliffe. Might be—" Abruptly his eyes closed and his body twitched convulsively.

And then his head slid back and he did not move again.

DOMINIC'S FACE WAS GRIM as he watched the medical team carry out Richard Severance's body. "What was it?" he asked the doctor making notes in a small black pad.

"Impossible to say for certain, not until the blood tests and tissue samples are complete." The man closed his pad with a snap. Dominic thought his eyes looked tired and slightly bitter. "Myself, I suspect a fast-acting alkaloid. Probably something in the curare family, since you say it happened over a matter of minutes."

"What about the guard?"

The doctor shrugged. "He's in the clear. Someone phoned down and told him to come upstairs in order to show Severance's lawyers down here, in preparation for his release. He waited until a relief guard took his place and then he left."

"And that relief guard who brought the coffee has long since disappeared, no doubt," Dominic said grimly.

"Right again."

Dominic looked down at the floor. There were still a few beads of coffee dotting the old, cracked tile. The paper cup had been removed for evidence, of course, but Dominic doubted there would be any found. Whoever was behind this wasn't the sort to leave any clues.

Slowly he sank onto the table, his hands clenched. Who

wanted Severance out of the picture and had the knowledge to see it done so cleanly?

And then Dominic sat forward. *Cathlin.* Whoever had gotten to Severance could just as easily get to Cathlin. He had to get back to Draycott.

The tired man with the notepad watched him rush from the room, then sighed and went back to his grisly report.

CATHLIN MOVED QUICKLY AS the wine cellar was plunged into darkness. She crouched by the new security system and punched in the code Dominic had programmed to retrigger the alarm. At least its secondary power source was secure for the moment.

Nearby she heard a thump, the kind that came from a body stumbling into something heavy. Tensely, she pinpointed the noise, four yards to her right. If she made her way along the far wall past the champagne racks, she would be in reach of the stairs.

She caught her breath and inched through the darkness. When her fingers met the cool wood of the stair rail, she threw caution to the winds and bolted straight up, calling hoarsely for Marston and the friend of Dominic who was supposed to be on watch by the front door.

But neither the butler nor the other man was anywhere to be seen. The abbey was empty.

"My dear, what's wrong? You look quite distraught."

Cathlin spun around, gasping in relief as she saw Joanna Harcliffe's anxious face. "Where's Marston? There's someone down in the cellars and I have to get help."

"Oh, I assure you no one has gone down there. I've been sitting here for at least twenty minutes. Marston said he had to go into town with that nice friend of your husband. I believe they had to pick up some new equipment. Marston seemed quite delighted to be involved, actually." The older woman touched

Cathlin's arm. "You're not looking at all well, my dear. Come into the study and sit down while you tell me all about it."

Perhaps she *had* been mistaken, Cathlin thought. Lord knows, her nerves were stretched thin these last days. Given her anxiety in the darkness, she might merely have imagined the noise.

She followed the older woman into the study, sank into a chintz armchair, and took the glass of water that Joanna Harcliffe had poured from a nearby carafe.

"I was certain I heard something. Just my imagination, I suppose. I've been imagining all *sorts* of strange things since I came to the abbey."

"Have another drink."

Cathlin took the glass, studying the woman's competent hands. She noted every line and texture, from the square, unpolished nails to the expensive but out-of-date Baume and Mercier wristwatch.

"Just close your eyes. It will help, you know. It will let you forget."

Cathlin stared at the silver watchband flashing in the sunlight as Joanna's Harcliffe's voice murmured on, soft and rhythmic. "Sleep. Sleep now." Sunlight glinted back and forth across the silver links. It was the kind of expensive and classic watch that would last a lifetime, Cathlin thought dimly.

Then her eyes sank closed. Her breathing grew deep and regular.

When the phone rang, the older woman reached out and unplugged it. "There's no need for us to be disturbed," she said gently. "Just sleep, Cathlin, my dearest. Close your eyes and sleep. Exactly the way your mother did."

JAMES HARCLIFFE KNOCKED at the door of his wife's study, then pushed it open. He did not go into this room as a rule. Medical confidentiality had to be strictly preserved, as his wife had repeatedly explained to him. Because Harcliffe had his own office at home, this had never bothered him before. But lately Joanna was spending more and more time in here, and he feared she was overworking.

But today she was not at her office and she should have been home hours ago.

He looked down, surprised to see a torn sheet of paper crumpled on her desk. Nearby a little crystal jar with paper clips lay overturned.

Harcliffe frowned. His wife was usually the soul of neatness, entirely a creature of habit. It annoyed her when something was not in its place. This was not at all like her. He picked up the paper and studied the single word that ran across it, written in his wife's neat handwriting.

Cathlin.

Beneath he saw a file and skimmed the first sheet. His frown grew as he turned sheet after sheet. When he finally snapped the file shut and sank down in the chair at his wife's desk, his face was grim.

He grabbed the phone and punched the number for Draycott Abbey. A mechanical voice came on the line, informing him that there was a circuit malfunction and would he please try his call again later.

Cursing softly, Harcliffe broke the connection, studying the unbelievable information he held in his hands. For the first time in twenty years there was fear in his eyes.

THE SUN BURNED AWAY OVER the hills, leaving Draycott's windows a blaze of crimson. The air was still and silence covered the sweeping hills like a veil.

Out of that veil came a shimmering wave of light that worked into black satin and white lace, into a face with brooding eyes and hard jaw. Adrian Draycott stood on the rise overlooking his beloved abbey, a gray cat at his feet.

His hands clenched to fists. They had no right to be here, severing the peace of this place, threatening those who had come back to heal a long-forgotten wound. He had tried to warn Cathlin and her stubborn husband, stirring their sleeping minds with fragments of their bitter past. He had hoped that with his warning, they might be better prepared for the dangers to come.

But the evil that had waited for two hundred years had only grown stronger. Now the dark past was about to be repeated and in spite of every shred of will and ghostly inclination, Adrian Draycott feared he would not be allowed to interfere.

CHAPTER TWENTY-SIX

"YES, SHE WAS VERY beautiful, your mother."

Joanna Harcliffe sat beside Cathlin, her voice friendly. She spoke with the detached calm of a professional, but her eyes were expressionless and flat. It was nearly dark now, and she liked the dark best. It was the perfect time to make plans. "She had every man at Oxford dogging her steps, even those who didn't care for women. Everything was wonderful then. We were two privileged women with the grandest of prospects before us. Then Elizabeth grew immersed in her art studies and I found myself with a new set, people who had different ideas. I began to see the larger world and all the weaknesses of England. And I came to see that increasing those weaknesses was the key to making a better world for all of us." She carefully unsnapped her silver watch, then held it before Cathlin's eyes, moving it slowly. "Yes, you're sleeping deeply now, my dear. Just as you were all those years ago when we had our discussions. You remember now, don't you?"

Cathlin frowned, her fingers tensing.

"Answer me, Cathlin."

"Y-yes. I'm sleepy now, very sleepy."

"Excellent. We've gone through all this before, of course, all about your memories of that day here at the abbey. And we discovered a different set of memories in our sessions, didn't we? Memories of a woman named Geneva Russell."

Cathlin's fingers moved restlessly over the chair arm, but she did not speak.

"Tell me, Cathlin." There was an iron undercurrent in the older woman's voice now.

"Yes. I remember. Geneva. Geneva Russell."

"Excellent. And do you know how she died?"

Cathlin frowned. "No, I—I can't remember. Only pieces. Painful even now…"

Harcliffe moved the watch rhythmically, her voice like a smooth wave. "Then I'll tell you. Listen well. She jumped from the abbey roof, distraught at her lover's death. Such a sad conclusion to the tale, just like your own past. How unfortunate that you and your mother saw me that day in London, speaking with a man I shouldn't be speaking with and giving him a file I most certainly shouldn't have been giving him. What a bad bit of luck for you that you were there by the duck pond in Regent's Park when your mother saw me. It all had to end, of course," she said softly. "I'd put far too much time into the government position I'd secured as a confidante and medical adviser to cabinet-level ministers—even to several members of the royal family. The secrets I held were of incredible value to those determined to see change brought about here in England. Nothing—nothing at all—could be allowed to interfere with that process. You do understand, don't you, Cathlin?"

No answer.

"*Tell* me, Cathlin."

"Yes, I…understand." It was the soft voice of a child of ten.

"And you do remember seeing me that day. It's coming back to you, isn't it? You remember the ducks, dirty and clamorous, while you tossed in the bread your mother had crumbled up for you."

Cathlin's face softened and she nodded. "I liked the ducks. I slipped and got mud on my new shoes, but she told me it didn't matter. We'd have them like new before my father saw them. She seemed worried, though. And she didn't want me to know."

"Yes, Elizabeth was quite the perfect mother. That's why I had to come up with a very special way to dispose of her." Joanna Harcliffe's eyes moved over the room, detached, analytical. "One of my new compatriots volunteered to take on the assignment. He was careful to lay all the clues to suggest it was the work of one of your father's enemies. Yes, it was a most satisfying conclusion to a nasty little problem and no breath of suspicion ever fell upon me."

Cathlin's fingers moved restlessly as the hypnotic words continued.

Abruptly the woman beside her frowned. "What are you holding there in your hand?"

Cathlin's fingers opened, revealing a small piece of silver.

"My God, you found it, after all those years. I broke my watch down there that day and had no time to find all the pieces. You didn't see me, but you heard my voice, didn't you?" Joanna Harcliffe laughed softly. "You were such a clever little girl."

Cathlin's eyes went very wide. Pain flared through their unfocused depths. After a moment she nodded jerkily.

"But I saw to that too. During our little sessions, I blocked out those memories and gave you a different set, didn't I?"

Cathlin nodded. "You—you told me I was responsible. You said if I hadn't insisted on stopping to feed the ducks that day, my mother would still be alive. You said it was all my fault."

Harcliffe sat back with a small hiss of triumph. "Excellent. A perfect textbook case of deep conditioning that has held up perfectly all these years. Guilt made you the perfect block for your memories, right up until I gave you the code to change it. You do remember the code, don't you, my dear? We went over it so many times."

Cathlin frowned, looking out into empty space, struggling with burning memories and painful images that threatened to shred her sanity.

"There is a dove on my mother's hill,
By oak and ash and bonny doe;
And though to me she sings full sweet,
No one else can know, oh,
No one else can know."

She spoke the words flatly, mechanically.

"Well done. And in the wake of those words, all the memories began coming back, didn't they?"

Cathlin nodded, her fingers tight on the piece of silver she'd found in the dust, her connection to the buried secrets of her past.

"Unfortunately, Richard Severance was also interested in what had happened to you, and he had access to information at very high levels. I soon found that he could be a formidable opponent. He had to die, of course, since he'd become a nuisance. But I had to keep you silent, too, until I was ready to clear the slate, and the best way was by keeping you offbalance, by making you question your sanity."

She looked at the watch, her face hard. "And now, my dear, we're going down into the cellars to look at that wine everyone is so interested in. It is authentic, isn't it?"

Cathlin's fingers tightened with strain. She fought the seductive force of that low voice.

"Come, now, tell me everything. I must insist."

Cathlin caught a jerky breath. She shuddered, then nodded slowly. "Real. Priceless…" She swallowed, her voice trailing away.

"Excellent. They'll ensure my welcome in the rather unstable country where I'm going tonight. Yes, they *must* be real." She seemed to rouse herself. "And now, Cathlin, we will go down and you will turn off the alarm system. You know the sequence, don't you? Your dear husband must have told you."

After a moment Cathlin nodded.

Joanna Harcliffe laughed softly. "Then after we load the wine in my car, we're going to take a nice, careful walk up to the roof, just you and I. Won't that be lovely?"

Cathlin's hands clenched.

And then slowly, painfully, she nodded.

DOMINIC CURSED AND SLAMMED his foot to the floor. His hands were white, locked on the wheel, as he went back and forth over Severance's final muttered warning.

Who? Who was behind this horror?

Frowning, he reached for the mobile telephone by his knee. Like all the other times, the result was the same, only static. Even the radio brought no response.

Damn it, where were Marston and the men he'd called in to keep an eye on the abbey? His jaw was set in a hard line as he shot past an approaching fuel truck, barely scraping his fender past in time, and roared south toward the abbey.

"GO AHEAD, MY DEAR." Cathlin was in the entrance hall, her hands locked at her waist. Joanna Harcliffe carefully smoothed a few wisps of hair back into her bun and leaned closer, speaking gently. "The stairs are right behind that door. Push it open, Cathlin. It's a lovely night for an airing on the roof."

Cathlin faltered.

"Now, my dear. You must do exactly as I say."

Cathlin nodded and moved forward.

"You do see that you can't be allowed to live. It was amusing to know that I had such power over your future, that with a single string of words I could heal you or destroy you." Joanna Harcliffe laughed softly. "It was my final, perfect revenge against Elizabeth, who'd always had everything. Everyone delighted in her presence, everyone hung on her every word. After a while there was nothing left for the rest of us." The elder woman's mouth flattened, settling into an ugly line. "And now her dear little daughter is in another world, every aspect of her mind under my control. It makes a most satisfactory ending, indeed. How sad that I won't be able to see my husband's face when he finds out." She laughed coldly. "My poor, stupid, unsuspecting husband. You've done very well, Cathlin," she crooned, patting her arm. "Very well."

Behind them came a light footstep.

"Ah, there you are, Hayes."

Hayes pointed to the rear of the abbey. "The wine's all loaded. We can leave any time."

"Very good. I shall be out shortly, after I've finished here."

After a moment her husband's assistant, who was in truth Joanna Harcliffe's assistant, turned and went back out to the waiting truck.

Silently the two women entered the narrow staircase, darkness closing in around them. Dust rose in dancing flecks as they moved up the broad steps to the abbey's roof.

"Hayes is a fool, I'm afraid. I shall dispose of him, too, once I have no more use for him. By this time tomorrow I expect to be comfortably ensconced somewhere far, far away from England. I can never be happy here, in a place where I have had to fight for every advancement and every bit of security."

Cathlin kept moving.

"But you don't see, do you?" The older woman laughed coldly. "I was there too, part of that whole, tragic tale. After your unexpected regression during our hypnosis sessions, I grew curious and did a regression of my own. Most interesting, it was." Joanna Harcliffe's voice hardened. "That's how I discovered my own part in your past. I was the one who convinced you to betray the man you loved."

They had reached the top of the stairs now. "Here we are, my dear. Push open the door."

A cool wind tore over the parapets as Cathlin shoved the door open. Outside the roof was shrouded in shadows and the countryside spread like a dark velvet sea below them, a few lights shimmering in the distance.

"And now it's finally time to bring our circle closed. You do understand, don't you, Cathlin? Or should I call you Geneva?" The older woman smiled coldly. "Yes, your lover is gone, you're distraught, and everything you value in life is lost. There's only one answer for you now, isn't there?"

Cathlin's fingers moved restlessly at her waist. She scrubbed at her skirt, fighting stains that weren't visible. "I—yes, I understand."

"And what is it that you must do?"

"Jump. Jump like *she* did. Because it's my fault."

Behind her James Harcliffe's wife laughed softly. "Very, very good, my dear. The lie worked then, too. Everyone in London was convinced that Gabriel had killed the innocent Geneva Russell and then vanished. My plan was perfect, in fact. But now we're almost finished. Yes, I think this corner will do."

Below them stretched the dark tangle of Draycott's hills. In the distance the moon hung cold and silver, its light thrown in broken webs across the moat.

"It is time, my dear."

"Yes—I understand." Cathlin moved forward, her hands restless. "He is waiting for me and I must go. First Gabriel, then my mother, now myself."

Without warning, a long shape hurtled from the darkness, ripping at Cathlin's skirts and knocking her backward, away from the roof's edge. She cried out, thrown down against sharp gravel and upturned stones, her head striking the edge of the parapet.

"Get up!" The order was sharp with fury. "You must complete the work you've agreed to."

Cathlin swallowed. Her hands pressed at her head. She looked down and saw the blood staining her palms. Looked—but did not really see. "Of course," she said mechanically.

"Be quick about it. I have a great many miles to cover before morning. I must be far away before that clever husband of yours suspects anything. Closer, my dear, that's right." Moonlight glinted on the gun in Joanna Harcliffe's fingers. "I would hate to see you change your mind now, after all this time. Yes, take another step, Cathlin." She laughed softly. "Only a few feet more and everything will finally be complete. Then your sad memories will trouble you no more."

CHAPTER TWENTY-SEVEN

DOMINIC ROARED UP TO Draycott's wrought-iron gates and leaped from the car. Instantly a uniformed figure moved to block his way.

"Sorry, sir. No one to go in or out. Strict orders."

"Orders from whom?"

"James Harcliffe, sir." The man looked nervous. As he spoke he bent down to finger the holster holding a standard-issue Beretta.

Dominic didn't give him a chance to finish. He didn't trust Harcliffe or anyone else at that moment. He spun sideways and flashed his leg up in the high, twisting *chassé* kick of *savate*. A sharp elbow parry followed a punishing right jab, and a clean follow-through brought his adversary into the full weight of his bent knee.

Dominic let him fall and took his Beretta, then ran grimly for the abbey. The moon hung like a chalk disk in the black night as he broke through the last line of trees. Now the moat lay just above him, ablaze with moonlight. When he looked up, a slender black form was silhouetted against the stark black line of the parapets.

Dominic knew as he stared upward that the bitter past was about to be repeated.

CATHLIN MOVED NEARER TO the edge of the roof.

Pain burned through her palms and shoulder. She swallowed, feeling her hair flung by the wind, feeling her mind flung just as wildly by a rush of cruel memories.

Her mother. The park. The ducks quacking as they surged around her feet.

And then an older woman, her face first bland, then wrinkled and ugly with rage.

Joanna Harcliffe.

It all slid back into Cathlin's mind then, the angry words, her mother's white face as they'd left the park, though she'd tried to hide her fear from Cathlin.

That evening they had gone as planned to the abbey. The incident was forgotten until Cathlin awoke in the night and heard her mother's voice raised high in anger and fear. Cathlin had gone to the door, listening to the angry words of two women who had once been friends. With sleepy eyes she had seen a brawny man pulling her mother down the hall. Screaming, she had flung herself at him, only to be thrown back into her room with the door locked.

After that…only silence.

Only the horror of bleak seconds ticking past as she whimpered softly for the mother who did not come. Eventually she had cried herself to sleep, and when she awoke hours later, the house was still silent, but now her door was open.

She had run through the dark corridors, shadows at her back, calling vainly for her mother.

Then Cathlin found her.

Motionless, broken, silent, her body lay sprawled against the long grass by the moat. That image had shattered Cathlin's hold on sanity.

And the initial trauma was soon cleverly reinforced by Joanna Harcliffe's weeks of cold-blooded conditioning until the memories were completely blocked.

"Come, my dear, you are too slow. The edge is so near now. It calls to you, beckons you."

Cathlin's fingers tightened. She had to fight the words and all those years of monstrous control. The pain had helped her begin, but even now it was nearly impossible. The child in her wanted to obey, to do everything this gentle, kindly voice ordered.

Something brushed past her leg, sleek and powerful.

The cat. The cat she'd seen that day beside the moat.

Cathlin swallowed, taking courage from the warm contact. She had to fight! With her past restored, she could finally have a future.

A future with Dominic.

"Yes. I'm—coming. But my foot is caught."

"Where?" Sharp. The irritation beginning to show. "Let me see." The older woman bent over, and as she did Cathlin shoved her away, kicking wildly at the gun.

Metal struck stone and then the night blurred, speed and shadow and cool moonlight bleeding together. A feline shape hurtled through the air, striking Cathlin's shoulder, ripping out with claws bared.

Fire burned in her arm. She cried out in pain and fell backward, striking the sharp granite of the roof.

And then only darkness. A darkness where cruel memories lay waiting.

HENRY DEVERE STOOD IN THE candlelight studying Geneva's bound hands.

"Where is he? Where is Gabriel?"

"He's escaped again, damn his soul. After he was shot, I had him transferred to a traveling carriage with two guards. But he tossed the incompetent fool outside, then jumped himself, no matter that the carriage was at the gallop. But I'm not worried. I know exactly where he'll head—to find you, my dear, right here at Draycott. And thanks to my story about the dreaded smallpox affecting the abbey, no one will be making any visits here. Now that Adrian Draycott has gone off to escort that impertinent American diplomat to sea, we will be quite alone here."

"*Monster!*"

*Devere only smiled coldly, playing with the lace at his cuff.
"Now all we have to do is wait for your brave cavalier to return
from France."*

TWO DAYS PASSED. THEN A *week.*

*Finally Henry Devere received the news he craved: the brave
Englishman had returned from his daring French mission with
a beautiful Englishwoman and her three children in tow and was
already on his way out of London.*

*Laughing wildly, Devere half carried and half shoved Geneva
down to the moat. Throwing open the gatehouse door, he made
her stand before him on the abbey's little bridge, with his pistol
against her back. There they had stood, while the minutes ticked
past, both waiting for the man Geneva loved to come plunging
through the gate.*

Both knowing that he would die when he did.

Geneva's hands tightened. Forgive me, my love, *she prayed.*
Forgive me and know that this is the greatest gift I can give you.
Accept it and remember that I shall love you always.

*Beyond the gate came the sound of a horse plunging over
gravel and then the hammer of boots.*

*Suddenly Gabriel was there, eyes wild, cloak flying. "Geneva!
They said you had gone with Adrian and Jefferson. I've just left
your sister in London and came as fast as I could. The wine is
following by coach."*

*Devere stepped into the moonlight, a pistol at Geneva's head.
"So I find you again at last, Ashton."*

*Gabriel cursed. "You can have me, Devere. Let her go and
you can take me where you like."*

*Devere threw back his head and laughed wildly. "So simple?
Come, this is hardly any challenge." Slowly his face darkened
with rage. "I've outplanned you at every step, and you'll not*

elude me now! That reward will be mine, as all that money should have been already. I worked all those years in India, slaving for Thomas Russell in the savage heat. 'Do your work well, Henry. Keep your accounts clear, Henry. Someday if you are very good, you will marry my daughter and all my money will be yours.'" Devere laughed wildly. *"But he died before I could fix her hand in marriage, blast his soul."*

Gabriel saw his moment. He lunged toward Devere, who had stepped away from Geneva during his mad harangue. The blow caught Devere in the side and sent him hurtling backward against the granite bridge across the moat.

They struggled desperately, breaths hoarse. Then there was a blur of blue silk and the bark of a gun.

"Geneva, no!"

But it was too late. She lay between them, blood staining the edge of her gown. Beside her lay Henry Devere, collapsed from the force of the rock she had flung against his head.

"You must go now." Her voice was already growing weak. "Know that I love you, my dearest Gabriel, with every fiber of my soul until the very end of time." She clutched at his sleeve. "You must go now. He'll be waking up soon!"

But Gabriel didn't move. He held her head to his chest as her breath slowly stilled and her blood leaked onto the cold granite.

He was still holding her locked to him, lost in a haze of pain, when Henry Devere's gun barrel swung down on his head and the world crashed into utter darkness around him.

BRICK BY BRICK THE WALL was raised. Bound and gagged, blood flowing from the gaping wounds Devere had inflicted, Gabriel watched without any flicker of emotion.

It was over. Devere had won, monster that he was. He was totally mad now.

But it mattered not, in truth.

With Geneva gone, Gabriel lost his own life and any hope of happiness.

"How does it feel to be caged, Montserrat? How does it feel to know the cold is climbing inside you and your blood stains the gray stones?" Devere moved clumsily before the unfinished wall, his face wild, demonic. "You'll make your tomb in there with that wine of yours, and Adrian Draycott will never be the wiser. When he returns he'll learn only that a wall of his cellar collapsed and had to be quickly buttressed with a new one." Devere laughed coldly. "And in one week's time all London will be abuzz with the sad story of Geneva Russell, who was flung from the abbey roof by her love in a jealous rage. Yes, the story will be on everyone's lips. I'll see to that." He stopped abruptly, his eyes anxious as he stared into the shadows of the cellar. "Who's there? Who's there, damn it?"

But no voice rose in answer. The only sound came from the mason's trowel, scraping new mortar over fresh bricks.

And then Devere's eyes darkened. His laughter echoed through the cold cellar, wild and ragged, as the last brick was set in place.

NOW, TWO HUNDRED YEARS later, Dominic Montserrat stood looking up into the night sky, into the moon that hung chill overhead, feeling his blood run to ice. Memories lay sharp upon him and once again he felt fate cheating him of all that he had ever loved and dreamed of.

Above him came a cry, then the slow, silent twist of a body as it plummeted from the parapets, end over end, to strike the stones at the edge of the moat.

Catching a wild breath, Dominic plunged toward the abbey.

IT TOOK LONG, PAINFUL seconds for her consciousness to return. There were stones digging into her fingers and a burning pain at her neck where the cat's sharp claws had ripped through her blouse.

Cathlin slowly opened her eyes.

Nothing but shadows. Nothing but darkness and pain.

Then memory returned, and with it the chill reality of the last hours. She sat up slowly and looked around her. The roof was empty—no cat, no Joanna Harcliffe. She put her hand to her head, brushing aside a line of blood.

She was struggling to rise when the door to the roof was thrown open and a tall figure appeared, silhouetted in the light from the stairs.

"Cathlin? Sweet God, are you there?"

"Dominic!" she cried hoarsely. "I'm here—waiting for you, just as I promised, my love."

In the distance came the wail of sirens, then the roar of a car. Brakes screamed on gravel and a door was thrown open against the angry stacatto of urgent questions. Somewhere James Harcliffe's voice rose in a harsh rain of commands, countered sharply by Nicholas Draycott.

But Dominic and Cathlin heard none of it.

Their bodies were locked where they stood on the cool granite of the abbey's roof, a perfect purity of line against the burning silver light of the rising moon.

"Together," Dominic said hoarsely, his fingers buried in her hair, his heart racing.

"Forever," Cathlin answered softly. To the night. To the golden future. To the man she loved more than her very life.

Most of all, to the two lovers who had been parted here by tragedy so long ago.

And as she said the words, Cathlin felt the hole in her mind begin to close. The shadows she had lived with for so long now wavered and began to recede. She knew then that the circle had finally been broken and they had found their way home at last.

CHAPTER TWENTY-EIGHT

"I'M FINE."

"Be quiet."

"No, really, Dominic. I'm fine."

But Cathlin's protests were ignored, muffled against Dominic's chest as he carried her into the abbey's rose-filled study. "Until I'm convinced of that, you're staying right here," he said tartly. "That madwoman came too bloody close out there. She was the one behind all of it, the intruders at Seacliffe, the men in the car, even that letter you found under your door with the ragged bit of plaid." His jaw hardened. "If she weren't dead already, I'd have serious trouble resisting the temptation to do the job myself."

Cathlin's fingers tightened on his shoulder. She didn't want to think about the nightmare of the last hours, not until the horror of the memories had begun to fade. She looked up at Dominic, seeing the lines of tension at his mouth and jaw that marked the worry that still gripped him. "You can't mean that."

"Just be glad we won't have to find out." He settled her in a chintz couch in front of the window, then sank down beside her. After a moment, he cursed and hauled her onto his lap.

"Dominic, I'm fine, really."

"Well maybe I'm not. I don't think I'll ever forget looking up and seeing the two of you silhouetted up there on the edge of the roof. As I watched, it all came back." His eyes hardened. "I saw the cellar, Cathlin. I saw the bricks going up one by one and I heard the scrape of the mortarman's trowel. And when I looked down I saw my own blood pooling over the granite floor."

"So close. Then and now." Cathlin brushed back a dark comma of hair from his forehead. "But I knew you'd come, Dominic. And until you did thank heavens the cat was there to frighten me back from the edge. The pain cut through the mental blocks somehow and when I got up, Joanna Harcliffe's control was broken."

"Cat?" Dominic frowned.

"A great creature, gray with black paws."

"Funny, I don't remember Nicholas keeping a cat here at the abbey." Dominic shrugged and eased Cathlin against his chest, trying to ignore the immediate ache that their contact kindled. "So it was Harcliffe's wife all along. No one would have guessed her capable of such tortured planning. Probably you weren't the only one she had her claws into either. In a way I can almost feel sorry for her husband, because James Harcliffe looked totally broken when he left in the ambulance with her body. Clearly all of this took him by surprise." His breath slid out slowly. His fingers crossed over Cathlin's waist. "But it's finally over now, my love. Gabriel and Geneva are at peace at last, with their old, sad mystery solved." Cathlin's fingers stole into his as he pressed a hard, protective kiss to her hair.

Outside the moon shone cloudless from a cobalt sky. Wind fluttered the roses cascading along the moat. And somewhere in the quiet darkness a nightingale began to sing.

"BUT SOMETHING *MUST* BE wrong. They've been in there for hours already!" Nicolas's voice was tight with worry as his wife patted his arm.

"They're fine, Nicholas."

"What if something happened to them? After all, Cathlin has

been under a terrible strain. First she had to come back here and face the memories of her mother's death. Right on top of that comes this mad attack by Joanna Harcliffe."

"I'm sure that Dominic is very well equipped to soothe any trauma that Cathlin might be feeling right now."

"No, I can't take a chance, Kacey. I'm going in."

Even as Nicholas fingered the ancient silver key to his study, a ripple of muted laughter drifted from behind the closed double doors, followed by the sound of a pillow hitting the floor.

Nicholas's frown wavered, but he didn't give up. "What if you're wrong? What if Cathlin—"

"Sometimes, my love, for someone so vastly intelligent, you can be very, very dim," his wife said tenderly.

Another wave of laughter emerged from behind the oak study doors. This one was decidedly masculine.

"I suppose you might be right," Nicholas said slowly, returning the key to his pocket. "So what do we do now?"

"We do nothing at all." His wife took his arm and led him off toward the kitchen. "Except perhaps to have a word with Marston. Unless I miss my guess, those two are going to be famished when they finally come out." She gave her husband a knowing smile. "As I recall, *we* certainly were."

The viscount's gray eyes took on an answering gleam. "You're right, we were, But not for food, my love."

"DOMINIC, WE CAN'T. IT'S almost ten o'clock."

Skin moved slowly over warm skin. Sunlight spilled over the moat and filtered past the damask curtains to fill the study. "What will Nicholas and Kacey think of us?"

Dominic laughed darkly. "That we are very much in love, I hope." He slanted Cathlin a wolfish smile. "And that we're embarking on the honeymoon we never had."

"But my dress. Your shirt." Her face filled with color as she gazed down ruefully at the crumpled shirt at her feet, now entirely buttonless. Her own dress had fared little better.

"You *were* rather impatient, weren't you?"

"Me? What about *you?*" Cathlin held up the shredded remains of her lace camisole. "This isn't exactly the sign of a patient man."

Dominic's smile grew even more wolfish. "Fantastic, wasn't it?"

After a moment Cathlin's lips slid into a smile. "Entirely. Especially when you…" She pushed onto her toes and whispered something in her husband's ear.

His eyes darkened. "No more, Irish. Otherwise, we'll never get out of here. And I don't plan to spend another night on this cold floor, no matter how valuable its eighteenth century Peking carpet." He studied the room thoughtfully, then swept a muted wool throw of tartan plaid from a nearby wing chair. After whisking it around Cathlin's shoulders, he cinched the long folds with his belt. "Very nice. Lady Macbeth incarnate."

"Snake."

"Witch." His voice grew husky. "Enchantress. You must be, woman. You've certainly stolen my heart and all vestiges of sanity, Cathlin O'Neill."

Her finger traced his lips, light as thistledown. "Cathlin O'Neill *Montserrat,*" she corrected softly.

Dominic looked upward, as if pleading for celestial assistance. "One look, one tiny touch, and she makes me putty. No, she makes me the most ineffectual mound of blancmange."

"How the mighty have fallen," Cathlin said silkily, moving her shoulder so that the soft wool gaped and afforded her beloved husband an intimate look at the skin he had worshiped and explored so thoroughly through the long hours of darkness.

The Earl of Ashton muttered beneath his breath and tugged the tartan closed. "March, O'Neill. You may be the keeper of the wines, but I'm the one dedicated to protecting your luscious body." His mouth hardened as he gathered up the shredded remains of their clothes. "If we stay in here one minute longer, protecting you is going to be the very last thing on my mind."

Her brow cocked. "So?"

"So you need a break. You've got beard burns over most of your body."

"Mmm. The memory alone is lovely."

"Damn it, Cathlin, I saw you wince when you stood up. And I have a fair idea of how you're feeling right now. After all, I wasn't exactly feeling very civilized last night." Dominic unlocked the study doors and threw them open. "I'm not very proud of that fact," he added grimly. He looked out into the shadowed corridor, frowning as his eyes adjusted to the darkness.

Someone cleared his throat.

"Marston, is that you?"

"I hope I have not disturbed you, my lord." The butler's face was impassive as he gazed at a rather ugly eighteenth-century oil portrait just to the left of Dominic's head. "However, I confess I am delighted to see you. The viscount has been rather distressed, you understand."

Cathlin caught a quick breath. "Nothing's wrong, is it? Genevieve hasn't—"

"No, the family is quite healthy," Marston hastened to reassure her. "Actually, it was you two he was concerned about."

"Us? But why—" Her voice fell away and color flared through her cheeks.

"Locked in the study in utter silence for six hours, eh?" Dominic chuckled. "Nicholas, concerned host that he is, was busy imagining all sorts of tragedies."

Marston's lips took on a faint curve. "His lordship has always had a rather active imagination. But now everything is settled." With one quick look he took in Dominic's bare torso, the shredded clothes caught beneath his arm, the rosy hue of Cathlin's cheeks. He also noted the stubble that had caused that color. He nodded contentedly, then turned. "And now if you will come this way, everything is prepared."

Dominic frowned. "Prepared?"

"Quite." Impassively, Marston gestured for Cathlin to precede him. "My lady?"

Seeing no alternative, Cathlin tugged at her makeshift robe, then moved self-consciously toward the front of the house.

"The limousine is waiting at the front door."

"Limousine? Limousine for where?"

"I believe you will have to ask the viscount and his wife about that."

"Damn it, Marston, don't go bloody butlerish on me now."

No answer. Marston managed to hide his smile; he was not so successful with the twinkle in his eye.

Dominic was just steeling himself to drag the truth out of the tight-lipped retainer when Nicholas himself appeared, a broad smile lighting his handsome face. "So the recluses finally emerge. Hunger got to you, didn't it? Kacey said it would."

Cathlin's stomach gave a telltale rumble.

Nicholas pretended not to notice. "Everything's arranged." His eyes lingered on their rather eccentric attire for a moment, before he turned to lift a large woven hamper from the polished floor of the foyer. "You should find everything you need in there. Caviar. Wild strawberries. French bread and foie gras. Belgian lace napkins and champagne on ice." Nicholas's brow arched wickedly as he shoved the heavy hamper at Dominic's chest. "The champagne is Veuve Clicquot, of course. Sorry I didn't have any more La Trouvaille on hand. Damnably hard to build up much stock with that perfectionist in charge. I presume you *do* have enough strength left to carry all that, Dominic."

"I believe I can summon up the requisite energy," the earl said dryly.

"Wonderful. Meanwhile, Kacey has gone for your clothes. Amazing how she can predict these things." He gave a contented nod, well pleased with his plans. "Now off with the two of you. Everything is set."

"Set?" Cathlin tugged uneasily at the folds of the tartan throw at her chest. "Set for what?"

Dominic's eyes took on a shimmer of humor. He eyed the two well-worn Burberry raincoats tossed over an oak peg by the door. "Forget the clothes. We'll just take these."

The viscount gave a low chuckle. "Be my guest."

Briskly Dominic pulled Cathlin out into the rose-filled court-yard. As they disappeared toward the limousine that purred in front of the gatehouse, the viscountess padded down the stairs, an old Louis Vuitton bag under her arm. "They've gone? But they can't. Their clothes will be in no shape to travel in."

"I doubt they'll be needing any more clothes, my love. Not the way Dominic was looking at Cathlin. Come to think of it," he mused, "she was looking at *him* the same way."

"But—"

Viscount Draycott smiled broadly and pulled his wife against him.

After a moment she laughed softly, catching his hand in hers. Together they watched the car disappear over the wooded hill. "It all worked out just as Gabriel hoped. Those two were meant for each other, weren't they?" Kacey said wonderingly. "How could he possibly have known?"

IT IS SAID THAT NO ONE AT London's elegant Dorchester Hotel can be surprised by anyone or anything.

Which was true. Usually.

But not on this sunny spring morning as the daffodils tossed in elegant Park Lane window boxes and waves danced along the Serpentine Lake where it lapped against the blinding green expanse of Hyde Park. When two people emerged smiling from the limousine that purred up to the venerable hotel's front steps, the liveried attendant broke into a broad grin of surprise. "Welcome back, Lord Ashton! It's been too long since you've come for a stay." The man's eyes crinkled as he nodded to Cathlin in turn.

If he thought their raincoats unusual attire for this bright sunny day, Leo was far too well trained to show it. Briskly he moved to sweep open the doors, at the same time motioning discreetly to a bellman inside. His eyes twinkled as he watched the new visitors stroll off hand in hand. Yes, *now* things would start to happen. Just the way they always did when Lord Ashton was about.

IT WAS A PLEASURE TO BE back at the Dorchester, Dominic thought. Trust Nicholas and Kacey to plan something perfect like this. He smiled as his steps were cushioned in the deep velour plush of the art deco carpet. The hotel staff was discreet and unflappable. Nothing ever surprised or upset them. Dominic had enjoyed the elegance of this grand old hotel ever since his father had brought him for the first stay at the ripe age of eight. That first morning he had eaten crisp Belgian waffles and raspberry crêpes in bed and fallen in love for life.

Now, as mellow golden light bounced off elegant banks of mirrored glass, Dominic gave a sigh and finally allowed himself to accept the happiness that had been stealing through his soul ever since he'd found Cathlin safe the night before.

"Good morning, Lord Ashton." A bright-cheeked attendant in a crisp linen apron nodded to Dominic.

"Good morning. Mary, isn't it?"

Her cheeks creased with pleasure. "So it is. I'm sure you'll have a lovely stay." Her voice dropped confidentially. "Everything is all arranged." Before Dominic could say another word, she was gone, giggling softly.

Cathlin slanted Dominic a measuring look. "Quite a regular

here, are you?" She smoothed a dark strand from his forehead and feigned a frown. "Should I be upset by this?"

"I stayed here several years ago, but it was a job, simply a job, Cathlin."

"I'm listening."

"A French actress appearing in a popular London play had been receiving some nasty threats and I was assigned to protect her." He mentioned a name that made Cathlin's eyes widen.

"You worked with *her?*"

"She's not exactly what you might imagine. She was convinced that soap of any kind promoted wrinkles. As a result her, er, hygiene was somewhat less than exemplary."

"But she's *beautiful.*"

"Not," Dominic said tenderly, "half so beautiful as you." He was just bending down to plant a kiss on her welcoming mouth when he heard a voice at his back.

"Welcome back to the Dorchester, Lord Ashton." An elderly woman with twinkling eyes and a serviceable navy dress smiled as she pushed a tray of pastries past.

"Thank you, Mrs. Hopkins."

Cathlin's brow rose. "*Very* familiar."

Dominic shrugged, grinning crookedly. "I did a few favors while I was here. I had to keep busy, since I was spending a lot of time avoiding being caught alone with Madame X."

"A predicament half the male population of the United States would have killed to experience."

"It was business, Cathlin." Dominic's eyes darkened. "All business. No matter what act I had to play or what lies the tabloids printed. No matter what everyone here at the hotel was led to believe. Do you believe me?" he asked, suddenly serious.

Cathlin knew what she said next was very important. "I believe you. But only because I know how ruthlessly competent you are in your work. Heaven help the female who tries to break one of Ashton's rules." Her brow creased. "She really didn't believe in using soap? Not *ever?*"

"Never." Laughing softly, Dominic pulled her close and set off for the gleaming marble expanse of the front foyer, where he was instantly hailed by a small man with very regular teeth and a suit that was a masterpiece of Italian understatement. The red rose in his lapel bobbed as he shook Dominic's hand.

"My lord, it is such a *pleasure* to see you again."

"Thank you, George."

"Things have been far too quiet since you left."

"Quiet?" Cathlin eyed Dominic.

"But madam does not know? First, there was the crazed fan who tried to climb a rope from the balcony to the window of Lord Ashton's, er, female friend. Lord Ashton had to climb up and bring the man down when his foot got caught in the rope."

"He struggled every inch of the way," Dominic said reflectively.

"And don't forget the horse." The red rose bobbed as the hotel's concierge went on.

"Horse?"

"A circus act," Dominic said tersely to his wife, clearly uncomfortable with the trend of the conversation.

"Oh?" Cathlin purred.

"It was nothing much." Dominic shrugged. "The horse broke away from its handlers and tore into Hyde Park, then bolted across Park Lane at rush hour and raced into the lobby. I helped quiet things down, that's all."

"You caught him single-handedly, my lord," the concierge protested. "And just as he was about to mow down three duchesses and a very senile member of the House of Lords! Incomparable, you were."

Cathlin's lips twitched. "Incomparable, was he?"

"George is exaggerating. He always exaggerates."

"And then there was the time that very lovely actress friend of yours was locked out of her room—very much as God made her. You gallantly offered your jacket, but she seemed to want a great deal more from you. I had heard she was a very passionate woman, of course, but I never expected she would indulge in such a display in public."

"Display?" Cathlin breathed.

"But, yes. She was most curious to assess the lordship's, er, lordly assets before she—"

"Thank you, George. I think we can find our own way upstairs."

"But the security keys."

Dominic patted his pocket. "Right here."

"And the new codes."

"George, you offend my professional pride."

"Of course. I forgot those unusual skills of yours."

Cathlin didn't move. "So she wanted to assess your 'lordly assets,' did she?"

"It was a lifetime ago, Cathlin. And nothing happened, I assure you. Now why don't we head upstairs before—"

The dapper hotelier interrupted enthusiastically. "Oh, yes, Lord Draycott was most specific in his requests. You will find everything *molto bene*." He kissed his fingers. "And the flowers, so lovely. I myself shall escort you up."

"There's no need, truly, George. I'm certain we can find our way to the room."

"Oh, not just *any* room. To the penthouse suite, you understand."

At that moment a handsome man with mahogany skin and a rum-soft Jamaican accent strode past. "Welcome back, Lord Ashton." He gave a quick grin. "Things always do happen when you're here, that's for certain. I hear they got something pretty special waiting for you and your lady upstairs, mon. Yes, it's a true pleasure to have *you* back."

Cathlin's eyes narrowed. "Lord Ashton?"

"Yes?" Anxious. Definitely anxious.

At that moment Cathlin decided she'd had enough. She ran her arms slowly along her husband's shoulders and twined her fingers at his neck. Then she moved to tiptoes, sliding closer with every tormentingly sensual inch of her progress.

A deep silence fell over the gilt lobby. Bellboys paused over their luggage. Bemused guests slowed their steps. The uniformed attendants at the desk put down their pens and studied the new arrivals with blatant curiosity.

Cathlin made the kiss long, slow, and roughly the temperature of Cajun *sauce piquante*.

When her air finally gave out and she eased away from Dominic, she noted with satisfaction that his pupils were dilated and his pulse was definitely ragged. "Just so you don't forget that you're a married man now," she said silkily.

Dominic cleared his throat and studied her glowing face.

Behind them the silence was deafening.

"Meet my new wife, everyone," he said hoarsely.

The sound of clapping broke over the polished lobby as Dominic turned and, with a determined look on his face, tugged his wife toward the gleaming bank of elevators.

THE PENTHOUSE WAS INDEED prepared. Roses spilled from crystal dishes and china vases, filling the air with lush perfume. The doors to the balcony were thrown open, overlooking the green sweep of Hyde Park.

Dominic barely noticed. With a supreme effort of will, he pulled away from Cathlin. "I'll run a bath, then call room service."

"I'm not hungry. Not for food at least," she said raggedly.

Dominic ran a hand through his hair. "But we barely ate in the car. And after what happened yesterday, you—"

Cathlin touched his mouth. "No. Not ever again. It's done, put away in the past, where it belongs. The future is all I want to think about now. The future with you."

"But—"

At that moment the shrill clamor of the doorbell brought Dominic around, cursing. "Yes?" he demanded of the liveried attendant outside.

"Flowers, Lord Ashton. They're from housekeeping." The man held out a huge expanse of white and pink carnations. "Mrs. Morrison said to thank you again for your help with those men who were threatening her son."

Dominic gave a distracted smile, trying not to look at Cathlin. "Just a small favor," he muttered.

The door had barely closed when the buzzing began again. This time a buxom woman in a neat gray uniform held out a bottle of champagne chilling in a bucket of etched silver. "For you, *Monsieur. Merci mille fois,*" she said hoarsely. "Without you, my Pierre would still be undergoing questioning for a crime he did not commit. Thank you for believing when no one else did." She wiped her eye, pressed a quick kiss on Dominic's cheek, curtsied, then withdrew without another word.

Dominic set the bucket on a gilt table beside the balcony doors. As he did, the buzzer sounded yet again. Outside a small and very round man in a pristine white chef's hat stood moving from one foot to the other.

"So they were right. You've come back, Lord Ashton." The chef shot a glance at Cathlin, who was watching this parade of gifts with a bemused look on her face. After a courteous nod, he pulled a foil covered box from behind his back. "For you, my lord." His cheeks grew red. "Not that it's half enough, not after all you did when those goons came after me. I did owe them a lot of money, of course." He looked at Cathlin and gave an unhappy shrug. "Gambling debts, you understand. Without Lord Ashton?" The man gave an expressive shrug. "No more crêpes or Grand Marnier soufflés," he finished grimly. "He is a special man, this one. The truffles, they are small, for I owe him my life. That is why I want to wish you both every happiness." He pressed Dominic's arm awkwardly, then backed from the room, eyes misted.

Dominic stood staring at the foiled box in his hands, shoulders stiff, legs braced. After a moment he sighed and turned to face Cathlin. "I didn't know they'd, well—" He waved at the gifts.

Cathlin felt a burn in her throat. "Don't apologize, you crazy, stubborn man. I've been too selfish to see you as you really are. And that, my dear Lord Ashton, is wonderful. *Incomparable.*"

"No." Dominic's voice was harsh as he sank into a plush damask armchair and tugged Cathlin across his lap. "I'm going to do this right, by heaven. There's something I have to tell you."

Another shrill buzz sent lines down his forehead. "Come in," he called curtly.

A uniformed teenager stood self-consciously in the foyer. "Lord Ashton? I have the package you requested from Harrods."

"Put it on the end table." Dominic's eyes didn't leave Cathlin's face as he counted out change for a tip. When the door closed softly, he gathered an unsteady breath. "The truth is that I'm a fake, Cathlin. I think I've always been a fake. I've never belonged anywhere. When I was young I felt too French among my schoolmates here and too English when I went back to my family in France. I learned to play a role, hiding my pain—no, denying it ever existed. That's why being a bodyguard was perfect. My life evolved into one great act."

"Dominic, you don't have to tell me this."

"No, let me finish. I want you to believe that the act ended that day in Italy when those teenagers died. Serita told you about it, I know. I had to face myself then, Cathlin—what I was and what I wasn't. And that sight made me turn around and never go back. You must believe that. I'm out for good. I will *never* be what your father became."

"But why didn't you tell me about La Trouvaille?" Cathlin asked gently.

"Because in a way that, too, was an act. My mind still runs back to the crowded parade grounds where I'm watching the eyes, waiting for the flash of an automatic weapon and steeling myself to take the bullet if it comes." He shook his head. "It doesn't change overnight. But it will. One day La Trouvaille will be natural for me. The grass will feel right beneath my feet and the wind over the hill will be the most ordinary thing in all the world. But for now it's still an amazing gift every second of every day I pass there, and until that changes I guess I'll feel like a fake."

"You *are* truly blessed, Dominic. I have no doubt that your sense of being blessed is what makes that wine of yours so special."

He gave her a slight smile. "Keep telling me that often enough and I might begin to believe you, Irish. Until then—" Dominic held the box out to her "—believe that this is no act. What I feel for you is as natural as breathing—and every bit as necessary." He took out a ring with three emeralds separated by tiny diamonds and slid it onto Cathlin's finger, where it rested next to the Ashton family ring which it had been designed to match.

"This is real Cathlin. My throat goes dry whenever I look at you. My hands get clammy when I see you shove your hair back out of your eyes. I have loved you from the first moment I saw you at that blasted wine auction, so sleek and confident and utterly American. I resented that wine you were so in love with and I wanted to put that same glow in your eyes." He drew a ragged breath. "I'm making a mess of this, I'm afraid." He went down on his knee before her. "I've never been good at facing my deepest feelings, much less expressing them. But I want to now, Cathlin. What I feel for you is so real it makes my eyes burn. Somehow you reached into my chest and found the heart I wasn't sure I had. That's what I had to explain to you. I had to show you how much you've changed my life." His eyes darkened. "So will you marry me? For us, this time. Because of this feeling, not because of wine or wills or dead ancestors creeping through our heads. Will you, Cathlin?"

She rose and pulled him into her body, her eyes misty. "I will. Because I love you. Because I love how you try to hide every single good thing about yourself and then get angry when you can't. For such a big, tough guy, you're a pushover, Montserrat. And now…" She started to tug at the belt of her raincoat.

Dominic's eyes blazed. "No, Cathlin. Not yet. I'm not done."

"Yes you are. I've heard enough explanations for one day. Besides, if we stand here any longer that buzzer is going to ring again and a dozen new people will flood in with gifts. Then we'll never have any privacy. Just go put out the Do Not Disturb sign."

An arrested gleam in his eyes, Dominic did as she asked.

When the sound of jetting water drew him into the vast marbled bathroom, he saw Cathlin's raincoat discarded on the floor and her body half-hidden beneath a froth of bubbles in the creamy marble tub.

Dominic's mouth filled with cotton gauze. "I hope the ring fits." Sweat broke over his brow. "I tried to estimate your size."

"It's fine."

"And about La Trouvaille, we can split our time there. I have a handpicked staff who can manage things at the vineyards during the slack season. If you prefer to focus your work here in London, then—"

"Dominic?"

"What?"

Her toe climbed from the froth. "London's out."

"It is? So you want Philadelphia? We could manage it, I suppose. Tricky, but not entirely impossible."

"Dominic?"

"Yes?"

White foam slid back to one sleek calf. "Not Philadelphia either."

"No?" He nodded, after a moment's reluctance. "I understand, Cathlin. Your job is very important. I never meant to take it from you."

"Not *anywhere* but with you, at La Trouvaille."

Dominic's eyes took on a rush of primitive, elemental shock. "Truly?"

Cathlin rose slowly, foam in every sleek curve, her eyes awash with love. "Truly."

"You're certain?"

"Without a doubt. And now I've got a confession of my own to make."

"I knew it. You're already married?" His voice was husky.

Cathlin shook her head silently.

"You're wanted for armed robbery in three countries?"

She kept approaching; as she did Dominic's hands kept getting tenser.

"Be quiet and let me confess, tough guy." When she moved into him, it felt as natural as ice cream melting on an August afternoon.

"I'm listening," Dominic said hoarsely, his body hardening instantly at the wet pressure of her naked skin.

"What I've been trying to tell you is that you can guard my body anytime you like, Officer. In fact I've been having fantasies about your guarding me. Ever since that first day at Seacliffe."

"No kidding."

Her hands feathered over his broad chest. They kissed, long and slow. Linen fell and cotton fled. Skin melted against hungry skin.

Two bodies met the scented waters. Dominic's foot accidentally triggered the jets, which screeched into activity, water and foam flying everywhere.

He groaned as he sank into her, his blood churning, hot and wild as the water jetting around them.

Cathlin arched against him, endlessly pliant, endlessly welcoming. She sighed huskily, taking the whole demanding length of him.

Dominic closed his eyes, fighting for sanity. "But the ring—are you sure it fits? If not I can—"

Her ankle eased over his thigh. Her muscles tensed, catching him up in a rush of pure, exquisite torture.

Cathlin's eyes gleamed. "As a point of future information, Officer Montserrat, *this* is as perfect a fit as I ever expect to find anywhere in this life."

And when she spoke, the emerald and diamond ring Dominic had slipped on her finger was nowhere in sight.

EPILOGUE

France
The Garonne Valley

IT WAS A PLACE OF SUN AND stone and heat. The sky was shimmering and cloudless as the wind ran over the green hills, rich with orange blossoms and lavender.

La Trouvaille spread over the hillside and covered the valley carved out by a curve of the Garonne River. Every fertile inch was consigned to neat rows of grapes that hung on emerald vines.

A bird screeched angrily. Tired and dusty, Dominic Montserrat pushed from beneath a layer of leaves and surveyed the netting he had been tying to keep off pests. "That should do it."

"Now you're going to rest." Cathlin's face was tanned and radiant as she eased out of the spot where she'd sat to help him. Of course, Dominic could have turned the backbreaking work over to one of his staff, but by habit he chose the hardest work for himself. Cathlin had long since given up trying to persuade him to do otherwise. Stretching her shoulders, she sat back and surveyed her dusty, but very satisfied, husband.

"Not yet. There are three more rows yet to finish."

Cathlin sniffed. "I knew you'd say that. That's why I took matters into my own hands."

"*What* matters?"

"Lunch, for a start." Cathlin pulled a hamper from beneath a neighboring vine. "Caviar. Wild strawberries." Her eyes rose to Dominic's face. "Belgian lace napkins. Unless, perhaps you've forgotten a certain drive to London in a certain limousine?"

"Oh, Irish, I haven't forgotten. Not in a thousand years."

"Good. Then relax while I open this bottle. You might remember it from a certain London wine auction? Château d'Yquem 1870. Marvelous texture and wonderful finesse."

"It was a very expensive way to get your attention. And not very effective, as I recall."

"You might be surprised about that." Her eyes turned thoughtful. "I thought you had to be the best-looking man I'd ever seen." Cathlin touched the smudge of dirt at his chin. "I still think so."

Heat swept between them. The distant hum of a tractor, the backfiring of a truck, the high shrill cry of a hawk, all melted away to nothingness as Cathlin stared at Dominic's deeply tanned face and thought how lucky they were to be alive and together and here in this beautiful valley filled with golden light.

Happiness. She had finally begun to trust that it wouldn't go away, that she had the right to be happy. The change hadn't come immediately. She still awoke sweaty and breathless sometimes, expecting to hear Joanna Harcliffe's cool, hypnotic voice telling her that she was the cause of her mother's death.

But now that Cathlin's shadows had faces, she was finally able to fight them. Every day brought greater strength and deeper understanding. And every velvet night brought new textures of pleasure shared in the arms of the man beside her.

Happiness. Cathlin smoothed the soft blue linen of her dress and looked out over La Trouvaille. The reddish soil was warm and pungent in the sun and the grape leaves whispered in their neatly trellised rows astride the hills above the river.

"Dominic?" Cathlin's fingers moved in restless circles. "I have to talk to you."

"I thought we were."

"No, really talk."

The seriousness of her voice made him sit up, frowning. "You miss England, don't you? Blast it, I knew keeping you cooped up here at La Trouvaille was a bad idea. I can—"

"It's not that." Her fingers went back and forth on the sun-warmed linen.

"You want to go back to Philadelphia?" He took her face between his palms. "You should have told me, Cathlin."

"No, you don't understand." Her eyes darkened.

"Say it. Whatever you want, we'll manage it somehow, I promise."

"It's not a matter of my wanting. That is, not myself alone. It takes two to manage what I'm talking about, Dominic."

"Two? Is something wrong, Cathlin?" He sat up sharply. "Damn it, if you lifted those old casks after I told you not to—" Abruptly he went very still. "Two. Are you trying to tell me that you're—that we're—" He swallowed.

"I am. A baby."

"A baby?" He looked at her face and then his eyes slid inexorably to the slender waist where her fingers were still moving restlessly. "A baby," he whispered, half disbelieving. "You're sure?"

Cathlin nodded. "I got the results today."

A moment later she was gathered to his chest, his lips pressed to her hair. "You should have told me sooner!"

"I wanted to be sure."

His fingers tightened and Cathlin felt a long sigh of contentment heave from his chest. "Just when I thought things couldn't possibly get any better. You are seriously altering my gloomy view of the world, do you know that?"

"You're glad? Truly?"

"I have no words to tell you how glad." Their fingers locked. "I only hope she looks like you," he said in a besotted voice.

"I hope *he* looks like *you*."

"Sweet God, a baby. I think I need a drink," Dominic said blankly. "Aunt Aggy will be ecstatic. She's got chest upon chest of baby clothes she's been saving neatly in lavender. I think she'd just about given up hope on me."

"You *are* a hard man to tame. I nearly gave up, too."

Dominic gave a crooked grin. "I've been conquered territory from the first moment I saw you, O'Neill. My heart shattered the second I saw you slithering past me in that black velvet suit."

"Slithering! I did no such thing. How dare you—"

He cut her off with a kiss, fierce and hard, possessive and protective at the same time, as if he couldn't quite trust his good fortune and needed to persuade himself this was not some kind of dream. When he finally pulled away, his face was hard with desire. "Let's go back." There was no mistaking his intention.

"But it's barely noon, Dominic. We still have three more rows to finish up here."

"To hell with the vines," he said thickly. "I want to undress you slowly, and kiss you until you moan my name. I want to hear that soft cry you make when I take you over the edge. And then I want to start all over again." Suddenly his eyes narrowed. "Unless—maybe you shouldn't. Now, I mean."

Cathlin laughed huskily. "I can't imagine why not."

"You're sure? God, I wouldn't want to hurt…"

"We've got months yet, my love."

"We do?" He gave her a wolfish grin. "Then what are we waiting for? Come to think of it, why go all the way back down to the château?"

"But, what if one of the staff comes by? Besides, today is the day the mayor is going to—"

"To hell with the staff. To hell with the mayor, too."

The tablecloth from Cathlin's hamper hit the ground with a *whoosh*. Dominic spread it carefully, then worked Cathlin back beneath the leafy shade of the trellised green vines.

"What about that Château d'Yquem I've got cooling on ice?"

"Forget it, Irish. I've got something with greater complexity and far more staying power in mind."

"I hope you're prepared to demonstrate the proof of that statement, Lord Ashton."

"You can damned well bet I am, Lady Ashton."

The green leaves shuddered. A single cloud marched across the crystal sky. Down the hill cicadas droned from the darkness of the woods.

Husky laughter spilled from the high vines. "Sorcery, Lord Ashton? Is this primitive ritual how you manage to keep producing those amazing vintages?"

"Be quiet and kiss me, wife of my heart, mother of my child."

She did, and the love they made between them was fine and sweet and unforgettable.

Tempered in pain, anchored in joy, it was stronger than any wine that would come from even La Trouvaille's hardy vines.

THEY SPILLED OUT OF THE sunset an hour later like a ragged circus parade, two Citroëns lurching along at the fore followed by an old farm truck. Behind that, tethered with a stout rope, trotted a donkey in a straw hat with holes cut for his ears. The backfiring motors roused the two figures half-asleep beneath a row of grape vines.

"Dominic, did you hear that?"

"I bloody well did." Dominic sat up and squinted into the sun, watching a cloud of dust swirl over the gravel drive and across the mellow golden walls and blue shutters of the beautiful old château at the foot of the forest. As the lead car lurched to a halt, he held his hand to his eye and frowned. "But that's—"

"Nicholas and Kacey," his wife finished breathlessly. "And there's Marston. Did you know about this?" she demanded. "Really, Dominic you should have told me." She sat up quickly, brushing twigs from her hair. "We'll have to hurry down."

"I'm totally in the dark." His eyes lovingly ran over her body, slender and shadow dappled. "But maybe you should put something on before you go running down to greet our guests."

"Maybe *you* should too."

They wriggled into their clothes clumsily, shielded by the low vines, then went down to welcome the visitors spilling over the lavender-edged lawns of the château.

Nicholas was leaning at ease against a dusty Citroën, elegant in a sherry-colored tweed jacket and deep brown trousers. "So the recluses of La Trouvaille emerge from their vines at last." Nicholas's sharp eyes ran from Dominic's dusty shirt to the bits of grass and leaves caught in Cathlin's hair. "I trust we haven't interrupted anything," he said blandly.

His wife was frowning. "I told you we should have phoned ahead, Nicholas. If it's a dreadful nuisance, we can always go back to the last town. But the farmer insisted on showing us the way personally. Then the mayor had to come along, too." The official in question was already hailing Dominic in a torrent of voluble French, detailing the arrival of his English friends, who had clearly been lost. Meanwhile, the farmer, after untying his donkey, launched into his own account of the story, shrugging expressively as he talked.

In the midst of this cheerful chaos of explanations and hugs and kisses from a sleepy-eyed Genevieve, Marston moved off to make the acquaintance of the housekeeper, who was just emerging from the château.

Dominic would permit no talk until all were settled at the old stone tables under a pair of poplar trees at one side of the house. Cathlin's Château Climens was opened and a first glass lovingly savored.

"Celebrating something special, were you?" Nicholas asked.

Dominic looked at Cathlin. "We were, actually." He took his wife's hand. "I've just found out—" He stopped and cleared his throat. "Lord, Nicky, I'm to be a father."

Another interval of chaos ensued. Soon the two friends were perched on the old table while the farmer and mayor wandered off to argue over the best choice of name for the coming child. Kacey and Cathlin, meanwhile, moved off to the bank of the brook that wound along the foot of the forest.

The viscountess touched Cathlin's arm. "You look positively radiant, my dear."

"I can't think why. I've been eating like a pig," Cathlin confessed. "I think that's how I first realized."

"Lucky you. I couldn't eat for weeks. Besides, your husband doesn't seem to mind in the slightest. In fact, he looks utterly exhilarated with the news."

"Do you think so?" Cathlin studied Dominic tenderly as he sat shoulder to shoulder beside Nicholas.

"Without a doubt. Men have a habit of getting that way about this time. Just wait until the first dirty diaper appears," Kacey added sagely.

Insects droned from the rows of lavender and banked rosemary. The mayor and the farmer had dispensed with female names and now were moving through a weighty selection of boys' names. Didier and Alexandre had emerged as the front contenders when Marston returned bearing a tray of watercress sandwiches and a bottle of La Trouvaille.

"Marston, you are impossible. Do sit down and be waited on like everyone else," Cathlin scolded good-naturedly.

"I'm afraid I can't, my lady. Some deficiency in my character, I fear. Would you care for more wine?" he asked in the same breath, the sun glinting off his purple running shoes.

Cathlin sighed and let Kacey take a turn at trying to bully the butler into taking the vacation he richly deserved.

The viscountess was no more successful than Cathlin.

Only when Genevieve tugged at his trousers and demanded that he pour her some of that "sparkly stuff all the grown-ups were drinking" did he put down his tray. Smiling faintly, he took her off to the kitchen in search of something "much better than that nasty sparkly stuff that was making the grown-ups laugh so much."

Nicholas bent closer to Dominic. "And now for my news. We've found the man who pushed Cathlin's mother. He and quite a few other members of Joanna Harcliffe's nasty little group are going to spend a long time behind bars."

Dominic looked at Cathlin, who was laughing at something that Kacey had said. "I don't think she needs to know, do you? Not yet at least. So much of her memory is returning. It's as if she's rediscovered her mother now that the mental logjam Joanna Harcliffe engineered has been broken. Thank God for it. And thank you, Nicky, for all you've done."

"I've got even better news. I've been sifting through the offers for your wine, as you asked."

"I hope it hasn't been a bloody bother. With my being away, it's been madness here."

Nicholas waved a hand. "It's been quite exciting. If Marston becomes any more impassive when he announces that the palace is on the phone, I think his face will freeze in a perpetual mask. I don't think he's ever had quite as much fun. Do you know that he got to argue with a member of Parliament and two U.S. senators yesterday?"

"Marston, argue?"

Nicholas chuckled. "He's determined that the wine should go to the Queen Mother and no one else." His eyes narrowed on the silver line of the stream. "There's no doubt that your estimate will be met, Dominic, and probably a great deal more. You see, we took apart the wooden slats of the case last week. Do you know what we found? Two pieces of paper—one from Thomas Jefferson, specifying an order of Château d'Yquem for himself and his friends. He listed a number of American patriots by name in the request, including George Washington. If that kind of written

provenance doesn't drive the buyers to a bidding frenzy, I don't
know what will."

Dominic's eyes played over the distant hills, wreathed in
golden light. "He seemed a thoroughly decent fellow. Once again
I owe him my thanks."

"Seemed? Have you been reading up on Jefferson? You speak
as if you know him personally."

Dominic smiled. "You might be surprised, Nicky. Now what
was that other letter you mentioned?"

Nicholas reached into his jacket and drew out a small sheet
of yellowed vellum protected in plastic. "I thought you'd want
to read it yourself."

Dominic took the sheet with quiet reverence, thinking of
blood and loss and shadows that had finally been overcome. His
eyes watered as he stared at the bold words scrawled across the
old paper and he knew without a doubt that he was looking at
the work of his own hand, mere minutes before his death.

If you have found this, unknown friend, then you must
also know the rest. Geneva Russell was murdered before
my eyes by a madman named Henry Devere as she stepped
before a bullet meant for me. Now I am to die, too, and no
doubt Devere will name me her killer. See that history
knows the truth, my unmet friend, so that our souls may
finally lie at rest. You will find the Ashton necklace pressed
into a recess I made in the wet plaster at the bottom of the
north rim of this wall. See that it goes to Geneva's descendant and to none other, on pain of my curse. And when that
is done, friend whom I shall never meet from a time that I
shall never see, then drink deep—to life, to us, and to the
truth that cannot stay hidden despite all of the work of evil
hearts. Know then that Geneva and I are finally at peace
in that place where souls meet and dance forever in the

light. I have seen it briefly, just now. It is beautiful beyond describing. Already my heart sings with an eagerness to go, for I know Geneva is there, waiting for me.

We send you our joy, unknown friend, and with it the assurance that forever is far more than just a word.

Farewell

Dominic held the page tightly, unashamed of the tears that covered his cheeks. He drew a deep breath, feeling peace steal over him, knowing that Gabriel had gone joyfully to meet his death.

He looked up to find Cathlin at his side, her eyes full of concern. "Dominic?"

"It's nothing, love. Just an end—and a beginning, the way life always is." He brushed a black strand from her cheek. "I'll tell you later. Now I want to offer a toast to two lovers who have finally found their peace." He refilled the glasses, then raised his own. "To Gabriel and Geneva. May all their good live on."

Cathlin offered him an answering smile full of silent understanding. Even the old farmer and the mayor stopped arguing long enough to join in the toast, for love is something that any Frenchman treats with greatest seriousness. Both knew love when they saw it, of course. And they saw it now, shining in Cathlin's and Dominic's eyes as their fingers intertwined.

FAR AWAY A PLAYFUL WIND danced over the quiet pools and reeds along the English coast, where twilight was just beginning to gather in the hollows below Seacliffe.

Suddenly a shimmer that was not quite sun and not quite water's reflection slid along a row of roses bordering the long gravel drive.

And then a man stood staring over the sweep of hills and sea, looking far to the southeast as if he could see all the way to France.

Which, of course, Adrian Draycott could, thanks to his special awareness of anything that concerned the abbey and its owner.

"So it is finally done. The lies are broken and the past is brought full circle. It pleases me well."

Behind him the roses whispered and a great gray cat emerged into the last rays of the blazing red sun.

Adrian Draycott smiled faintly. "I expect two boys."

The cat's tail arched.

"Girls? Nonsense, my friend."

The cat sat back and studied his black-clad master with unblinking eyes.

"Three of them? And they'll grow up to do *what?*"

The cat's whiskers quivered slightly in the wind and if ever a cat could be said to smile, then this one did.

"Amazing," Adrian murmured. He fingered the fine lace at his wrist, looking at two newly carved headstones. Where Gabriel and Geneva lay side by side, a pair of roses had begun to cast up their first, tentative buds. "But now perhaps it's time for a little of my own magic, such as is left to me so far from my abbey."

Adrian's eyes narrowed as he raised his hands over the low boughs. A cloud passed across the sun and somewhere a thrush called out a persistent tune.

When the cloud moved away, there were dozens of new leaves and tight buds clustered against the pair of roses. And now a row of lilacs spilled their white blooms along the foot of a nearby wall of warm granite.

Maybe the flowers had been there before, or maybe they hadn't. Afterward no one could remember clearly.

But Adrian knew. He smiled faintly and studied his handiwork, while the gray cat pressed against his polished boots. "Rather nice, I think. And now, Gideon, it is time that we were on our way home."

Beyond the witch's pool, beyond the hill and the moat, a dying sun gilded the weathered granite walls of Draycott Abbey and light seemed to shimmer along the silent, darkened corridor that led to the long gallery. The radiance gathered slowly, settling over the hard-faced portrait of a man in black damask and white lace.

Only a sharp eye would have seen the gray cat that ghosted through the day's last beam.

Only a sharp eye would have noticed the single petal of white lilac that fell dreamlike and pale upon the old carpet beneath the painting.

And only the very keenest observer would have seen the way Adrian Draycott's mouth lifted in a smile as the great cat curled up on the carpet beneath his feet.

A carpet that now carried a rain of crimson rose petals.

REQUEST YOUR FREE BOOKS!

2 FREE NOVELS FROM THE ROMANCE/SUSPENSE COLLECTION PLUS 2 FREE GIFTS!

YES! Please send me 2 FREE novels from the Romance/Suspense Collection and my 2 FREE gifts. After receiving them, if I don't wish to receive any more books, I can return the shipping statement marked "cancel." If I don't cancel, I will receive 4 brand-new novels every month and be billed just $5.49 per book in the U.S., or $5.99 per book in Canada, plus 25¢ shipping and handling per book plus applicable taxes, if any*. That's a savings of at least 20% off the cover price! I understand that accepting the 2 free books and gifts places me under no obligation to buy anything. I can always return a shipment and cancel at any time. Even if I never buy another book from the Reader Service, the two free books and gifts are mine to keep forever.

185 MDN EF5Y   385 MDN EF6C

Name _____ (PLEASE PRINT) _____

Address _____ Apt. # _____

City _____ State/Prov. _____ Zip/Postal Code _____

Signature (if under 18, a parent or guardian must sign)

Mail to **The Reader Service:**
IN U.S.A.: P.O. Box 1867, Buffalo, NY 14240-1867
IN CANADA: P.O. Box 609, Fort Erie, Ontario L2A 5X3

Not valid to current subscribers to the Romance Collection,
the Suspense Collection or the Romance/Suspense Collection.

Want to try two free books from another line?
Call 1-800-873-8635 or visit www.morefreebooks.com.

* Terms and prices subject to change without notice. NY residents add applicable sales tax. Canadian residents will be charged applicable provincial taxes and GST. This offer is limited to one order per household. All orders subject to approval. Credit or debit balances in a customer's account(s) may be offset by any other outstanding balance owed by or to the customer. Please allow 4 to 6 weeks for delivery.

Your Privacy: Harlequin is committed to protecting your privacy. Our Privacy Policy is available online at www.eHarlequin.com or upon request from the Reader Service. From time to time we make our lists of customers available to reputable firms who may have a product or service of interest to you. If you would prefer we not share your name and address, please check here. ☐

BOB07

CHRISTINA
SKYE

77123	CODE NAME: BLONDIE	___	$6.99 U.S. ___	$8.50 CAN.
77069	CODE NAME: BABY	___	$6.99 U.S. ___	$8.50 CAN.

(limited quantities available)

TOTAL AMOUNT	$ _____
POSTAGE & HANDLING	$ _____
($1.00 FOR 1 BOOK, 50¢ for each additional)	
APPLICABLE TAXES*	$ _____
TOTAL PAYABLE	$ _____

(check or money order—please do not send cash)

To order, complete this form and send it, along with a check or money order for the total above, payable to HQN Books, to: **In the U.S.:** 3010 Walden Avenue, P.O. Box 9077, Buffalo, NY 14269-9077; **In Canada:** P.O. Box 636, Fort Erie, Ontario, L2A 5X3.

Name: _____
Address: _____ City: _____
State/Prov.: _____ Zip/Postal Code: _____
Account Number (if applicable): _____

075 CSAS

*New York residents remit applicable sales taxes.
*Canadian residents remit applicable GST and provincial taxes.

HQN™

We *are* romance™